PRAISE FOR THE NOVE...
ACROSS TH...

"So good it hurts. Benford pu...
adult characters, rich writing, innovative science, a grand phil
osophical theme—it's all here..."

"Confirms again Benford's u...
ously sustain literary values a...

GREAT S...

"A challenging, pace-setting ...
should not be missed."

"Overwhelming power . . . i...

TIDES ...

"Mr. Benford is a rarity: a sc...
insight not only about black h...
human desires and fears."

"*Tides of Light* is at once Be...
philosophical and most scien...
the best SF novel published s...

Gregory Benford's Galactic ...novels are a triumph
of worldbuilding and hard science, brimming with com-
pelling characters and rousing adventure. Don't miss the
other books in this critically...
saga: ACR...

Bantam Spectra Books by Gregory Benford

ACROSS THE SEA OF SUNS
GREAT SKY RIVER
FURIOUS GULF
TIDES OF LIGHT
IN THE OCEAN OF NIGHT

HEART OF THE COMET (with David Brin)
IF THE STARS ARE GODS
TIMESCAPE
AGAINST INFINITY
THE JUPITER PROJECT

IN THE OCEAN OF NIGHT

GREGORY BENFORD

BANTAM BOOKS
NEW YORK • TORONTO • LONDON • SYDNEY • AUCKLAND

*This edition contains the complete text
of the original hardcover edition.*
NOT ONE WORD HAS BEEN OMITTED.

IN THE OCEAN OF NIGHT

*A Bantam Spectra Book / published by arrangement with
the author*

PUBLISHING HISTORY
*Bantam Spectra edition / July 1987
Bantam reissue edition / August 1994*

*SPECTRA and the portrayal of a boxed "s" are trademarks of Bantam Books,
a division of Bantam Doubleday Dell Publishing Group, Inc.*

Lines from "Little Gidding" in Four Quartets *by T. S. Eliot, copyright © 1943 by T. S.
Eliot; copyright © 1971 by Esme Valerie Eliot. Reprinted by permission of Harcourt
Brace Jovanovich Inc. and of Faber and Faber Ltd.*

*Portions of this work first appeared in substantially different versions in the following
publications:* Worlds of If, The Magazine of Fantasy and Science Fiction, *and in* Threads
of Time, *an anthology edited by Robert Silverberg.*

ISBN 0-553-26578-4

Published simultaneously in the United States and Canada

*Bantam Books are published by Bantam Books, a division of Bantam Doubleday Dell
Publishing Group, Inc. Its trademark, consisting of the words "Bantam Books" and the
portrayal of a rooster, is Registered in U.S. Patent and Trademark Office and in other
countries. Marca Registrada. Bantam Books, 1540 Broadway, New York, New York
10036.*

PRINTED IN THE UNITED STATES OF AMERICA

RAD   12   11   10   9   8   7   6

To Joan
who knows what it means

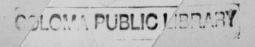

We shall not cease from exploration
And the end of all our exploring
Will be to arrive where we started
And know the place for the first time.

—T. S. Eliot

IN THE OCEAN
OF NIGHT

PART ONE 1999

From *The Encyclopaedia Britannica*, 17th Edition, 2073: *Icarus* (ik'-ə-rəs)

Minor planet 1566. Had the most eccentric elliptic orbit of all the known asteroids (e = 0.83), the smallest semimajor axis (a = 1.08) and passed closest to the sun (28,000,000 kilometers). It was discovered by Walter Baade of Mt. Palomar Observatory in 1949. Its orbit extended from beyond Mars's to within Mercury's; it could approach to within 6,400,000 kilometers of the Earth. Radar observations showed it to have a diameter of about 0.8 kilometer and a rotation period of about 2.5 hours. The unusual orbit attracted only minor interest until June 1997, when Icarus suddenly began emitting a plume of gas and dust. Since it was presumably a typical rocky Apollo asteroid, this evolution into a cometary object excited the astronomical world. The oddity became of intense concern when calculations in October 1997 showed that the momentum transferred to the escaping cometary tail was altering the orbit of Icarus. This orbital perturbation could, within a few years, cause a portion of the comet to collide with the Earth. Impact of the tenuous gas would be harmless. But the head of the comet Icarus was by then obscured, and some conjectured that a solid core could remain, in which case . . .

Icarus

> In Greek legend, the son of Daedalus. After
> Daedalus, an architect and sculptor, built the
> labyrinth for King Minos of Crete, he fell out of
> favor with the king. He fashioned wings of wax
> and feathers for himself and Icarus, and es-
> caped to Sicily. Icarus, however, flew too near
> the sun and his wings melted; he fell into the
> sea and drowned. The island on which his body
> was washed ashore was later named Icaria. The
> legend is often invoked as a symbol of man's
> quest for knowledge and fresh horizons, what-
> ever the cost. Icarus was invoked in van
> Hoven's masterwork, *Icarus Descending* (1997),
> as an emblem for the decline of Western
> cultural eminence . . .

ONE

He found the flying mountain by its shadow.

Ahead the sun was dimmed by a swirling film of dust,
and Nigel first saw Icarus at the tip of a lancing finger of
shadow in the clouds.

"The core is here," he said over the radio. "It's solid."

"You're sure?" Len replied. His voice, filtered by
sputtering radio noise, was thin and distant, though the
Dragon module waited only a thousand kilometers away.

"Yes. Something bloody big is casting a shadow
through the dust and coma."

"Let me talk to Houston. Back in a sec, boy-o."

A humming blunted the silence. Nigel's mouth felt
soft, full of cotton: the thick-tongued sensation of mingled
fear and excitement. He nudged his module toward the
cone of shadow that pointed directly ahead, sunward, and
adjusted attitude control. A pebble rattled against the
aftersection.

He entered the cone of shadow. The sun paled and
then flickered as, ahead, a growing dot passed across its
face. Nigel drifted, awash in yellow. Corona streamed and

shimmered around a hard nugget of black: Icarus. He was the first man to see the asteroid in over two years. To observers on Earth its newborn cloak of thick dust and gas hid this solid center.

"Nigel," Len said quickly, "how fast are you closing?"

"Hard to say." The nugget had grown to the size of a nickel held at arm's length. "I'm moving to the side, out of the shadow, just in case it comes up too fast." Two stones rapped hollowly on the hull; the dust seemed thicker here, random fragments bled from Icarus to make the Flare Tail.

"Yeah, Houston just suggested that. Any magnetic field reading?"

"Not—wait, I've just picked up some. Maybe, oh, a tenth of a gauss."

"Uh oh. I'd better tell them."

"Right." His stomach clenched slightly. *Here we go*, he thought.

The black coin grew; he slipped the module further away from the edge of the disk, for safety margin. A quick burst of the steering jets slowed him. He studied the irregular rim of Icarus through the small telescope, but the blazing white sun washed out any detail. He felt his heart thumping sluggishly in the closeness of his suit.

A click, some static. "This is Dave Fowles at Houston, Nigel, patching through *Dragon*. Congratulations on your visual acquisition. We want to verify this magnetic field strength—can you transmit the automatic log?"

"Roger," Nigel said. Conversations with Houston lagged; the time delay was several seconds, even at the light-speed of radio waves. He flipped switches; there was a sharp beep. "Done."

The edge of the disk rushed at him. "I'm going around it, Len. Might lose you for a while."

"Okay."

He swept over the sharp twilight line and into full sunlight. Below was a burnt cinder of a world. Small bumps and shallow valleys threw low shadows and everywhere the rock was a brownish black. Its highly elliptical orbit had grilled Icarus as though on a spit, taking it yearly twice as close to the sun as Mercury.

Nigel matched velocities with the tumbling rock and activated a series of automatic experiments. Panel lights winked and a low rhythm of activity sounded through the cramped cabin. Icarus turned slowly in the arc light-white sun, looking bleak and rough . . . and not at all like the bearer of death to millions of people.

"Can you hear me, Nigel?" Len said.

"Right."

"I'm out of your radio shadow now. What's she look like?"

"Stony, maybe some nickel-iron. No signs of snow or conglomerate structures."

"No wonder, it's been baked for billions of years."

"Then where did the cometary tail come from? Why the Flare?"

"An outcropping of ice got exposed, or maybe a vent opened to the surface—you know what they told us. Whatever the stuff was, maybe it's all been evaporated by now. Been two years, that should be enough."

"Looks like it's rotating—ummm, let me check—about every two hours."

"Uh huh," Len said. "That cinches it."

"Anything less than solid rock couldn't support that much centrifugal force, right?"

"That's what they say. Maybe Icarus is the nucleus of a used-up comet and maybe not—it's rock, and that's all we care about right now."

Nigel's mouth tasted bitter; he drank some water, sloshing it between his teeth.

"It's knocking on one kilometer across, roughly spherical, not much surface detail," he said slowly. "No clear cratering, but there are some shallow circular depressions. I don't know, it could be that the cycle of heating and cooling as it passes near the sun is an effective erosion mechanism."

He said all this automatically, trying to ignore the slight depression he felt. Nigel had hoped Icarus would turn out to be an icy conglomerate instead of a rock, even though he knew the indirect evidence was heavily against it. Along with a few of the astrophysicists, he hoped the

Flare Tail of 1997—a bright orange coma twenty million miles long that twisted and danced and lit the night sky of Earth for three months—had signaled the end of Icarus. No telescope, including the orbiting Skylab X tube, had been able to penetrate the cloud of dust and gas that billowed out and obscured the spot where the asteroid Icarus had been. One school of thought held that a rocky shell had been eroded by the eternal fine spray of particles from the sun—the solar wind—and a remaining core of ice had suddenly boiled away, making the Flare Tail. Thus, no core remained. But a majority of astronomers felt it unlikely that ice should be at the center of Icarus; probably, most of the rocky asteroid was left somewhere in the dust cloud.

NASA hoped the controversy would stimulate funding for an Icarus flyby. The Agency, ever press-conscious, needed support. It had come a long way from the dark days of 1986, when the explosion of the *Challenger* had begun a fundamental shift in Agency thinking. NASA went on to develop the transats—trans-atmospheric rocket-airplane combinations that flew a good piece of the way to the upper atmosphere, then boosted into orbit on rocket thrust—but it had been badly mauled. As soon as it could, it edged away from the milk-run, commercial and military business of carrying tonnage into orbit. NASA was trying to become a primarily scientific agency now.

Icarus seemed a pleasantly distant spectacle. Its sudden, bright, fan-shaped coma was larger and prettier than Halley's Comet's rather disappointing apparition in 1985. The *Los Angeles Times* dubbed it "the instant comet." People could see it, even through suburban smog. It made news.

But in the winter of 1997, the question of Icarus's composition became more than a passing, academic point. The jet of gas spurting from the head of what was now Comet Icarus seemed to have deflected it. The dust cloud was moving sidewise slightly as it followed Icarus's old orbit, and it was natural to assume that if a core remained, it was somewhere near the center of the drifting cloud. The deflection was slight. Precise measurements were difficult and some uncertainty remained. But it was clear that by mid-1999 the center of the cloud and whatever remained of Icarus would collide with the Earth.

"Len, how's it look from your end?" Nigel said.

"Pretty dull. Can't see much for the dust. The sun's a kind of watery color looking through the cloud. I'm off to the side pretty far, to separate your radio and radar image from the sun's."

"Where am I?"

"Right on the money, in the center of the dust. On your way to Bengal."

"Hope not."

"Yeah. Hey—getting a relay from Houston for you." A moment's humming silence as the black pitted world turned beneath him. Nigel wondered whether it was made of the original ancient material that formed the solar system, as the astrophysicists said, or the center of a shattered planet, as the popular media trumpeted. He had hoped it would be a snowball of methane and water ice that would break up when it hit Earth's atmosphere—perhaps filling the sky with blue and orange jets of light and spreading an aurora around the globe, but doing no damage. He stared down at the cinder world that had betrayed his hopes by being so substantial, so deadly. The automatic cameras clicked methodically, mapping its random bumps and depressions; the cabin smelled of hot metal and the sour tang of sweat. No leisurely strolling and hole-boring expeditions with Len, now; no measurements; no samples to chip away; no time.

"Dave again, Nigel. Those magnetic field strengths sew it up, boy—it's nickel-iron, probably eighty percent pure or better. From the dimensions we calculate the rock masses around four billion kilograms."

"Right."

"Len's radar fixes have helped us narrow down the orbit, too. That ball of rock you're looking at is coming down in the middle of India, just like we thought. I—"

"You want us to go into the retail poultry business," Nigel said.

"Yeah. Deliver the Egg."

Nigel lit a panel of systems monitors. "Bringing the

Egg out of powered-down operation," he said mechanically, watching the lights sequence.

"Good luck, boy," Len broke in. "Better look for a place to plant it. We've got plenty of time. Holler if you need help," he said, even though they both knew full well he could not bring the *Dragon* module into the cloud without temporarily losing most communications with Houston.

Nigel passed an hour in the time-filling tasks of awakening the fifty-megaton fusion device that rode a few yards behind his cabin. He repeated the jargon—redundancy checks, safe-arm mode, profile verification—without taking his attention fully from the charred expanse below. Toward the end of the time he caught sight of what he had anticipated: a jagged cleft at the dawn edge of Icarus.

"I think I've found the vent," he called. "About as long as a soccer field, perhaps ten meters wide in places."

"A fracture?" Len said. "Maybe the thing's coming apart."

"Could be. It will be interesting to see if there are more, and whether they form a pattern."

"How deep is it?"

"I can't tell yet; the bottom is in shadow now."

"If you have the time—wait, Houston wants to patch through to you again."

A pause, then: "We've been very happy with the relayed telemetry from you, Nigel. Looks to us here in Control as though the Egg is ready to fly."

"Has to be hatched before it can fly."

"Right, boy, got me on that one," Dave said with sudden exuberant levity.

A pause, then Dave's tones became rounded, modulated. "You know, I wish you could see the Three-D coverage of the crowds around the installation here, Nigel. Traffic is blocked for a twenty-kilometer radius. There are people everywhere. I think this has caught the imagination of all humanity, Nigel, a noble attempt—"

He wondered if Dave knew how all this sounded. Well, the man probably did; every astronaut a member of Actor's Equity.

He grimaced when, a moment later, the smooth voice described the sweaty press of bodies around NASA Houston, the heat strokes suffered and babies delivered in the waiting crowds, the roiling prayer chains of New Sons, their nighttime vigils around bonfires of licking, oily flames. The man was good, no possible qualm over that; the millions of eavesdroppers thought they were listening to the straight stuff, an open line between Houston and Icarus meant for serious business, when in fact the conversation at Dave's end was elaborately staged and mannered.

"Anybody you'd like to talk to back here on Earth, Nigel, while you're taking your break?"

He replied that no, there was no one, he wanted to watch Icarus as it turned, study the vent. While, simultaneously, he saw in his mind's eye his parents in their cluttered apartment, wanted to speak to them, felt the halting, ineffectual way he had tried to explain to them why he was doing this thing.

They still lived in that dear dead world where space equaled research equaled dispassionate truth. They knew he had trained for programs that never materialized. He'd put in time in orbit as a glorified mechanic, and that had seemed quite all right.

But this. They couldn't understand how he'd come to take a mission which promised nothing but the chance to plant a bomb if he succeeded, and death if he failed. A scrambled, jury-rigged, balls-up of a mission with sixty percent chance of failure; so the systems analysts said.

They had emigrated from England, following their son when he was selected for the US-European program, hard on his final year at Cambridge. As an all-purpose scientist he'd seemed trainable, in good condition (squash, soccer, amateur pilot), agreeable, docile (after all, he was British, happy to have any sort of career at all) and presentable. When he showed superior reflexes, did well in flight training and was accepted into the aborted Mars program, his parents felt vindicated, their sacrifices redeemed.

He would lead in the new era of moon exploration, they thought. Justify their flight from a sleepy, comfy England into this technicolor technocrat's circus.

So when the Icarus thing came, they'd asked: Why risk his Cambridge years, his astronautics, in the high vacuum between Venus and Earth?

And he'd said—?

Nothing, really. He had sat in their Boston rocker, pumping impatiently, and spoken of work, plans, relatives, the Second Depression, politics. Of their arguments he remembered little, only the blurred cadences of their voices. In memory his parents blended together into one person, one slow Suffolk accent he recalled as filling his adolescence. His own voice could never slide into those smooth vowels; he could never be them. They were a separate entity and, no matter that he was their son, he was beyond some unspoken perimeter they drew in their lives. Within that curve was certainty, clear forms. Their living room had pockets of air in it, spots smelling of sweet tea or musty bindings or potted flowers, things more substantial than his words. There in their damp old house his jittery, crowded world fell away and he, too, found it difficult to believe in the masses of people who jammed into the cities, fouling the world and blunting, spongelike, the best that anyone could do or plan for them.

There was precious little money for research, for new ideas, for dreams. But his parents did not sense that fact. His father shook his head a millimeter to each side, listening as Nigel talked, the older man probably not aware that he gave away his reaction. When Nigel was through describing the Icarus mission plan, his father had cast one of those unreadable looks at his mother and then very calmly advised Nigel to sign off the mission, to wait for something better. Surely something would come along. Surely, yes. From inside their perimeter they saw it very clearly. He had given them no daughter-in-law as yet, no grandchildren, had spent little time at home these past years. All this hovered unspoken behind his father's millimeter swaying, and Nigel promised himself that when Icarus was over and done he would see more of them.

His father, obviously well read up on the matter, mentioned the unmanned backup missions. Robot probes, ready with a series of nuclear shoves. Why couldn't

Houston rely on them alone? A matter of probabilities, Nigel explained, glad to be on factual ground. But he knew, despite the committee reports, that the odds were cloudy. Perhaps a man was better, but who was sure? Even if only men could ferret out the core of Icarus, amid all that dust, why should it be Nigel? Easy answers: youth, reflexes; and, finally, because there weren't all that many trained men left. Nigel mentioned not a word of this as he pumped the rocker, drank tea, murmured into the layered still air of the old house. He was going, one way or another. They knew it. And that last evening ended in silence.

On the airplane back to the anthill of Houston, he took up the one volume that he'd noticed in his old bedroom bookcase, and brought along on an impulse. The yellowed hardback was cracked, the pages stiff and stained by the accidents of adolescence. He remembered reading it shortly after applying for the US–European program, to get a feel for the Americans. He paged through remembered scenes and near the end came upon the one passage he had involuntarily memorized.

> And then Tom he talked along and talked along, and says, le's all three slide out of here one of these nights and get an outfit, and go for howling adventures amongst the Injuns, over in the territory for a couple of weeks or two; and I says, all right, that suits me . . .

Sitting in the contoured airplane seat, he felt more like Huck Finn than the calculating European others thought him to be.

Dave Fowles's voice broke in.

"We have a recalculation of the impact damage, Nigel. Looks pretty bad."

"Oh?"

"Two point six million people dead. Peripheral damage for four hundred kilometers around the impact site. No major Indian cities hit, but hundreds of villages—"

"How is that famine going?"

He sighed. "Worse than we expected. I guess as soon as word filtered down that Icarus might hit, all those dirt farmers left their crops and started preparing for the afterlife. That just aggravated the famine. The UN thinks there'll be several million dead inside six months, even with our airlifts, and our sociometricians agree."

"And that movement out of the impact area?"

"Bad. They just give up and won't walk a step, Herb said. It must be their religion or something. I don't understand it, I really don't."

Nigel thought, and something came to an edge in him.

"Dave, I have an idea."

"Sure, we just went off open channel, Nigel, the networks aren't getting this. Shoot."

"I'm going to plant the Egg after this rest period, aren't I? This thing is solid metal ore, the magnetic field proves that. No point in waiting."

"Correct. The Mission Commander just gave me confirmation on that. We have you scheduled to begin descent in about thirteen minutes."

"Okay. This is it: I want to put the Egg in that vent I've found. It's a long, irregular fissure. The Egg will give us a better momentum transfer if it goes off in a hole, and this one looks pretty deep."

A whisper of static marked the line. Some tiny facet of Icarus gave him a quick white flash and vanished; he ached to seek it out, take a sample. He felt himself suspended beneath the white sun.

"How deep do you estimate?" Dave's voice was guarded.

"I've been watching the shadows move as the vent rotates into the sun. I think its floor must be forty meters down, at least. That'll give us a good kick from the Egg. I can take some interesting specimens out of there at the same time," he finished lamely.

"Let you know in a minute."

Len broke the wait that followed. "Think you can handle that? Securing that thing might get tricky if there's not enough room."

"If I can't get it down to the bottom I'll leave it

hanging. The Egg won't weigh even a kilo on the surface, I can simply hang it to the fissure wall like a painting."

"Right. Hope they buy it."

And then the carrier from Houston came in.

"We authorize touchdown near the edge. If the vent is wide enough—"

He was already readying his board.

TWO

It was a world of straight lines, no serene parabolas. He brought his module—cylindrical, thin radial spokes for stability, an insect profile ending in a globular pouch that was the Egg—in slowly, watching his radar screen. It was difficult to sense in this pebble of a world below him the potential to open a crater in the Earth forty kilometers across. It seemed sluggish, inert.

"Sure you don't need any help?" Len called.

Nigel smiled and his tanned face crinkled. "You know Houston won't let us get out of contact. The *Dragon*'s high gain antenna might not work in all this dust, and—"

"I know," Len said, "and if we were both on the sunward side of Icarus, Earth would be in my radio shadow. Fine. Just let me know if—"

"Certainly."

"Get'em, boy-o."

The textured surface grew. He flew toward the dawn line and the small pocks and angles became clearer. Steering rockets murmured at his back. He concentrated on distance and relative velocities, and upon speeding up the automatic cameras, until he was hovering directly above the vent. He rotated the module to gain a better view and inched closer.

"It's deeper than I thought. I can see fifty meters in and the mouth is quite wide."

"Sounds encouraging," Dave said.

Without waiting for further word, he took the module down to the top of the vent. Blasted stone rose toward him, brown discolored into black where minute traces of gas had been baked away.

His headphones sputtered and crackled. "I'm losing your telemetry," Len's voice came.

Nigel brought the module to a dead stop. "Look, Len, I can't go further in without the rock screening you out."

"We can't break contact."

"Well—"

"Maybe I should move in."

"No, stay outside the dust. Move sunward and behind me—there'll still be a cone of good reception."

"Okay, I'm off."

"Listen, you guys," Dave said, "if you're having trouble with this maybe we should just for—" Nigel switched him off. Minutes were being eaten away.

He rotated the module to get a full set of photographs.

Icarus was a bumpy, round hill that sloped away wherever he looked. Burnished mounds and clefts made a miniature geography, seeming larger than they were as the eye tried to fit them into a familiar perspective. He glanced at the clock. It had been long enough; he flipped a switch and the burr of static returned.

"How's it going, Len?" he said.

"Hey, having transmission trouble? I lost you there for a minute."

"Had some thinking to do."

"Oh. Dave says they're having second thoughts back there."

"I guessed as much. But then, they're not here, are they?"

Len chuckled. "I guess not."

"How far around are you? Ready for me to go in?"

"Almost. Take a few more minutes. What's it like down there?"

"Pretty bleak. I wonder why Icarus is so close to spherical? I expected something jagged."

"Can't be gravitational forces."

"No, there's not enough to hold down even gravel—everything is bald, there's no debris around at all."

"Maybe solar erosion has rounded the whole asteroid off."

"I'm going in," Nigel said abruptly.

"Okay, I guess I can track you from here."

The rotation of Icarus had brought the left wall closer. He nudged the craft back to center, remembering the first time he had learned in some forgotten science text that the Earth rotated. For weeks he had been convinced that whenever he fell down, it was because the Earth had moved beneath him without his noticing. He had thought it a wonderful fact, that everyone was able to stand up when the Earth was obviously trying to knock them down.

He smiled and took the craft in.

Jaws of stone yawned around him. Random fragments of something like mica glinted from the seared rocks. Nigel stopped about halfway down and tilted his spotlights up to see the underhang of a shelf; it was rough, brownish. He glided toward the vent wall and extended a waldoe claw. Its teeth bit neatly with a dull snap and brought back a few pounds of desiccated rubble. Len called; Nigel answered with monosyllables. He nudged the module downward again, moving carefully in the shadowed silence. He used a carrier pouch on the craft's skin to store the sample, and added more clawfuls of rock to other pouches.

He was nearly to the bottom before he noticed it.

The pitted floor was a jumble of rocks that rose from pools of ink. Nigel could not make out detail; he turned his spotlights downward.

A deep crack ran down the center of the rough floor. It was perhaps five meters wide and utterly black.

At irregular intervals things protruded from the crack, angular things that were charred and blunted. Some gave sparkling reflections, as though partially fused and melted. Nigel glided closer.

One of the objects was a long convoluted band on a coppery metal that described an intricate, folded weave of spirals.

He sat in the stillness and looked at it. Time passed.

Ten meters away a crumpled form that had been square was jammed in the crack, as though it had been partly forced out by a great wind. There were others; he photographed them.

Len had been calling for some time.

When he was through Nigel pressed a button to transmit and said, "We're going to have to recalculate, Len. Icarus isn't a lump of ice or a rock or anything else. I think"—he paused, still not quite believing it—"it has to be a ship."

THREE

It took Houston an hour to agree that he had to leave the module. Both he and Len had to argue with a Project Director who thought they had wasted too much time already; the man obviously didn't believe anything they reported, thinking it a cock-and-bull story designed to give Nigel more time for sample collecting. Len could only barely be restrained from coming into the cloud himself and only the necessity for reevaluating the mission stopped him.

Even after agreeing, Houston demanded a price. The Egg had to be secured to the vent floor first. This could be done without Nigel's leaving the module and, rather than argue, he moved quickly and efficiently to make short work of it.

The Egg was a dull gray sphere with securing bolts sunk into its skin. Nigel maneuvered it near the dark fissure wall and fired the bolts that freed it. The sphere coasted free.

Before it could glide very far he shot the aft securing bolts and they arced across the space to the wall and buried themselves in the stone. Steel cables reeled in and pulled the Egg to the rock face. Nothing could move it now and only Len or Nigel could detonate its fifty megatons.

Nigel ate before he left the module. Houston was divided about contingency plans; Dave gave him a summary to which he half listened. He and Len had another twenty-two hours' margin of air, and some changes could be made in their braking orbit back to Earth.

The two unmanned backup missions were being stepped up, but they looked less promising now. The radar sensing modules had to close on Icarus at high velocity, and the dust and pebbles inside the cloud, impacting at those speeds, could disable the warheads before they searched out Icarus itself.

"Popping the cover," Nigel called, and switched over to suit radio. The hatch came free with a hollow bang. He inched gingerly out, went hand over hand down the module's securing line, and stood at last on Icarus.

"The surface crunches a little under my feet," he said, knowing Len would pester him with questions if he didn't keep up a steady stream of commentary. They had both ridden in a small, sweaty cabin for five weeks to intercept Icarus, and now Len was missing a payoff larger than anything they had dreamed. "It must be something like cinder. Dried out. That's the way it looks, anyway."

A pause.

"I'm at the edge of the crack. It's about two meters across here, and the sides are pretty smooth. I'm hanging over it now, looking in. The walls go on for about four meters and then there's nothing but black. My lights can't pick up anything beyond that."

"Maybe there's a hole in there," Len said.

"Could be."

Before Dave could break in, Nigel added, "I'm going inside," and caught a lip of rock to pull himself into the crack.

As the rock fell away behind him there was only a faint glimmering reflection ahead. A white rectangle loomed up as he coasted on. It seemed to be set into the side of some larger slab, flush against the rock on one end and at least a hundred meters on a side. There were odd-shaped openings in it, some with curlicues and grainy stone collars like raised parentheses. Nigel lost his bearings as he approached and had to spin his arms to bring his feet around. There was a faint ring as he landed.

The white material had the dull luster of metal. Nigel used a cutting tool to gouge out a sliver. Nearby, a contorted thing of red and green appeared to grow smoothly out of the white metal, with no seam. To Nigel it looked like an abstract sculpture. When he touched it there was a faint tremor in his fingers; an arm of it moved infinitesimally, then was still. Nothing more happened.

He moved on, examined other objects, then shone a light down one of the holes in the face. The opening was a large oval and in the distance he could see where other dark corridors intersected it.

He went in.

A long tube of chipped rock. He took a sample. Volcanic origin? Something strange about its grainy flecks.

A vault. Gray walls, flash-burned brown.

Coasting.

Stretched lines shaping up . . . through . . . an eager bunching into swells. Should he go further? Beneath his torch light shadows swung with each motion of his arm, like eyes following every movement. Rippling patterns.

Patterns.

In the walls?

Should he? Behind each smile, teeth await.

Down, down now. Level. Gliding. Legs dangling
                                        dangling
                                        soft

something like a cushion but he sees nothing, only the shadows now melting something.   *hot*
                                    then cold   old

drawing him down again, telescoping him into fresh cubes of space, all aslant, a spherical room now, glowing red where his torch touches or is that a trick of the eyes?—he has difficulty focusing, probably loss of local vertical, an old problem in zero g, just a turn of the head will fix it—

Worn stone steps leading impossibly up, up into a ceiling now crumpled, spattered with orange drops that gleamed like oil in his murky light. Nigel remembered abruptly, dimly . . . An old film. A film of the Tutankhamun tomb, the jackal god Anubis rampant above nine defeated foes. Within the Treasury, tossed against a wall near the burial chamber by the necropolis guards after a robbery, lay a chest. Dried wood. It held the mummified bodies of two stillborn babies, perhaps Tutankhamun's children, in resins, gums and oils.

* * *

Opening the tomb.
Stepping inside.

And up from the Valley of Kings, from Karnak and
Luxor, winding with the Nile to Alexandria, a woman,
ancient, wrists rouged and walking with legs numb in the
grip of a gnawing, eating disease—
Nigel shook his head.

The steps were only markings. They led nowhere. He
photographed them *click whirr* and moved on.

The odd humming, again. There was no air in here—
how did he hear it? He coasted down a narrowing tube. The
humming was stronger. Ahead loomed a sphere. It was not
connected to the walls. Nigel touched it. It did not move.
The humming increased. He stuck the adhesive webbing
on the backs of his gloves to the sphere and used the
leverage to swing himself around it. The space beyond
yawned black. His torch licked into it and found nothing.
The light simply faded away. Nothing was reflected back.
The humming continued.

He moved to the far face of the sphere and peered into
the abyss beyond. Nothing.

Abruptly the humming rose, shrieked, wailed—and
stopped.

Nigel blinked, startled. Silence. Around him was a
pocket of darkness. The sphere, when he turned to face it,
seemed somehow inert, exhausted.

Nigel frowned. He jetted back to the sphere, worked
his way around it and returned through the tunnel the way
he had come, searching.

FOUR

Three hours later, when he had exhausted his film cannis-
ters and was beginning to tire, he headed back. The
network of corridors was a simple but space-saving web of
spherical shells, intricately intersected, and he had no
difficulty finding his way out.

"I'm back in the cabin," he said, sighing with a leaden fatigue.

"My God, where have you been, Nigel? Hours without a peep—I was almost ready to come in after you."

"There was rather a lot to see."

"Houston's patched through—and mad as hell, too—so start talking."

He took them through it all, describing the small rooms with elaborate netting that might have been sleeping quarters, the places like auditoriums, the ceilings with dancing lights, all the similarities he could find.

And the strangeness: spaces clogged with an infinitely layered green film that did not dissipate into the vacuum around it, but rippled as he passed by; rooms that seemed to change their dimensions as he watched; a place that gave off shrill vibrations he felt through his suit.

"Was there any illumination?" Dave said.

"Nothing I could see."

"We picked up a strong radio pulse several hours ago," Dave said. "We guessed you were trying to transmit from inside."

"No," Nigel said. "I couldn't raise Len or anything else on suit radio, so I packed it in and simply looked about."

"The signal wasn't on our assigned frequencies," Len said.

"We missed recording it—only lasted a second or so, and all our monitoring is in the telemetry bands," Dave said.

"Never mind," Len said. "Look, Nigel, it's just abandoned in there? No signs of occupants?"

Nigel paused. There were things he wanted to tell them, things he had felt. But how could he convey them? Earthside wanted facts.

Nigel had a sudden image of himself blundering hamfisted through those strange stretching corridors. The sphere. That humming. Had he accidentally triggered something?

"Nigel?"

"I think it's been vacant for a long time. There are big open vaults inside, hundreds of meters on a side. Something must have been in them—maybe water or food—"

"Or engines? Fuel?" Len said.

"Could be. Whatever it was, it's gone. If it was liquid it probably evaporated when this vent opened."

"Yes," Dave said, "that could be what made the cometary plume, the Flare Tail."

"I think it was. That, and the atmosphere that blew out through the crack. There's a lot of disorder inside—things ripped off the walls, strewn around, some gouges in the corridors that could have been made by things flying by. I picked up some of the smaller stuff lying around and brought it out."

No one said anything for a while. Nigel put a hand to the cabin wall near him, feeling the wholeness of it. He looked out at a burnished rock shelf and sensed the problem before him. It was something he could hold in one palm and turn to watch its facets catch the light, much as he had once seen in his mind Icarus slipping silently toward the Earth at thirty kilometers a second, himself and Len arcing out to meet the tumbling mountain, administer the kick, race home. That had been a clean problem with easy solutions, but now it crumpled and fell away from him, replaced by another, darker vision that slowly formed, coming to clarity in his mind—

Just before he had entered the dust plume, while Len was still in view, Nigel had taken a sighting on prominent stars to fix his inertial gyros. It was a simple process, easily done in the allotted time. Before swinging the telescope away from the port, a point of light caught Nigel's eye and he focused on it. It swelled into a disk, blue and white and flat, and he realized that he was looking at Earth. A featureless circle, complete and serene. Alone. A target, unnoticing. Its smooth, certain curve seemed more than a blotch on a star background; no, it was the center. A hole through which light was pouring from the other side of the universe. Complete. He had looked at it for a long moment.

Through scratchy static, Dave said, "Well, we can give you the time for another trip inside, Nigel. Haul out everything you can, take some more photos. Then you and Len can rendezvous and get clear of the Egg and—"

"No."

"What?"

"No. We're not going to set off the Egg, are we, Len?"

"Nigel—" Dave started, then paused.

"I don't know," Len said. "What have you got in mind?"

"Don't you see that this changes everything?"

"I wonder," Len said distantly. "We're trying to save millions of lives, Nigel. When Icarus hits it's going to wipe out a big chunk of territory, throw dirt into the air and probably change the climate. I kind of—"

"But it won't! Now now, anyway. Don't you see, Icarus is *hollow*. It has only a fraction of the mass we thought it did. Sure, it'll make a pretty big blast when it gets to India, but nothing like the disaster we thought."

Len said, "Maybe you've got something there."

"I can estimate the volume of rock left—"

"Nigel, I've been talking to some people here at Houston. We started reevaluating the collision dynamics and trajectory when you found the core was hollow. We'll have the results pretty soon, but until we do I just want to talk to you about this." Dave paused.

"Go ahead."

"Even if the mass of Icarus is a tenth of what we thought, its energy of impact will still be thousands of times larger than Krakatoa. Think of the people in Bengal."

"What's left of them, you mean," Len said. "The famine cycles have killed millions already, and they've been migrating out of the impact area for over a year now. Since the Indian government broke down nobody knows how many souls we're talking about, Dave."

"That's right. But if you don't care about them, Len, think about the dust that will be thrown into the upper atmosphere. That might bring on another Ice Age alone."

Nigel finished chewing on a bar of food concentrate. He felt a curious floating tiredness, his body relaxed and weak. The stimulants he had taken left him alert, but they could not wash away the lassitude that seeped through his arms and legs.

"I don't want to kill them, Dave," Nigel said. "Stop being melodramatic. But we've got to admit that what we can learn from this relic may be worth some human life."

"What do you propose, huh? What jackass scheme have you got?"

"That we stay here for a week, ten days, stripping the inside of whatever we can. You fly us additional air and water—use one of the unmanned intercepts that's carrying a warhead right now. We'll get clear of Icarus in time for the other interceptors to home on it, and we'll use the Egg, too."

"Sounds like it might work," Len said, and Nigel felt a surge of anticipation. He was going to do it; they couldn't turn him down.

"You *know* those interceptors aren't reliable in that dust cloud—that's why you guys are out there now. And the closer to Earth we hit Icarus, the less the net deflection before zero hour. If anything screws up at the last minute it might still smack into us."

"The risk is worth it, Dave," Len said.

"You're really going along with him, Len? I had hoped—"

"We've got hopes, too," Nigel said with sudden feeling. "Hopes that we might learn something here that will get the human race out of the mess it's in. A new physical concept, some invention that might come out of this. The beings who built this were superior to us, Dave, even in size—the doorways and corridors are big, wide."

"The *risk*, Nigel! If the Egg doesn't do the job and—"

"We've got to take it."

"—we sent you men out there to do a job. Now you're—"

Nigel wondered why Dave sounded so calm, even now. Perhaps they had told him to be deliberately cool and not provoke anything more. He wondered what his parents thought of this, of his taking a stand for exploration at the cost of people's lives. Or whether they knew of it at all— NASA had probably stopped news coverage as soon as they knew something was wrong; it wasn't just a heroic life-saving mission any more. He noticed his hands were trembling.

"Wait a minute, wait," Dave said. "I didn't mean to blow up that way, you guys. We all know you think you're doing the right thing." He paused amid the quiet burr of static, as though marshaling his words.

"Something new has come into the picture, though. I've just been handed the recomputed trajectory, allowing for the reduced Icarus mass. It makes a difference, a big one."

"How's that?" Nigel said.

"It was coming in pretty oblique to the top of the atmosphere already, you remember. With less mass, though, it's going to skip a bit—not much, but enough. It'll skip like a flat rock on a pond, and then drop. That takes it clear of the Indian subcontinent, and moves the impact point west."

Nigel felt a thick weight of dread form in his stomach.

"The ocean?"

"Yes. About two hundred miles out."

The finality of it consumed him. An ocean strike was vastly worse. Instead of dissipating energy as it ripped through the mantle rock, Icarus would throw up from the sea floor a towering geyser of steam. The steam jet would fan out across the upper atmosphere, leaving a planet swathed in clouds, driving great storms over a sunless world. The tidal wave splashed up would smash every coastal city on Earth, and most of civilization would vanish in hours.

"They're sure?" Len said.

"As certain as they can be," Dave said, and something veiled in his voice brought Nigel back out of his contemplation.

"Cut off Houston for a minute, Len," he said.

"Sure. There. What is it?"

"How do we know David isn't lying?"

"Oh . . . I guess we don't."

"It seems a little funny. A big rock skipping on the top of the atmosphere—one of the astrophysicists mentioned it in a briefing, but he said for a mass as large as Icarus it couldn't happen."

"What about for a tenth of that mass?"

"I don't know. And—damn it!—it's crucial."

"An ocean strike . . . If that happens, billions of people . . ."

"Right."

"You know . . . I don't think I want to . . ."

"I don't either." Nigel paused. And something flitted across his mind.

"Wait a second," he said. "Something odd here. This rock is hollow, that makes it lighter."

"Sure. Less mass."

"But that will make it easier to fragment, too. The chances of having a big chunk of rock left around after we set off the Egg is less, too."

"I guess so."

"But why didn't Dave mention that? It makes the odds *better*."

A silence.

"He's lying."

"Damn right he is." Saying the words made Nigel sure of it.

"So our chances are good."

"Better than Dave says, anyway. They must be."

"*If* the Egg goes off at all. We've hauled it all this way, maybe it's crapped out by now. They told us there would be a seven percent probability of that even before we left, remember? The thing might not work at all, Nigel."

"I'll bet it's going to, though."

"How much?"

"What?"

"How much will you bet? The lives of the rest of the human race?"

"If I have to."

"You're crazy."

"No. The odds are good. Dave is lying to us."

"Why would he do that?"

Nigel frowned. Len's doubts were beginning to reinforce his own. How sure *was* he? But he shook off the mood and said, "They don't want any *risk*, Len. They want two heroes and a lot of lives saved and no worries. They want to just keep it simple."

"And you're after—"

"I want to know what this thing is. Who built it. How they propelled it, where they came from—"

"That's a lot to expect of a bunch of artifacts."

"Maybe not. I saw some panels and consoles in there, I think. Could be the computerized records they used are still around."

"If they used computers at all."

"They must've. If we could get to some of the storage units—"

"You really think we could?"

Nigel shrugged. "Yes, I think so. I don't *know*—nobody does. But if we can find out something new here, Len, it could pay off. New technology could get us out of the mess the world is in."

"Like what?"

"A new power source. Maybe something with higher efficiency. That would be worth the chance."

"Maybe."

"Well . . ." Nigel felt his energy begin to drain away. "If you're not with me, Len . . ."

There came a silence.

Ping went the capsule, stretching with the sun's uneven heating. A metallic voice, asking *tick ping* its own questions. Could he really do it? No, absurd. Pointless. For what, after all? Why this comical risk? (Why leave England? Why go into space? *Ping*.) His parents had wondered that, he knew, though they'd never said it. Worried, even as they nudged him onward, where it would lead. And what *was* he going to look for in there? New wine, in this rocky old bottle? Or had humanity had enough wine already, thanks, hand held flat over the mouth of the glass, no. No, absurd. He was being impolite. All this stuff he'd done, all the work, really, you see, what was the point? Very well to search, but who pays the bill? Did he know—here his hands clenched, whitening—did he know what he was

looking for? Step aside for a moment. Look at this matter.
Was it rational? No. Absurd. No. He couldn't. He spun
from *tick* the voice but could not escape it. No. *Ping*. He
spun . . . spun . . .

Nigel wet his lips and waited. The sun lay hot on the
rock rim above. Its light reflected in the cabin and
deepened the lines of strain in his face. He found he was
holding his breath.

Then: "Nigel . . . look . . . don't put me on the
spot like this."

Nigel sealed his suit again, automatically. He reached
up and popped the hatch cover.

"I . . . I've got to go with Dave, buddy. This thing is
too big for me to—"

"Okay," Nigel said abruptly. "Okay, okay."

"Look, I don't want you to feel—"

"Yeah." He reached up and pulled himself through the
hatch, into the full glare. Looking up, his inner ear played a
trick and he suddenly felt as though he was falling down a
narrow canyon and into the sun, drawn by it. Automatically
he clung to the hatch and twisted himself out, letting his
equilibrium return with the sense of motion. He felt
curiously calm.

"Nigel?"

He said nothing. Halfway along the module's length
was a flat brown box the size of a typewriter. He went for it
hand over hand, legs free, his breath sounding abnormally
loud. The clamps around the box opened easily and with
one hand he swung it to his side and clipped it to his utility
belt.

"Nigel? Dave wants to know—"

"I'm here. Wait a second."

He found the extra food and air units to the aft of the
module—emergency supplies, easily portable. He felt
clumsy with all of them clinging to his waist, but if he
moved carefully he should be able to carry them some
distance without tiring. Sluggishly he made his way to the
brownish-black rock below.

"Nigel?"

He checked his suit. Everything seemed all right. His shoulder itched around his suit yoke and he moved, trying to scratch.

The irony was inescapable: the blowout of gases through the vent made the cometary tail flare out from this ancient vessel, causing him and Len to come here and discover it—but that same eruption deflected Icarus enough to strike the Earth, and made necessary its destruction. Fate is a double-edged blade.

"Nigel?"

He started toward the vent and then stopped. Might as well finish it.

"Listen, Len—and be sure Dave hears this, too. I've got the arming circuits and the trigger. You can't set off the Egg without them. I'm taking them into the vent with me."

"Hey! Look—" Behind Len's voice was a faint chorus of cries from Houston. Nigel went on.

"I'm going to hide them somewhere inside. Even if you follow me in, you won't be able to find them."

"Jesus! Nigel, you don't under—"

"Shut up. I'm doing this for time, Len. Houston had better send us more air and supplies, because I'm going to use the full week of margin I think we've got. One week—to look for something worth saving out of this derelict. Maybe those computer banks, if there are any."

"No, no, listen," Len said, a thin edge of desperation in his voice. "You're not just gambling with those Indians, man. Or even with everybody who lives near the seacoasts, if you even care about that. If the Egg doesn't work and Houston can't reach that rock with the unmanned warheads, and it hits the water—"

"Right."

"There'll be storms."

"Right."

"Enough to keep a shuttle from coming up to get us back into Earth orbit."

"I don't think they'd want to bother, anyway," Nigel said wryly. "We won't be too popular."

"*You* won't."

"The search will be twice as effective if you come down here and help, Len." Nigel smiled to himself. "You can gain us some time that way."

"You son of a bitch!"

He began moving toward the vent again. "Better hurry up, Len. I won't stick around out here for long to guide you in."

"Shit! You used to be a nice guy, Nigel. Why are you acting like such a bastard now?"

"I never had a chance to be a bastard for something I believed in before," he said, and kept moving.

PART TWO 2014

ONE

He awoke, basking in the orange glow of sun on his eyelids. A yellow shaft of light streamed through the acacias outside the window and warmed his shoulder and face. Nigel stretched, warm and lazy and catlike. Though it was early, already the heavy, scented heat of the Pasadena spring filled the bedroom. He rolled over and looked appreciatively at Alexandria, who was seriously studying herself in the mirror.

"Vanity," he said, voice blurred from sleep.

"Insurance."

"Why can't you simply be a scruff, like me?"

"Business," she said distantly, smearing something under her eyes. "I'm going to be far too busy today to pay attention to my appearance."

"And you must be spiffy to face the public."

"Ummm. I think I'll pin up my hair. It's a mess, but I don't have time to . . ."

"Why not? It's early yet."

"I want to get into the office and thrash through some paperwork before those representatives from Brazil arrive. And I have to leave work early—have an appointment with Dr. Hufman."

"Again?"

"He's got those tests back."

"What's the upshot?"

"That's what I'm to find out."

Nigel squinted at her groggily, trying to read her mood.

"I don't think it's really important," she volunteered.

The bed sloshed as he rolled out and teetered on one foot, an arm extended upward in a theatrical gesture.

29

"Jack be nimble," Alexandria said, smiling and brushing her hair about experimentally.

"You didn't say that last night."

"When you fell out of bed?"

"When *we* fell out of bed."

"The party on top is in charge of navigation. Code of the sea."

"My mind must have been elsewhere. Silly of me."

"Um. Where's breakfast?"

Naked, he padded across the planking. The yielding, creaking feel of oiled and varnished wood was one of the charms of this old trisected house, and worth the cost of leasing. He went into the bathroom, lifted the ivory toilet seat and peed for a long moment; first pleasure of the day. Finished, he lowered the seat and its magenta cover but did not push the handle. At thirty-five cents a flush, he and Alexandria had decided to let things go until absolutely necessary. As an economy measure the savings weren't necessary for them, but the waste of not doing so seemed inelegant.

He slipped on his sandals where he'd stepped out of them the night before and walked through the archway of thick oak beams, into the kitchen. The tiled room held the night chill long after the remainder of the house had surrendered to day. The slapping of his sandals echoed back at him; he flipped on the audio channels and dialed first music, then—finding nothing he liked, this early—the news spots.

He grated out some sharp cheddar cheese while a calm, undisturbed voice told him that another large strike was brewing, threatening to cut off shipping again. He rapped open six eggs, thought a moment and then added two more, and rummaged through the refrigerator for the creamy, small curd cottage cheese he'd bought the day before. The President, he heard, had made a "tough, hard-hitting" speech against secret corporate gestation-under-glass programs; the newscaster made no mention of similar government projects. Two of the recent hermaphrodites had married, proclaiming the first human relationship free of stereotypes. Nigel sighed and dumped the lot into the blender. He added some watery brown sauce he'd made up in batches for just this purpose and sprinkled in marjoram, salt and pepper. The blender purred it all into a smooth soup. He fetched tomato sauce while the audio went on about a new industrial coalition which had linked up with an equally massive crowd of labor unions, to back a bill granting extraordinary protectionist import taxes on goods from Brazil, Australia and China. For variety and in the name of pure blind experiment he added coriander to the mix, poured it into a souffle dish and started it baking. The oven popped with industrious heat.

Alexandria was showering as he dressed. He put the bedroom in order; last night, tumbling toward the bed, they'd scattered oddments of underclothing like debris from some domestic collision. He rolled up his flared shirt cuffs in anticipation of the day's warmth and Alexandria emerged from the vapor shower, her expressive bottom jiggling beneath a sheen of moisture.

She slipped the shower cap from around her knotted hair and said, "Read me my horoscope, will you? It's on the end table, there."

Nigel grimaced. "I prefer entrails, myself. Shall I nip out for a small goat, put him to the knife and give you a prognosis for the day?"

"Read."

"Much more satisfying, I should think. Gutsy—"

"Read."

"Gemini, April twentieth to May twentieth." He paused. "Let's see, 'You are quick, intelligent and well organized. Try to use these to advantage today. Unfortunately, people will probably tend to think you are overly aggressive. Try not to flaunt your power, and resist the impulse to hurt small animals—this is a bad character trait. Avoid orange juice pits and dwarfs today.' Sound advice, I'd say."

"Nigel . . ."

"Well, what good's advice if it's not specific? A lot of vapid generalities won't tell you much about what stock to buy for those Brazilian fellows—if there were stocks any more, that is."

"They want to buy *us*, that's the point."

"The whole airline?"

"Yep. Lock, stock and et cetera."

"And your job—?"

"Oh, they just want to own us, not run the company."

"Ah. Well—" He glanced at his watch. "Nearly time for the Catnapper's Soufflé."

He went into the kitchen, dealt out forks, plates and napkins and took them into the dining nook. The nook had been a spacious closet in the old house, in those days a single-family dwelling, and now featured a mitred window giving on the back yard. A jacaranda tree, showing signs of an interest in blossoming into a velvety blue-and-white, bracketed one side of the green swath of lawn.

Nigel checked his watch again, which mutely informed him that this was the thirty-first of April. Was that right, under the new calendar? He ran the old rhyme through— thirty days hath November, and, and—? He never could summon up those fiendish little aids to memory when they'd be handy. But he knew April well enough, certainly: next week would mark fifteen years since Icarus.

Fifteen. And for all the conferences and international symposia and doctoral theses, scant reward had come of the Icarus adventure. He and Len had managed to lash a fair quantity of interesting artifacts into various crannies of the *Dragon* module, and even more outside, in the superstructure. But in dealing with the totally strange, how could they possibly make the right judgments? What seemed a complex web of electronics turned out to be a series of idiot circuits; the greenish fog that permeated the vast caverns within Icarus was an organic chain molecule, probably a high-vacuum lubricant.

Interesting, yes; but not keys to a fundamental discovery. Some odd technical tricks came out of it all—an advanced substrate for microelectronics, resistant alloys, some sophisticated chemicals—but somehow the *alienness* of the thing had slipped through their fingers. None of their haul bore silent witness to Icarus's origin. Everything in it could have been made from Earth materials, far in the past—and a fraction of the scientists who worked on the trove thought it had been. No one had come up with convincing evidence of an earlier civilization on Earth, but the sheer ordinariness of Icarus seemed to argue for it.

For Nigel and Len it had been a slowly dawning defeat, particularly following on the storm of controversy that waited for them when the shuttle brought them down from Earth orbit. NASA had shielded them at first, but too many people were horrified at Nigel's risk-taking. The Indians broke off relations, even after he and Len fired the Egg and pulverized Icarus into harmless gravel. Congressmen demanded prison sentences for the two of them. *The New York Times* ran three editorials within one month, each calling for progressively stronger measures against NASA, and Len, and especially Nigel.

He spoke a few times before largely hostile audiences, defendings his ideas and emotions, and gave up. Words weren't actions, and never would be. Luckily, he was a civilian. His offense against the moral equilibrium fell awkwardly between statutes. A Federal prosecutor introduced a charge, based on deprivation of the civil rights of everyone in the United States, but it was thrown out; after all, it was the Indians who'd been threatened. And in the public scuffle NASA kept very quiet, stepping gingerly around the fact that Dave had been lying behind that media-measured Cheshire-cat grin of his. The whole story about Icarus skipping on the upper atmosphere, like a child's accurately skimmed rock, was a hastily improvised song and dance.

And so it had passed.

After a year and a final receding volley from the *Times* ("Remembering the Abyss"), other worries furrowed the world's brows. Once out of the limelight, NASA began gently easing Len and Nigel out. Oddly enough, in obscurity lay more threat. Exposure of Dave's lie in full view would have cost NASA support on all sides. But if the facts wobbled into view before an obscure committee, years later, it would do little harm; timing was everything. The trump cards he and Len held slowly devalued, like an inflated currency. Thus the worst time came when he could finally walk into a supermarket without being harangued, insulted, treated to a garlic-breathed debate.

That, too, he had survived.

"Ready yet?" Alexandria said, bringing the jug of orange juice into the dining nook. It rattled with ice cubes.

"Right." Nigel shook off his mood and fetched the souffle. As he served it up with a broad wooden spoon, the crust cracked and exhaled a cloud smelling of omelette. They ate quickly, both hungry. It was their policy to eat virtually no supper and a thorough breakfast; Alexandria felt the body would use the breakfast through the day, and simply turn a supper into fat.

"Shirley's coming over after supper tonight," Alexandria said.

"Good. You finish that novel she gave you?"

Alexandria sniffed elegantly. "Nope. It was mostly the usual wallowing in postmodernist angst, with technicolor side shows."

Nigel popped a Swebitter grape into his mouth; his lips puckered at its tartness.

Alexandria reached for a grape and winced. "Damn."

"Wrists still hurting?"

"I thought they were getting better." She held her right wrist in the other hand and wriggled it experimentally. Her face pinched for an instant and she stopped. "Nope, it's still there, whatever it is."

"Perhaps you sprained it."

"Both wrists simultaneously? Without noticing it?"

"Seems unlikely."

"Damn," Alexandria said abruptly. "You know, I don't believe I want those Brazilians to get our company after all."

"Uh? I thought—"

"Yes, yes, I started it all. Made the first moves. But damn it, it's *ours*. We could use the capital, sure . . ." She twisted her mouth sidewise in a familiar gesture of irritation. ". . . but I didn't realize . . . !"

"That was part of the soft sell, though. They'd get something thoroughly American—*American* Airlines."

"Compared to us, the way we do things, those preening dandies can't tie their shoelaces without an instruction manual. They don't *know*."

"Ah." He enjoyed watching the flush of eagerness and zest stealing the cool and proper manner from her features. Watching her this way, chattering on about indices and margins and accountable funds, suspended halfway between the soft and easy Alexandria of the night, emerging into the precise, efficient executive of the day, he knew again why he loved her.

He left for the Lab a few minutes after Alexandria, as soon as he could finish the dishes, and barely caught his bus. It meandeared along Fair Oaks, three-quarters filled even this late in the morning. Nigel pulled his personal earjacks out of his pocket and plugged into the six-channel audio track. He tuned out a jingle suitable for morons, a sportscast ditto, paused at the news—psychologists were worrying about a sudden surge in infanticide—and flicked over the "classical" channel. A short trumpet voluntary ended and a soupy Brahms symphony began, heavy with strings. He switched off, pocketed his earjacks and studied the view as the bus labored up the Pasadena hills. A ruddy-brown tinge smothered the land. He slipped his nose mask on and breathed in the sweet, cloying smell. Some things never improved. He was aware that the political situation was worsening, people were jittery about imports/exports, but it seemed to him that air smelling fresh-scrubbed, as though from the night's rain, and a bit of Beethoven on the way to work were, all in all, more important issues.

Nigel smiled to himself. In these sentiments he recognized an echo of his mother and father. They had moved back to Suffolk shortly after the Icarus business, and he had seen them regularly. Their compass had shrunk into the comfortable English countryside: clear air and string quartets. The more he rubbed against the world, the more he saw them in himself. Stubborn he was, yes, just like his father, who had refused to ever believe Nigel should have gone to Icarus or, indeed, should have stayed on in America after that. It was precisely that same stubbornness that made him remain, though. Now, when he spoke amid these flat American voices, he heard his father's smooth vowels. Angina and emphysema had stolen those two blended figures from him, finally, but here in this sometimes alien land he felt them closer than before.

The Jet Propulsion Laboratory was a jumble of rectangular blocks perched on a still-green hillside. As the bus wheezed to a stop he heard chanting and saw three New Sons handing out literature and buttonholing at the main gate. He took one of their handouts and crumpled it up after a glance. It seemed to him their promotional field work was getting worse; overtly mystical appeals wouldn't work with JPL's staff.

He passed through three sets of guards, grudgingly showed his badge—the Lab was a prime target for the bombers, but it was a nuisance nonetheless—and made his way down chilly, neon-bleached corridors. When he reached his office he found Kevin Lubkin, Mission Coordinator, already waiting for him. Nigel moved some issues of *Icarus*, the scholarly journal, out of a chair for Lubkin, pushed them into the heap of papers on his desk and raised the blinds of his window to let one pale blade of light lance across the opposite wall. He worked in a wing without air conditioning and it was a good idea to get some cross-ventilation going as soon as possible; the afternoon was unforgiving. Then, too, he adjusted the blinds each morning as a ritual beginning of work, and so uttered nothing more than a greeting to Lubkin until it was done.

"Something wrong?" he asked then, summoning up an artificial alertness.

Kevin Lubkin, distracted, closed a folder he had been reading. "Jupiter Monitor," he said tersely. He was a burly, red-faced man with a smooth voice and a belly that had recently begun to bulge downward, concealing his belt buckle.

"Malfunction?"

"No. It's being jammed."

He flicked a blank look at Nigel, waiting.

Nigel raised an eyebrow. An odd tension had suddenly come into the room. He might still be relaxed from breakfast, but he wasn't so slow that he could be taken in by an office sendup. He said nothing.

"Yeah, I know," Lubkin said, sighing. "Sounds impossible. But it happened. I called you about it but—"

"What's the trouble?"

"At two this morning we got a diagnostic report from the Jovian Monitor. The graveyard shift couldn't figure it out, so they called me. Seemed like the onboard computer thought the main radio dish was having problems." He took off his creamshell glasses to cradle them in his lap. "That wasn't it, I decided. The dish is okay. But every time it tries to transmit to us, something echoes the signal back after two minutes."

"Echoes?" Nigel tilted his chair, staring at titles on his bookshelves while he ran the circuit layout of the J-Monitor's radio gear through his mind. "Two minutes is far too long for any feedback problem—you're right. Unless the whole program has gone sour and the transmissions are being retaped by Monitor itself. It could get confused and think it was reading an incoming signal."

Lubkin waved a hand impatiently. "We thought of that."

"And?"

"The self-diagnostics say no—everything checks."

"I give up," Nigel said. "I can tell you've got a theory, though." He spread his hands expansively. "What is it, then?"

"I think J-Monitor is getting an honest incoming signal. It's telling us the truth."

Nigel snorted. "How did you muddle through to that idea?"

"Well, I know—"

"Radio takes nearly an *hour* to reach us from Jupiter at this phase of the orbit. How is anyone going to send Monitor's own messages back to it in two minutes?"

"By putting a transmitter in Jupiter orbit—just like Monitor."

Nigel blinked. "The Sovs? But they agreed—"

"No Soviets. We checked on the fastwire. They say no, they haven't shot anything out that way at all in a coon's age. Our intelligence people are sure they're leveling."

"Chinese?"

"They aren't playing in our league yet."

"Who, then?"

Lubkin shrugged. The sallow sagging lines in his face told more than his words. "I was kind of thinking you might help me find out."

There was a faint ring of defeat in the way the man said it—Nigel noted the tone because he had never heard it before. Usually Lubkin had an aspect of brittle hardness, a cool superior air. Now his face was not set in its habitual aloof expression; it seemed open, even vulnerable. Nigel guessed why the man had come in himself at 2 A.M., rather than delegating the job—to show his people, without having to tell them in so many words, that he could do the work himself, that he hadn't lost the sure touch, that he understood the twists and subtleties of the machines they guided. But now Lubkin hadn't unraveled the knot. The graveyard shift had departed into a gray dawn, so now he could safely ask for help without being obvious.

Nigel smiled wryly at himself. Always calculating, weighing the scales.

"Right," he said. "I'll help."

TWO

The solar system is vast. Light requires eleven hours to cross it. Scattered debris—rock, dust, icy conglomerates, planets—circles the ordinary white star, each fragment turning one face to the incandescent center, receiving warmth, while the other faces the interstellar abyss.

The craft approaching the system in 2011 did not know even these simple facts. Swimming in black vastness, it understood only that it was once again nearing a commonplace type of star and that the familiar ritual must begin again.

Though it was carrying out a long and labored exploration of this spiral arm, it had not chosen this particular star at random. Long before, cruising at a sizable fraction of light speed somewhat below the plane of the galaxy, it had filtered through the whispering radio noise a brief signal.

The message was blurred and garbled. There were three common referents the craft could piece together, however, and these resembled an ancient code it had been taught to honor. The machine began to turn in a great arc which arrowed toward a grouping of stars; the jittery message had not lasted long enough to get a precise fix.

Much later, during the approach, a stronger radio burst peaked through the sea of hydrogen emission. A distress call. Life system failure. A breach in the hull, violation of the vital integrity indices—

There it ended. The signal's direction was clearer. But did it come from this system ahead, or from some much more distant source lying behind it? In such circumstances the craft fell back on its habitual patterns.

Its first duty was simple. It had already decelerated until interstellar dust would no longer plow into it with blistering, destructive velocity. The craft could now safely cut off the magnetic fields encasing it and begin to extend sensors. A port opened to the utter cold and peered ahead. A blinder drew across the image of the nearing star, so that tiny flecks of light nearby could register.

The telescope employed was 150 centimeters in diameter and did not differ markedly from those used on Earth; some facets of design, bounded by natural law, are universal. The craft crept along at far below light speed. Isotopes met with a low mumble in the throat of its exhaust. Fingers of magnetic fields, extended forward, plucked the proper atoms from the interstellar gas and funneled them in. Only this carving of a cylinder in the dust disturbed the silent reaches.

The craft watched patiently. Any planets orbiting the star ahead were still far away, and picking out their movements against the speckled background of stationary stars was difficult. At four-tenths of a light year away, the activated circuits and their consultation backup agreed: a yellow-brown patch near the white star was a planet. Higher functions of the computers felt the prickly stirrings of activity and heard of the discovery. A background library of planetary theory was consulted. The blurred, dim disk ahead shimmered as the ship swept through a whisper-thin cloud of dust, while the machine bracketed and measured its objective in methodical detail.

The planet was large. It might have enough mass to ignite thermonuclear fires in its core, but experience argued that its light was too weak. The computers pondered whether to classify the system as a binary star and eventually decided against it. Still, the waxing point of light ahead held promise.

The morning passed in puzzled argument.

Nigel wasn't totally willing to abandon the hypothesis that Jupiter Monitor had malfunctioned. The flight engineers—a flinty crew, skeptical of nonspecialists, fond of jargon—thought otherwise. They gave ground grudgingly, pitting sweet cool reason against Nigel's vague doubts. A complete run-through of J-Monitor's error-detection modes, a new diagnostic analysis, a hand-check of transmissions—all showed nothing wrong. There was no mechanical flaw.

The quirky echo had faded away a little after 3 A.M. The Monitor was no longer in its original ellipse around Jupiter; a month earlier its engines had stirred awake and fired, to nudge it into orbit around Callisto, fifth moon of Jupiter. Now it spun an elaborate orange-slice orbit, lacing over the icy glare of Callisto's poles every eight hours.

Nigel snapped a cracker in half, swallowed it with some lukewarm tea, hardly noticing the mingling of sweet and tart. He closed his eyes to the *ting* and clatter of telemetry. The flight engineers had finally gone back to their burrows and he and Lubkin sat in the main control bay, at one of the semicircular tables; digital arrays ringed them.

"That puts paid to the simple ideas, then," Nigel said. "I suppose we'd best have a glance at the Callisto orbit."

"Don't follow," Lubkin said.

"If the signal came from a source *outside* J-Monitor, something cut it off. The echo must've faded because Callisto came between the source and J-Monitor."

Lubkin nodded. "Reasonable. The same thing had occurred to me, but—" he looked at his watch. "It's almost noon. Why didn't the echo return around seven or so this morning, when J-Monitor came *out* from behind Callisto?"

Nigel had the uncomfortable feeling that he was playing the role of dull-witted graduate student to Lubkin's learned professor. But then, he realized, that was precisely the impression a skillful administrator would try to create.

"Well . . . maybe the other source is occluded by Jupiter itself. Now *it's* blotted out."

Lubkin pursed his lips. "Maybe, maybe."

"Can't we rough out some sort of orbit for the source, given a triangulation with Callisto?"

Lubkin nodded.

Around every star stretches a spherical shell of space, and somewhere within the thickness of that shell, temperatures are mild. For an Earthlike world, given the right primordial nudge, water will be liquid on the planet's surface.

One-third of a light year from the burning nugget of the star, the craft surveyed this livable zone and found it good. There was no sign of a large planet like the yellow-brown gas giant circling further out. This was a crucial test, for a massive world, close in, would have made another stable orbit impossible within the life-giving volume. Had the ship found such a planet, it was under standing orders—encrusted, ingrained, so old they functioned as instincts—to accelerate through the system, gathering all possible data for the astrophysical index, and chart a course for the next in a lengthy record of candidate suns.

Instead, the ship quickened the rumble of deceleration. It uncapped its telescope more frequently and peered ahead for longer intervals. A blue-white splotch revolved into another gas giant planet, smaller than the first and further out. Its image resisted precise definition. The craft noted a blurred circlet of bluish light—the body was ringed, a not uncommon occurrence among heavy planets.

Another massive planet was found, thinly ringed, and then another, each further away from the star. The ma-

chines began lowering their estimates of the possibility of
life in this system. Still, past experience held out a glimmer
of hope. Small, dim worlds might lie further in, even if the
weight of theory and observation made it seem unlikely. By
a fluke, the ship could be approaching from the night side of
a world and miss it entirely. The craft waited.

At one-sixth of a light year out the computers found an
ambiguous smear of blue and brown and white: a planet
near the star. Reward circuits triggered. The machines felt
a spasm of relief and joy, a seething electric surge within.
They were sophisticated devices, webs of impulses pro-
grammed to want to succeed, yet buffered against severe
disappointment if success eluded them.

For the moment they were content. The ship flew on.

Spherical trigonometry, the vectoring line of J-Monitor's main dish, calculus, orbital parameters, estimates,
angles. Check and recheck.

Slowly, the most probable answer emerged—3:30 P.M.,
an hour away. By then the source should arc into view of
J-Monitor's main dish. Nigel imagined it as a dot of light
slowly separating from the churning brown bands of
Jupiter, rising above the horizon. As it traced its own
ellipse, J-Monitor would be surveying the snow fields of
Callisto below with its own mechanical intensity; craters,
wrinkled hill lines, fissures, glinting blue ice mountains.

"One hour," Lubkin said.

"Can we realign the main dish that quickly, without
disturbing the surveying routine?" Nigel asked.

"We'll have to," Lubkin replied firmly. He picked up
the telephone and dialed Operations Control.

"Tell them to rotate the camera platform, too," Nigel
said quickly.

"You think there'll be anything to see at that range?"

Nigel shrugged. "Possibly."

"The narrow-angle camera? We can't move both in—"

"Right. We should work out a set of shots. Use the
filters, stepping down from ultraviolet to IR. They can
sequence automatically."

Lubkin began speaking rapidly and precisely into the

telephone, smiling confidently now that there were orders to be given, men to be told.

The ship was still cruising in deep silence, far from the star's warmth, when it began to discern radio waves. More of the higher functions of the craft came alive. The weak signals were weighed and sifted. Filtering away the usual sputtering star noise, they found a faint trace of emission localized to the planets.

The most powerful source was the innermost gas giant. This was an optimistic sign, for the world did orbit fairly near its star. If it had merely a transparent atmosphere it would be too cold, but analysis showed it to be cloaked in thick, deep clouds. Such planets could warm themselves, the ship knew, by gravitational contraction and by heat-trapping—the greenhouse effect. Life could well evolve in their skies and seas.

Still, such clotted blankets of gas and liquid meant awesome pressures. Life in similar worlds rarely developed skeletons and thus could not manipulate tools; the ship's log carried many instances of this. Trapped in their deep bowl of ammonia and methane, free of technology's snarls, such creatures could not communicate—and the ship could assuredly not fly into such pressures in search of them.

A smaller source of radio waves lay further inward. It was the third planet, blue and white. The signals wove complex overlapping patterns, faint tremors that could be atmospheric phenomena: thunderstorms, lightning flashes, perhaps radiation from a magnetosphere. Still, the world was wrapped in a clear gas, a hopeful sign. The craft flew sunward.

By 6 P.M. they became discouraged. The Monitor's main dish was reprogrammed to carry out a methodical search pattern around the spot where the unknown radio source should appear.

It was functioning. The data were coming in. All operations were proceeding smoothly.

And there were absolutely no results.

The flight engineering staff was milling about, writing

day summary reports, ready to go home. To them, the echo problem was a temporary aberration that cleared up of itself. Until it reappeared, no cause for alarm.

The target should have emerged from Jupiter's rim at 3:37 P.M., according to revised estimates. Given the time lag in signals from Jupiter, Operations Control began receiving data slightly before 4:30 P.M. The main dish's search was completed within an hour. They couldn't use the narrow-angle camera—not enough technicians were free from the Mars Burrower and the planetary satellites. In any case, nothing indicated that there was anything worth seeing.

"Looks like balls-up on that," Nigel said.

"Either the whole ideas is a pipe dream—" Lubkin began.

"Or we haven't got the orbit right," Nigel finished. An engineer in portable headphones came down the curved aisle, asked Lubkin to sign a clipboard, and went away.

Lubkin leaned back in his roller chair. "Yeah, there's always that."

"We can have another go tomorrow."

"Sure." Lubkin did not sound particularly enthusiastic. He got up from the console and paced back and forth in the aisle. There wasn't much room; he nearly bumped into a technician down the way who was checking readouts at the Antenna Systems console. Nigel ignored the background murmur of the Control Bay and tried to think. Lubkin paced some more and finally sat down. The pair studied their green television screens, which were tilted backward for ease of viewing, where sequencing and programming data were continually displayed and erased. Occasionally the computer index would exceed its allowed parameter range and the screen would jump from yellow-on-green to green-on-yellow. Nigel had never gotten used to this; he remained disconcertingly on edge until someone found the error and the screen reverted.

The console telephone rang, jarring his concentration still further. "There's an external call for you," an impersonal woman's voice said.

"Put them off a bit, will you?"

"I believe it's your wife."

"Ah. Put her on hold."

He turned to Lubkin. "I'd like to get the camera free tomorrow."

"What's the use?"

"Call it idle speculation," he said shortly. He was rather tired and wasn't looking for an argument.

"Okay, try it," Lubkin said, threw down his pencil and labored to his feet. His white shirt was creased and wrinkled. In defeat he seemed more likable to Nigel, less an edgy executive measuring his moves before he made them. "See you tomorrow," Lubkin said and turned away, shoulders slumped.

Nigel punched a button on the telephone.

"Sorry I took so long, I—"

"Nigel, I'm at Dr. Hufman's."

"What's—"

"I, I need you here. Please." Her voice was thin and oddly distant.

"What's going?"

"He wants to talk to both of us."

"Why?"

"I don't know, really. Not totally."

"What's the address?"

She gave him a number on Thalia. "I'm going down for some lab tests. A half hour or so."

Nigel thought. "I don't know which bus serves that—"

"Can't you . . ."

"Certainly. Certainly. I'll sign off for a Lab car, tell them it's for business tomorrow."

"Thank you, Nigel. I, I just . . ."

He pursed his lips. She seemed dazed, distracted, her executive briskness melted away. Usually the efficient manner did not seep from her until evening.

"Right," he said. "I'm leaving now." He replaced the telephone in its cradle.

THREE

A gray haze layer cut off all buildings at the fourth story, giving Thalia Avenue an oddly truncated look. The cramped car labored along with an occasionally irregular *pocketa-pocketa* as Nigel leaned out the window, searching for building numbers. He had never become accustomed to the curious American reticence about disclosing addresses. Immense, imposing steel and concrete masses stood anonymously, challenging the mere pedestrian to discover what lay inside. After some searching, 2636 Thalia proved to be a low building of elegant striated stonework, the most recent addition to the block, clearly assembled well after the twentieth-century splurge of construction materials.

Dr. Hufman's waiting room had the hushed antechamber feel to it that marked a private practice. A public medical center would have been all tile and tan partitions and anonymous furniture. As he walked in, Nigel's attention returned to Alexandria's unspoken tension and he looked around the waiting room, expecting to see her.

"Mr. Walmsley?" a nurse said from a glass-encased box that formed one wall of the room. He advanced.

"Where is she?" He saw no point in wasting time.

"In the laboratory, next door. I wanted to explain that I didn't, we didn't know Miss Ascencio was, ah . . ."

"Where's the lab?"

"You see, she filled out her form as Single and gave her sister as person to be notified. So we didn't know—"

"She was living with me. Right. Where's—"

"And Dr. Hufman likes to have both parties present when . . ."

"When what?"

"Well, I, ah, only wanted to apologize. We, I would have asked Miss Ascencio to come with you if we had—"

"Mr. Walmsley. Come in."

Dr. Hufman was an unremarkable man in an ill-fitting brown jacket, no tie, large cushioned shoes. His black hair thinned at the temples, showing a marble-white scalp. He turned and walked back into his office without waiting to see if Nigel would follow.

The office differed in detail but not general theme from every other doctor's office Nigel had ever seen. There were old-fashioned books with real bindings, some of them leather or a convincing synthetic. Long lines of medical journals, mostly out of date, marched across the shelves on one wall, punctuated by a model ship here and there. On the desk and a side table were collections of stubby African dolls. Nigel wondered if physicians were given a course in med school in interior decorating, with special emphasis on patient-soothing bric-a-brac, restful paintings and humanizing oddments.

He began to sit down in the chair Hufman offered when a door opened to his left and Alexandria stepped in. She hesitated when she saw Nigel and then closed the door softly. Her hands seemed bony and white. There was in her manner something Nigel had never seen before.

"Thank you, dear, for coming so quickly."

Nigel nodded. She sat in another chair and both turned toward Hufman, who was sitting behind a vast mahogany desk, peering into a file folder. He looked up and seemed to compose himself.

"I've asked that you come over, Mr. Walmsley, because I have some rather bad news for Miss Ascencio." He spoke almost matter-of-factly, but Nigel sensed a balanced weight behind the words.

"Briefly, she has systemic lupus erythematosus."

"Which is?" Nigel said.

"Sorry, I thought you might have heard of it."

"I have," Alexandria said quietly. "It's the second most common cause of death now, isn't it?"

Nigel looked at her questioningly. It seemed an unlikely sort of thing for Alexandria to know, unless— unless she'd guessed.

"Yes, cancer of all sorts is still first. Lupus has increased rapidly in the last two decades."

"Because it comes from pollution," she said.

Hufman leaned back in his chair and regarded her.

"That is a common opinion. It is very difficult to verify, of course, because of the difficulty in isolating influences."

"I think I've heard of it," Nigel murmured. "But . . ."

"Oh. A disease of the connective tissue, Mr. Walmsley. It strikes primarily the skin, joints, kidneys, heart, the fibrous tissue that provides internal support for the organs."

"Her sprained wrists—"

"Exactly, yes. We can expect further inflammation, though not so much as to create a deformity. That is only one symptom, not the total disease, however."

"What else is there?"

"We don't know. It's an insidious process. It could reside in the joints or it could spread to the organs. We have very little diagnostic capability. We simply treat it—"

"How?"

"Aspirin," Alexandria said mildly with a wan smile.

"That's absurd!" Nigel said. "Fixing up a disease with—"

"No, Miss Ascencio is correct, as far as she goes. That is the recommended course for the mild stages. I'm afraid she is beyond that now, though."

"What'll you give her?"

"Corticosteroid hormones. Perhaps chloroquine. I want to stress that these are not cures. They offer only symptomatic relief."

"What does cure it?"

"Nothing."

"Well, hell! There's got to be—"

"No, Nigel," she said. "There doesn't have to be anything."

"Mr. Walmsley, we are dealing with a potentially fatal disease here. Some specialists attribute the rise of lupus to specific pollutants such as lead or sulfur or nitrogen compounds in auto exhausts, but we truly do not know its cause. Or cure."

Nigel noticed that he was clenching the chair arms. He sat back and put his hands in his lap. "Very well."

"Miss Ascencio's condition is not acute. I must warn you, however, that the subacute or chronic stage of this disease has been getting shorter and shorter as its frequency among the population increases. There are cases in which the disease persists but is not ultimately fatal."

"And—?" she said.

"Other cases sometimes go to completion within a year. But that is *not* an average. The course of the illness is totally unpredictable." He leaned forward earnestly to emphasize the point.

"Simply take the drugs and wait, is that what you advise?" Alexandria said.

"We will keep close track of your progress," Hufman said, glancing at Nigel. "I assure you of that. Any flareup we can probably control with more powerful agents."

"What is it that kills people, then?" she said.

"Spread to the organs. Or, worse, interception of the connective tissue in the nervous system."

"If that happens—" Nigel began.

"We often don't know right away. Occasionally there are early convulsions. Sometimes a psychosis develops, but that is rare. The clinical spectrum of this disease is broad."

Nigel sat and listened with pressed lips as the man went on, Alexandria with her hands folded neatly, the man's voice droning in the soft air with facts and theories, his broad forefinger occasionally tapping Alexandria's file to reinforce a point, his sentences paraded out to display a new facet of systemic lupus bloody erythematosus, more lockjawed Latinisms, words converging like a pack of erudite wolves to devour some new snippet of causation, diagnosis, remission, exacerbation. Nigel took it all, numbly, sensing a dim tremor within his chest that went unnamed.

During the drive home he concentrated. Traffic was always thin since the demise of the private automobile, and the broad avenues of Pasadena seemed an infinite plane over which they skated with Newtonian skill. He played the game of his youth, when everyone drove but fuel was excruciatingly short. He watched the lights flick yellow red green and timed his approach, seeking the path of minimum energy. It was best to glide the last third of a block, letting road friction and the gentle brushing wind slow them until the red popped over to green. If his timing was off he would down-shift to third, then second, storing the kinetic life that he envisioned as a precious fluid moving within the car, poured into temporary bottles somewhere between engine and axle. Making a turn, he would wait until the last moment before shifting, hoping to stretch the green time, then slapping the stick forward as his leg pumped the clutch, bringing the turgid car to a humming peak, tires howling slightly with expended energy. They arced into a new linear path, vectoring on the Pasadena grid toward the hills. Thus he played again the game of his youth, lines creasing his face.

"You can't accept it, can you, Nigel?" she said in the long silence.

"What?"

She reached over and caressed his forearm, fluffing up the blond hair. Her own gesture; no other woman had ever touched him that way. "Ease into it," she said.

He let the silence between them grow as several blocks of neon consumer gumbo passed, the sandwich parlors pooled in wan yellow.

"I'll try. But sometimes, I . . . I'll try."

Something blazed ahead. As they approached they could make out a large bonfire in a ruined field, flames licking at the cup of darkening sky. Figures moved against the lemon flickering.

"New Sons," he said.

"Slow," she said. He lifted his foot and she studied the fire.

"Why is it round?" she murmured.

"It's an annular flame. One of their symbols."

"The secret center. Godhood in every person."

"I suppose."

Several figures turned from the playing flames and waved their arms toward the car, beckoning.

"They pile their scrap wood in a circle, leaving the center clear. One pair is left there when they light it. For the duration of the fire they are free. Nothing can reach them. They can dance or—"

"How do you know all this?" he said.

"Someone told me."

A tall woman detached herself from the weaving line of figures and moved toward the street, toward their car. She was the focus of multiple, shifting shadows.

Nigel shifted into first and they surged away into the dim and desiccated night.

"Freedom at the center," he murmured. "License for public rutting, I'll wager."

"So I've heard," she said mildly.

When they let themselves into the apartment, Shirley was lying on the couch, reading. "You're late," she said sleepily.

Nigel explained about the car, about Dr. Hufman, and then it all came out in a rush, Alexandria and Nigel alternating in the telling. Lupus. Sore wrists. Connective tissue. Chloroquine. Swelling joints.

Shirley got up wordlessly and embraced each of them. Nigel chattered on for a bit, filling the room with busy, comfortable sound. Into the darting talk Alexandria inserted a mention of supper and their attention deflected to the practicalities of the meal. Nigel offered to do up some simple chopped vegetables in the wok. Rummaging through the refrigerator revealed a total absence of meat. Alexandria volunteered to walk down the two blocks to a grocery store and, without debating the issue, slipped out. Nigel was busy with an array of celery and onions on the chopping block as the door closed behind her and Shirley was washing spinach, snapping off the stems as she went.

At once a silence descended between them.

"It's serious, isn't it?" she said. He looked up. Shirley's dark eyebrows were compressed downward, forming long ridges beneath her towering stack of black hair.

"I gather so." He went back to chopping. Then, suddenly: "Shit! I wish I knew, really knew."

"Hufman doesn't sound very sympathetic."

"He isn't. I don't think he intended to be. He simply told us the bloody facts in that flat voice of his."

"It takes a while," she said softly, "to come to terms with facts."

He rapped the block with the cleaver, scattering onion cuttings. "Right."

"What do you think we ought to do?"

"Do?" He stopped, puzzled. "Wait. Go on, I suppose."

Shirley nodded. She rolled up the sleeves of her shimmering blue dress, bunching it above the elbows. She handed him the spinach in aligned stacks, ready for cutting. "I think you ought to travel," she said.

"Eh? What for?"

"To take her mind off it. And yours."

"Don't you think her usual, settled routine is more the thing?"

"That's just the point," Shirley said abruptly, an edge to her voice. "You two are stuck here because you don't want to leave your work at JPL—"

"And she doesn't either," he said evenly. "She has a career."

"Damn it!" She threw down a wad of spinach. "She could be dead in a year! Don't you think she realizes that? Even if you don't?"

"I realize it," he said stiffly.

"Then act like it!"

"How?"

Shirley's mood changed abruptly. "If you become more flexible, Nigel, she will, too. You're so absorbed in that damned laboratory, those rockets, you can't see it." Her lips parted slightly, puckering outward infinitesimally. "I love you both, but you're so fucking blind."

Nigel put his chopping knife aside. He was breathing in quick little gasps, he noted, and wondered why. "I . . . I simply can't throw it all over—"

Shirley's eyes moistened and her face seemed to draw downward. "Nigel . . . you think all this space research is so important, I *know* that. I've never said anything until now. But now your obsession can hurt Alexandria, damage her terribly in ways you may never even *see*."

He shook his head dumbly, blinking.

"If the work was so vastly important, I wouldn't say anything. But it isn't. The real problems are here on Earth—"

"Buggering nonsense."

"They *are*. You slave away at this business, after all they've done to you, and act as though it's somehow crucial."

"Better that, than a job handing out the daily dole."

"Is *that* what you think I do?" she said, voice teetering between acid and genuine curiosity.

"Well . . ."

"No backing and filling. Is it?"

"Not quite. I *do* know it's not my sort of thing."

"With your intelligence, Nigel, you could make real contributions to—"

"Human problems, as you call them, are seldom accessible to intelligence alone. It takes patience. A warm touch, all that. You've got it. I don't."

"I think you're very warm. Below that surface, I mean."

"Uh," he said wryly.

"No. You are. I, I know you are in some ways, or else you and I and Alexandria wouldn't be possible, it couldn't work."

"*Does* it work?"

"I think so," she said in almost a whisper.

"Sorry. I didn't mean that. Just lashing out."

"We need people in the project at Alta Dena, in Farensca. It's not easy, creating a sense of community after all that's happened. Those sociometricians—"

"Haven't a clue about making it work, I know. Good for diagnostics and precious little else."

"Yes." Her fine-boned face took on a bleak, introspective look.

"I think you should stay over tonight."

"Yes, of course."

The front door clicked open then, Alexandria returning with lean cuts of flank steak. The mere presence of so much meat implied that the occasion was festive, and Nigel resumed chopping, silent, pondering the details of whether to open a bottle of red wine before the cooking began. Without having time to absorb the meaning of what Shirley had said, he slipped into the routine and ritual of evening.

* * *

Each time with Shirley he found some new depth, some unexplored flavoring, a sea change. The revelation always came at that place where all parts of her converged; his head cradled between her thighs, the salt musk aswarm in his nostrils. Alexandria's presence was a warm O sliding on him. He was an arched segment of their ring. His hands stretched toward where Shirley and Alexandria intersected, Shirley's black hair mingling with Alexandria's pubic brown. His arms made an unsuccessful chord to the circle, too short; he turned his hands and felt the puckering of Shirley's nipple. His tongue worked. Shirley was moist and cool under his massaging hand. The equilibrium between the three shifted and resolved: Alexandria's tongue fluttered him to new heat; Shirley drew down Alexandria's breasts, cupping them and rolling the perked nipples between her long fingernails, like marbles. Here they were at their best, he knew. Here the machinery of their bodies spoke what words could not or would not. He felt Shirley's edgy tension in her hip which trembled with concealed energy. He sank into Alexandria's encased calm, her mouth fluid and impossibly deep. He felt his own knotted confusion focus in a thrusting jerk, battering against her slick throat. Yes, here was their center. Loving, they hauled each other's bodies as though they were sacks of sand, stacking them against the waters that surrounded Alexandria, and thus now enveloped all three of them. Shirley moved. Her legs released him and her hand caressed the back of his neck where two rigid bands of muscle formed a valley between. She smiled in the dusky light. Their bodies moved to a new geometry.

FOUR

Since having an auto available was an unusual treat, Nigel took Alexandria to work the next morning. Shirley had waved away the invitation to drop her in Alta Dena; it would be wasteful, and anyway she had her motorbike with her. She coasted down the street for a block, started the engine with a preliminary rattle, rounded a corner and was gone.

Alexandria was intent on the Brazilians, getting ready for the second day of negotiations. The employees' committee was divided on the terms American Airlines should ask, afraid that control would slip out of the country and into hands they didn't understand. Alexandria's job was to soothe their fears without endangering the course of the bargaining. She still didn't know whether she agreed with the deal or not.

Nigel took his time driving up the gentle sloping hills. He took a route shaded by long stands of eucalyptus, and rolled down the window to breathe the fresh, minty smell. To his surprise he found that the subject of Alexandria and lupus did not float unbidden to the surface of his mind, again and again. Somehow the night had washed him free of it, for the moment.

This area was unfamiliar; he passed by several blocks of gutted ruins. Only the blackened corners of buildings remained, jagged spires thrusting from a sea of lush weeds. He slowed to study them, to determine whether they were remnants of the earthquake, or the result of one of the "incidents" that had raged over the last two decades. The quake, he guessed; there were no obvious, yawning craters, and the flaking walls were unpocked by heavy-caliber fire.

By the time the craft entered the system it knew the planetary population. Of the nine planets, four held promise. All but the farthest inward could be resolved into a disk now. There was a completely clouded world near the star. Next outward came the smaller radio-emitter; it showed sharp oxygen lines and an occasional blue glint hinted at oceans. A smaller world came next, dry and cold, with odd markings.

But for now the craft's attention focused on the fourth possibility, the huge banded giant. Its radio emissions were broad, covering much of the spectrum, as though the source were natural. But they seemed keyed to an amplitude pattern that repeated nearly identically, at a constant period.

The pinkish-brown world seemed an unlikely site for a technological society. Other considerations entered here, however: time and energy. The craft's engines worked inefficiently at these low speeds. Yet it needed to alter momentum and flatten its trajectory into the plane of the ecliptic. A flyby of the large planet could save engine strain and time. Looping through its gravitational field, picking up momentum from the vectoring forces, would allow a detailed study while the ship was launched sunward along a more desirable course.

Its higher functions debated.

With a mild rumble it altered the timbre of its engines. Gas giant or no, the radio pattern could not be ignored. It swung smoothly toward the waiting world.

"The aft camera nailed it," Nigel said.

"What? You found the trouble?" Lubkin got up with surprising agility and walked around his desk.

"No malfunction. Those echoes were real, the engineers pegged it right. We've got a Snark."

Nigel tossed a shelf of fax sheets on the desk. They were shiny even in the muted office light, yellow squiggles on green stripping.

"Snark?"

"Mythical English creature."

"Something's really out there?"

"These are optical and spectroscopic analyses. Telemetry errors already corrected and numerically smoothed." He pulled one sheet from the pile and pointed at several lines.

"What is it?"

"Our Snark gives off all the lines of a fusion torch burning pretty bright. Nearly a billion degrees."

"Come *on.*" Lubkin gave him a skeptical look, eyes screwed up behind his pale glasses.

"I checked it with Knapp."

"Damn," Lubkin said. He shook his head. "Funny."

"J-Monitor got one clear look at it before Callisto came

into the way again. Couldn't avoid that, even with the new orbit we put it into."

He slid a glossy optical photograph out of the stack.

"Not much to see," Lubkin said.

Near one corner was a tiny orange splotch against a dead black background. Lubkin shook his head again. "And this was through the *small*-angle telescope? Must be pretty far away."

"It was. Almost all the way diagonally across the Callisto orbit. I don't think we'll be able to spot it again on the next pass."

"Any radio contact?"

"None. No time. I tried when I first came in this morning, registered something—didn't know what, right away—couldn't get a good enough fix on it, with that photo. The narrow radio beam that Monitor's main dish puts out needs a better fix."

"Try again."

"I did. Callisto got in the way, then Jupiter itself."

"Shit."

Both men stood, hands on hips, staring down at the fax sheets. Their eyes traced through the matted patterns, noting details, neither of them moving.

"This is going to be pretty big news, Nigel."

"I expect."

"I think we ought to sit on it for a while. Until I get a chance to speak to the Director."

"Ummm. Suppose so."

Lubkin looked at him steadily.

"There's not much question about what this thing is."

"Not one of ours," Nigel said. "Dead on about that."

"Funny, you discovering it. You and McCauley are the only men who've ever seen anything alien."

Nigel glanced up at Lubkin, surprised. "That's why I stayed in the program. I thought you knew. I wanted to be where things were happening."

"You guessed something would?" Lubkin seemed genuinely startled.

"No. I was gambling."

"Some people are still pretty hot about Icarus, you know."

"I've heard."

"They might not like your being—"

"*Up* theirs." Nigel's face hardened. He had answered Lubkin's questions about Icarus years before and saw no reason to reopen the past now.

"Well, I was only . . . I'll be seeing the Director—"

"I found it. I want in on it. *Remember that,*" he finished savagely.

"The military is going to remember last time." Lubkin spread his palms open in a conciliatory gesture.

"And?"

"Icarus was dangerous. Maybe this thing is, too."

Nigel scowled. *Politics. Committees. Jesus.*

"Bugger all," he said. "Hadn't we best figure where it's going? Before fretting about what to do if it gets here?"

The gas giant had been a disappointment. The nonrandom radio emissions were natural in origin, keyed to the orbital period of its reddish inner moon. Methodically, the craft analysed the larger moons and found only ice fields and gray rock.

As it whipped by the giant planet on an artful parabola, it decided to focus on the water world. The signals from there were clearly artificial. But as it did so, a brief radio burst caught its attention. The signal showed high correlations, but not enough to rule out a natural origin; there were many well-ordered phenomena in nature. Incredibly, the source was nearby.

Following standing orders, the ship retransmitted the same electromagnetic signal back at the source. This happened several times, quite quickly, but with no sign from the source that the ship's transmission had been received. Then, abruptly, the signal stopped. Nothing spiked up from the wash of static.

The ship pondered. The signal might well have had a natural cause, particularly in the intense magnetic fields surrounding the gas giant planet. Without further investigation there was no way to decide.

The source seemed to be the fifth moon, a cold and barren world. The ship was aware that this moon was tidelocked to the gas giant, keeping the same side eternally facing inward. Its revolution with respect to the ship was therefore rather slow. It seemed unlikely, then, that the source of the radiation would have slipped below the visible edge so quickly.

As well, the signal strength was low, but not so weak that the ship could not have detected it before. Perhaps it was another radiation pattern from the belts of trapped electrons around the planet, triggered by the fifth moon rather than the first.

The ship thought and decided. The hypothesis of natural origin seemed far more likely. It would cost fuel and time to check further, and the region near the gas giant was dangerous. Far wiser, then, to continue accelerating.

It moved sunward, toward the warming glow.

Nigel worked late on a search-and-survey program to pick up the Snark's trail. He hadn't much hope of it working because Jupiter Monitor wasn't designed for the task, and the Snark's departing velocity would carry it out of range soon. But there was a lift to his steps as he left and he hummed an old song in the darkened corridors. As a boy he'd watched the old film cassettes and had an ambition to be John Lennon, to strut and clown and warble and become immortal, launch himself into history with his vocal cords. It had been years since he'd remembered that obsession. The period lasted for a year or so: gathering memorabilia, hiring a guitar by the week, rummaging through a song or two, posing in profile for the mirror (backlighting himself in blue, sporting a cap, fluffing out his hair), learning the surprisingly undated slang. The dream faded when he learned he couldn't sing.

Near the entrance he did a little two-step, whistling, lifting, lilting, and then pushed out into the dimming spring sunlight.

The exit guard stopped him. She looked at his badge photograph and then back at his face.

"Can't match up this ruined visage with that cherubic photograph?"

"Oh, sorry. I knew you worked here, sir, and I'm new, I hadn't seen you. I saw you on Three-D when I was a girl."

She smiled prettily at him and he felt suddenly considerably older.

He trotted for the bus, snagged it and waved to the guard as he swung aboard.

Fame. Lubkin envied him for it, he knew, and that fact alone was enough to make him wince and laugh at the same time. Hell, if he'd wanted the limelight he'd have stayed in the most visible part of the program, the cylinder cities being built at the Lagrange points. Create a world, fresh and clean. (*Cylcits*, the 3D called them, a perfectly American perversion of the admittedly whorish language—almost as bad as *skyscraper*, from the last century.)

No. He'd been lucky, is all, fearsomely lucky, to get even this post.

When they pried him and Len out of the shoe-box accommodations of the *Dragon*, and then tiptoed away from the legal scuffle, Nigel had learned a lot. The attacks from *The New York Times* were mosquitoes compared to what awaited them at NASA. Still, the public experience prepared him for private infighting. Parsons, who was head of NASA at the time, had sent Nigel off as a boy, really, quick and serious, able to lower his breathing rate and slow his metabolism at will with self-hypnosis. The Icarus furor made him a man, gave him time to water the bile that built up inside him, so that some humor remained.

Admittedly, he was less than a second Lindbergh. But he slicked down his hair and when the Night of the Long Knives loomed up within NASA, he went public with the facts. He snared a retrospective interview on 3D, made some well-timed speeches, flashed his teeth. When asked about Cheshire-cat-David's role in the mission, he invented a limerick about him that NBC cut from their early evening show, but CBS left in.

Business picked up. He appeared on a mildly intellectual talk show and revealed a better than passing acquaintance with the works of Louis Armstrong and the Jefferson Airplane, both of whom were coming back into vogue. He was interviewed during a long hike through the Sierras' Desolation Wilderness, wearing a sweat suit and talking about meditation and respect for closed lifesystems (such as

Earth). Not great material, no. But 3D execs proved to be an odd breed; anything that tickled their noses they thought was champagne.

He was inordinately lucky. Something would boil up from his subconscious and he would put it into a sentence or two, and suddenly Parsons or Cheshire Dave would be in trouble. He hit them about duplicity in the Icarus incident, about cutting the cylinder cities program (truly stupid, that; the first city was already giving birth to whole new zero-g and low-temperature industries that could save the American economy).

And in the sweet rushing fullness of time, Parsons was no longer director of NASA.

Cheshire Dave was execing somewhere in Nevada, his grin slowly coming unstuck.

A news commentator said Nigel had a talent for telling the right truth at the right time—right for Nigel—and it was doubly surprising when the faculty left him, utterly, after Parsons resigned. Some NASA execs urged him to keep it up, kick over a few more clay-footed troglodytes. But they did it in secluded corners at cocktail parties, muttering into their branch-water-and-bourbons about his maneuvering skill. He shrugged them off, and knew their feral admiration was misplaced. He had done in Parsons and Dave out of sheer personal dislike, no principle at all involved, and his subconscious knew it.

As soon as the irritants vanished, the sly Medici within him slid into slumber, the venom drained from him and Nigel returned to being a working astronaut.

Such as it was.

NASA sensed his potential power (once stung, twice paranoid) and—lo—retained him and Len on active status. Len opted for orbital maintenance work. Nigel wangled for the moon.

The older men were thoroughly married and nearing forty, reeking of oatmeal virtues. NASA was having to pay its way in economic payoffs, so they wanted the moon explored quickly, for possible industrial uses. The cylcits needed raw materials, Earth needed pollution-free manu-facturing sites, and it all had to come at low rates. So into an

age leached of glory came the return of gallant men,
bleached hair cropped close to the skull. Into their ranks he
wormed his way, for an eighteen-month sojourn at Hipparchus Base on the moon.

His rotation schedule back on Earth turned into a
permanent post. The economy was reviving, men could be
trained who were younger, quicker of eye, leaner and
harder. He and Len still kept up their minimum capability
requirements in the flight sim at Moffatt Field, and every
three months flew to Houston for the full two-day primer.

Someday he might get back into zero-g work, but he
doubted it. His waist thickened, the loyal sloshing of his
heart now ran at a higher blood pressure and he was forty-
one.

Time, everyone hinted, to move on.

To what? Administration? The synthetic experience of
directing other people's work? No; he had never learned to
smile without meaning it. Or to calibrate the impact of his
words. He said things spontaneously; his entire life was
done in first draft.

He stared out at the carved Pasadena hills. Some other
career, then? He had written a longish piece on Icarus,
some years back, for *Worldview*. It had been well received
and for a while he'd contemplated becoming immersed in
litbiz. It would give him a vent for his odd, cartwheeling
verbal tricks, his quirky puns. Perhaps it would drain the
occasional souring bile that rose up in him.

No, thumbs down to that. He wanted more than the
act of excreting himself onto pieces of paper.

He snorted wryly to himself. There was an old Dylan
lyric that applied here: the only thing he knew how to do
was to keep on keepin' on.

Like it or not.

FIVE

"It started in on my ankles this afternoon."

He stopped, his hand halfway raised to beckon a
waiter. "What?"

"My ankles ache. Worse than my wrists."

"You're taking the chloroquine?"

"Of course, I'm not *stupid*," Alexandria said irritably.

"Perhaps it takes a few days to settle in. To have an effect," he said with false lightness.

"Maybe."

"You may feel better after you've had a bite. What about the birani?"

"Not in the mood for that."

"Ah. Their curries are always sound. Why don't we share one, medium hot?"

"Okay." She sat back in her chair and rolled her head lazily from side to side. "I need to unwind. Order me a beer, would you? *Lacanta.*"

In the layered air, heavy with incense, she seemed to hover at a dreamy distance. Two days had passed since he'd spotted the Snark and he hadn't told her yet. He decided this was the right moment; it would distract her from the ache in her joints.

He caught a waiter's eye and placed their order. They were cloistered near the back of the restaurant, sheltered by a clicking curtain of glass beads, unlikely to be overheard. He spoke softly, scarcely above the buzz of casual conversation provided by the other diners.

She was excited by the news and peppered him with questions. The past two days had revealed nothing new, but he described in detail the work he'd done in organizing the systematic search for further traces of the Snark. He was partway through an involved explanation when he noticed that her interest had waned. She toyed with her food, sipped some amber beer. She glanced at diners as they entered and left.

He paused and dug away at the mountain of curry before him, added condiments, experimented with two chutneys. After a polite silence she changed the subject. "I, I've been thinking about something Shirley said, Nigel."

"What's that?"

"Dr. Hufman recommended rest as well as these pills. Shirley thinks the best rest is absence from the day-to-day." She gazed at him pensively.

"A vacation, you mean?"

"Yes, and short trips here and there. Outings."

"This Snark thing is going to snarl up my time pretty—"

"I know that. I wanted to get in my bid first."

He smiled affectionately. "Of course. No reason we can't nip down to Baja, take in a few things."

"I have a lot of travel credit built up. We can fly anywhere in the world on American."

"I'm surprised you want to give up a great deal of time, with these negotiations going on."

"They can spare me now and again."

As she said it the expression altered around her brown eyes, her mouth turned subtly downward and he saw suddenly into her, into a bleak and anxious center.

It was late when they left the restaurant. Some of the more stylish stores were still open. Two police in riot jackets checked their faxcodes and then passed down the street. The two women stopped most of the people they met, taking them into the orange pools beneath the well-spaced street lamps and demanding identification. One woman stood at a safe distance with stun-club drawn while the other dialed through to Central, checking the ferrite verimatrix in the faxcodes. Nigel was not looking when, a short distance away, a woman suddenly bolted away from the police and dashed into a department store. The man with her tried to run, too, but a policewoman forced him to the ground. The other policewoman drew a pistol and ran into the store. The man yelled something, protesting. The woman rapped him with her stunclub and his face whitened. He slumped forward. Muffled shots came from inside the department store.

Their bus arrived. Nigel climbed on.

Alexandria stood still, hand raised halfway to her face. The man was trying to get to his knees. He rasped out a few words. Her lips curled back in distaste and she started to say something. Nigel called her name. She hesitated. "Alexandria!"

He reached down toward her. She climbed the steps numbly, legs stiff. She sat down next to him as the bus doors wheezed shut. She breathed deeply.

"Forget it," Nigel said. "That's the way it is."

The bus hummed into motion. They glided past the man on the sidewalk. The policewoman's knee was in his back and he stared glassily at the broken paving. All the details were quite clear in the faintly orange light.

Before Lubkin could finish his drawling sentence Nigel was out of his chair, pacing.

"You're damned right I object to it," Nigel said. "It's the most stupid bloody—"

"Look, Nigel, I sympathize with you completely. You and I are scientists, after all."

Nigel thought sourly that he could quite easily marshal a good argument against that statement alone, at least in Lubkin's case. But he let it ride.

"We don't like this secrecy business," Lubkin went on. He chose his words carefully. "However. At the same time. I can understand the need for tight security in this matter."

"For how long?" Nigel said sharply.

"Long?" Lubkin hesitated. Nigel guessed that the rhythm of his prepared speech was broken. "I really don't know," the other man said lamely. "Perhaps for the indefinite future, although"—he speeded up, to cut off Nigel's reaction—"we may be speaking of a mere matter of days. You understand."

"Who says?"

"What?"

"Who has the say in this?"

"Well, the Director, of course, he was the first. He thought we should go through military channels as well as civilian."

Nigel ceased pacing and sat down. Lubkin's office was illuminated only around his desk, the corners gloomy. To Nigel's mind's eye the effect of the pooled light was to frame him and Lubkin as though in a prizefighter's ring, two antagonists pitted across Lubkin's oaken desk. Nigel hunched forward, elbows on knees, and stared at the other man's puffy face.

"Why in *hell* is the goddamned Air Force—"

"They would find out about it *any*way, through channels."

"Why?"

"We may need their deep space sensor network to track the, ah, Snark."

"Ridiculous. That's a near-Earth net."

"Maybe that's where the Snark is heading."

"A remote possibility."

"But a nonzero one. You have to admit that. This *could* be of importance in world security, too, you know."

Nigel thought a moment. "You mean if the Snark approaches Earth, and the nuclear monitoring system picks up its fusion flame—"

"Yes."

"—and thinks it's a missile, or warhead going off—"

"You must admit, that is a possibility."

Nigel balled his fists and said nothing.

"We keep this under our hats by telling no one extra," Lubkin said smoothly. "The technicians never got the whole story. If we say nothing more they'll forget it. You, I, the Director, perhaps a dozen or two in Washington and the UN."

"How in hell do we *work*? I can't oversee every flamin' planetary monitor. We need shifts—"

"You'll have them. But we can break the work down into piecemeal studies. So no one technican or staff engineer knows the purpose."

"That's inefficient as hell. We've got a whole solar system to search."

Lubkin's voice became hard and flat. "That's the way it's going to be, Nigel. And if you want to work on this program . . ." He did not finish the sentence.

She shook him gently in the night, and then more roughly and finally he awoke, eyes gummy and mind still drifting in fog.

"Nigel, I'm afraid."

"What? I . . ."

"I don't know, I just woke up and I was terrified."

He sat up and cradled her in his arms. She burrowed

her face into his chest and shivered as though she were cold. "Was there a dream?"

"No. No, I just . . . my heart was pounding so loud I thought you must have heard it and my legs were so cramped . . . They still hurt."

"You had a dream. You simply don't remember it."

"You think so?"

"Certainly."

"I wonder what it was about?"

"Some beastly bit from the subconscious, that's always what it is. Settling the accounts."

She said in a weak, high voice, "Well, I wish I could get rid of this one."

"No, the subconscious is like the commercial bits on Three-D. Without them sandwiched in, you'd get none of the good programming."

"What's that sound?"

"Rain. Sounds like it's pissing down quite heavily."

"Oh. Good. Good, we need it."

"We always need it."

"Yes."

He sat that way the remainder of the night, finally falling asleep long after she did.

At the Los Angeles County Museum:

Alexandria leaned over to study the descriptive card beneath the black and gray sculpture. "Devadasi performing a gymnastic sexual act with a pair of soldiers who engage in sword-play at the same time. This scene records a motif for a spectacle. South India. Seventeenth Century." She arched her back in imitation of the Devadasi, getting about halfway over.

"Looks difficult," he said.

"*Impossible*. And the angle for the fellow in front is basically wrong."

"They *were* gymnasts."

Reflectively: "I liked the big one back there better. The one who carried men off in the night for 'sexual purposes'— remember?"

"Yes. Delicate phrasing."

"Why did she have a touch-hole in her vulva?"

"Religious significance."

"Ha!"

"Maintenance purposes, then. It probably short-cir-cuited the occasional desire to carve one's initials in her."

"Unlikely," she said. "Ummm. 'The eternal dance of the Yogini and the lingam,' it says, on this next one. Eternal." She gazed at it for a long moment, and then turned quickly away. Her mouth sagged. She wobbled uncertainly on the glossy tiles. Nigel took her arm and held her as she limped toward a row of chairs. He noticed that the gallery was oddly hushed. She sat down heavily, air wheezing out in a rush. She swayed and stared straight ahead. Her forehead beaded with sudden perspiration. Nigel glanced up. Everyone in the gallery had stopped moving and stood, watching Alexandria.

"She ought to quit that damned job *now*," Shirley said adamantly.

"She likes it."

Nigel sipped at his coffee. It was oily and thick, but still probably better than what he could get at work. He told himself that he should get up and clear away the breakfast dishes, now that Alexandria had left for her meeting, but Shirley's cold, deliberate anger pinned him to the dining nook.

"She's holding on, just *barely* holding on. Can't you *see* that?" Her eyes flashed at him, their glitter punctuated by the high, arching black eyebrows.

"She wants to have a hand in this Brazilian thing."

"God damn it! She's frightened. I was gone—how long? five minutes?—and when I came back she was still sitting there in that gallery, white as a sheet and you patting her arm. That's not healthy, that's not the Alexandria we know."

Nigel nodded. "But I talked to her. She—"

"—is afraid to bring it up, to show how worried she is. She feels *guilty* about it, Nigel. That's a common reaction. The people I work with, they're guilty over being poor, or old, or sick. It's up to you and me to force them out of that. Make them see themselves as . . ."

Her voice trickled away. "I'm not reaching you, am I?"

"No, no, you are."

"I think you ought to at least persuade her to stay home and rest."

"I will."

"When she's feeling better we'll take a trip," Shirley said quickly, consolidating her gains.

"Right. A trip." He stood up and began stacking plates, their ceramic edges scraping, the silverware clattering. "I'm afraid I haven't noticed. My work—"

"Yes, yes," Shirley said fiercely, "I know about your damned work."

He awoke in a swamp of wrinkled, sticky sheets. July's heat was trapped in the upper rooms of this old house, lying in wait for the night, clinging in the airless corners. He rolled slowly out of bed, so that Alexandria rocked peacefully in the slow swells of the water's motion. She made a foggy murmur deep in her throat and fell silent again.

The cold snap of night air startled him. The room was not close and stifling after all. The sweat that tingled, drying, had come from some inner fire, a vaguely remembered dream. He sucked in the cool, dry air and shivered.

Then he remembered.

He padded into the high-arched living room and switched on a lamp where the light would not cast into the bedroom. He fumbled among the volumes of the *Encyclopaedia Britannica* and found the entry he wanted. Reading, he groped for the couch and sat down.

> *Lupus erythematosus.* May affect any organ or the overall structure of the body. Preference for membranes which exude moisture, such as those of the joints or those lining the abdomen. Produces modified antibodies, altered proteins. For long intervals symptoms may subside. Spreading through the body is usually undetectable until major symptoms arise. Communication to the central nervous system has become a consistent feature of the

disease in recent years. Studies relating disease
incidence and pollution levels show a clear connection, though the precise mechanism is not understood. Treatment—

Until this moment it had not seemed truly real.

He read through the article once, then again, and
finally stopped when he found that he was crying. His eyes
were stinging and watery.

He put the volume back and noticed a new book on the
shelf. A Bible bound in ridged acrylic. Curious, he opened
it. Some pages were well thumbed. Shirley? No, Alexandria. Had she been reading it, even before their conference
with Hufman? Had she suspected in advance? He sat down
and began reading.

SIX

"The President does not *know* how long, Nigel," Lubkin
said sternly. "He wants us all to hold on and try to find it."

"Does he think anybody can suppress news about
something this big *forever*? It's been *five* months now. I
don't think the Washington or UN people will keep quiet
much longer."

Once more they were framed in the pool of light
around Lubkin's desk. The one window in the far wall let in
some sunlight, giving Lubkin's sallow skin a deeper cast of
yellow. Nigel sat stiffly alert, lips pressed thin.

Lubkin casually leaned back in his chair and rocked for
a moment. "You aren't hinting that you might . . . ?"

"No, rubbish. I won't spill it." He paused for a second,
remembering that Alexandria knew. She could be trusted,
he was sure. In fact, she didn't seem to quite grasp the
importance of the Snark, and never spontaneously spoke of
it. "But the whole idea is stupid. Childish."

"You wouldn't feel that way if you had been with me at
the White House, Nigel," Lubkin said solemnly.

"I wasn't invited."

"I know. I understand the President and NASA wanted
to keep the number of attendees down. To avoid attracting
notice from the press. And for security reasons."

The trip had been the high point of Lubkin's career, clearly, and Nigel suspected he burned to tell someone about it. But at JPL only Nigel and the Director were privy to the information, and the Director had been present at the White House, anyway. Nigel smiled to himself.

"The way the President put it was really convincing, Nigel. The emotional impact of such an event, coupled with the religious fervor afoot in the country, in fact in the *world* . . . those New Sons of God have a senator to speak for them now, you know. They would kick up quite a bit of dust."

"Which wing of the New Sons?"

"Wing? I don't know . . ."

"They come in all colors and sizes, these days. The fever-eyed, sweaty-palmed ones can't count to twelve without taking off their shoes. If they have any. The intellectual New Sons, though, have a doctrine cobbled together about life existing everywhere and being part of the Immanent Host and that sort of thing. So Alexandria says. They—" Nigel stopped, aware that he'd begun to rattle on about a side issue. Lubkin had a definite talent for deflecting from the point.

"Well," Lubkin said, "there are also the military people. They're pretty nervous about this thing." Lubkin nodded unconsciously to himself, as though this last statement needed added weight.

"That's bloody *simple-minded*. No species from another star is going to come all this way to drop a bomb on us."

"*You* know that. *I* know that. But some of the generals are worried."

"Whatever the hell for?"

"The danger of triggering the Nuclear Warning Net, though that is reduced now that more participants know of the, ah, Snark. There is also the possibility of biological contamination if this thing should enter the atmosphere . . ."

Lubkin's voice trailed off and both men stared moodily for a long moment at a eucalyptus tree that dripped steadily from the light gray fog outside the window. The continuing alteration in the world weather cycle made these fall fogs more intense each year; the process was understood but beyond control.

Lubkin tapped his pen on his desk's polished sheen and the ticking rhythm echoed hollowly in the still room. Nigel studied the man and tried to estimate how Lubkin was dealing with the politics of this situation. He probably saw it as a matter of containment, of separate spheres of activity. Lubkin would do what he could to keep Nigel toeing the line, keeping mum, and rummaging around the solar system after the Snark. Meanwhile, Lubkin could play the steely-eyed, competent, can-do type back at the UN. To harried diplomats someone like Lubkin, with hard, sure answers, must seem like a good bet, a bright candidate for better things.

Nigel twisted his lips and wondered if he was becoming cynical. It was hard to tell.

"I still believe we have an obligation to tell the human race about this. The Snark isn't merely another strategic element," Nigel said.

"Well, I'm sorry you feel that way, Nigel."

There was no reply. Outside drops pattered silently in a moist, gray world, beading the pane.

"You *do* acknowledge the need for secrecy in this, don't you? I mean, despite your personal feelings, you *will* maintain security? I would—"

"Yes, yes, I'll go along," Nigel said testily.

"Good, very good. If you hadn't, I'm afraid I would have had to remove you from the group. The President was *very* firm about it. We, nothing personal, of—"

"Right. Your only concern is the Snark."

"Uh, yes. About that. There was a little concern about attaching such an odd, mythical name to it. Might excite interest, you know, if anybody overheard. The UN Chancellor's office suggested we give it a number, J-27. With twenty-six discovered Jovian moons, this is the next, you see—"

"Um." Nigel shrugged.

"—but of course, the main interest expressed by the Chancellor lay in finding out where we can expect it next."

Nigel saw he could wait no longer. The card in his hand couldn't be turned into a trump, so he might as well play it. "I think I may already know," he said evenly.

"Oh?" Lubkin brightened and leaned forward gingerly.

"I guessed the Snark would follow a reasonably energy-saving orbit. No point in squandering essentials. Given that, and the crude Doppler shift measurement we got of its fusion flame, I figured it for a long, sloping orbit in toward Mars."

"It's near *Mars?*" Lubkin stood up excitedly, his distant manner forgotten.

"Not any more."

"I don't—"

"I've been putting in a lot of hours on the Mars Monitors. Used that blanket budget charge and had the camera and telescope rigs doing a piecemeal scan of the available sky around Mars. The program ran round the clock and I'd check the results each day. I got behind. Yesterday I found something."

"You should've told me."

"I *am* telling you."

"I'll have to call Washington and the UN at once. If the object is in orbit around Mars now—"

"It isn't." Nigel folded his arms, a faint sour taste in his mouth.

"I thought you—"

"The Snark was outward bound, away from Mars. I got two shots, spaced hours apart. The data was from seven days ago. I looked again today, when I finally read that week-old readout, but it's gone, out of resolving range."

Lubkin seemed dazed. "Already left," he said slowly.

"Even with only two points, the flight path is pretty clear. I think it must've done a gravitational rebound, looping in for a quick look and picking up momentum from the encounter."

Nigel was standing now, and he walked leisurely over to Lubkin's blackboard. He leaned against it, hands behind his back and resting on the chalk tray, elbows cocked out. He stood in the dim light, where Lubkin could not quite make out the expression of wry superiority on his face. He brushed away drifting swirls of yellow chalk dust and studied the other man. He was glad for once to have Lubkin on the defensive, in a way. Perhaps the Snark riddle could deflect the man from his fascination with generals and presidents.

Lubkin looked puzzled. "Where is it going next?"

"I think . . . Venus," Nigel said.

The ship knew, even before leaving the banded giant planet, that the next world inward was barren, a place where reddish dust stirred under the touch of cold, thin winds. Absence of a natural life system did not rule out inhabitants, however. The craft recalled several other such worlds, encountered in the distant past, which supported advanced cultures.

It elected to fly past the planet without orbiting. This would subtract more angular momentum during the gravitational "collision," readying the ship for the venture further inward.

This loomed all-important now, for the blue and white world demanded most of the craft's attention. Many overlapping radio signals chorused out from it, a babble of voices.

A debate ensued within the ship.

Matters of judgment were decided by vote between three equally able computers, until intelligent signals could be deciphered. Only a short while remained until a preliminary breakdown of the incoming transmissions was complete. Then, still higher elements of the craft would be warmed into life.

One of the computers held out for an immediate change of orbit, to skip the dry pink world and drive on, burning more fuel, toward the blue world.

Another felt that the bewildering torrent of radio voices, weak but all different, bespoke chaos on the third planet. Best to allow ample time for deciphering these confusing signals. The minimal energy course involved yet another flyby, looping by the second planet, the world which was shrouded in thick, creamy clouds. This path would trade time for fuel, a clever bargain.

The third computer wavered for a moment and then cast its lot with the second.

They hurried; the parched disk ahead swelled quickly. The craft swept by this world of drifting dust and icy poles, storing the collected data on tiny magnetic grains deep within itself; one more entry in a vast array of astronomical lore.

The craft damped the rumble of its fusion torch and began the long glide toward the wreathed second planet. Intricate steps began in the final revival of its full mental capacity. Meanwhile, electromagnetic ears cupped toward the blue world, catching whispers of many tongues. Understanding a single language without knowing any common referents would require immense labor. Indeed, the attempt might fail. The craft had failed before, in other systems, and been forced to leave in the face of hostility and misunderstanding. But perhaps here . . .

The machines set to work eagerly.

He and Shirley sat on the hard-packed sand and watched Alexandria gingerly wade into the foaming white waves. She held her forearms up with each successive wash of cold water in a curious gesture, as though the lifting motion would pull her, loft her up and away from the chilling prick of the ocean. Her breasts swayed and jounced.

"It's good to see her getting in," Nigel said conversationally. He and Shirley had spent a good ten minutes coaxing Alexandria into activity.

"It *is* cold," Shirley said. "You suppose there's some runoff from . . . ?" She waved a lazy finger at the blue-white mountain that peaked above the rippling surface of blue. The iceberg floated a few kilometers offshore, slightly south of Malibu.

"No, they ring it pretty tight. Float most of the fresh water in on top of the ocean water." A slight cooling wind stirred the sand around them. "That breeze might be coming over the berg, though," he added.

Alexandria was now bouncing in the scalloping waves. A spray of surf burst over her. She emerged, hair stringy and now a darker brown, shook her head, blinked and resolutely dove into the deepening trough of the next wave. She breast-stroked out with sudden energy.

"This was a good idea, Shirley," he said. "She's responding to it."

"I knew she would. Getting her *away*, out of that deal with the Brazilians, is the only thing that'll work."

"Is that what you learned during these nightly jaunts of yours?"

"Ah *ha*," she said with a slowly drawn smile. "You're wondering where we go."

"Well, I did . . ."

Nearby, an old man, barrel chest supported by wiry tanned legs, pointed offshore. "Hey. Ya," he said.

Nigel followed the man's trembling index finger. Alexandria was floundering in the undertow. An arm appeared, grasping. She rolled in the soapy white. Her head jerked up, jaws agape to suck in more air. She paddled aimlessly, arms loose.

Nigel felt his heels digging into the gritty sand. From the dunes to the hissing water's edge was downhill and he covered it in a few strides. He leaped high and ran through the first few breaking waves. He tumbled over the next wave, regained his feet and blinked back stinging salt.

He could not see Alexandria. A curving wall of water rose up, sucking at his feet. He dove into it.

As he surfaced something brushed his leg, soft and warm. He reached down into the frothing white suds and pulled up. Alexandria's leg poked out of the surf.

He set his feet solidly and heaved upward. She came up slowly, as though an immense weight pinned her. He stumbled in the riptide, blue currents rushing around his legs.

He got her face clear. Awkwardly he manhandled her body until she was facing down. He swatted her on the back and a jet of water spurted from her throat.

She gasped. Choked. Breathed.

He and Shirley stood just inside the ring of strangers. Their blunt stares fixed on the young man who was talking to Alexandria calmly, filling out spaces in his clipboarded form. Afternoon sunlight bleached the scene and Nigel turned away, his muscles jumping nervously from residual adrenalin.

Shirley glanced at him with a mingled look of fear and relief. "She, she said there was a feeling of weakness that came over her," Shirley said. "She couldn't swim any more. A wave picked her up and slammed her into the bottom."

Nigel put an arm around her, nodding. His body felt jittery, urging him to action. He looked at the clotted gathering of beachgoers, abuzz with speculations, eyeing the two of them with unasked inquiry. A ring of naked primates. Far down the rectilinear beach a huge restaurant sign promised ERNIE'S SUDDEN SERVICE. Shirley huddled closer to him. Her hand clenched and relaxed, clenched and relaxed. Absurdly, he noticed that this gesture occurred scarcely centimeters from his penis. At the thought it swelled, thickened, swayed, throwing him into a confusion of emotions.

He hired a cab to drive them from Malibu to Pasadena. It was immensely expensive but Alexandria's wan and drained expression told him the bus would be intolerable.

On the long drive Alexandria told the story over and over again. The wave. Choking on the salt water. Struggling at the bottom. The pressing, churning weight of water.

In the midst of the fifth telling she fell asleep, head sagging to the side. When they reached home she woke in a fumbling daze and allowed herself to be led upstairs. He and Shirley stripped and bathed her and then tucked her into bed.

They made a meal and ate silently.

"After this, I . . . ." Shirley began. She put down her fork. "Nigel, you should know that she and I have been going to the New Sons in the evenings."

He looked at her, stunned. "Your . . . jaunts?"

"She needs it. I'm beginning to think *I* need it."

"I think you need . . . ." But he let it fade away, the sharp edge left his voice. He reached across the table and touched the sheen of her cheek, where a tear was slowly rolling down.

"God knows what we need. God knows," he said hollowly.

Dr. Hufman looked at him blankly. "Of course I can put her into the hospital for a longer time, but there is no need, I assure you, Mr. Walmsley."

He reached out for one of the stubby African dolls grouped at the corner of his desk. Nigel said nothing for a moment and the other man turned the doll over in his hands, studying it as though he had never seen it before. He wore a black suit that wrinkled under the arms.

"More time wouldn't help? A few more tests in hospital—"

"The complete battery is finished. True, we shall have to monitor these symptoms more frequently now, but there's nothing to be gained—"

"Damn it!" Nigel leaned over and swept the collection of dolls off the mahogany desk. "She doesn't *eat*. Barely makes it to and from work. She's, she's got no *zest*. And *you* tell me there's nothing for it—"

"Until the disease equilibrates, that is so."

"Suppose it doesn't?"

"We're giving her everything we can now. Hospitalization would only—"

Nigel waved him silent with a hand. Abruptly he heard the distant swishing of traffic on Thalia outside, as though suddenly the volume control had been turned up somewhere.

He stared at Hufman. The man was a technician, doing his job, not responsible for the reddening and swelling attacking Alexandria. Nigel saw that, had never doubted that, but now in the compressed airless space of this office the facts smothered him and he sought a way out. There had to be a release from the arrowing of events.

Hufman was gazing steadily at him. In the man's constricted face he read the truth: that Hufman had seen this reaction before, knew it as a stage in the process, something to be passed through as surely as the aches and spasms and clenching tremors. Knew that this, too, was one of the converging lines. Knew that there was no release.

SEVEN

Lubkin did not react well when Nigel requested an extended leave.

He appealed to Nigel's duty to the project, loyalty to the President (forgetting his British origins), to JPL. Nigel shook his head wearily. He needed time to be with Alexandria, he said. She wanted to travel. And—casually, not quite looking into Lubkin's eyes—he was behind in his flight simulations. To maintain his astronaut status he needed a solid week at NASA Ames, splicing it up so that he was never gone from Alexandria more than a few hours.

Lubkin agreed. Nigel promised to call in at least every two days. They were bringing in new men, Ichino and Williams, to supplement the survey program. If Nigel wanted to interview them now—

Nigel didn't.

The three of them went to the beach again, partly to exorcise the experience, partly because it was October and the crowds were gone. They lounged, they waded. The women were doing their meditations regularly now. They would face each other, draw the annular circle in the sand between them, link hands and go off into their own mesmerized world. Nigel closed his eyes, back pressed to the sand and dreamed. Of Alexandria, of the past. Of the years after Icarus.

What put off *The New York Times* attracted women. They would drift his way at a party, lips pursed, seemingly inspecting Cezanne prints, and abruptly come upon him, round doe eyes widening in polite surprise at his mumbled identity (yes, he was the one), hand unconsciously going to the throat to caress a necklace or scarf, an oddly sensual gesture to be read if he cared.

Often, he did. They were electric women, he thought, yet they sensed in the Icarus even something basic and feral, some mysterious male rite performed beyond the

horn-rimmed gaze of pundits and, most importantly, away
from women.

They were of many kinds, many types. (*How mas-
culine*, one of them said, patting blue hair into place, *to
think of women as types*. Embarrassed—this was in New
York, where differences were unfashionable that year—he
laughed and threw some chablis at the back of his throat
and left her soon thereafter, reasoning that, after all, he did
not quite like her type.) He sampled them: the Junoesque;
the wiry and intense; the darkly almond sensual; the
Rubens maiden; the others. How not to call them types?
The urge to classify washed over him, to analyze and
inspect. At last he came to look upon himself as from a
distance, pacing his responses, never moving wholly with
the moment. There, he quit. The NASA flack who hovered
ever-present at his elbow tried to keep him "alive" on the
3D, circling through the talk shows, to retain his "saturated
image," but Nigel dropped out. And after a while, found
Alexandria.

He went for long runs on the beach between La Jolla
and Del Mar, keeping in training, churning doggedly by
forests of firm young thighs, sun shimmering through a thin
haze of sweat that ran into his eyes from bushy eyebrows.
Cantilevered breasts—or, more stylishly, bare ones, brown
painted nipples pouting in the stinging sun—swung to
follow his progress. He loped along the ocean's foaming
margin, feet slapping in water, arms and legs growing
leaden, his throat awash in dry pinpricks. He diverted
himself by studying the faces that wheeled by, moving
stride by stride into his past. Small families, leathery men,
dogs and children: he picked roles for them all, ran small
plays in his head. He glimpsed them frozen in laughter,
boredom, lazy sleep.

One of them had stared straight at him, seen in an
instant what his mind's eye was up to and given him a
crooked insane grin, eyes crossed. He slowed, stopped.
Tried to read the deliciously red lips. Came closer. And met
Alexandria.

The past was really not a scroll or an ornament for the
mind to do with as it liked; no. It was a fog, a white cloud

made of pale dead brain cells that once stored memory, their loss a sloughing off of detail and everyday incident, until only a few moments, warm random yellow lights, shine through the fog. Whether he had met Shirley first, or Alexandria, was not clear to him any longer. He had been reeling away from the whole oppressive NASA thing, without realizing it, and when Alexandria appeared he washed up on the shore of her. He remembered talking to her, very earnestly, over clear glasses of Vouvray, chilled so that it almost numbed the lips to drink it. Remembered hikes on the southern slopes of Palomar Mountain, past the ruins of the great telescope, lizards scuttling in the sunlight. And dry nights, dim and strange after the setting sun, with that cool stagnancy that pervades the California coastal towns.

Early on, when things were still cementing, Shirley and Alexandria still saw each other separately, in elaborately arranged schedules, but soon they saw the comedy of it and became more natural. Their circle of friends constricted until he and Alexandria became a circle of two, complete together, though not obsessive, not clutching at each other. They each lived in the world, moving and doing, she at American Airlines and he at NASA, but each in an orbit that defined the locus of the center: the place where they both met. About this center Shirley orbited, a moon bound to their planetary influence. Always changing, always shifting, the spaces around the three had still a Pythagorean simplicity, a unity centered on the two—

"Nigel. Wake *up*, Nigel!"

Shirley loomed over him, blotting out the sun. "We've got to go. She's feeling nauseous again."

He sat up. Alexandria smiled wanly a few meters away, eyes hollowed and dark, a shadow of the woman he had conjured up a moment before. He wrenched his eyes away.

They took the express coach to the Orange County Fall Fair, coasting high on the Santa Ana freeway above the punctured, burnished ruins of La Mirada and Disneyland, now asprawl with groves of oranges again.

Alexandria potted earnestly at moving dummy targets,

felling three with wadded paper bullets and winning a wooden doll that grinned with manic love. They rode the looper, relishing the seconds of delicious free fall. They inspected the implausibly fattened cattle, stared into the blank brown eyes of lambs, stroked the matted heads of baby goats.

A ring of singing New Sons accosted them. Nigel brushed them off and Alexandria lingered behind to speak to them, beyond his earshot.

They sat under cloth umbrellas and ate fair food: tacos, paste salad, crisp *sansejens*. Nigel slurped at a tankard.

And Alexandria said with sudden finality, "We should have had children."

"Alexandria, *no*, we thought it through. Our jobs—"

"But then there would have been *some*thing . . ."

She blinked rapidly, swallowed and bit into her simbani and noodles.

Uncomfortably, Nigel glanced at the next table. A mother was urging her son to finish his taco so that the family could go see the cattle show. "Ummm, mmmm, mommy." The boy artlessly fumbled the taco into his left hand and dropped it theatrically on the ground. The maneuver was well timed; his mother looked back to see the taco tumble, but not early enough to see his preparations. "Oh," he said unconvincingly.

"All through," Alexandria said.

Nigel turned and found she was smiling again.

"Right, I see that. What I can't make out is why *I* must have a telltale installed." Nigel leaned forward, shoulders hunched, elbows on Hufman's desk. Alexandria sat silent, hands folded. Hufman grimaced and started over:

"Because I can't rely on Alexandria carrying her pickup monitor everywhere. Her telltale is much more complex than yours—it taps directly into the nervous system—but its radio transmitter hasn't got enough range. If she got beyond her pickup, she could have a brain stem hemorrhage, go into coma, and you'd think she was just dozing. But with a pickup telltale inset behind your ear, you'd know something was wrong even if she'd left her monitor behind."

"And fetch you."

"An emergency team, not me." Hugman sighed, looking frayed and tired. "If you two are going to travel or even go on long walks, the telltales are necessary."

"It won't screw up my inner ear or my balance, anything like that? NASA has to approve any—"

"I know, Mr. Walmsley. They'll okay it; I checked."

"Nigel, yours is only an—" Alexandria glanced at Hufman.

"Acoustic transducer," Hufman supplied.

"Yes. Mine is a complete diagnostic communicator. We'll both be tagged with the same transmission code, but yours will be, well, just a warning light for mine. You—"

"I know, right," Nigel said, jerking to his feet. He paced nervously. "You say mine can come right back out, just pop the cork and I'm good as new?"

"Painless." Hufman regarded him steadily. "We'll be able to interrogate Alexandria's diagnostics, or check yours to see if it's receiving properly, without touching either of you."

Nigel blinked rapidly, jittery. He hated operations of any kind, could barely tolerate the NASA physicals. But what upset him here was the calm, assured way Hufman and Alexandria talked about the possibility of massive damage to her nervous system. Of a wasting disease, a slow seeping away of function. Then the hemorrhage. Then—

"Of course. Of course I'll do it. Now that I understand. Of course."

He flew to Houston for his routine tests and workout. Nigel arrived with two other astronauts, all doing ground work but remaining on standby for deep space operations. They flew in on commercial transport; the days of private planes for astronauts had vanished long before. The other two men were of the usual mold: robust, good-humored, competitive. Nigel weathered the physical tests, including the long-standing worst—cold water, poured in an ear, causing the eyeballs to whirl as the confused brain struggles with input from two semicircular canals, one warm and the other cold; the world tilted madly. Then a day in a practice module, immersed in a universe of switches, manifolds, pipes, tanks, sensors, valves, connectors, hardware without end. They centrifuged him in it, timed his reflexes. He relearned the tricks of breathing under high gs: balloon the lungs and then suck in air in rapid little pants, breathing off the top. Finally, on the fifth day, he arced into a low orbit on a milk-run shuttle craft. In zero g his blood pooled in different parts of his body, fooling the body into thinking that his blood volume had increased. His urine output rose, hormones accumulated, all within the acceptable parameter range. He passed, renewed his credentials, and sped earthward. The shuttle landed in Nevada. He arrived back at their apartment to find that Alexandria had entered the hospital for an overnight biopsy, all standard, and that Shirley was alone there, reading.

He puttered about, unpacking. As they went to bed Nigel realized this was the first time they had spent the night together since the days when he'd first met Shirley, through Alexandria. Even then their intimacy had a forced quality to it, a seeming inevitability without its own intrinsic momentum. Touching her, he worked awkwardly for the right rhythm. They fumbled with each other's bodies, unfamiliar packages they could not open. At last they gave it up with mumbled apologies, a half-muttered theory about fatigue and the lateness of the hour, and sank into a relieved sleep, back to back, the sheets making a loose tent over the space between them.

In the long afternoons as Alexandria rested, he pored over decades of scientific research and speculations. There was a cycle, he saw: as the twentieth century wore on, the assertion that life was common in the universe rose from the status of an improbability to a common assumption, until the radio listening programs began. Then, after several decades of null results, a certain zest went out of the search. Expensive radio telescopes cupped an ear to the fizzle of interstellar hydrogen, and then, as budgets ran short, the programs died. There was no dramatic change in the scientific underpinning—the evolution of matter seemed to almost require that life arise in many sites—but faith lagged. If the galaxy swarmed with life, why were there no prominent radio beacons left to guide us? Why no galactic library? Perhaps man was simply too impatient; he should listen for a century, calmly, without counting the cost. Nigel wondered how the debate over use of the radio telescopes would shift when word of the Snark became widespread. Did one example of a visitor change the odds that much? Emotionally, perhaps so. The key was the Snark itself.

They still attended parties in the homes of friends, or visited Shirley's cramped apartment in Alta Dena, but Alexandria found her tolerance for alcohol weakened. She tired early and asked to be taken home.

Her work schedule slipped from three days a week, to two, then one. The Brazilian deal went on, gathering legal complexity, like a ball of wool picking up lint. She fell behind and was given more and more circumscribed tasks to complete.

Nigel resisted Shirley's persuasions to attend New Sons . . . meetings? rallies? services? He could not tell whether Shirley went because of Alexandria, or the other way around. Alexandria, knowing him, scarcely mentioned it.

He rose in the early morning and read the New Son books, the *New Revelations*, the intellectual super structure. It seemed a tinkertoy religion to him, assembled from the detachable sprockets and gears of earlier faiths. Through the center of it ran the turbine he'd suspected: a parody of the Old Testament God, obsessed with the power of His own name, capable of minute bookkeeping in the lives of the devout, to decide their salvation. This God carried the whole suitcase full of wars, disease, floods, earthquakes and agonizing death to visit upon the unconvinced. And, apparently, believed in preposterous connections between Buddha, Christ, Joseph Smith and Albert Einstein; indeed, had caused them all, with a tweak of the holy hand.

Nigel slammed the *New Revelations* shut on this mean-minded God, rose and padded quietly into the bedroom. Alexandria lay sleeping, head tilted back and mouth open.

He had never seen her sleep this way before. The thrust of her body seemed to belie the fact of rest. Tense yet vulnerable. He had a sudden perception of death: a small thing moving in from the distance, winging slowly in the night air as she slept. Searching out the house. Through a window. Into the shadowed bedroom. Silent, slow. Fluttering. Fluttering into her sagging mouth.

EIGHT

Lubkin called frequently. Nigel listened but volunteered little; nothing more had been learned about the Snark, so there seemed no purpose in speculating. Lubkin was all atremble over the President's appointment of an Executive Committee, headed by a man named Evers, to monitor the situation. ExComm, Lubkin called it. The Committee was meeting at JPL in a week; would Nigel come?

He did, begrudgingly. Evers proved to be a deeply tanned, athletic-looking sort, well groomed and noncommittal. He carried the air of one who had been in charge of things for so long that his leadership was assumed, a fact hardly worth remarking upon. Evers took Nigel aside before the formal meeting and pumped him for an estimate of what the Snark was up to, where it would go. Nigel had his own ideas, but he told Evers that he hadn't a clue.

The meeting itself proved to be a lot of talk with precious little new data. The Venus rendezvous seemed quite probable now, after detailed analysis of the Mars encounter. Why the Snark should be doing this was another matter. Since the communications satellite nets were completed in the 1990s, Earth was no longer a strong radio or TV emitter. A magnetic implosion-induced rainbow artfully produced in Saudi Arabia was transmitted to Japan by direct beaming through a satellite; no signals leaked out of the atmoshpere anymore. It was conceivable that the Snark hadn't picked up intelligible electromagnetic signals from Earth until it was near Mars. But still, why Venus? Why go there?

Nigel felt a certain wry amusement at Evers and his scientific advisors. When pressed on a point they would hedge and slip into their neutral jargon; a simple "I think" became "it is suggested that"; opinions were given in the passive voice, devoid of direct authorship.

It came to him as the meeting broke up that, compared to this slippery committee and the unreadable Evers, he probably preferred the riddle now riding toward Venus, a thing known only by its blossoming orange fusion flame.

Lubkin called. The Snark did not respond to a beamed radio signal, or to a laser pulse.

Of course not, Nigel thought. The thing isn't naive anymore. It's had a squint or two at daytime 3D and grown cautious. It wants time to study us before putting a toe in the water.

More news: Evers was upping the budget. New specialists were being called in, though none was given the whole picture, none knew what all this was really about. The Ichino fellow was working out well. Tracking went on. No sign of the Snark.

Nigel nodded, murmured something and went back to Alexandria.

And Alexandria was right, he saw: the two of them had been on a plateau for years. He recalled the boy at the Orange County Fall Fair. People with children had a natural benchmark. They grew, developed; you could see your effort giving into a living human being, a new element in the world's compound. Alexandria had climbed up through a corporate anthill. Her progress was merely vertical, without human dimension. The Brazilians would buy the damned airline, that much was clear by now, and how, precisely, could that enter the sum of her life?

Nigel usually left the ExComm meetings as soon as they formally broke up. Without a firm fix on the Snark's trajectory, there seemed little to discuss. At one of them

Lubkin followed him out of the conference room and into an elevator. Nigel nodded a greeting, distracted. He absently scratched his cheek, which was shadowed by a day's growth of beard, and the rasp sounded loudly in the elevator.

"You know," Lubkin said abruptly, "the thing I kind of like about a thing like this, a group effort like this with not many people in on the thing, is the way it makes people fall back on each other."

"So does gin."

Lubkin laughed in short, sharp barks. "Man, I'm glad Evers didn't hear you say that. He'd be angry as a toad with the warts filed off."

"Oh? Why?"

"He, well, he wants to be sure we got a solid group."

"Then he must be having doubts about me."

"Naw, I wouldn't say that. We all sort of feel different about you."

"Why?"

"Well, you know." Lubkin looked at him earnestly, as though trying to read something in Nigel's face. "You were there. At Icarus. You've seen some things that, well, nobody else in the human race ever will."

Nigel paused. He chewed his lip.

"You've seen the photos I took. They—"

"It's not the same. Hell, Nigel—what you did—going into Icarus—may have brought the Snark."

"That radio burst, you mean?"

"Yeah. Why would a derelict send out an intense signal like that?"

Nigel shrugged, lifting his eyebrows in a faintly comical way that he hoped would break Lubkin's mood. "Beyond me, I'm afraid."

The elevator door slid aside. "If it's beyond you, I'm pretty sure it's beyond all of us, Nigel." He shuffled his feet, as though vaguely embarrassed. "Look, I've got to run. Give my best to Alexandria, will you? And don't forget the party, eh?"

"Certainly."

As Nigel left the building he felt good to be getting away from Lubkin, a man he basically found difficult to like, but who had somehow touched him for a moment in that brief conversation. The look on Lubkin's face reminded him of other people at NASA who had spoken to him in the past, sometimes buttonholing him in lunchrooms or corridors, total strangers, really, some of them. They wanted to know an odd point or two about Icarus, or ask a technical question that hadn't been adequately covered in the reports; or so they said. Some were dry and businesslike, others would leave phrases hanging for long moments as if, acutely conscious of Nigel (who was balancing a tray of food, or waiting to go into a meeting, and still did not want to seem rude), they nonetheless could not let him go. Some would mumble for a moment and then beat a retreat, while others, after a moody phrase or two about a detail, would suddenly boom out jovial phrases, wring his hand and be gone before he could reply. And from those encounters would come the same phrases: *you were there . . . you've seen some things that . . . the pictures, not the same . . . not what it was really like . . . you were there . . .*

Lubkin and the rest truly did respect him and hold him apart, he saw. Nigel could deduce that people felt some aura around him. He ignored it pretty successfully. Now and then the thought would crop up that this must have happened to the early astronauts. He'd gone and read the books from that era; they didn't teach him much. He retained a vision of Buzz Aldrin withdrawing into depressive-alcoholic binges, divorcing his wife, living alone, securing the doors and windows of his apartment, unplugging the telephone, and drinking, for days at a time, simply drinking and the thinking and drinking. Had his own personality picked up a tinge of whatever demon stalked Aldrin? From the subtle weight of expectations people had? . . . *you've been there . . . touched it . . .* Well, so he had. And perhaps been changed by it. And changed by what people thought of it.

* * *

Some days later, Nigel's home console sigmaed a
reminding nudge for him, from its memorex. CATEGORY:
ASTRONOMY, 1b (Planetary); periodic events, as requested. A
partial eclipse of the sun by the moon would be visible from
the southern California coast, 2:46 P.M. Pacific Coast Zone
Time, two days in the future. So they delayed lunch and
made an elaborate picnic on the back lawn. A casserole of
beans, onions, chunky beef and spices; cheese, pale yellow;
tomatoes, sliced cucumbers; gazpacho; artichoke frittatas
with lime sauce; a sound Pinot Noir; finally, macadamia-nut
ice cream. Alexandria ate with gusto. She forked the
frittatas between her teeth in precise, squarely cut wafers,
leaning back on one stiffened arm, an extended hand buried
to the wrist in fresh grass. Her red skirt slid off her raised
knees and down, exposing thighs of parallel whiteness to
the sun's sting, a sun already bitten at its edge. This lazy
motion, laying bare the ashy white inside of her thighs as
though they were a new and secret place, caught at
something in his throat. Above them, the moon devoured
the sun. She lay back on the grass with a sigh and motioned
to him to put on the filmed glasses they'd bought. Nigel
rested his head against the firm and rounding earth, feeling
it curve away beneath him and roll off toward the horizon.
He realized for a moment that he was, indeed, pinned by
Mr. Newton to what was in fact a ball, a sphere, and not the
misleading flatland men thought themselves to inhabit (and
reminded himself that a savage, according to Dr. Johnson,
was a person who saw ghosts, but not the law of gravity).
Some of the earliest observations of eclipses, he recalled
from the memorex, were made from the intellectual
fulcrum of ancient Alexandria. There, in Ptolemaic times
and after, the great library blending Greece and Rome had
stood—until, in some minor scramble of a war, it had
burned. He blinked. Darkness gnawed at the sun. Alexandria beside him asked questions and he answered, his
words slurred by the Pinot Noir and the muzzy haze of
afternoon sunlight. But the warmth ebbed. A chill came
across the lawn. The eating above continued, an abiding
darkness chewing the center from the sun. It was a partial
eclipse. Slowly a curtain drew across the dead but furious

matter above, carving the star into a crescent, Nigel saw suddenly, an incomplete circle with horns that yawned open and unconnected, its tips burning bright with mad energy. Something in him turned, *I am dying, Egypt, dying*, it squeezed his throat, and he blinked, blinked to see the chewing everlasting pit that hung above them.

NINE

Alexandria insisted that they go to the Lubkins'. The idea somehow caught her interest and brought a glinting life to her eyes. She had always gotten into the spirit of holidays with more zest than he, and now the early weeks of December lifted her mood. Nigel mentioned it to Hufman. The doctor, relying on lab reports, thought she might have reached a stable plateau. Perhaps the drugs were working. The disease might go no further.

As if on cue, Alexandria improved more. She bought a dress that artfully exposed her left breast and found a shirt for Nigel with ruffled black-and-tan sleeves. Nigel felt conspicuous in it when they arrived at the Lubkins' party, but within half an hour he had knocked back the better part of a bottle of a Chilean red he'd found at the bar. Alexandria was her old self; she took up a corner position in the living room and the guests, mostly JPL-related, gradually accumulated around her. Nigel talked to a few people he knew but somehow the flow of words between mind and tongue never got going. He prowled Lubkin's home, staring out at the evening fog that seeped uphill toward them through a stand of jacaranda trees. The house was in the new style, worked stone and thin planking, with huge oval windows overlooking the hazy view of Pasadena.

"Say, Nigel, I thought you'd like to know Mr. Ichino."

Nigel turned woodenly. Lubkin's introduction had come unexpectedly and Nigel was not prepared for the short, intense man who held out a hand. He normally thought that Japanese faces were impassive and unreadable, but this man seemed to radiate a quiet intensity before he'd even said anything.

"Ah, yes"—they shook hands—"I gather you're to look into the telemetry and computer hookups to Houston."

"Yes, I shall," Ichino said. "I have been overseeing the general aspects of the problem so far. I must say your programming for the Snark search pattern was admirable."

At this last sentence Lubkin stiffened.

"I am sorry," Ichino said quickly. "I shall not mention such terms again in public."

Lubkin's face, drawn and strained, relaxed slightly. He nodded, looked at the two men indecisively for a moment and then murmured something about looking after the drinks and was gone. Ichino compressed his lips to hide a smile. A glance passed between him and Nigel. For an instant there was total communication.

Nigel snickered. "Art has been defined"—he sipped at his wine—"as adroitly working within limitations."

"Then we are artists," Mr. Ichino said.

"Only not by choice."

"Correct." Mr. Ichino beamed.

"Have you picked up the, ah, object yet?"

"Picked up . . . ?" Mr. Ichino's walnut-brown forehead wrinkled into a frown. "How could we?"

"Radar. Use Arecibo and the big Goldstone net together."

"This will work?"

"I calculate that it will."

"But everyone knows we cannot follow deep space probes with radar."

"Because they're too small. Admittedly we've never seen the, the thing, so we don't know its size. But I used the apparent luminosity of its fusion flame and estimated what mass that exhaust was pushing around."

"It is large?"

"Very. Couldn't be smaller than a klick or two on a side."

"Two kilometers? Using Arecibo we could easily—"

"Precisely."

"You have told Dr. Lubkin of this?"

"No. I rather thought somebody would've looked into it by now."

From the look on Mr. Ichino's face, Nigel could see quite clearly that the usual Lubkin style was still in force; Lubkin was doing what he was told. Innovation be damned and full speed ahead.

A tray of edibles passed by. Nigel took some violet seascrape paste and smeared it on a cracker. He felt suddenly hungry and scooped up a handful of wheatmeats. He asked the waiter after more of the Chilean red. Ichino was partway through a delicately phrased recital of what was happening in the Snark search—apparently, damned little—when the red arrived. Nigel allowed an ample quantity to slosh into his glass and gestured expansively: "Let's move round a bit, shall we?"

Ichino followed quietly, ice tinkling in his watery drink. Nigel ducked down a hallway, nudged open a door that was ajar. The family rec room. He peered around at the usual furniture netting, console desk and sim-sensors.

"Big screen, isn't it?" He crossed over to the pearly blank 3D. He thumbed it on.

—A man in an orange and black uniform, holding a long, bloody sword, was disemboweling a young girl—

—The thing in silvered dorsal fins made an explicit gesture, grinning, eyes fixed. Male? Female? Ambig? It murmured warmly, twisting—

"Bit juicy, looks like," Nigel said, switching away.

"Perhaps we should not be witnessing his private channel selections . . ." Mr. Ichino said.

"True enough," Nigel said. He flipped over to full public circuits. "Haven't seen one this big in quite a while."

A gaudy picture swam into being. The two men watched it for a few moments. "Ah, he's a hibernation criminal, you see," Nigel said, "and he is set on destroying this underwater complex, so's the woman there, the one in red—" He stopped. "Dreadful stuff, isn't it?" He spun the dial.

—The oiled bodies snaked in long lines. They formed the sacred annular circles under the glare of spots, off-camera, which did not wash out the log fire that blazed angrily at the center, sparks showering upward. Feet pounded the worn earth. A hollow gong carried the beat. Spin. Whirl. Stamp. Sing.

"Even worse than before," Mr. Ichino said mildly. He reached out to the dial. Nigel stopped him. "No," he said.

—Chanting, spinning in a dizzy rhythm, the bodies glistened with sweat. Their ragged chorus swelled into new strength.

> Running living leaping soaring
> Brimming loving flying dying
> Only once and all together
> Joyful singing love forever

Annular circles orbited about the central fire. Spin. Whirl. Stamp. Sing.

"Overall," Nigel drawled, "I think I would prefer opium as the religion of the masses."

"But you err there, sir," a voice said from the doorway. A roly-poly man stood there with Alexandria. His eyes glimmered out from folds of flesh and he laughed deeply.

"Bread and circuses we need. We cannot provide infinite bread. So—" He spread his hands expansively. "Infinite circuses."

Introductions: he was Jacques Fresnel, French, completing two years of study in the United States. ("Or what's left of it," Nigel added. Fresnel nodded uncertainly.) His subject was the New Sons in all their branches and tributaries. So Alexandria had struck up a conversation with him and, sensing an interesting confrontation, led him to Nigel. (And Nigel, despite the fact that the New Sons were not a favorite topic, felt a surge of happiness at this sign of her new liveliness. She was mixing and enjoying things again, and socializing better than he was at this party.)

"They are, you see, sir, the social cement," Fresnel said. He held his glass between two massive hands as though he would crush it, and gazed at Nigel intently. "They are *necessary*."

"To glue together the foundations," Nigel said blandly.

"Correct, correct. They have only this week unified with numerous Protestant faiths."

"Those weren't faiths. They were administrative structures with no parishioners left to keep them afloat."

"Socially, unification is paramount. A new binding. A restructuring of group relationships."

"Nigel," Alexandria said, "he thinks they are a hopeful sign."

"Of what?"

"The death of our Late Sensate culture," Fresnel said earnestly.

"Passing into—what?—fanaticism?"

"No no." He waved the idea away. "Our declining Sensate art is al*ready* being swept aside. No more emptiness and excesses. We shall turn to Harmonious-Ascendant-Ascetic."

"No more Nazis gutting blonds for a thrill on the Three-D?"

Alexandria frowned and glanced at Lubkin's pearly 3D, now blank.

"Certainly not. We shall have mythic themes, intuitive art, work of sublime underlying intent. I do not need to stress that these are the feelings we all sorely lack, both in Europe and here and in Asia."

Alexandria said, "Why does that come next, after Sensate?"

"Well, these are modified views, taken from the strictly schematic outline of Sorokin. We could pass into a Heroic-Promethean, of course"—he paused, beaming around at them—"but does any of us expect that? No one feels Promethean these days, even in your country."

"We are building the second cylinder city," Mr. Ichino said. "Surely construction of another world—"

"A fluctuation," Fresnel said jovially. He touched a fingertip to his vest. "*I* am always in favor of such adventures. But how many can go to the—the cylcits?"

"If we build them fast enough with raw materials from the moon—" Alexandria began.

"Not enough, not enough," Fresnel said. "There will always be such things, and they are good, but the main drift is clear. The last few decades, the horrors of it—what have we learned? There will always be dissenters, schismatics, deviants, holdovers, dropouts, undergrounds, heretics even, and of course the reluctant or nominal conformers."

"They are the majority," Mr. Ichino said.

"Yes! The majority! So, to do *any*thing useful with them, to channel and funnel that stu*pen*dous energy, we, we must place—how is it said?—all these under one roof." Fresnel made a steeple of his hands, his stone rings like gargoyles.

"The New Sons," Nigel said.

"A true cultural innovation," Fresnel said. "Very American. Like your Mormons, they add whatever elements are missing from traditional religions."

"Stir, season to taste and serve," Nigel said.

"You're not truly giving it a chance, Nigel," Alexandria said with sudden earnestness.

"Bloody right. Anyone for drinks?" He took Alexandria's glass and made off toward the bar.

The carpet seemed made of spongy stuff that lifted him slightly into the air after each step. He navigated through knots of JPL people, flashing an occasional automatic smile and brushing away from contact with others. At the bar he scooped up a basket of pumpkin seeds, roasted and salty and crisp. The Chilean red was gone; he switched to an anonymous Bordeaux. Mr. Ichino materialized at his elbow. "You remain an active astronaut, Mr. Walmsley, I understand?"

"So far." He downed the Bordeaux and held out his glass to the bartender for a refill.

"Should you be watching your weight?"

"A good eye you have. Quite good." Nigel prodded a finger into his stomach. "Gaining a bit."

"Alcohol has a remarkable number of—"

"Right. Apart from stuff like cement, which I presume you aren't taking in by the handfuls, strong drink—love that phrase—is the worse thing possible for cramming on the kilos. But wine—the dryer, the better—isn't. Scarcely more in a glass than in a few grams of macadamia nuts. If you could *get* macadamias any more, I mean."

He stopped, aware that he was probably talking too much. Mr. Ichino nodded solemnly at Nigel's advice and asked the barman for beer. Nigel watched owlishly as the icing of suds rose. "Back to the sociometrician?" he said, and the two of them returned to the rec room.

A small knot of people had formed around Fresnel. Most of them had fashionably midnight-black hair, trimmed exactly to the shoulders. They were discussing Humanistic-Secular. The prime point in question seemed to be the use of electronically enhanced gloves by the Pope, and whether this meant he would throw in with the New Sons. Media said the two were jockeying over the issue; a computer-human linkup had predicted absorption of the Catholics within three years, based on assignable sociometric parameters.

Nigel beckoned to Alexandria and they drifted away. Shirley appeared, arriving late. She kissed Alexandria and asked Nigel to fetch her a drink. When he returned, Alexandria was talking to some Soviets, and Shirley drew him aside.

"Are you going with us?"

"Where?"

"The Immanence. We do so want you to go with us to see him, Nigel."

He studied her eyes, set deep above the high cheekbones, to read how serious she was. "Alexandria has mentioned it."

"I know. She said she's making no progress. You just clam up about it."

"Don't see much point in talking nonsense."

"You apparently don't like talking to us at *all*," she said with sudden fire.

"What's that mean?" he asked, bristling.

"Ohh." She slammed her fist against the wall in dramatic emphasis. She rolled her eyes and Nigel couldn't stop himself smiling at the gesture. *She should have been an actress*, he thought.

"Nigel, damn it, you are not *flexing* with this."

"Don't follow the slang, sorry."

"Ohh." Again the rolling eyes. "You and your language fetishes. Okay, in one syllable. Alexandria and I don't know where you *are* any more."

"Hell, I'm home with her most of the day."

"Yes, but—Lord!—emotionally, I mean. You keep working on this thing, whatever it is, at JPL. Reading your

damned astronomy books. Alexandria needs more of you
now—"

"She's getting plenty," Nigel said a bit stiffly.

"You're closed off in there, Nigel. I mean, *some* gets
through, but . . ." Shirley knitted her eyebrows together
in concentration. "It never struck me before, but I think
that might be why you fit into a triad. Most men can't, but
you . . ."

"I'd imagine a triad requires *more* communication, not
less."

"Of a kind, I suppose, yes. But Alexandria is the
center. We orbit around her. We don't have a true three-
way."

She leaned against the padded hallway wall, shoulders
slumped forward, studying the carpet. Her left breast,
exposed, teardropped in the soft shadows, its tip a brown
splotch. Nigel suddenly saw her as more open, more
vulnerable than she had seemed in months. Her pastel
dress bunched at hips and breasts and somehow made her
appear nude, as though the material protected without
concealing. The oval on her left breast hung as an eye into a
deeper layer of her.

He sighed. He was aware of the breath leaving him as
a thick alcoholic vapor, a liter of stuff so substantial he half
expected to see the cloud hang in the hallway, unmixed
with the customary air. "I suppose you are right," he said.
"I will go and see this fellow if you wish. It must be before
we leave though—a week from now."

Shirley nodded silently. He kissed her with an odd
gravity.

Three people, chattering, came out of a nearby room
and the mood between them was broken.

Mr. Ichino left early. Damned early, Nigel thought
muzzily, for he had liked the man on sight. It was a good
party, too, quite good. Lubkin's affairs in the past had been
straightway the most boring of a sad lot of parties that
sprouted up around the moribund jollity of the Xmas
season. *Keep the X in Xmas*, he thought, making another
round to the bar. The Bordeaux was finished off but a

passable California claret went down nicely. Lubkin wasn't being mean-minded about his wine, much to his credit. No poisonous California rotgut reds, no mysterious mixtures. Nigel realized dimly that he was pretty well into a substantial piss-up. Better yet, all done at Lubkin's expense. He had half a mind to search out Lubkin and thank him profusely, meantime sloshing down a gratifyingly large quantity directly in his presence.

He set out on this mission and found himself negotiating a surprisingly difficult corner getting out of the rumpus room. (Did Lubkin allow an occasional rumpus in the rumpus room? Just a sweet beheading or two, in full color, Chinese cleavers and all? No, no; the disorderly nature of the cleaning-up would offend the man.) The angle of the corner was obtuse, opaque. He had noticed the floor plan was pentagonal, with occasional jutting intrusions, but how was he to get his bearings?

He sat down to clear his head. People drifted by as if under glass.

He pondered the opaque angle. Oddities of the language: *angle*, with two letters interchanged, spelled *angel*. Easy, so easy. One transposition rendered the comfortably Euclidean into—pop—the orthodoxly religious. Two letters alone could leap that vast, abiding chasm. Absurdly easy.

Up again, and off. In the living room he sighted land, in the persons of Shirley and Alexandria. They were foci for the usual knot of JPL engineers, men with close-cropped hair and cheap ballpoint pens still clipped in their shirt pockets. They smiled wanly as he approached, looking as though they had just been shaken awake.

Nigel skimmed past these constellations on a flyby, then ricocheted from conversation to conversation in the hollow living room:

—So Cal lost its appeal to the regional EIB?

—Sure. I expected it.

—So our water quote's cut again?

—Sure. Factors into an eighteen thousand-person popdrop, mandatory. We'll make it up from fractional decline. Slowed immigration laws will come through. And the Federal Regional Support Allotments will be shaved. We—

Onward:

—Suppose we've got the terrorists stopped on pluto-nium 240? So what? Since the New Delhi incident we know the damned Asians can't be trusted to—

Onward:

—and I loved that scene with the semen all *over* the stage, just frozen CO_2 really but what an *effect*, jizzing into the *au*dience—

Here and there Nigel began talking, feeling the sentences form whole inside before he'd begun them. He unzipped the floppy covers from words, made them pop out quick and shiny. People peered at him as though down a pit, from a height. Words smerged together.

Nigel: You pronounce "clothes" as though it were "close."

Woman: Well, aren't they the same?

Nigel: How about "morning" and "mourning"?

And then away, to the bar, where some decent hock burbled out into his uplifted glimmering glass. He sipped. A riesling? Too sweet. Gewürztraminer? Possibly.

The room was unsuitably warm. He moved through the heavy, cloying air. Crescents of sweat had blossomed under his armpits. He made for the rec room.

Vacant. The 3D. He thumbed it on. The screen flickered wetly at him and melted into an overview of the two annular circles. Bodies laced together. A voice boomed out over the crowd. Bread and wine. Come to fullness.

No communion rail and wafer, not here. No baptismal dunking, no empty Jewish phrases muttering about a Pharaoh in a tongue they can't understand. No ritual. The *real* religion straight from the wellsprings. Only once and all together. Joyful singing love forever. Sic transit, Gloria.

Nigel reeled away to the opposite wall, yellowed by a spotlight. He punched at a button, stabbed another. Family Music Center, it said.

Good, right. Try for a bit of Eine Kleine Krocked-musik.

He dialed. Wellsby's choral improvisations swelled out of the speaker. He stabbed again. Jazz: King Oliver. Brassy trumpet, drums. But where was the Bach? The sixties, one of his favorite Beatles? Or did he have to settle for some modern cacophonist?

He turned back to the 3D. Stabbed once more.

The writhing New Sons, again. Make a joyful noise unto the horde.

He punched at the buttons.

The black swastika vibrated against the orange uniform. The gleaming tip of the sword bit into the girl's stomach. She begged, crying. The man shoved upward and the sword sank deep. Blood spattered from her. She lunged against the cords binding her hands but this only made the sword slice crosswise. She screamed. The crimson laced down her legs.

Nigel wrenched it off. He was sweating; it ran into his eyes. He wiped his brow and wheeled away.

He paused in the hallway to steady himself. Malt does more than Milton can, to justify God's ways to man. Welcome to the 21st century. Sic transit, Gloria. Or was it Alexandria?

He made his way to the patio. Cool air washed over him. The fog below had layered above the jacaranda trees, haloing the lights of Pasadena. Nigel stood, breathing deeply, watching the gathering mist.

"Mr. Walmsley? I wanted to continue our discussion."

Fresnel advanced from the opened slideway, framed by the murmuring party beyond.

The frog comes in on little flat feet, Nigel thought. He tossed his wine glass away and turned to meet the man.

"Surely you understand, don't you, that we have all, all of us, come at last to terms with ourselves? With our finiteness? Our little amusing perversions? Mr. Lubkin's Three-D was demonstrative. It illustrates how far we have come. Progressed. Econometrics—"

Nigel watched his fist blossom in midair and home with elliptical accuracy on Fresnel's forehead. There was a fleshy smack. Fresnel staggered. Lurched. Did not fall. Nigel set himself and estimated the geometry of the situation with a precise eye. Fresnel was wobbling, a difficult, challenging target. The man's face beaded with

perspiration in the silvery light. Nigel launched his left fist
along an ascending parabola. Angle into angel. There was a
jolting impact. Flesh colliding, wetly. His hand went numb.
Lick the lips: salty. Fresnel melted away. His nostrils
sucked in a rasping new breath. Nigel tottered. Relaxed.
He studied the fog layer. It was tilting. Tilting in the
smooth air. It seemed to take a long time.

TEN

His Immanence resided in a recently purchased Baptist
church. The building squatted on a scruffy, midwestern-
looking street corner among the flatlands of lower Los
Angeles. Nigel squinted at it skeptically and slowed his
walk, but Alexandria and Shirley, on either side of him,
tugged him on.

They'd never have gotten him here but for a moment
of contrition over Fresnel. Scarcely anyone at the party'd
noticed except Alexandria, who glimpsed Nigel tipping
over. Fresnel had been insulted but surprisingly, dismay-
ingly unhurt; the women had been shocked; Nigel had
rather enjoyed the whole bash, and still relished the
memory of Fresnel going down, ass over entrails.

He braced himself for the ordeal to come. They
entered through a side door and passed through a large
auditorium packed with saffron-robed figures being lec-
tured. Shaved heads, bright garlands of flowers. The salty
tang of Japanese food. Through a clicking beaded curtain,
out the back door, around the temple. They entered a small
garden through a bamboo gate, nosily slipping the latch.

A small, browned man sat in lotus position on a broad
swath of green. A breeze bestirred the trees overhead. The
man regarded him with quick, assessing yellow eyes. He
gestured for the three of them to sit and Alexandria
produced three round yellow pads for them. Nigel sat in
the center.

They exchanged pleasantries. This was a wing of the
New Sons, those who felt in tune with the eastern roots of
man's religious heritage. This seated man with his face of

sagging flesh was an Immanence, for there was no one sole Immanence, just as a universal God had an infinite store of representations.

Nigel explained, with long uncomfortable pauses, his own rational skepticism about religion in any form. Most men sought some undefinable something, and Nigel admitted he did too, but the grotesque distortions of the New Sons—

The Immanence plucked a leaf from a bush and held it to Nigel's eyes. He blinked and then stared at it steadily.

"You are a scientist. Why would anyone spend his life studying this leaf? Where was the gain?"

"Any form of knowledge has a chance of resonating with other kinds," Nigel replied.

"So?"

"Suppose the universe is a parable," Nigel said uncertainly. "By studying part of it we can read the whole."

"The universe within a grain of sand."

"Something like that. I feel the laws of science and the way the world is put together can't be accidents."

The Immanence pondered a moment.

"No, they are not accidents. But except for their practical use, they were always unimportant. The physical laws are but the bars of a cage."

"Not if you understand them."

"The central point is not to study the bars. It is to get out of the cage."

"I think the act of reaching out is everything."

"If you would come to fullness you must stop reaching and manifest a more basic spirit."

"By dancing in two circles?"

"Another facet of the Many Ways. Not ours, but a Way."

"I have my own way."

"This world can best be understood as an insane asylum. Not an asylum for the mind, no. For the *soul*. Only the flawed remain here. Are still here."

"I have my reaching out to do here. Out between the bloody bars, if that's the way—"

"That is nothing. You must try to escape and transcend the cage."

Nigel began to speak rapidly and the old man waved away his points.

"No," he said. "That is nothing. Nothing."

Rubbish, Nigel thought. *Utter rubbish, what that dried prune of a man had said.*

So thinking, he dipped a wing.

The airfoil caught and he felt a tug, pressure. Up he went, the momentary image of that dreadful Immanence bloke fading as quickly as it had come (*odd, to think of it here, now*) and the wind sang through the struts.

"How is it, Nigel?" Alexandria's voice came in his ears.

"Incredible," he said into his throat mike. He peered down at the spinning earth—which the instructor had warned him against, but what in hell was the point, really, if you couldn't do that?—and saw her, an orange speck.

"Can you hold the spiral?" she called.

"Bit tough on the arms," he grunted.

"The instructor says to relax into the harness."

"Right. I'm trying. Oops—" He lurched. The glider bit into a surge of wind and climbed sharply. The invisible funnel of air, warm as it swept in from the Pacific, lofted him further up his lazy spiral. The wind rose like a transparent fountain here on the coast, where breezes moving landward struck first the steep hills and then the westward wall of Arcosoleri, the kilometer-high city of cubes and apses. Nigel glanced at the glittering windows of the Arc as he swooped nearer it, judging the distance. He still had a safe margin of distance from the pinkish concrete face. The circling tunnel of air held him in check.

Below, the turning world.

Purple-ripe clouds mottled the arc of the sea's horizon, showers of rain like skirts beneath them. And here, Nigel, banking and rising, felt a sensation like a *swoosh* of breath leaving him as his spirit lifted free of this spiraling body and joined the air. He shook himself. It was as though he had stopped struggling, stopped trying to swim through mud. The scooping wind moaned at the slit in his face mask and he tilted his wings to rise higher, Icarus reborn as he left behind everything below him. It was all in the past now, he hoped—Alexandria was recovering, the Snark was on its way. A pure blind joy possessed him. The unacknowledged fear that had gripped him at the beginning of the flight now fell away like a weight and he felt smooth and sleek, birdlike, darting in these high winds. Corkscrewing up, up from the enveloping earth. Soundless happiness. Mortality seeped out of him, froze in the chill high air and fell to shatter with a crystal tinkling on the California below. He turned in a slow circle, carving Earth's skin of air, glinting ocean waves below waving at him randomly. A wing foil flapped, then straightened. Icarus. Wax wings. Do not go softly into this good sky. Soaring. The spinning Earth a basket below. The twin dots of Shirley and Alexandria like pins on a map

coins in his lap
Yes.
He lofted free.

They stayed overnight in a luxury suite of the Arc, rather than catch a bus southward to Los Angeles. Shirley dialed a holo and Nigel lay back in their room's center pit, letting the delicious ache that came from exercise seep through him.

"Do you really think NASA will approve of your taking a chance like that?" Shirley said.

"Ummm? Flying a one-man glider, you mean?" Nigel shrugged. "Whacking lot they can do now."

"I thought you were supposed to check with them on anything dangerous."

"Piss on 'em and leave 'em for dead." Nigel sighed noisily and watched quick splashes of color flick, jewel-like, across the inside of his eyelids.

"You don't feel boxed in by what they'll think?"

"Hardly."

"Then you wouldn't mind signing an endorsement of a People's Referendum?"

Nigel opened his eyes lazily. The holo abstract was a

seething vision two meters above the pit, like an oozing ruby in oil. "What for?"

"To prohibit sale of LHS foods."

"LHS?" Nigel frowned. A signer of a People's Referendum Call guaranteed that he would help pay for the cost of having a nationwide vote on the issue in question, if it was turned down by the voters.

"Left-Handed Sugars. *You* know. We digest only sugars with a right-handed spiral molecule in them."

"That's what natural sugars are—right-handed."

"Yes. Only now they're making left-handed ones to use in food, so the body doesn't turn them into fat. It's a kind of diet food."

"So what?"

"Well, it's an insult to other countries to have that happening. When people are starving, I mean, almost everywhere. Will you sign, Nigel?"

He tilted his head back and studied the seamed concrete vault above them. Someone had once asked him to sign a Referendum Call against this Arc, even while it was becoming obvious that the first one, Arcosanti, was already an enormous success. It was still growing faster than Phoenix, which lay sixty klicks to the south of it, and yet wasted no space or energy on transportation systems. Everyone who lived inside it was within a fifteen-minute walk of work, play, entertainment, shopping. It had the urban complexity without the Losangelization, the separation from nature. But somebody had opposed it, for reasons now forgotten.

He sighed. "Think not."

Her "Oh?" was carefully put.

He opened his eyes again and studied her. She wore the simplest of black dresses. Long panels of gossamer cloth hung down from a deep neckline. They were artfully arranged to hint at the tanned flesh beneath. She had a well-scrubbed sheen on her nose but her face was clouded by an odd, compressed tension.

"Shirley, old girl, you know I'm no revolutionary."

"Do you feel the same way about what those Brazilians want to do?" she said sharply. "They've got great little ideas about how to make the airline cost-effective again."

"How?" Nigel said guardedly.

"During peak periods, when the computers don't have enough solid-state electronics banks left to do the job, they're planning to use human neural inventories."

Nigel blinked, surprised. "Alexandria didn't tell me."

"She probably doesn't want to bother you while you're busy planning your trip."

"Probably . . . But look, why not use animals to tap into, for computer memory?"

"They don't have—what's it called?—anyway, they lose detail too easily."

"Holographic data-storing capability, you mean." He paused. "I'd heard about the experiments, but . . . With the cost of manufacturing computers these days, and the power drain, I suppose it's smart economics . . ."

"Is *that* what you say? *Economics?* To hook poor people into machines, rent out their frontal lobes?"

"Granted, it's unappealing. A zombie life, I suppose."

"It's beneath human dignity."

"How dignified is it to starve to death?"

Shirley leaned forward and said fiercely, "Do you really believe such a simple-minded—? You *do*, don't you? Nigel, you're greedy. You don't know a thing about social problems and you want your life undisturbed."

"Greedy?"

"Of course! Look at this room. It's packed with every rich man's amusements—"

"I didn't notice you hanging back at the threshold."

"Okay, I enjoy a holiday too. But—"

"Why aren't you down in Brazil? That's what those types are going to do, isn't it?—use grunt labor from Brazil to beef up—you'll excuse the phrase?—American computers? Why not go down there and work with the poor people on the spot, in some little dimple of a burg?"

"This is my home," Shirley said stiffly. "The people I love are here."

"So they are. And you have wondrous thighs, Shirley, but they can't encompass all the world's teeming troubles."

"Sarcasm won't—"

"Listen." Nigel cocked his head. "Alexandria's coming

in from her walk. I don't want a chuffup over this, Shirley. I want no bother before we go off. Right?"

She nodded, her mouth twisted slightly as though under pressure.

Nigel saw that the mood in the room would be detectable when Alexandria came in, so he leaned back, yawned elaborately and began in a heavy Welsh accent,

> "Aw-ee lasst mah-ee hawrt een ahn Angleesh gawrdaan,
> Whaar thah rawzaz ahv Anglahand graw . . ."

ELEVEN

He and Alexandria lifted three days later. They had booked well in advance to get a flight over the poles; they reentered the atmosphere as a flaring pink line scratched across the sky of the north Atlantic.

Matters were a bit better in England than during their last visit several years before. There were only a few shambling beggars at the baggage checkout, and they seemed to have valid licenses. Most of the terminal was lighted, though not heated. Their helicopter to the southlands lifted free with a clatter into the chilling winds. Coal smoke blotted out the London sprawl.

They reached their destination easily: a well-preserved English inn about three hundred and fifty years old, well run and securely guarded. They spent Christmas there, snug in the battering winds. The next day they hired a guard and a limousine and visited Stonehenge.

Nigel found the experience oddly moving. In spirit he was scarcely an Englishman anymore after the welfare state had turned into the farewell state. These massive thrusting columns, though, spoke to him of a different England. The heel stone was so marvelously aligned, the celestial computer so accurate, he felt a kinship with the men who had made it. They had thrust these gray measuring fingers at a clockwork sky, to understand it. The New Sons had long since played up the pantheistic side of the Druids, popularly thought to be the builders of this stone heap, never mentioning the rest—that these were not men who followed others' ideas senselessly.

Nigel looked out at the road where a gang of altered chimps was repairing wash damage. They cradled their special shovels and flicked mud thirty meters in one toss. Alexandria stood beside him, biting absently at a fingernail: evolutionary remnant of animal claws. He shivered and took her back to the inn.

Paris was depressing. The second day of freezing in a darkened hotel ended with a shutdown of water pressure throughout the city for the rest of the week.

The pleasure domes of the Saudis were thronged. Cloud sculptors flitted over the desert, carving erotic white giants that coiled ponderously into vast orgasms.

Over South Africa the display was more modest. At evening the swollen elders appeared, wrinkled financial barons, and enjoyed an orchestrated weatherscape as they dined. Nigel and Alexandria watched a vibrating rainbow that framed purple thunderheads, clouds moving with the stately grace of Victorian royalty.

In Brazil, in a restaurant, Alexandria pointed: "Look. That's one of the men we're negotiating with for the airline."

"Which one?"

"The stocky man. Tiltlens glasses. A sway shirt. The briefcut jacket with highlighted trim. Khaki—"

"Right, I see."

She looked back at Nigel. "Why are you smiling?"

"I've missed that eye for clothes you have. I never see those things, really." He reached out to take her hand. "I've got you back again."

A lot of the planet they couldn't see. In the large areas without resources or industry a white man was an automatic enemy, a child-starver, a thief; the politics of the past thirty years had seen to that. In Sri Lanka they went a block from the hotel to eat. Partway through their curry the muttering in the restaurant and a gathering tension drove them into the sinking street. A passing cab took them back, and then to the airport, and then to Australia.

They were baking on Polynesian sands when his pager buzzed. It was Lubkin. Ichino had relayed the radar search idea to him. They had a blip. It was bigger than two klicks, and spinning. It would rendezvous with Venus inside eleven days if it didn't accelerate. Lubkin asked if Nigel would return early to run the Main Bay team. Nigel told him he would think about it.

Outside Kyoto, walking a country lane, Alexandria suddenly threw up into a ditch. A two-day biopsy showed no change in her condition from three months before. Her organic systems seemed stable.

Her pocket telltale hadn't made a sound. Nigel checked his skull set. It was active. It beeped on command. Alexandria simply hadn't been ill enough to trigger it.

The next day she felt better. The day after that she was eating well. They went on a hike. As she slept, afterward, Nigel called ahead and cancelled the rest of their reservations. He fluxed through to Hufman; the man's face showed on the screen as a wobbling mask. Hufman thought Alexandria needed a rest near home.

They took the next jet to California, arcing high over the pale Pacific.

TWELVE

The Main Bay: a crescent of consoles, each sprinkled with input boards like a prickly frosting. Men sitting in roller chairs were stationed at each console, watching the green/yellow screens flicker with a blur of information. The Bay was sealed; only staff members directly involved in the J-27 project were present.

"Arecibo has acquisition," Nigel said.

The knot of men around his chair buzzed with

exclamations. Nigel listened to his headphones. "They say the Doppler confirms a flyby orbit."

"You check with Arecibo?" Evers said at Nigel's elbow.

Nigel shook his head. "Our satellite, Venus Monitor, can't get a radar fix. This is all we have." He tapped in programming instructions on his keyboard.

"Spectrographic reading," Lubkin explained. A tele-metered photo was being drawn on the screen line by line. At the top edge of the screen was a tiny point of light, scarcely more than a few bright dots on the picture tube.

"Spectral intensity shows it's hot. Must be a pretty fiendish fusion torch." Nigel looked up at the men from NASA, Defense and the UN. Most of them clearly couldn't make sense of the wavelength plot being displayed; they scowled in the fluorescent glow of the Main Bay, looking out of place in their stylish green suits.

"If it *is* on a flyby course it will almost certainly come here next," Evers said to the other men.

"Possibly," Nigel said.

"It may attempt to land, bringing unknown diseases with it," Evers went on smoothly. "The military will have to be able to stop such an eventuality."

"How?" Nigel said, ignoring a raised finger from Lubkin that plainly told him to remain silent.

"Well, ah, perhaps a warning shot." Evers's expression pinched slightly. "Yes," he said more brusquely, looking at Nigel. "I'm afraid we will have to determine that for ourselves."

The group broke into conversation.

Lubkin tapped Evers's arm. "I think we should try to signal again."

Evers nodded. "Yes, there is that. The ExComm will work out the message. We have some hours left to discuss it, don't we?" He turned to Nigel.

"Three or four at least," Nigel said. "The men need a break. We've been at it over ten hours."

"Good. Gentlemen," he said in a booming voice, "this area is not secure for further discussions. I suggest we retire upstairs."

The group began moving off under Evers's direction. Lubkin beckoned Nigel to follow.

"I'll stay here for a bit. Set up the watch schedule. And I want to go home to rest. I'm not going to be needed in your deliberations."

"Well, Nigel, we could use your knowledge of . . ." Lubkin hesitated. "Ah, maybe you're right. See you later." He hurried to catch up to the group.

Nigel smiled. Lubkin clearly didn't relish the prospect of a cantankerous Nigel in the ExComm meeting. Feisty subordinates do not reflect well on their superiors.

He took a JPL scooter home. The tires howled on the corners as he banked and shifted down the hillside avenues, slicing through the dry evening air. Stars glimmered dimly behind a layer of industrial haze. He piloted without goggles or helmet, wanting to feel the rush of wind. He knew handling the Snark-Venus encounter would be tricky, particularly if Evers and Lubkin and their faceless committee designed some transmission. Nigel would then have to sandwich his own in somehow before the Committee caught on. He had been working for months on the code; he'd read all the old literature on radio contact with extra-terrestrial civilizations and adapted some of their ideas. The transmission had to be simple but clearly a deliberate signal to the Snark. Otherwise the Snark would probably assume it had picked up another conventional Earthside station, and ignore it.

Or would it? Why did Snark remain mute? Couldn't it easily pick up Earth's local stations?

Nigel gunned the scooter, swooping down the hills. He felt a rising zest. He'd check on Alexandria, who would be home from work soon, then wait for Shirley to arrive and keep Alexandria company while he was gone. Then back to JPL and Venus and the Snark—

He coasted into the driveway, kicked back the stand and bounded to the front door. The lock snapped over and he ran up the winding staircase. At the landing he stopped to fit his key into the apartment lock and was surprised to find his ears ringing. Too much excitement. Maybe he really would need to rest; the Venus encounter would last through until morning at least.

He let himself in. The living room lights glowed a soft white.

Now only one of his ears was ringing. He was more tired than he thought.

He walked through the lving room and into the arched intersection of kitchen and dining nook. His steps rang on the brown Mexican tiles, the beamed arch echoing them. The ringing in his head pitched higher. He cupped his hand to an ear.

A woman's shoe lay on the tiles.

One shoe. It was directly under the bedroom arch.

Nigel stepped forward. The ringing pierced his skull.

He walked unsteadily into the bedroom. Looked to the left.

Alexandria lay still. Face down. Hands reaching out, clenched, wrists a swollen red.

The ambulance wove through darkened streets, shrieking into the night mists. Nigel sat dumbly beside Alexandria and watched the attendant check her life functions, give injections, speak in a rapid clipped voice into his headset transmitter. Lights rippled by. After some minutes Nigel remembered his telltale. It was still keening at him. Alexandria's unit was running down, the attendant said, using most of its power to transmit diagnostics into the ambulance cassette. He showed Nigel the spot behind Nigel's right ear where a rhythmic pressure would shut it off. Nigel thumped at it and the wailing went away. A thin beeping remained; his telltale continued to monitor Alexandria's diagnostic telemetry. He listened, numb, to this squeaky voice from the very center of her. Her face was slack with a gray pallor. Here, now, linked by bits of microelectronics, he and she spoke to each other. The indecipherable chatter was a slim chain but he clung to it. It would not stop even if she died; still, it was her only voice now.

They swerved, rocked down a ramp, jolted to a stop under red neons. The bubble surrounding him and Alexandria burst—the ambulance tail door popped open, she was wheeled out under a white blanket, people babbled. Nigel got out awkwardly, ignored by the attendants, and followed the trotting interns through a slideway.

A nurse stopped him. Questions. Forms. He gave Hufman's name but they already knew that. She said bland, comforting things. She led him to a carpeted waiting room, indicated some magazine faxes, a 3D, smiled, was gone.

He sat for a long time.

They brought him coffee. He listened to a distant hum of traffic.

Very carefully he thought about nothing.

When he next looked up Hufman was standing nearby, peeling away transparent gloves.

"I'm sorry to say, Mr. Walmsley, it's as I feared."

Nigel said nothing. His face felt caked with dense wax, stiff, as though nothing could crack through.

"An incipient brain stem hemorrhage. The lupus *did* equilibrate in her organs, as I thought. She would have been all right. But it then spread into the central nervous system. There has been a breakdown in the stem."

"And?" Nigel said woodenly.

"We're using coagulants now. That might possibly arrest the hemorrhage."

"What then?" a female voice said.

Hufman turned. Shirley was standing in the doorway. "I said, what then?"

"If it stabilizes . . . she might live. There is probably no significant brain damage yet. A spasm, though, induced by the lupus or our treatment—"

"Would kill her," Shirley said sharply.

"Yes," Hufman said, tilting his head back to regard her. He plainly wondered who this woman was.

Nigel made a halting introduction. Shirley nodded at Hufman, arms folded under her breasts, standing hipshot with tense energy.

"Couldn't you have *seen* the lupus was getting worse?" she said.

"This form is very subtle. The nervous system—"

"So you had to wait until she *collapsed.*"

"Her next biopsy—"

"There might not *be* a next—"

"Shirley!" Nigel said sharply.

"I must go," Hufman said stiffly. He walked out with rigid movements.

"Now you've fair well muddled it," Nigel said. "Shaken up the man whose judgment determines whether Alexandria lives."

"Fuck *that*. I wanted to know—"

"Then *ask*."

"—because I just got here, I didn't talk to anybody and—"

"How did you know Alexandria collapsed?"

Nigel had thought he could gradually deflect the conversation and calm her down. He was surprised when Shirley glared at him and fell silent, nervously stretching her arms to the side. Her face was ashen. Her chin trembled slightly until she noticed the fact and tightened her jaw muscles. In the distance he could hear the staccato laboring of some machine.

"Shirley . . ." he began, to break the pressing silence between them.

"I saw the ambulance leaving when I came back from my walk."

"Walk?"

"I got to the apartment early. Alexandria and I had a talk. An argument, really. Over you, your working late. I, I got mad and Alexandria shouted at me. We were fighting, really fighting in a way we never had before. So before it got any worse I left."

"Leaving her there. Wrought up. Alone. When Hufman had already said she couldn't take stress in her condition."

"You don't have to . . ."

"Rub it in? I'm not. But I'd like to know why you harp away on my taking time for JPL. *You* work."

"But you're her, well, she leans on you more than me, and when I got to the apartment and she was so weak and pale and waiting for you and you were late I—"

"She could lean on *you*. That's what we three are all about. Extended sharing, isn't that the proper jargon?"

"Nigel—"

"You know what I think? You don't want to face the fact

that you'll lose Alexandria and you're blaming me in some
buggered-up way."

"You're so damned independent. You don't *share*,
Nigel, you—"

"Can that *shit*." He took a convulsive, mechanical step
toward her and caught himself. "That's, that's your own
illusion."

"A pretty convincing one."

"I've tried—"

"When you *do* let go it's something seamy. Like getting
drunk that night."

Nigel held his breath for a moment and let it out in a
constricted, wheezing sigh. "Maybe. It all stacked up on
me there. Alexandria, I mean. And this New Sons, I
couldn't—" He stared directly at Shirley. In the bleached
light her skin seemed translucent, stretched thin over the
bones of her face. "We've never supported each other, have
we? Never."

She studied him. "No. I'm not sure I'd want to, now."

Silence. A clink of glassware from down the corridor.

"Me either," he said across the pressing space that had
formed between them.

"It shouldn't be that way."

"No."

"We weren't, weren't growing together. Ever."

"No."

"Then . . . no matter what happens to Alexandria, I
think . . ."

"It's finished. You and me."

"Yes."

With each exchange he had felt a pane of glass slide
snugly into place between them. There was no going back
from this.

"There's some, some *knot* in you, Nigel. I couldn't
reach it. Alexandria could."

She closed her trembling eyelids, tears swelling from
under them. She began to cry without a sound.

Nigel reached out toward her and then a soft, padding
shuffle caught his attention. Several people were coming
down the corridor.

"Oh," Shirley said, the word coming from her like a

thick bubble. "Oh." She turned, arms straightening to her sides, and went to the door.

Two robed men entered. Each held an arm of His Immanence. The small browned man between them moved with arthritic slowness but his yellowed eyes moved quickly from Shirley to Nigel, judging the situation.

"Alexandria may want to see him again," Shirley said to Nigel. "I called from the apartment and asked him to come."

"You can tell him to clear off," Nigel said tightly.

"*No*," Shirley said. "She needs him more, more than she needs you—"

"Bugger that. Th—" and something clutched at his throat, stemming the words. His mind spun. He dimly sensed Alexandria lying nearby somewhere, near death, and Shirley here, these men, the awful sagging flesh of the old one. Pressing at him. Pressing. He turned, a hand out to steady himself. Sit down. Rest.

But he knew they would wear him down if he sat there meekly and listened to their droning talk. The room suddenly was a clotted, airless place, thick with the sweet incense of the New Sons coiling into everything. He swayed on his feet and gulped for air. Something tugged at his memory. The Snark. Venus. The shallow curve he'd plotted, now coming to its apex. Time ticking, the Snark—

"No." He raised his hands, palms outward. He pushed the cloak of air away from him. Pushed at Shirley and the men, who now receded in the watery light. Swerved away and lurched out the door. A destination formed in his mind. The shiny plastiform walls of the corridor slid past. The dense antiseptic air of the hospital parted before him and closed behind, his passage a spreading ripple.

THIRTEEN

He hunched over in the back of the cab and planned. He rubbed his hands together, each palm momentarily clenching the other in the chilling air. His teeth chattered slightly until he clamped his jaw shut. The past fell away from him and left only a clear, geometrically precise problem. He could not allow Evers and the ExComm to blunder when they tried to communicate with the Snark. Granted they'd had the sense to adopt Nigel's scheme, a set of primes denoted in binary code. When arrayed in a rectangle the long string of numbers formed pictures: a plot of Snark's path through the solar system, with circles for the planetary orbits; a breakdown of simple terrestrial chemistry; a recognition code for fast transmission, once the Snark understood that someone was trying to communicate.

But when the Snark responded, how would ExComm answer? Then it would be out of Nigel's hands. Well, he had a partial answer for that, too. He had made up another message cube, identical to his earlier, ExComm-approved cube, except that it allowed the Snark's return signal to be routed through the JPL communications board to whatever receiver the board operator selected. And that receiver would be Nigel, through the only private channel he had—his telltale. Simultaneously, the message would be stored and then, when it was finished, replayed for the JPL crew in the Main Bay.

Nigel grimaced. Granted, Evers had accepted Nigel's message. Granted, getting early reception was a small betrayal, of sorts. But it would give Nigel a few moments to understand before ExComm got into the act—a precious margin of minutes so he could hear the Snark through the telltale, try and guess what the proper response must be. And then, if he could follow what the Snark said, he would have to head off the ExComm reply; those men would almost certainly jump the gun. Any error could be disastrous. The Snark had probably been silent all this time because it was cautious. If the ExComm reply was unclear or seemed unfriendly, the Snark might simply pass through the solar system and away. Gone. Forever.

The yellow sprinkling of lighted windows at JPL made a beacon amid the shadowed hills. Nigel paid the cab, checked through the guards and, instead of going directly to the Main Bay, walked quickly to his office. He unlocked

his desk and reached far back in the left drawer. He fished
out the second ferrite message cube, identical in appearance to the one ExComm now had. He pocketed it and
stopped at the men's room to check his appearance in the
mirror. His eyes were red and his face seemed all angles,
stark and sharp. He combed his hair with jittery strokes and
practiced looking relaxed. Must be smooth. Calm. Yes.

He froze, breathing shallow gasps as he looked at
himself. Back there lay Alexandria, beyond his help but not
beyond his caring. And here he stood, dealing an ace from
under the deck to the men he'd worked with, not trusting
them, a fine film of perspiration cooling the skin below his
eyes. If he could step outside his mind he was sure it would
all appear stupid, blind. What was the Snark to him,
anyway? Round the bend, he was. He curled a fist and
pressed it against his thigh. Alexandria was now in their
province, the world gnawing away at her. Let it come.
Relax, he told himself. Be reasonable, Nigel. *Ping*. It's gone
way past tea, now. Things are well past the realm of pure
bloody fucking sweet reason. Oh yes, oh yes.

Outside the Main Bay door he pressed the spot behind
his ear. His telltale beeped on. He opened the door.

The Committee was there, and Evers, and Lubkin.
Nigel moved among them, consulted, advised. He checked
recent developments with the technicians. Lubkin showed
him some ExComm work on a second signal to Snark—
awkward, ambiguous, too complicated. Nigel nodded,
murmured something. Lubkin gave him the ferrite cube
with their signal in it and Nigel made a show of logging it
into the communications board.

The casual air of the bay had evaporated. The Snark
was still on the plotted course. Minutes ticked by. A half
hour. The Committee buzzed with speculations and worries. Nigel fielded their questions and watched the Snark
approach. Venus Monitor still showed only an unresolved
dot of light.

Nigel spoke into his head microphone, ordering Venus
Monitor out of the tandem control scheme JPL usually
used; now the satellite would respond only to Nigel's board.

He ordered the Monitor's main radio dish to rotate and fed in aiming coordinates.

Casually he fished his own ferrite cube from his pocket and logged it into the board. He punched in orders and the ExComm cube was retired into storage, while his own came to the fore, ready to transmit.

"What are you doing?" Lubkin said. The men around Nigel's roller chair fell silent.

"Transmitting," Nigel said.

He tapped in the crucial part: recognition code. He had memorized his telltale code months before, in Hufman's office, and now he instructed his board to relay the Snark's reply to him. The board would transmit directly to the telltale, so that Nigel could hear the reply before it was replayed in the Main Bay for the Committee.

"Here it goes," Nigel said. He pressed a button and the board transmitted a recognition signal; his telltale beeped in sympathy in his ear.

He ordered Venus Monitor to begin signalling the Snark.

The ship was coasting smoothly when the strong signal found it.

It was a clever code, beginning with a plot of the ship's own trajectory through this planetary system. So the beings of the third planet had followed all along, waiting. To reveal this now was a clear sign of nonhostile intentions; they could have kept their capabilities secret.

The craft quickly located the source of the pulse, circling this shrouded planet. Was this world occupied, too? It recalled an ancient amphibian race that evolved on a world not too dissimilar, whose inability to see the stars through the blanket of clouds had retarded them forever. And it thought of other worlds, encased in baking layers of gases, where the veined rock itself attained intelligence, laced together by conducting metals and white-hot crystals.

The machines studied the radio pulse for a fraction of a second. There was much here to understand. Elaborate chains of deduction and inference led to a single conclusion:

the third planet was the key. Caution was no longer justified.

The computers would have to revive the slumbering intelligence which could deal with these problems. They would become submerged in that vast mind. There was a bittersweet quality to the success of their mission; their identity would cease. The overmind would seek whatever channel it needed to understand this new species, and these more simple computers would be swept up in its currents.

The revival began.

The craft readied itself to answer.

The ferrite cube emptied itself. Nigel heard a blur of stuttered tenor squeals.

"Hey! What're you—"

Lubkin had noticed the switch in cubes. Some indexing error? Lubkin reached over Nigel's shoulder toward the board controls.

Nigel lunged upward. He caught Lubkin's arm and twisted it away from the board.

Someone shouted. Nigel swung out of his chair and pulled on Lubkin's arm, slamming him into another man. Lubkin's coat sleeve ripped open.

His telltale beeped. The Snark was answering. Nigel froze. The pattern was clear, even though speeded up: the Snark was sending back Nigel's original message.

Nigel wobbled. In the enameled light the faces of Evers and Lubkin swam toward him. He concentrated on the burbling in his head. There; the Snark had finished retransmitting Nigel's signal. Nigel felt a surge of joy. He had broken through. They could reply with—

Someone seized his arm, butted into his ribs. He opened his mouth to say something, to calm them. Voices were babbling.

His telltale squealed. Shrieked.

Sound exploded in his mind. The world writhed and spun.

He felt something dark and massive move through

him. There was a bulging surge, filling— The torrent
swallowed his identity.

Nigel gasped. Clawed the air. Fell, unconscious.

FOURTEEN

Lubkin was talking to him. Meanwhile fireflies of blue-
white banked and swooped and stung his eyes. They were
distracting. Nigel watched the cloud of singing fireflies
flitting between him and the matted ceiling. Lubkin's voice
droned. He breathed deeply and the fireflies evaporated,
then returned. Lubkin's words became more sharp. A
weight settled in his gut.

They understood Nigel's state of mind, Lubkin said.
About his wife and all. That explained a lot. Evers wasn't
even very angry about Nigel's maneuver with J-27. It was a
better idea, the committee admitted, once they'd had a
chance to study it. What the hell, they could understand . . .

Nigel grinned dizzily, ironically.

The fireflies sang. Danced.

Evers was pretty pissed at Nigel's suckering them,
Lubkin said, forehead wrinkling. But now J-27 had responded. That made things better. Evers was willing to
ignore Nigel's deception. Considering, that is, Alexandria.

"What?" Nigel sat upright in the hospital bed.

"Well, I—"

"What did you say about Alexandria?"

Nigel saw that he was stripped to the waist. Lubkin
licked his lips in an uncertain, edgy way. His eyes slid away
from Nigel's.

"Dr. Hufman wants to see you as soon as I'm through.
We brought you here from JPL, after we got that call,
asking where you were. I mean, we understood then."

"Understood what?"

Lubkin shrugged uneasily, eyes averted. "Well, I
didn't want to be the one . . ."

"What in hell are you saying?"

"I didn't know she was that *close*, Nigel. None of us
did."

"Cl . . . close?"

"That's what the call was about. She died."

A nurse found him a stiff blue robe. Dr. Hufman met him in the corridor where he was saying goodbye to Lubkin and shook hands solemnly, silent. Nigel looked at Hufman but he could not read any expression.

Hufman beckoned to him. They moved down the hallway. Somewhere a summoning bell chimed. The sleek walls reflected back to Nigel the face of a haggard man, a day's growth of beard sprouting, upper face fixed in a rigid scowl. The two men walked.

"She . . . she died right after I left?" Nigel asked in a croaking whisper.

"Yes."

"I—I'm sorry I left. You tried to call me . . ."

"Yes."

Nigel looked at the other man. Hufman's face was compressed, eyes unnaturally large, his features pinched as if under pressure.

"You . . . you're taking me to view her?"

"Yes." Hufman reached a gray metal door and opened it.

His eyes fixed on Nigel. "She died, Mr. Walmsley. Uncontrollable hemorrhage. The operating room was busy. There were other patients. We put her aside for the orderlies to carry away. A half hour passed."

Nigel nodded dumbly.

"Then she began to move, Mr. Walmsley. She rose from the dead."

Alexandria sat alone. She was in an elaborate diagnostic wheelchair; it bristled with electronics. Her white hospital smock was bunched above her knees and probes touched her at ankles, calves, forearms, neck, temples. She smiled wanly.

"I knew. You would return. Nigel."

"I . . . I was . . ."

"I know," she said mildly. "You. Spoke. To Shirley. You became. Frightened. By what was. Happening." She spoke slowly, the words individually formed and separated by a perceptible pause. She had to work for each syllable.

"The New Sons . . ." Nigel began and then did not know how to continue.

"You need not. Have. Become. Excited. Nigel. He had told. Me. That you sensed it. Too. Briefly."

"He? Who . . ."

"Him. What you felt. Before you. Rejected the Immanence."

Nigel was aware of Hufman closing the door behind them, standing where he could hear but not interrupt. Alexandria seemed delicately balanced, fragile, suspended by some inner certainty. Encased.

"You felt Him. Nigel. My love. Perhaps. You did not. Recognize. Him. To you. For a long while. He was the Snark."

Nigel was silent for a long, stunned moment. "The telltale," he said out of the corner of his mouth, toward Hufman.

"Yes. Yes," Alexandria said in a flat voice. "That is. How He entered me. But I. Recognized Him. For His true nature."

She closed her eyes and her chest rose in shallow, rapid breaths. Nigel glanced at Hufman. His legs were numb and he felt pinned to this spot, unable to advance toward Alexandria or retreat. Her wheelchair readouts blinked and shifted.

"Can someone—some*thing*—do that?" he said in a quick whisper. "Transmit over that telltale circuit?"

Hufman's voice was a resonant bass in the small room. "Yes, certainly. Hers has both acoustic and electric contact with her nervous system. It functions passively most of the time, but we can use it to send echo signals through the central nerves."

"Is that what's happening?"

Hufman moved to Nigel's side and, to Nigel's surprise, put an arm over his shoulders. "I believe so. I've told no one about this because, well, at first I thought I had made some awful mistake."

"Something is going *into* her. Through that telltale."

"Apparently. You collapsed, didn't you? At JPL? Probably an overload. Or whoever is transmitting shorted out your input and concentrated on her."

"But she was *dead*."

"Yes. All functions ceased. I estimate she suffered oxygen deprivation only five or ten minutes, at most. Somehow a stimulus through the telltale jolted her breathing. Restored it to function. Her renal overload has subsided, too."

"I don't see how . . ."

"Neither do I. There is work going on in the use of neurological startups, yes, but they are highly dangerous. And unreliable."

"It's bringing her back to life," Nigel said distantly.

"*What* is? Who's doing this?"

"I can't say."

Hufman looked at him piercingly. "You won't, you mean. You and that other woman have some—"

"What other woman?"

"The one I met. You introduced us earlier. Alexandria asked for her. I wasn't thinking very clearly, I let her in, and—"

"Nigel?" Alexandria's eyelids fluttered, mothlike, and she moved her right hand weakly in a beckoning motion. Nigel went to her.

"He is. Seeing. Through me. Nigel. He wants. You. To know that."

Nigel looked back at Hufman helplessly.

"No, do not be. Afraid. He wants to see. To feel. To walk. In this world."

"Who is he, Alexandria?" Nigel's voice broke as he said her name.

"He is the Immanence," she said, as though to a child. "I know. What He has done. You and the Doctor. Do not need. To whisper. I know."

"He—it—brought you back."

"I know. From the dead. To see."

"*Why?*"

She looked at him serenely. Her eyes crinkled with some inner mirth. "In the sense. You mean. Darling. I do not. Know. But I do not. Question Him. Or question. Moving. With this moment."

In the antiseptic light her bloodless face shone both strange and familiar, each pore sharp and clean.

Hufman's voice intruded: "As nearly as I can determine, she is kept alive by the telltale stimulus. Somehow the synaptic breakdown is being offset. Perhaps the telltale is providing control functions for her heart and lungs, taking the place of the damaged tissue. I don't believe that can last long, however."

Alexandria gazed at him steadily. Her smile was thin and pale. "He is here. With me. Doctor. That is all. That matters."

Nigel took her hand, squatting beside the heavy wheelchair, and studied her, frowning. Conflicting emotions played on his face.

There was a knock on the gray metal door.

Hufman glanced at Nigel uncertainly. Nigel was lost in his own thoughts. Hufman hesitated and then opened the door.

Shirley stood firmly in the doorway. Behind her were a half a dozen New Sons clad in dhotis and jackets. A man in a business suit shouldered his way to the front of them.

"We've come for her, Doctor," Shirley said. Her voice carried a hard, brittle edge. "We know her wishes. She wants out, she told me. And we have a lawyer to deal with your hospital."

FIFTEEN

Imagine thin sheets of metal standing vertically, separated by millimeters. In the stark light they become lines of metallic white. In slow motion a projectile, spinning, the color of smoke, strikes the first sheet. The thin metal crumples. The sheet is rammed back into the second layer, silently, as the film goes on. Though it moves with ponderous slowness you can do nothing. The second sheet folds. At the point of impact the bullet is splattering, turning to liquid. But it goes on. The third silvery line is

compressed into the fourth, the lines form a family of
parabolas, shock waves focused at the head of the tumbling,
melting bullet. And you cannot stop it. Each sheet presses
on the next. Each act—

Nigel saw this dream, lived through it each night, yet
could do nothing. Events compressed. Each moment of
those days impinged on the next, carrying him forward in a
stream of instants.

—At the hospital. Hufman objecting between
clenched teeth. The lawyer smooth, voice resonant with
certainty. Nigel had no legal rights over Alexandria; he was
not her husband. And Alexandria said she wished to leave.
The law, thin sheets compressing, was clear. She wished to
live—or die—among the New Sons. They understood.
They wished her to walk with Him.

—The wheelchair. Winking its update metric lights,
purring, ignored. The New Sons in dhotis wheeling her
from the ambulance toward the Baptist church. The old
man, the Immanence. His face a leadened silver, lit by arc
lamps ringing the church. He cupped his hands and
nodded to Shirley. Alexandria was between them, the focus
of a swelling crowd. Shirley spoke reverently to the
stooped, gnarled Immanence. In the moving shadows
Nigel thought he caught a glance from those yellow eyes. A
look of weighing, judging, assessing. The old man gestured.
There was a subtle shifting in the crowd. The tide of bodies
that opened before Alexandria's wheelchair now lapped
around behind her. Sealing her off. Shirley on the edge, the
Immanence, sagging face aglow, at the center. Toward the
church. An excited babble, a murmur. And the liquid
crowd swirled between Nigel and the others. Cut him off.
Slowly him. *Shirley*, he cried out. *Alexandria!* Shirley had
mounted the steps into the church. She turned, looking
back over the tossing sea of faces. She called out something,
something about love, and then was gone. Into the
shadows. Following the winking wheelchair.

* * *

—On 3D.

She was the same—calm, compact, radiating an inner sureness. The snowballing of interest around her had not touched that core. The eyes were set back, away from the questions put to her by her interrogators; viewing, studying. Nigel watched her in their darkened apartment, lit only by the glowing 3D. He saw Shirley in the background crowd. Her face was rapt, like those around her. Three individual Immanences of the New Sons escorted Alexandria down a ceremonial ramp. They were each tall and stately men, sunken cheeks, palms turned outward in ritual gesture; ascetic; lean. They were very careful of her, their first confirmed miracle. The program paused to run a fax of Hufman, angry, jaw muscles clenching. He admitted under direct questioning that Alexandria had died. Was certified. Abandoned. And then rose.

"Did she have an explanation?" the interviewer asked.

Hufman's weary face faded from the screen, to be replaced by Alexandria's.

She smiled, shook her head, no. And something shifted far back in her eyes.

—At the church they would not let him in. To Nigel all doors were barred.

When his story reached the 3D people they interviewed him, paid attention, promised results. But when the interview was broadcast Nigel came through as a bitter, hostile man. Had he really said these things? he wondered, watching himself. Or were they adroitly rearranging his words? He could not remember. The metallic lines compressed, converged.

—At JPL, alone with Evers and Lubkin. Outside sunlight glinted on trucks as they hauled in new equipment. The facility was being beefed up.

Lubkin: We heard about Alexandria recovering, Nigel. That's great news. We were kind of wondering if, well . . .

Evers: J-27 transmits on two channels, Walmsley. Using a circuit *you* logged into the board. We've got Ichino working on the main signal, but we're afraid to tamper with this other one. Whatever's receiving it—

Nigel: It's my telltale. You know that, don't you?

Evers: Yes. We just wanted to give you the chance to admit it.

Lubkin: You're receiving J-27? Directly?

Nigel: No. It's found some way to sidestep me.

Evers: We'll cut it off then.

So he had to tell them about Alexandria. And beg them to allow the transmissions through JPL. Otherwise she would die.

Stony-jawed, Evers nodded. He would let the beeping thread of life go on. They would even monitor it, eavesdrop, try to decipher what they could. The code was a dense thicket of complexity.

After Nigel had left Evers's office he could remember little of whatever else was said. Events had become so constricted, so compressed, that he confused people and moments. But he could recall Evers's calculating bland expression, the pursed lips, the hint of forces finding a new balance.

SIXTEEN

He sat on the dusty hillside and watched the people streaming into the V of the canyon. Most of them had made the two-hour ride from Mexico City, carrying box lunches. There were bunches from Asia, though, carefully shepherded by guides. And Europeans, identifiable by their brown standard-issue trousers and wooly shirts, severely cut. Separate rivulets which emptied into the canyon.

A flight of birds entered the canyon from the south, fluttering higher as they came. Probably disturbed by the hum of the vast crowd, Nigel thought. He licked his lips. The morning air already shimmered, far warmer than it had been in Kansas two days before. Or had that been Toronto? He had difficulty keeping the days straight. Each of Alexandria's appearances drew a larger crowd; these, he'd been told, had encamped days in advance.

A hundred meters away men labored to frame up more bleachers. It was pointless; people were sitting on the jutting rock ledges already in immense numbers, far more than last-minute measures could accommodate.

The hills swarmed with life, the ripplings of the throng like cilia on an immense cell. On the narrow floor of the valley the impassioned performed: tumblers, self-flagellators, psi acrobats, chanters with their hollow booming sound, dancers. The annular rings turned. Brimming loving flying dying. Fling. Shout. Moan. Stamp.

At last, the excited babble came. At the head of the canyon a white dot blossomed. Alexandria in her wheelchair, wrapped in glittering robes. She occupied a platform among the banked rock shelves. Four Immanences flanked her.

"To fullness!" chanted the crowd. "Oneness!" In the sky a winged dot burned orange at one end. Against the pale desert blue a cloud formed. A white sculpture for the occasion: an immense alabaster woman. Wings. Hand raised in greeting, blessing, forgiveness. Alexandria.

Words from an Immanence. Music. Trumpets blared and echoed from the stones. Stamp. Sing. Running living leaping soaring. Salvation in the shimmering, enchanting heat.

He knew the litany well. It washed over him without effect. He was numb from following her. He knew he should leave but he could not give up when he could still stay close, still see her in the distance. A white dot. The walking, talking dead. Come and see. Have your hopes raised. Regain your faith. Joyful singing love forever.

And yet, and yet . . . he envied her. And loved her.

He grimaced.

Her voice suddenly rolled down the canyon, booming, silencing the mob. She spoke of Him, the One, and how He saw through each of us. Of a vision—

She crumpled. Something banged the microphone. A man shouted hoarsely. Nigel squinted and could make out a knot of robed, milling figures clustered where Alexandria had stood the moment before. Shrill voices called out orders.

She was going at last. Woodenly he stood, brushed away dust from his pants, staring fixedly ahead. Going. Going.

* * *

In his room in Mexico City he let the 3D play while he showered and packed. A short balding man, pink skin, fleshy cheeks, said that Alexandria had suffered a relapse but had not yet joined the Essential One, as she herself had predicted she soon would.

His telephone rang.

"Walmsley? That you?" Evers's voice was high and ragged. Nigel grunted a reply.

"Listen, we just heard the news. Sorry, and all that, but it looks like she's dying. We know you've been following her. Security's tracked you. Have you been able to find out what she's told the New Sons? I mean, about J-27?"

"Nothing. As far as I can tell."

"Ah. Good. I've gotten word from higher up to be pretty damned sure nothing gets out. Particularly not to those . . . well, it looks okay, then. We'll—"

"Evers."

"Yeah?"

"Don't cut the second channel. She isn't dead yet. If you do, I'll tell the Three-Ds about . . . J-27."

"You're . . ." Evers's voice cut off as though a hand had cupped over the speaker. In a moment Evers said, "Okay."

"Keep it on indefinitely. Even if you hear she's dead."

"Okay, Walmsley, but—"

"Goodbye."

For a long time he stood at the hotel window and watched pedicabs lace through the lanes of the Paseo de la Reforma, mostly the late crowd streaming out of Chapultepec Park. The hivelike comings and goings of man.

So he had made one last gesture, threatened Evers. Perhaps kept her alive a few more hours or days. For what? He knew he would never see her again. Only the New Sons would relish those last moments of her.

So . . . back to JPL? Begin over? The Snark still waited.

Eventually, yes. He needed to know. Always the clean and sure, the definite; that's what he sought. To *know*.

Something that Shirley, and perhaps even Alexandria, had never quite understood.

Or . . .

He fluxed the window and a seam parted in the middle. At least two hundred meters down. Into a pool of racing yellow headlights. Compressing lines, snuffing him out like a candle burned too low.

He looked down for long moments.

Then turned. Picked up his bags and took the shuttle down to the lobby. He checked out, smiling stiffly, tipped a porter, left his bags and went out onto the sidewalk. Soft air greeted him. He shoved his hands into his pockets and decided to take a walk around the block, to clear his head.

From his pocket he took a wedge of plastic. It contained microminiature electronics, a power source and transducer. He clipped it into a holder beneath his collar and made sure it did not show. It rubbed as he walked.

He wanted to be in the open when he tried this. A building might shield the signal at these distances, or blur it. He could take no chances. When Alexandria died, the Snark could still use the channel . . .

He reached behind his ear and pressed. The telltale hummed into life. The bit of plastic and electronics he'd had made at such expense rubbed his neck. He pressed a thumb against it and heard a faint ceramic click.

He walked. Stepped. Felt a massive, bulging surge—

Stepped—

Love and envy.

Stepped—

SEVENTEEN

A day later: he steps—

—steps

—onto the sheets of folded rock. Stone decks of an earthen ship, adrift in this high desert. A craft of baking rock. The ages have layered and compressed this wrinkled deck; life skitters over it. Chittering. Leaping.

He mounts the flaking rock. A scorpion scuttles aside. Boots bite into crunching gravel.

—plants licking, foamlike, at the coarse crust—
> *The looming presence*

> *peers out*

sucks in

> *understands*

—*and is quiet*.

In this brittle Mexican desert he marches on. The air is crystalline; puddles from a recent rain splinter the descending light.

Poppies, mallows, zinnias, cacti, sand mats and yellow splashes of lichen—

—*soil awash in life*—

—*sun spinning over the warped earth*—

Nigel smiles. The being rides back, behind the eyes. His legs make easy strides. A bootheel rubs. Leather creaks. Arms rocking, calves bunching. Heart pumping lungs whooshing skin warm boot turning on a stone sky flat shirt tugging in the damp armpits waxy cactus in the path canteen rattling as he turns—

From this awareness Nigel selects. The being does not. He eats it all.

A rabbit bounds to the side. A claret-cup cactus beckons. Nigel stops. Unscrews canteen. Drinks.

—*feels the rushing silvery quilted reddening flavor on his tongue*—   .

—And senses some dim trace of what the other being must feel. It honored the sanctity of living creatures; it would not have bid Alexandria to rise again, but she was already gone, already dead to her own world. So to see this fresh planet, the being used a body that men had already cast aside.

In those first moments of contact with Nigel, on the street in Mexico City, the being had very nearly withdrawn. But when it saw the ruined canvas inside this man, it had stayed. Using the subtle knowledge, learned from thousands of such contacts with chemical life forms, it undertook some brush of contact. And remained. To taste this sweet world. To shore up this man.

—blue custard sky vibrant with flapping life, drifting splotches, writhing clouds—

This place is alien.

Pausing, the sharp jagged horizon dividing this world into halves, he reflects. And sees the rippling weave of Evers and Lubkin and Shirley and Hufman and Alexandria and Nigel. A play. A net. Gravid workings. Each a small universe in itself.

But each together. Exalted. Each a firmament. A clockwork.

So familiar.

So alien.

Deep, buried in the currents of the torrent, Nigel swims.

Swimming, he heals.

The looming presence sat astride the flood of perception and took it all. Before Nigel could apply the filters of his eyes, ears, skin, touch, smell—before all that, the being sponged up this new and strange world, and in the act of taking altered it for Nigel as well.

And someday the being would go. Pass through. Nigel would split his cocoon then. Emerge. Into the splintering day. On doddering feet.

He would pass through that lens. All would pass. But for the moment:

> *The Snark   feels the booming pulse*
> *unfolds the rocks before him*
> *carves the dry air*
> *smacks boots into yielding earth—*
> *seeing*
> *   tasting*
> *   opening.*
> *Eases him into the warming world.*
> *Pins him loving to the day*
> *— E v e r s L u b k i n S h i r l e y H u f m a n -*
> *AlexandriaAlexandria—*

Thinking of them, knowing he will return to that world someday, a weight slips from him and he rolls and basks and floats in these familiar waters of the desert. Evers-Hufman-Shirley—

Alien, they are, his brothers.

So alien.

PART
THREE

He woke, staring up into an iron-gray sky glowing with dawn.

He woke alone.

The being was gone. The faint trembling pressure had seemed to ride behind his eyes; now Nigel felt only a hollow absence of something he could scarcely recall.

He sat up in his sleeping bag, felt a buzzing dizziness, and lay back again. A horned lizard froze on a nearby rock and then, sensing his relaxation, darted away.

There were two places, he thought, where people feel closer to the source of things. The ocean, with its salty memory of origins. And in the desert—bleached, carved, turning beneath a yellow flame, a place reduced to the raw edge. And yet it was alive with a fine webbing of creatures. Perhaps that was why the being wanted to come here.

He remembered buying his backpack, goosedown sleeping bag and boots in a Mexico City shop. Remembered the short flight into the high desert. Remembered walking.

And sensed something behind his memories . . .

Of standing in a high place, looking down on a flat checkerboard of *things*, of *categories* and coordinate systems and forms.

He had watched himself. Seen a bird sheltering in a mesquite plant. Watched the first layer: Bird. Wings. A burnished brown. Phylum-order-class-genus-species.

Watched the second layer: Flight. Motion. Momentum. Analysis.

And saw at last that there was an essence in the way he filtered the world. That beyond the filter lay an ocean. A desert.

That the filter was what it meant to be human.

There was something more, something larger. He snatched at it but it . . . it brushed by him. He dimly saw the fabric of something . . . and then it was gone.

Nigel blinked. He lay on a shelf of worn rock, his body rubbed and warmed by the goosedown bag. The hill beside him glowed soft and golden; the horizon brimmed with light.

What had he learned? he thought. Factually, nothing. There were glimpsed aspects, nuances, but nothing concrete. The being had come. It provided some cushion for him during those dark hours in Mexico City (had he really fluxed the window? thought of jumping?). And the being had gone, seeped away in the night.

Nigel frowned, stretched, relaxed. His calves ached from walking. His stomach rumbled with hunger. He reached over to his backpack and fished out a dried fruit bar. His saliva wetted a bite and the flavor of strawberry filled his mouth.

What was it? After all he'd been through, Nigel still knew nothing about the alien that was useful. No facts, no data. One does not ask questions of a ghost.

He chewed, watching the filling sky.

Alexandria, Shirley—all behind him now. Ironic, how close you could be to someone, how much he'd thought he loved Shirley. Now, after all she'd done, there was only a dull, sour memory.

And questions. Had he really loved Shirley, or was that another illusion? The only person he had ever been sure of was Alexandria. And she was gone. Through the Snark he had known some faint trace of her, for a while. Perhaps some fraction of her remained in the Snark, some shadow.

He blew his nose on a handkerchief. The cloth came away with a smattering of blood; the night air had dried out his nasal passages.

Nigel smiled. Was the blood a sign of life? Or of death? Everywhere was ambiguity.

And yet . . . he wanted answers. He needed to know. Of his old world only one fragment remained: the Snark. There he must go. NASA and Evers would be stepping-stones outward and there would be others, other people who could help. There would be some resistance to him at NASA, he knew, particularly after the business about signaling the Snark first. Nigel Walmsley, the mad astronaut. But he would get through that.

He rubbed his eyes, smoothing the fretwork of crow's feet. What he needed, after these two days with the being-behind-the-eyes, was people. The simple touch of his own kind. And he needed help to deal with NASA. But most of all, people.

PART FOUR **2015**

ONE

Mr. Ichino paused at the entrance to the Pit. The calm murmur of technicians conversing mingled with the *ding* and chatter of typewriter inputs. The Pit was dark, its air stale. Hooded consoles spread dappled pools of light where men sat monitoring, checking, editing the river of information that flowed from this room, into the dancing rhythms of electrons and then out, riding electromagnetic wings to the Snark.

He noted a wall clock; twenty minutes until the meeting. Mr. Ichino sighed, willing himself to relax and not think of what lay ahead. He clasped his hands behind him in an habitual gesture amd walked slowly into the Pit, letting his eyes accustom themselves to the gloom. He paused at his personal console, froze a scrap of the transmission and read:

> In the service of the Emperor he found
> life, and fought the barbarians, and
> beat them into submission. When the Em-
> peror so commanded, he fought strange
> and evil fairy creatures, and these he
> conquered. Dragons he slew, and giants.
> He was willing to do battle with all
> enemies of the land, mortal or animal or
> creatures from another world. And he was
> always the victor.

He recognized the passage from the Japanese legend of Kintaro, even in this westernized form. The Snark had asked Mr. Ichino several days before for more of the ancient literature of the East, and he had brought in all the texts and translations he could find in his collection. They were now being transmitted when time allowed. Mr. Ichino wondered idly if this passage had been selected especially by a programmer, since it contained reference to "creatures from another world." Such an action would be lamentably typical; most of the men here understood nothing of what the Snark wished to know.

Mr. Ichino tapped his front teeth with a finger, thinking. The square, stylized yellow tape squatted against the green of the tube, a totally unfit medium for the delicate thread of a fairy tale. He wondered how it would be read—*was* read, by now—by a thing of copper and germanium, circling Venus. All this—the quiet intensity of the Pit, the compressed minutes he had lived through for months now, the unbalanced feel of what he was doing—seemed parts of a jumbled puzzle. If he could have but a few days to sort it out, to fathom what being could see so quickly to the core of his personal experience, and extract it—

He moved on. A technician nodded, an engineer saluted silently. Word would spread that the Old Man was in the Pit for his daily visit; the men would be a trifle more alert.

Mr. Ichino came to a large graphics tank and studied the intricate work being done inside it by the computer. He recognized the print at once: *Nude in the Sunlight*, Renoir, painted 1875 or 1876; Mr. Ichino had selected the painting only two days before.

Light, filtered to a blue-green, cast streaks across the breasts and arms of the naked girl, strangely altering the illuminating red glow of the skin that was Renoir's unmistakable signature. The girl gazed pensively downward, caught as she grasped at some ill-defined cloth. Mr. Ichino looked at her for a long moment, savoring the ambiguity of her expression with a wistful romanticism he knew as an old friend; he had been a bachelor all his life.

And what would the Snark make of it? Mr. Ichino did not venture to guess. It had responded well to *Luncheon of the Boating Party* and asked for more; perhaps it mistook them for a sort of photograph, despite his explanation of the uses men made of painting.

He shook his head as he watched the computer carefully breaking the picture down into tiny squares of color. The Snark spoke very little; many of Mr. Ichino's ideas about it were deductions. Still, there was something about the pattern of requests the Snark made—

"Anything you would like to see especially, sir?" a technician said at his elbow.

"No, no, everything seems to be going well," Mr. Ichino said softly, startled out of his contemplation. He waved the man away.

Other consoles flickered as the men in the Pit transmitted data to the Snark. At the moment they were working their way through a fresh edition of an encyclopedia, he recalled. Simply radioing the material would have been simple, but the men he supervised were charged with editing each line that found its way into code. The President had accepted the recommendation of the Executive Committee that no detailed scientific or technical information be given the Snark—the Pit was quickly built to ensure it.

Most of the consoles were operating with Mr. Ichino's own Code 4, a specially designed vocabulary and matrix of symbols that afforded high information density in each transmission to the Snark. The Executive Committee had searched Mr. Ichino out in the days following first contact, desperately trying to find a cryptologist who had enough experience with high flux signaling. Code 4 had been relatively simple to lay out, since it drew upon the codes Mr. Ichino had already developed for scrambled transmissions to Hipparchus Base on the moon. It was a simple, flexible code that seemed fairly secure from the Russians and Chinese and whoever else was listening in, but of course it had limited range. It soon became inadequate for the questions the Snark asked; past that point, only photographs and a wider vocabulary would suffice.

Because security was tight, many of the encoders and technicians were not told about the Snark; they thought they were working on something related to Hipparchus Base. So it fell to Mr. Ichino to speak to the Snark. Another cryptologist, John Williams, was brought in to ease the strain. Mr. Ichino had little contact with him, since he managed the other half of their round-the-clock schedule. The Snark never slept.

But Williams would be at the meeting, Mr. Ichino reminded himself. He stopped amid the comforting buzz of the Pit and made a quick survey of the remaining consoles. Images flickered there: a three-masted schooner in outline; stiff figures modeling sixteenth-century clothes; clouds layered over a boiling ocean. A river of information, shoveled at the Snark, to correlate as it liked.

He turned and made his way down a line of swivel chairs to the doorway, where he was passed by a guard. As he emerged into a bright corridor, he reached involuntarily for the lump in his jacket pocket and brought it out: a rubbing stone. He kneaded it with his right hand, feeling the smooth cool textures and focusing on them, calming himself by lifelong habit.

He walked. Mr. Ichino felt out of place in these garish crisp corridors, transfixed by the plastiform walls, the thin partitions, clatter of typewriters, distant whisper of air conditioning. He should be in a university by now, he thought, spending patient hours in a cloister far back in shadowed library stacks, peering into nuances of information theory. He was aging; the higher he rose, the more abrasive the men he dealt with, the more subtle their methods of combat. He was not made for this game.

But he played; he always had. For love of the crystalline mathematical puzzles he found in cryptography, for an avenue, an escape—it had, after all, brought him from an immigrant family in smalltown Oregon on to Berkeley, to Washington, and now finally to Pasadena. To meet the Snark. For that, the journey had been worth it.

He passed by another gray guard and into the conference room. No one there; he was early. He padded softly over thick carpets to the table and sat down. Mr. Ichino's notes were in order, but he looked at them without focusing on the individual words. Secretaries came and went, placing yellow scratch pads and pens before each chair. An urn of coffee was wheeled in and set in a corner. A slight hollow pop disturbed Mr. Ichino's muzzy meditations; it was a test of the pickup microphones inlaid at regular spacings around the conference table.

A secretary gave him the agenda and he studied it. There was only a list of attendees, no hint of the meeting's purpose. Mr. Ichino pursed his lips as he read the names; there would be men here whom he knew only as distant figures in the news magazines.

All because of a vessel many millions of kilometers away. It seemed mildly ironic, considering the immediate and serious problems of the administration in Washington. But Mr. Ichino did now dwell on politics. His father had learned a stringent lesson of noninvolvement in Japan and made sure his son followed his example. From his earliest days of adolescence Mr. Ichino remembered his reluctance to join the poetry and language clubs in high school, because he felt the sharing of the tenuous emotions these things brought him, the nuances they called up, could not be a public thing. To write about them, perhaps—that was possible. But how to describe haiku except with another poem? To use anything more—slabs of words, sentences of explanation without grace or lightness of touch—was to crush the butterfly beneath a muddy boot.

He did finally summon up the sheer bravery to join the poetry club—though not French Studies, the other possibility—and found in it nothing to fear. Girls read their own stilted lines in high, nervous voices and sat down to beamed approval, followed by mild criticism from the teacher/sponsor. There were only three boys in the club but he could not remember them at all, and the girls now seemed to have merged into one composite: thin, willowy, eternally cold even in her cashmeres, her nostrils a pinched pale blue.

There was no clash of wills there, so the club marked a transition for him: he learned to speak before a group in his halting English, to define and explain and finally to disagree.

That was before mathematics, before the long years of concentration at university, before Washington and the dozens upon dozens of machine codes he devised, the monographs on cryptography that consumed his days and nights. The thin girls became—he looked up—secretaries in fashionably short skirts, coffee-bearers. And what had he become, that shy Japanese-American boy? Fifty-one years old, well paid, responsible, a bachelor consumed by work and hobbies. All clear, precise measures, but beyond that he was not sure.

"Mr. Ichino, I'm George Evers," a deep voice said.

Mr. Ichino stood up quickly with a sudden release of unexpected nervous energy, murmured words of greeting and shook the man's hand.

Evers smiled thinly and regarded him with distant assessment. "I hope we aren't taking too much of your time today. You and Mr. Williams"—he nodded as Williams appeared and walked to the coffee urn, long legs scissoring awkwardly—"are our experts on the day-to-day behavior of the Snark and we thought we should hear what you have to say before proceeding with the rest of the meeting."

"I see," Mr. Ichino said, surprised to find his voice almost a whisper. "The letter I received yesterday gave me no details, so—"

"On purpose." Evers said jovially, hitching thumbs into his belt. "We merely want to get an informal idea of what you think that thing is up to. The committee here—the Executive Committee, actually, that's the President's title—is faced with a deadline and I'm afraid we're going to have to come to a decision right away, sooner than we thought."

"Why?" Mr. Ichino said, alarmed. "I was under the impression that there was no hurry."

Mr. Evers paused and turned to wave to other men entering the long room and Mr. Ichino had the sudden impression of a man impatient to be off, to have the waiting finished, as though Evers knew the decision ahead and wanted to get beyond that dead moment to the action that followed. He noticed that Evers's left hand, casually resting on the back of a chair, had a slight tremor.

"That machine isn't willing to wait any more," Evers said, turning back. "It gave us the word two days ago."

Before he could reply Evers nodded and moved away, clasping hands with men in suits and pastel sports jackets who were filling the room. Williams, seated directly across the table, sent him a questioning glance.

Mr. Ichino shrugged elaborately in reply, glad that he was able to appear so casual. He looked around. Some of the faces he recognized. None were as important as Evers, who bore the ambiguous title of Presidential Advisor. Evers moved to the head of the table, still talking to the men nearest him, and sat down. Others who had been standing took their places and the secretaries left the coffee urn to fend for itself.

"Gentlemen," Evers said, calling them to order. "We will have to hurry things along, as you know, in order to meet the President's new deadline. I spoke with him this morning. He is very concerned, and looks forward to reviewing the recommendations of this committee."

Evers sat with his arms folded on the table before him, letting his eyes rove up and down the two lines of men. "You have all seen—excuse me, all but Mr. Williams and Mr. Ichino here—seen the messages received from the Snark requesting a change of venue." He paused for the ripple of polite laughter. "We are here to go into possible scenarios that could be initiated by the Snark's arrival in near-Earth orbit."

He gestured toward Mr. Ichino. "These two gentlemen are guests of the Committee today and are here solely to bring us up to date on the nonessential information the Division has been sending the Snark. They are not, of course, members of the Executive Committee itself." In the bleached light his skin took on a high glaze as he focused on the aligned ranks of men, yellow pads scattered at random before them. A few were already taking notes.

Evers sat back, relaxing. "The Snark remained in Venus orbit to keep a strong channel to us, through our satellite. But we and it have transferred our, uh, dialogue to highflux channels now. We're communicating directly, bypassing the satellite. Now the Snark wants to come to Earth."

"To see our biosphere up close," a thin man said at Evers's left. "Which I don't believe."

Eyes turned to him. Mr. Ichino recognized the man as a leading games theorist from the Hudson Institute. He wore poorly-fitted tweeds; from an ornate pipe he puffed a blue wreath around himself.

"I believe the Snark—Walmsley's term, isn't it?—has been studying us quite well from Venus," he said. "Look at what it asks for—a welter of cultural information, photographs, art. No science or engineering. It can probably deduce that sort of thing, if it needs, from radio and Three-D programs."

"Quite right," a man further down said. There were more assents.

"Then why come to Earth?" Evers said.

"To get a good look at our defenses?" someone said halfway down the long table.

"Perhaps, perhaps," Evers replied. "The military believes the Snark may not *care* about our level of technology. For the same reason we wouldn't worry about the spears of South Sea natives if we wanted to use their island as a base."

"*I'd* worry," said a swarthy man. "Those spears are sharp."

Evers had a way of delaying his smile one judicious second, and then allowing it to spread broadly, a haughty white crease. "Precisely to the point. It can't be *sure* without a closer look."

"Snark has already *had* a look," the Hudson Insitute man murmured. "Through the Walmsley woman."

There was a low flurry of comment around the room, agreeing. Mr. Ichino had heard rumors about this, and here was confirmation.

"Gentlemen," Evers said, "we have seen the text of the Snark's demand. It was quite strong. Acting on your earlier suggestion"—he nodded toward the Hudson Institute man, who was relighting his pipe—"I spoke with the President. He authorized me to send the Snark a go-ahead. I wrote the message myself—there was no time to consult this committee on the exact wording—and I have learned that our Venus satellite now detects a reignition of the Snark's fusion torch."

The table buzzed with comment. Mr. Ichino slumped back, reflecting.

"I explained to this . . . being . . . that we did not know, at first, whether it was friendly. I *didn't* mention that we still don't know."

"What did it say?" the Hudson Institute man asked.

"It replied with a request to orbit Earth. Upon my advice, the President counter-proposed that the Snark orbit the moon for a while, so our men there—and in the vicinity—can observe it. A sort of mutual inspection, as it were."

The man in tweeds puffed energetically and said, "We could do the job better from a near-Earth orbit."

"True," Evers said. "I suppose I can merely summarize our earlier doubts?" He leaned forward, face furrowed. "About why it didn't try to get in touch with us first? ExComm had to make the first move. *Then*, and only then, it responded."

"Surveying strange solar systems must be a chancy business," the man in tweeds said mildly.

"For both parties," Evers said with a hollow jovial laugh. Mr. Ichino reflected that with success comes a reputation—if only in the mind's eye of the successful—for wisdom. "But perhaps I should explain. The moon orbit option came about because of an alternate plan the Joint Chiefs have in mind. I suppose I needn't add that we haven't discussed this with the United Nations?" The room rustled with chuckles. "Well, the plan works best if the Snark stops by the moon. That isolates it, pins it down, within our zone of operations."

"And?" the pipe smoker said, his lips pursed wryly.

"The Chiefs—and the theoretical staff behind them—regard it as highly suspicious that the Snark says it knows nothing—*nothing*—of its origins. A minimax factor analysis of this situation, I'm told, says that the Snark may simply be learning all it can about us without risking itself by giving away potentially useful information. I can't say anything more right now"—he glanced at Williams and Mr. Ichino and then, realizing that he had, looked quickly away—"but I'll bring it up later in the meeting. I'll only say that the President thinks it has some merit."

Mr. Ichino frowned. *The Joint Chiefs?* he thought. He

tried to understand the implications and lost track of Evers's words until:

"—we'll hear first from Mr. Ichino, who has shared the encoding and selection of information for the Snark. Mr. Ichino?"

His thoughts were a scramble. He said very carefully, "There is so much the Snark wants to know. I have only begun to tell it about us. I am not by any means the best qualified—"

Mr. Ichino stopped. He looked down the table at them. He had always had to hold himself in check before people like this, he realized, men of closed faces. And he could not speak to them, let the soft things within him come out.

"I have found," he said haltingly, mind filled with fleeting impulses and images, ". . . found something I never expected." He gazed at their blank eyes and set faces. They were silent.

"I began with a simple code, based on arithmetical analogies to words. The machine picked it up at once. We began a conversation. I learned nothing about it—that was not my assignment. I gather no one else has, either.

"But—what struck me . . ." Words, he could not find the words. ". . . was the *nimble* aspect it has. We spoke of elementary mathematics, physics, number theory. It gave me what I believe to be a proof of Fermat's Last Theorem. Its mind leaps from one subject to another and is perfectly at home. When it spoke of mathematics it was cool and efficient, never wasting a word. Then it asked for poetry."

The man in tweeds was watching Mr. Ichino intently and sucking on his pipe, which had gone out.

"I do not know how it discovered poetry. Perhaps from commercial radio. I told it what I knew and gave it examples. It seems to understand. What is more, the Snark began to ask for art. It was interested in everything from oils to sculpture. I undertook the encoding problems involved, even to the point of fixing for it the right portion of the electromagnetic spectrum for viewing the pictures we sent."

He spread his hands and spoke more rapidly. "It is like

sitting in a room and speaking to someone you cannot see. One inevitably assigns a personality to the other. Each day I speak to the Snark. He wants to know everything. And when we spoke of varying subjects, there was a feeling of *differentness*, as, as . . ."

Mr. Ichino saw the distilling eyes of Evans and hurried on, stumbling over his words.

". . . as if I was speaking to different personalities each time. A mathematician, a poet—he even wrote sonnets one day, good ones—and scientist and artist . . . He is so large, I . . ."

Mr. Ichino paused, for he felt the air tightening around him, the men at the table drawing back. He was saying things beyond his competence, he was only a cryptographer, not qualified—

The lips of the man in tweeds compressed and turned up slightly in a thin, deprecating smile of condescension.

Across the table from Mr. Ichino, Williams stared into the space between them, distracted, and said slowly, "I see, I see, yes. That is what it is like. I had never thought of it that way before, but . . ."

Williams put both hands flat on the table, as though to push himself up, and glanced with sudden energy up and down the table. "He's right, the Snark is like that. It's many personalities, operating almost independently."

Mr. Ichino gazed at this man who shared his labor and for the first time saw that Williams, too, had been changed by contact with the Snark. The thought lifted his spirits.

"Independently," Mr. Ichino said. "That is it. I sense many aspects to his personality, each a separate facet, and behind them there is something . . . greater. Something that I cannot visualize—"

"It's bigger," Williams broke in. "We're seeing parts of the Snark, that's all." Both men stared at each other, unable to put into words the immensity they sensed.

Evers spoke.

"I really think you gentlemen have strayed from the subject at hand. I *asked* you to describe the range of input the Snark requested, *not* your own metaphysical reactions to it."

There were a few nervous chuckles. Around the long
table Mr. Ichino saw minds sitting a sheltered inch back
from narrowed eyes, judging, weighing, refusing to feel.

"But this is important—" Williams began. Evers raised
a hand to cut him off. Mr. Ichino saw in the gesture the final
proof of why Evers was a Presidential Advisor and he was
not.

"I will thank you, Mr. Williams, to leave to the
Executive Committee the determination of what is or is not
important."

Williams's face went rigid. He looked across the table.
Mr. Ichino took a deep, calming breath and struggled up
out of his confusion.

"You have already decided, haven't you?" he said to
Evers. He peered at the man's face, the white shirt
bleaching out its shadows, and thought he saw something
shift deep behind the eyes. "This is a sham," he said with
certainty.

"I don't know what you think you're—"

"That may be true, Mr. Evers, you do not know.
Perhaps you have not admitted it to yourself yet. But you
plan something monstrous, Mr. Evers, or else you would
listen to us."

"Listen—"

"You do not want to know what we say."

There was an uncomfortable rustle in the room. Mr.
Ichino held Evers with his eyes, refusing to let the man go.
The silence lengthened. Evers blinked, looked away, too
casually brought a hand up to touch his chin and hide his
mouth.

"I think you two had better go," Evers said in an oddly
calm voice.

There was no other sound. Mr. Ichino, hands clasped
tightly to the notes before him, felt a sudden strange
intimacy with Evers, a recognition. In the lines around the
man's mouth he read an expression he had seen before: the
quick-witted executive, intelligent, who knew with a sure
instinct that he carried the necessary toughness to decide
when others could not. Evers loved the balancing of one
case against another, the talk of options and probabilities
and plans. He lived for the making of hard choices.

Mr. Ichino stood up. For such men it was impossible to do nothing, even when that was best. Power demanded action. Action gave drama, and drama . . . was glory.

Now it is out of my hands, he thought.

Williams followed him out of that room, but Mr. Ichino did not wait to speak to him. For the moment he wanted only to leave the building, to escape the ominous weight he felt.

There are storms that are felt before they can be seen. He doubted that he would be allowed back in the Pit to talk to the Snark again; he was now a risk. The thought troubled him but he put it aside. He signed out at the nearest exit and pushed out through the glass-paneled door, into the thin spring air of Pasadena. It was almost noon.

He still carried the yellow pad and his notes, pages crumpled in his fist. Butterflies beneath the boot. Going down the steps he felt a welling tide and, dropping the pages, dropping it all, he ran. Ran.

TWO

Mr. Ichino pushed on resolutely, despite his fatigue. He was aware that Nigel, nine years younger and in better physical condition, was setting a mild pace; still, he panted steadily and felt a knotting tension in his calves. They were hiking above the timberline in early June and each breath sucked in a chilled, cutting wash of air.

Nigel signaled for a stop and, wordless, they helped each other slip free of their packs. They broke out a simple lunch: cheese, nuts, sour lemonade made from a powder. They had stopped in an elliptical clearing bordered by snowpack. Above, wave upon wave of flecked rock marched skyward. Shelves of granite had been heaved and tossed and eroded into a swirl of patterns, notched here and there by blocks that had tumbled down, split off by an endless hammering, the melting and freezing of winter frost. On this raw cliff face small yellow scatterings drew Mr. Ichino's eye: rock-hugging bushes had begun to flower.

"So you think I should do it anyway," Nigel said abruptly.

Mr. Ichino nodded. He was glad to see this spontaneous interest from his friend; it was the first time Nigel had ever brought up the Snark on his own. "We cannot be sure what their intentions are."

"We can guess."

"Our judgment of Evers may be wrong."

"Do you honestly believe so?"

"No."

"Then, damn it—"

"We must give them some latitude. Perhaps they are right and taking precautions is absolutely necessary."

Nigel rested back against his bulging yellow pack, sipping at his steel Sierra Club cup of lemonade. "Equipping the rendezvous craft with a nuclear weapon doesn't strike me as a precaution. It's an act of insanity, buggering insanity."

"You have seen the list of reasons."

"Right. Fear of disease. Vague mutterings about a sociometric impact they can't predict. Even a bloody *invasion*, for God's sake."

"The last reason?" Mr Ichino asked quietly.

"Oh yes. 'Something unimaginable.' A *brilliant* category."

"That is why they need a man in the rendezvous module, not merely a machine."

"Not to imagine the unimaginable. No, they want some sod to give them a play-by-play."

"Which you can certainly do."

"Um. You're probably right, there. I'm a dried-up old raisin of an astronaut, but at least I'm in on the operation. I know the necessary astrophysics and computer encoding, if it comes to that."

"You are not a security risk, either. By using you, they are not forced to expand the circle of fully-informed people."

"Right." Some unseen pressure seemed to go out of Nigel as Mr. Ichino watched him. He loosened; a fine cross-hatching of wrinkles in his face faded. The two men lay for a while and listened to the tinkling of water, freed from the thawing ice, as it spattered down the cliffs.

"The nub of it is . . ." Nigel paused. "Did you ever read any Mark Twain?"

"Yes."

"Remember that piece where he describes getting to pilot on the Mississippi? Learning the shallows and sandbars and currents?"

"I believe I may."

"Well, there's the rub. After he'd mastered the analytic knowledge needed to move on the river, he found it had lost its beauty. He couldn't look at it any longer and see the things he'd seen before."

Mr. Ichino smiled. "So it is with you and"—he gestured—"out there?"

"Maybe. Maybe."

"I doubt that."

"I feel . . . I don't know. Alexandria . . ."

"She is gone. She would not want you to hang on to her."

"Yes. Yes, you're right. You're the only other person who knows the whole thing, about me and the hiking in the desert. Maybe you understand this better than I do, now. I was too close to the center of it."

"As Twain was? Too near to the river?"

"Something's lost, that's all I know."

Mr. Ichino said quietly, slowly, "I wish you the strength to let go, Nigel."

They hiked over a saddle-shaped crescent into the next valley. The lodgepole pines, their bark crinkled and dry and brittle, thinned out as the two men reached the high point of their passage. Here the air took on a new resolving clarity. Sierra junipers clung to the exposed overhangs, gaunt whitened branches following the streamlines of the wind. The gnarled limbs seemed dead to Mr. Ichino, but at their tips a mottled green peppered the wood. He stroked a trunk in passing and felt a rough, reassuring solidity.

This early in the season there were no other parties on the gravelly trails. They set a steady pace on the downward leg; the tiered glacial lakes below them flickered as blue promises through the shadowed woods. Mr. Ichino knew he would be even more stiff and sore tonight than he was yesterday; still, he would not have missed this rare opportunity to see the remaining Sierra wilderness. Nigel's reservations had come due and one evening, as they dined together—almost entirely in silence, as was usual with them—he had asked Mr. Ichino to accompany him. The invitation was a final cementing of their growing friendship.

In the last few months Mr. Ichino had found himself spending increasing spans of time in the company of this restless, amusing, moody astronaut. In retrospect the friendship had a certain interior logic to it, despite their differences in character. Both were alone. Both shared the Snark project as a hovering presence in their days. And now, after Mr. Ichino's behavior at the Executive Committee meeting, they both worked under the same faint shadow of suspicion from above.

They had met accidentally a few times after Nigel returned from his "rest" in the desert. They'd worked on computer problems together, ingressing and confluing matrices for the Snark, and spoken of the usual neutral subjects: books, weather, politics. They agreed that the United States and Canada should stand firm and sell satellite data to the World Food Reserve for whatever they could get. The same for orbital manufacturing, including the precious space on the cylinder cities. They talked, drank wine, argued small points in comfortable eddies of words.

Then, gradually, Nigel began to tell him of the Snark, of Alexandria, of things inside himself . . .

Mr. Ichino peered down the trail at the swaying bulk of Nigel's pack. Throughout this journey the other man had set an odd pace, moving too fast or too slow for the terrain, pressing himself unnecessarily on precarious, terraced slopes. He rested at strange times. He craned forward, chin thrust out. Always the lay of the land ahead occupied him, not what surrounded him. In their pauses he leaped from one subject to the next without a bridging thought, always speaking of something distant, some new idea unrelated to the free spaces around them. He was there, but not there. A slanting blade of sunlight that split the forest darkness would elude him even as he tramped through it, head bowed, the light striking a coppery glint from his hair. The suction of what lay ahead drew him through the present.

Abruptly, Nigel turned.

"The orbit they're planning—it's a near intersection, isn't it?" he said briskly.

"That was how Evers described it. I merely heard the summary talk, however. I know no details."

"I should've gone to it." Nigel chewed absently at his lip. "I dislike meetings, but . . ."

"You can still apply. Speak to Evers."

"I don't take it he's a terribly big fan of mine."

"He respects your past. Your knowledge."

Nigel crooked his thumbs into his backpack straps where they crossed his chest. "Perhaps. If I appear docile enough . . ."

Mr. Ichino waited, feeling a small tension stretching thin within Nigel.

"God damn, yes. Right. They want somebody to lie in wait by the moon, good enough. I'll go. Hunting for the Snark. Right."

With a quick, hearty gesture he clapped Mr. Ichino on the back. Beneath the canopy of pines the sound had a swallowed, muffled quality.

Nigel took the bus into central Los Angeles and spent a morning browsing in the old shops there. He turned up a book he only vaguely remembered, *The Hunting of the Snark*. It was an early edition, Macmillian, 1899, subtitled *an Agony, in Eight Fits,* including nine illustrating prints by Henry Holiday. The grotesque figures each seemed wreathed in their own preoccupations, staring inward even as they sharpened axes, rang bells and poked at bollards. Nigel bought the book at an enormous price—having any sort of bound volume not done out in faxprint, and over a decade old, was now fashionable—and took it along to Reagan Park, where he sat beneath the graying statue of a dead politician.

He opened the book gingerly, feeling less cavalier about this ancient artifact now that it was his, and began to

read. He relished the clean, stiff pages, the austere formal
march of words in old type. Had he ever really done this
poem through to the end? No, apparently, for whole
patches he could not remember.

> He had bought a large map representing the sea,
>   Without the least vestige of land:
> And the crew were much pleased when they found it
>   to be
>   A map they could all understand.

Nigel smiled, thinking of ExComm. He glanced up at
the granite politician, now the spattered colleague of
pigeons.

> For, although common Snarks do no manner of harm,
>   Yet I feel it my duty to say
> Beware if your Snark be a Boojum! For then
>   You will softly and suddenly vanish away.

Nigel enjoyed the crisp turning of pages, the contorted
line drawings of wrinkled dwarves fretting over their hunt.
Sitting here in this dry American park, he felt suddenly
very mild and English.

> For the Snark's peculiar creature, that won't
>   Be caught in a commonplace way.
> Do all that you know, and try all that you don't:
>   Not a chance must be wasted to-day.

THREE

The top floor at JPL was now executive country, entirely
given over to the management of the Snark problem.
Several corridors branched into warrens of cramped offices.
Nigel lost his way and, opening a conference room door by
mistake, disturbed an earnest circle of men. They looked
up and recognition of him crossed their faces, but they said
nothing. The blackboard behind them was covered with

indecipherable symbols. Nigel nodded, smiled and went away.

Ah, and here it was: Evers & Company. The anonymous tiled corridors changed to Mirrormaze. As he passed, the walls rippled with liquid light, responding to his body heat. A lacy pink cocoon followed him down the hallway until the walls flared out to form a reception center, dotted with bodyfit furniture. Nigel recognized the scheme and looked for the unobtrusive signature. There it was, inlaid in gold, tucked in a corner: WmR. He did Total Environments for those wealthy enough, or powerful enough, to commission him.

So Evers now had that kind of prestige. Interesting. With Snark still an official secret—and a remarkably tight one—Evers still had used it as a lever to get more attention from the government. Interesting.

"Dr. Walmsley?" a receptionist said to him.

"Mr. Walmsley."

"Oh. Well. Mr. Evers will see you in just a moment."

Nigel stopped watching the iridescent walls and studied her. "Fine." He turned to watch an inset 3D, ignoring the well-dressed young man who lounged in a nearby flexchair. The man flicked a casual appraising glance at Nigel and then relaxed again behind heavy-lidded eyes, thumbs hooked into his belt just above his fashionably padded crotch. Nigel guessed that he was Evers's bodyguard, one selected more for show than protection.

Nigel thumbed the 3D control. In brown: immense, prickly piles of garbage. On the far hillside, a glowing white dot of the fusion flame. In the foreground, a commentator, stylishly bare to the waist, told of three workers—hashslingers, she called them—who'd gotten caught in the belts that fed the recycling burner. There was no trace of them, of course, and the accident had to be reconstructed from their work schedules and approximate positions in the Wastepark. The fusion flame had ripped them down into their component atoms, and then the mass spectrometers had plucked the valuable phosphorus amd calcium and iron from the everlasting plasma and formed bricks. The hydrogen and carbon and oxygen became fuel and water, final useful burial for one man and two women who—one officially presumed—were a bit slow that particular day, or a bit stupid. But the focus of the news story was that they quite obviously weren't innocent victims. They'd hired on only weeks before. They'd been seen dangerously near the mouth of the fusion chambers, where radiation and plasma blowback were constant threats. So: a scavenger gang, rummaging the waste of decades past for durable antiques or precious metals. Wastepark workers didn't have tote-home rights, but who checked that close to the fusion torches? *How many others have sneaked into these landfill areas?* the commentator asked somberly. She swiveled to face the 3D snout, seemingly oblivious of the jeweled ornaments that swung from her artificially swollen nipples. Dangling gems winked blue and red at the 3D. *Systematically raking up and mining these hills, I think we uncover more than raw materials for the fusors. We find more than the opulent trash of the middle twencen. No*—she paused, face clouding—*we find ourselves. Our greed. Our longing for the decadent past. How many have died unknown in the automatic belts and claws? Been jammed and sucked slimmy-jimmy into the eternal flames?* The camera panned across the jumbled hills.

Nigel shook his head and clicked it off.

"Mr. Walmsley?"

He went through the burnished oak door held open by the receptionist and shook hands with Evers.

"I promised I'd get back to you," Evers said. "Sit down." He smiled warmly and moved to a comfortable chair away from the walnut desk.

"I bucked it upstairs," Evers said.

"To meet the Snark."

"Yes."

"Not merely be on the tracking team—to actually make the mission."

"Right."

"And?"

"Well, there were a lot of questions."

Nigel laughed, a barking sound. "There always are."

"Some people wondered if you were still in the top flight-training category."

"I go back to Houston and Ames regularly. I put in a lot of time on the simulators."

"True. How about exercise?"

"Hiking. Squash. Racquetball."

"Racquetball? How's that played?"

"A blend of handball and squash. Short, stubby racquet. Played in a room, shots off the ceiling are legal, and you have to return the ball to the forward wall after each bounce."

"I see. Fast?"

"Reasonably."

"As fast as squash?"

"No. The ball bounces a lot."

"You don't like me, do you, Nigel?"

Nigel sat silent. He kept his face stony and shifted his feet on the thick carpet.

"Can't say I've thought about it."

"Come *on*." Evers leaned forward, elbows on his chair's arms, hands knitted together.

"Well, I can't really—"

"I'm trying to level with you."

"I see."

"No, you *don't* see."

Nigel sat back, crossed his legs.

"You come to me and want the Snark rendezvous mission. Right? I think about it. I read your file."

"You buck it upstairs," Nigel said evenly.

"Damned right. It's an important decision."

"One you can make."

"*Not* by myself."

"You're in charge of this operation. You're the next rung up from NASA itself, so—"

"So *nothing*. I have to take the advice of the experts below me or else there's no reason to have experts in the first place."

"Well, then—take it."

"You wouldn't like it if I did."

Nigel grimaced. "The canonical punchup, eh?"

"Let's say the returns are mixed."

"Nice phrase."

"*Damn* it!" Evers slapped his chair arm. "You are *not* going to sit here and Gary Cooper your way through this thing."

"I don't know what you mean, but if you're asking me to be responsible, then ask me a bloody question."

"Nigel . . ." Evers looked at his hands. "Nigel. NASA remembers Icarus. They remember your private little communication gambit with the Snark—and so do I."

"I don't think that last bears on matters. I was under stress. My—"

"You'll be under stress out there, meeting the Snark."

"A different thing entirely."

"Maybe. That's it—*maybe*. You're unreliable, Nigel. You don't follow orders."

"I'm not a machine, no."

"There you go. That fucking British reserve, those distancing remarks. But I know you're not really like that, Nigel. Your personality profile from the psychtechs isn't that way."

"And they should know, of course."

"Okay, they're not perfect. But there has to be something to explain why a hell of a lot of people in NASA like you, Nigel. Why they'll go out on a limb and recommend you for the Snark rendezvous."

"Ah. So some did."

"Sure. I said you got mixed reviews, not uniformly bad ones."

"After what you've said, I honestly wonder why."

Evers looked at him quizzically. "Do you? Really?"

"Well . . ." Nigel murmured uncertainly. "Yes. Yes, I do."

"You don't have a clear idea what NASA—the people you've worked with—think of you?"

"Well . . ."

"You really don't. You don't know that to them you're a, a symbol?"

"Of what?"

"Of what the program's about. You've *been* there. You found the first alien artifact. And now, you're on the team that discovered the second—the Snark."

"I see."

"It's true. You don't notice it, do you?"

"I don't suppose I do."

Evers thought for a moment, studying Nigel. "I guess you wouldn't."

Nigel shrugged.

"It's my job to see things like that," Evers said, seeming to pull himself up. "I deal in people. And you're the person I've got to figure out right now."

"How?"

"By guess and by golly, as my Dad used to say."

"By asking me about racquetball?"

"Sure, why not? Anything to find out what makes Nigel run. And run pretty damned well, too. You're smart, you've kept up on spacecraft tech, you know the plumbing and the computers, the astronomy—you're a pro. The only thing you don't understand is folks like me."

"Like you?"

"Administrators."

"Oh."

"*Guessers* is a better word. Professional guessers."

"How so?" Nigel murmured, interested despite himself.

"You remember the Chinese Trigger incident?"

"I read Gottlieb's book."

"It's pretty near the facts."

"You should know. You stepped into that muck and figured out what was going to happen next."

Evers nodded. "There were clues. The Chinese had dispatched a large infantry force by submarine. It didn't make any sense that they'd be hitting Australia or anything reachable by more conventional methods."

"So you estimated they were bound for a clandestine landing in California."

"To say 'estimated' makes it more exact than it was. I guessed. Guessed they'd try to touch off a nuclear war with some well-placed tacticals and a commando raid to silence communications for a vital twenty minutes. Guessed."

Nigel nodded.

"It occurred to me that you maybe don't have a whole lot of respect for that kind of thinking."

Nigel blinked. "How'd that pop into your head?"

"You never seem very relaxed when you're talking to your, ah, superiors."

"You mean talking to you?"

"Among others."

"Umm." Nigel studied Evers and then looked aside, where a wall holo showed a glinting Eckhaus laser-carved iceberg sculpture, waves lapping at its base. Nigel breathed deeply and seemed to make a decision.

"Not really," he said slowly, searching for the words. "There's something poisonous in the way we do things, that's all."

"A strong word."

"Appropriate. There's a good lot here, individually fine people. But organizations have their own drives and that gets in the way."

"In the way of what?"

"Of the truth. Of what people really want out of all this. Look, remember the first years? The Apollo landings and all. What kind of genius did it require to take hold of the greatest event in the century—and make it boring?"

"Okay, so NASA wasn't and isn't perfect."

"No, it isn't just NASA. It's, it's whenever people deny their own interior visions. Or don't communicate them correctly."

"Organization is impossible without compromise," Evers said, the webbing around his eyes crinkling with amusement.

"Granted," Nigel said judiciously. "But I seem to've run smack into situations where I couldn't see the motivation—"

"You mean NASA has screwed up the Snark business."

"You were going to. Your message to the Snark was a balls-up."

"Probably. But that was because we didn't have your input."

"You weren't in the mood, it seemed to me."

"You've got to understand where I'm coming from here, Nigel," Evers murmured, hunching forward.

"How so?"

"I'm the kind of guy I am because of what I've done. I had a pretty bumpy career until the Chinese Trigger. I took a look at the intelligence estimates, sure, everybody did. Hell, I'll bet lots of guys had it cross their minds that the slants might have a joker in the deck. It's one thing to guess, it's another to *act*."

"Surely we agree on that."

"Check. You did, too, at Icarus."

"With middling results."

"Sure, but you followed your nose 'cause you had to. I respect that. I went out on a limb and depth-bombed those subs and I was right."

"So Commander Sturrock could become a national hero."

"Yeah. Well, you know . . ." A shrug. "Gottlieb got it straight, though."

"You've done pretty well in the government."

"So-so. That little venture when I was undersecretary—you know, in '97, breaking the back of that metals cartel—bought me more enemies than I thought it would." He paused and seemed to pull himself out of a private mood, straightening up as his flexchair moved to accommodate him. "But I'm back on my way again. Moving up. And I'm kind of a renegade myself, Nigel, I guess that's what I'm saying."

"I can see that. I never said I didn't respect you."

"No, you didn't. But then"—he chuckled—"I never asked."

"I suppose," Nigel murmured carefully, "we simply have different feelings about how organizations should be used."

"Check. Down where I come from, Nigel, near Mobile, there's an old story. Back in the days when the South was down, way down, there was a lot of trouble, over race, y'know. Somebody from the North, down to help straighten things out, asked a relative of mine if he didn't have to watch what he said in favor of black people, living down there, and considering the attitude of the police and so on."

"Yes."

"So my relative thought a minute and said, 'Why no, we don't have to watch what we say. We just have to watch what we *think*.'"

Nigel burst into laughter. "I take the point," he said, smiling.

"I can tell you've got your head screwed on right. All I'm sayin' to you is that getting along with NASA is going to be a tradeoff—but you don't have to watch what you think, not if you're careful. Things aren't that bad." He squinted at Nigel warmly. "I made my way so far by defending the West, Nigel, and that's the way I see this mission. Hell, only we may be defending the whole damned planet this time."

"Umm."

"Okay, I could be wrong." He waved a hand. "We won't argue. I've kind of let down my hair today so I could see what sort of guy you were, and it's settled my mind. You're a classy sort of astronaut, Nigel, the best and the oldest we've got. That British thing you've got going for you—it's a big help with Americans, y'know. A big help. It'll come in handy when I push this thing through."

"So you're going to back me."

"Sure." Evers relaxed. "I just decided. I want a guy out there I understand. I have a hunch the Snark isn't going to give us a lot of warning when it decides to come Earthside—probably on purpose, to be sure we can't set up eleborate defenses. So we'll be in a damned rush and there won't be time for a lot of talk amongst ourselves. I don't ask that you agree with me, but I have to understand *you* in order to know for sure what you're saying, when your voice comes over a squawk box."

Nigel nodded. Evers came to his feet and held out a hand, beaming. "Glad we had this talk, Nigel."

* * *

He let a secret smile crease his face as he made his way back through the fluxing Mirrormaze hallway. It had gone quite well, all things considered, and his prior careful rummaging into Evers's past now made sense. Nigel didn't for a moment believe he'd seen the core of Evers, but there had been another layer, certainly, deeper than the no-nonsense bureaucratic sheen. Evers very probably thought the down home, good-ole-boy persona was the real Evers; if you spend time developing a role, you become it. But Nigel sensed something further. Inside every hard-edged executive there seemed to lie a shadow of the ambitious boy, and beneath *that* lurked whatever made the boy step on the first rung. *Glad we had this talk, Nigel.* A clear signal that Evers now thought of him as an ally, a team player, cheerfully backing Evers for his next leap upward. *I want a guy out there I understand. Glad we had this talk.* But Evers had done very nearly all the talking himself.

FOUR

It was deliciously pleasant to drift, restrained by the buckles and pads, and spin soft coils of illusion. Zero-g did that. Below, the random splotchings of craters wheeled, each slipping below the arched horizon before he had memorized it. An old friend lost without a farewell handshake; memory of a million such. *When shaking hands, remember your manners, Nigel, take off your glove first* (cold snatching at your fingers) . . .

His mind wandered.

Which wasn't right, he told himself. He should stay alert. He was not here for the view. Nor did segmented tanks of high-energy fuel ride to the side of him, above, below, aft, for his own amusement. They waited for their signal, the soft percussion of a button, to apply the bootheel and send him straight into history.

Or into the abyss beyond Earth's web, he thought. Hipparchus Control—awesome name for six sheet-metal huts buried in twenty feet of dust—had been a touch vague about the margin of error they had allowed for getting him back. Maybe there wasn't any.

Off to his right the northmost rim of Mare Orientale slid into view, slate-gray sheets of lava cooled in their convulsions. The crater's center lay a good fifteen degrees south of his near-equatorial orbit, but even at this low altitude he could see the marching mountain ranges that curved away from him, inward, toward the focus. He wondered how big the rock had been that caused that eerie effect: crests of ancient waves that froze into mountains. An enormous bull's-eye in the moon's ribs. Assassin's knife. Death from an asteroid, a brother of Icarus—

"Hipparchus here," a voice rattled and squeaked in his ear. "Everything's okay?"

Nigel hesitated a moment and then said, "Shut up."

"No, it's okay. We've calculated it out. We're both of us in the moon's radio shadow, as far as the Snark is concerned. It can't pick up any of this."

"I thought we weren't taking any chances."

"Well, this isn't exactly a *chance*." The voice sounded a bit peevish. "We just wanted to see how things're going up there. We don't get any telemetry. You could be dead for all we know."

He couldn't think of anything to say to that, so he let it go. The radio man—who was it, that short fellow, Lewis?—seemed to think he was just making a neighborly call. The phones crackled and sputtered in his ears for a moment while he waited out the other man. Finally the voice came, a little stronger.

"Well, we have a good fix on the time, anyway. About five hours away. Squirting the scoop to your LogEx now."

There was a hum from the electronics beside him as the computer absorbed the orbital data. He was sure it was Lewis now; the man was addicted to jargon.

"Have you rechecked your missiles?" Lewis said.

"Yes. Uh, roger."

"We just had a squirt from Houston to remind you about priorities. Any piece of it is better than nothing, so hold off on the nuke if you can."

"Roger."

"Feeling okay? You've been up there over a day now, it must be getting cramped."

Nigel studied the scattering of stars outside.

"Nothing compared to the Icarus thing though, huh? Say, I never did ask you about that. I mean, with the drugs and that long a meditation to keep your oxy use down. I never did ask you."

"No, you never did."

There was another silence.

"Well, it must feel different, this one being almost a combat mission, you might say. Not the same."

"Sweating like a pig."

"Yeah, really?" The voice brightened at this evidence of human failing. "We'll get you back okay, don't worry, fella."

"Say hello to the crew down there." Nigel felt he ought to say something friendly. Lewis wasn't a bad sort, only too chummy.

"We're all rooting for you. Zap that thing if it does anything funny. The whole gig sounds flippo, if you ask me."

"I'd better go over that flight plan. Give me a fix on a translunar."

"Oh, okay." A blurred squeal from the electronics. "There she is. Uh, signing off."

"Roger."

Combat mission, Lewis had said. Sweet Christ. Marines wading ashore. Somebody always wondering where the medic is. Crawl along a clay ditch, rifle bullets zipping overhead like hornets. Hug the earth, align with the groin of the world. Images: a brown-skinned woman wrapped around a pudgy white man, he in spattered uniform, idly cleaning a rifle barrel, peering absently down the shiny bore as she rocks and humps and kisses him with her universal rhythm, her knotted hands feeling in his pockets . . .

Somewhere, a musical phrase of hunger.

He found one of the clear plastic tubes, squeezed it and ate. Carrot juice. NASA issue, lifegiving vegetables and hearty roots, no evil meat. Those who would meet God in his firmament shall be pure of intestine, live not from the flesh of dead animals. Rear your children on beans and berries; they too may ride to the stars. When they come home from a date, smell their breath for the aberrant trace of a hot dog. Unclean, unclean. And anyway, nobody had yet learned how to grow a chicken or cow on the moon, so soybeans it was.

For that matter, they couldn't do much else on the moon, either. It was all well and good to balance tomatoes with barley, coaxing forth from the lunar gravel enough protein and oxygen to support a small base, and yet another to regulate amino acids and plant sap, keep mildew from forming in the access pipes, conserve the thin, mealy loam. The optimistic biologists frowned at their soybeans: with the daily cycle of sun and tides removed, the beans grew gnarled roots and gray leaves, became miserly with their proteins. It was no simple trick to be an adversary of entropy in a land with black skies and winds that slept.

Somehow the cyclinder cities worked, grew their food and prospered. But the moon, truly alien, didn't. Still, the crew at Hipparchus carried on, searched the moon for water and ice, experimented. They had a burning optimism. Precisely what he lacked, Nigel thought. He shrugged, with no one to see. The loss did not seem to matter now.

To pass the time he meditated and read novels from the cabin's erasable slate. The module was well designed, considering the short time allowed for converting the blueprint into hardware. Nigel had brought a pack of four memorex crystals, each book length, and in the first day of waiting had devoured two of them, taking an hour apiece.

A phrase caught his eye:

at an attitude toward Ataturk

Later, musing down at the flinty plain of Mare Smythii, it came back to him. He treated the words like an algebraic expression; he factored out all the a's, then the t's. Rearranged, the words could yield amibiguity, incoherence, passable poetry.

He wondered if this was a neurotic habit.

Memories from reading: women who never passed a lamppost without touching it; men who balanced always on the ball of the left foot while urinating: outfielders who had to take a skip before throwing the ball into home plate. Fellow neurotics all; nerves skittering on a fine high wire.

He divided the phrase into thirds, quarters, eighths, thought of an anagram, fiddled. Alexandria. The desert, now a fading memory. He wondered what Ichino would think of this.

The moon's crumpled gray horizon swallowed a blue-white ice cream Earth.

"You're projected ignition time is holding firm." Lewis again, seven orbits later.

"What does Houston say?"

"Snark is holding to its promised course. Decelerating as our trajectory specified."

"What's it saying to Houston?"

"Nothing unusual, they said. The scenario calls for beaming a lot of hot stuff, things the Snark's been asking about, during the last stages of its approach. Distract it so's you can get in close."

"I know, but what is the new information?"

"What's it matter? It's all false anyway."

"*What?*"

"They're not giving it the straight stuff anymore. Houston says the President clamped down on them."

Nigel grimaced. "Perfectly predictable."

"Just you cripple it, Nigel, and *we'll* be picking *its* brains."

"Um hum."

"But remember, go for the big nuke if it looks like it's getting away. That's what Houston says."

"Sure, that's what Houston says."

"Huh?" Thin thread of surprise in the voice.

"A finger in the eye."

"I didn't track you on that one."

"Did you ever think how old it must be?" Nigel said, his words clipped. "Our lives are so short. To Snark we must look like bacilli. Whole eras and dynasties snuffed out in an instant. It looks at us with its microscope and makes lab notes, while we try to poke a finger in its eye."

"Uh, yeah. Well, you're coming out of radio shadow. We'd better shut up. I've already squirted your LogEx corrections."

"Check."

He was moving into the white sun's glare again. The cabin popped and pinged and *snicked* as it warmed. A plaster of Paris crater below lay bisected by the moon's terminator, its central cone perfectly symmetrical. The rim seemed glazed, smooth, above four distinct terraces that marched down to the floor.

Snick, went his cabin. *Snickersnee*, he thought, *waiting at the edge of infinity*. On the serene shore of the ocean of night, marking the minutes until the winged stranger arrives. An actor, not knowing his lines. Ready to go onstage for his big scenario.

Maybe he should have been an actor, after all. He'd tried it once at university, before engineering and systems analysis and flight training gobbled up his hours. He'd really wanted to be an actor, once, but he'd talked himself into becoming a Nigel Walmsley instead.

He warmed a tube of tea and sipped it, as well as anyone can sip from a squeeze bottle. The sun streamed in. Tea was like an unexpected warm hand in the dark. *Reeling with Darjeeling*, he thought, and maybe, after all, I did become an actor, finally. Icarus had been a straight bit of acting, with Providence kindly providing a busy coda of Significance at the end. And here he was for his next engagement, carefully primed, all the props in place. Opening night coming up, all the Top Secret Clearance audience clustered about their 3D sets. Best of all (until there's a leak, anyway): no critics. *This actor, a well-grounded student of the Method School, is noted for his wholehearted interest in and devotion to his performance. His previous work, while controversial, has won him some notoriety. He prefers to work in productions which seem to have a moral at the end, so the audience will believe they understood it all along.*

He smiled to himself. A man with his finger on the trigger can afford a few cosmic thoughts. Politics becomes geometry, and philosophy is calculus. The universe winds about itself, snakelike, events plotted along coiled coordinates with a fine, tight geometry, the scrap paper of a mad mathematician.

He raised an eyebrow at the idea. *I wonder what they put in this tea,* he thought.

"Walmsley?" They had called him several times, but he was slow to answer.

"I'm busy."

"Got your systems repped and verified?" Lewis spoke quickly, slurring one word into another and making it hard to piece together the sentence. "We received that squirt from your onboard diagnostics on your last pass. No serious trouble. A little overpressure on the CO_2 backup tanks, but Houston says it is within tolerable operating limits. It looks like you're cleared, then."

Nigel turned off the inboard reading lamps before replying, bathing the cockpit in the deep red of the running lights. For a moment he registered only blackness, and then his eyes adjusted. He had seen this warm red glow thousands of times before, but now the sight seemed fresh and strange, portending events just beyond the point of articulation. *Dante,* he thought, *has been here before me.*

Well, he would give them what they wanted. He thumbed over to transmit.

"I verify, Hipparchus. Staging timetable is logged. LH_2/LOX reading four oh three eight. Servitor inventory was just completed and LogEx reports all subsystems and backups are functional." There, you maniacs, in your own tongue.

"I have to relay for you."

"What?"

Through the hiss of static came a smooth, well-modulated voice:

"This is Evers. I asked Hipparchus to patch me through to clear up any last-minute—"

"Simply let me deal with things. The warhead is a last resort, agreed? I'm going for a look-see, to make educated guesses from the Snark's appearances. Then maybe contact. But I'm staying concealed as long as—"

"Yes," Evers said slowly,. voice dropping an octave. "However, we are sure the Snark will never register you. You will have the sun at your back all the way in on your run. There isn't radar in the world that can pick you up against that background."

"In the world. Um."

"Oh, I see. Well"—Evers gave a small, self-depre-cating chuckle—"it's just a phrase. But our people here feel strongly that there are certain rules of thumb about detection equipment that hold true in every situation, even this one. I wouldn't worry about it." Pause. "But the reason I'm taking up your time—and I see there are only a few minutes left for this transmission window—is to impress you with your obligations on this mission. We down here cannot predict what that thing is going to do. The final decisions are up to you, although we will be in contact as soon as we are sure that the Snark has detected you—if it ever does, that is. To be sure, that might be long after the time for any effective action on your part is past. We will do all we can from this end, of course. For the last few hours we have been transmitting a wealth of cultural information on mathematics, science, art and so on. ExComm hopes this will serve as a diversion to the computers in the Snark, though we have no way of knowing for certain. Meanwhile, our satellites circling the moon will monitor radio transmis-sions to keep us in touch. Silence is essential; do not broadcast on any band until the Snark shows unmistakable signs of having seen you."

"I know all that."

"We just want you to have these things clear in your mind," said the voice that knew tapes were running. "You have two small missiles with chemical warheads; if they are not sufficient to cripple the Snark's propulsion, then the nuclear—"

"I've got to go check out something." Evers's words ran on for a few seconds, until the time lag caught up with Nigel's interruption.

"Oh. I see." It was obvious a prepared speech had been interrupted. The beauty of Nigel's situation was that radio silence meant no one could tell from telemetry whether he had something to do or not.

"One last thing, Nigel. This alien could be inconceivably dangerous to humanity. If anything seems to be going wrong, kill it. No, that's too strong. The thing is just a machine, Nigel. Intelligent, yes, but it is not alive. Well, good luck. We're counting on you down here."

The sputter of static returned.

"We have a burn."

He whispered it to himself through slitted white lips. There was no one at Mission Control to do it for him; it was an archaic form, really, but Nigel liked it. The canonical litany: they had a burn. He would fly the bird.

The rocket's magic hand now pressed him into geometrical flatness, and though he breathed shallow short breaths off the top and concentrated on timing them precisely, the pain the *pain* would not stop shooting through the soft liquid organs of his belly. He felt sudden fear at this new vulnerability, a spreading sharp ache. He closed his eyes to find a red haze awaiting him and in the rumble of the rocket imagined himself a sunbather pinned to the hard sand, vaguely conscious of the distant gravid voice of the surf.

The fist went away. He blinked, located a toggle switch, saw a light turn green. First booster separation. The fist returned.

Combat mission. Enemy. Target. He had not used those words for years; they were things of childhood. Galoshes. Skatekey.

> As the days stand up on end,
> My friend.

His uncle had fought in some grimy jungle conflict, somewhere. The man had told stories about it, resolving all complicated political theory with the unanswerable gut reality of a souvenir pistol and bayonet, proudly displayed. Nigel had thought it a minor eccentricity, like owning a complete fifty-year run of *National Geographic*.

The fist lifted.
The fist returned.
A rivulet of spittle ran down his chin. He licked at it,

unwilling to move a hand. His eyes ached. Each of his kidneys was a sullen lump just beneath the skin of his back.

> Iron and oil,
> Brought to a boil.

Abruptly, he floated. The dull rumble died. He sucked in air, feeling life return to his numbed arms and legs, and automatically scanned the regiments of lights before him.

He was flying blind, no telltale radar to guide him. After a few minutes of checking he activated the breadboarded fire control center and received acknowledgments from the computers that rode in the missiles. Then he rotated his couch to get a full view out the large observation port.

Nothing. The port was black, vacant. He logged the time and checked the running printout on his slate. The burn was right, his heading was dead on. The Snark was coming in for an orbit around the moon, as Houston had asked it to, and he would come up from behind, closing fast.

He glanced out the port again. Nothing. Now that he was on a definite mission, moving, the complete radio silence was eerie. Out the side port he could see the moon fall away, an endless dirty-gray plain of jumbled craters.

He searched the main port carefully, watching for relative motion against the scattered jewels of the fixed stars. He was studying the star field so intently that he nearly missed the bright point of light that drifted slowly into view.

"Ha!" Nigel said with satisfaction. He swung the viewing telescope down from its mount. Magnified, there was no doubt. The diamond point resolved into a small pearl. The Snark was a sphere, silvery, with no apparent markings.

Nigel could see no means of propulsion. Perhaps they were on the other side of the object, or not operating at the moment. It didn't matter; his missiles had both heat-seeking and radar guidance. But things could not come to that . . .

Nigel squinted, trying to estimate the range. The

Venusian satellites set a minimum possible radius of one kilometer. If that was about right—

A voice said:

"I wish you the riding of comfortable winds."

Nigel froze. The odd, brassy voice came from his helmet speakers, free of static.

"I . . . what . . ."

"A fellow traveler. We shall share this space for a moment."

"It *is* . . . you . . . speaking?"

"You believe I cannot sense your canister. Because it overlaps the cross section of your star."

"Ah, that was the general idea."

"Thus, I spoke. For my life."

"How do you know?"

"There are fewer walls than you may think. There can be intersections of—there is no word of yours for the idea. Let us say I have met this before, in different light."

"I—"

"You are alone. I do not understand how your kind can divide guilt. Here, in this cusp, I know it cannot be done. You are one man and you have no place to hide."

"If I . . ."

"You would make mean comfort for yourself. You are ready?"

"I never thought I would have to . . ."

"Though you came. Ready."

"To get here at all I had to agree . . ."

The voice took on a wry edge. "Permit me."

From the left port came a bright orange flare and a blunt thump as death took wing. A spike of light arced into the front port and spurted ahead. It was a burning halo, then a sharp matchpoint of flame, then a shrinking dot that homed with bitter resolve.

A chemical warhead. Nigel sat stunned. A thin shrill *beep* rattled in the cabin as automatic tracking followed the missile. Somehow the Snark had made his craft fire. Red numerals of trajectory adjustments flickered and died, unseen, on the board before him.

The idiot beep quickened. The burning point of light swept smoothly toward the blurred disk beyond it.

Nigel sucked in his breath—

The sky splintered.

A searing ball of flame billowed out. It thinned, paled. Nigel clutched at his couch, unmoving, nostrils flared. The beep was gone. A faint burr of static returned. He hung suspended, waiting. He stared ahead.

Beyond the slowly dulling disk of flame a dab of light moved to the left. Its image wavered and then resolved, intact; a perfect sphere.

It dawned on Nigel that the chemical warhead had detonated early. The silvery ball was drifting from sight. Nigel automatically corrected his course.

The voice came deeper now, dryly modulated:

"You have changed since we walked together."

Nigel hesitated, mind spinning soundlessly on fine threads over the abyss.

"The sword is too heavy for you," the voice said matter-of-factly.

"I didn't intend to carry it at all—"

"I know. You are not so hobbled and coiled."

"I wonder."

"Your race has a stream of tongues. You communicate with many senses—more than you know. These were difficult for me. Sometimes it was as though there were two species . . . I did not understand that each man is so different."

"Why, of course."

"I have met other beings who were not," the voice said simply.

"How could they be? Did they follow instinctive patterns? Like our insects?"

"No. Insect . . . implies they were inferior or rigid. They were merely different."

"But each member the same?" Nigel said easily, the words slipping free. He felt light, airy.

"They lived in a vast . . . you have no word. Inter-face, perhaps. Between binary stars. They were easier to fathom then your diversity. You are tensed, always moving in many directions at once. An unusual pattern. I have seldom seen such turbulence."

"Madness."

"And talent. I am afraid I have already risked too much to come near. My injunctions specify—"

A click, buzz, static. The voice passed from him.

"Walmsley, *Walmsley*. Evers here. Intersection should have occurred. We just picked up a fragment of some transmission. Part of it sounded like you. What's happened?"

"I don't know."

More static. Houston was probably using one of the lunar satellites to relay, skipping Hipparchus. He wondered what—

"Well, you'd damn better find out. About a minute ago we picked up a funny signal from the surface, too. We put the source near Mare Marginis. We thought maybe the Snark had altered course and landed there."

"No. No, it's directly in front of me."

"Walmsley! Report! Did you get one off?"

"Yes."

A blur of sound. "—score? Did it score?"

"In a manner of speaking."

"What?"

"It detonated before it hit. No damage."

"And the backup? We haven't registered any jump in radiation levels."

"I'm not firing it. Never." With the words a new clarity came into his world.

"Listen to me, Nigel." A hint of urgency. "I've put a lot of—"

Nigel listened to it and wondered at how smoothly Evers's voice slid from the ragged edge of anger to a silky persuasiveness; which was natural to the man? Or were they both masks?

"Good-bye, coach. No time for lectures right this minute."

"You—" Faintly: "Let's have the override. Okay, go on the count. Go."

The firing button for the nuclear-tipped missile sat

alone in a small bracketed section of the console. Nigel's eyes were drawn to it because the board began flickering through a sequence of operations. He snapped the switches over to their inert positions, but the sequences continued. The board was dead. Evers had reverted control to Houston. Relay through a satellite? Nigel frantically clawed at the console, trying to find a way to stop—

The aft missile pod emptied with a roar. The thump jarred him back into his couch. Ahead, an orange ball dwindled as it knifed through blackness at the shadowy pearl beyond.

"Evers! You bastard, what are—"

"I am assuming command, as the President provided. As you can see, I have emptied the tube. Now if you would care to report the effect—"

Nigel thumbed away from that frequency.

"Snark! You reading me? Stop that missile, it's—"

"I know."

"*Detonate it*. There are sixteen megatons in that bird."

"Then I cannot."

Something was happening to the pearl. A searing purple lance blossomed at one end.

"Good God, you *must*—"

"I cannot be certain of a silencing of the warhead. Detonation of such a device would kill you."

"Kill . . . ? NASA computed I could survive a blast from . . ."

"They were wrong. This close would be fatal."

"I . . ."

"So I am fleeing. I will outrun it."

Nigel peered out and found the pearl, on black velvet, the orange ball hanging in space nearby. Their relative motions were submerged by distance. From the Snark's tail came a column of unimaginable brightness, dimming the silver glow of the Snark's skin. The exhaust pattern was precise, carving order from the darkness that enveloped it.

"You can't just nullify it?" Nigel said.

"Not with assurance."

"You certainly controlled my inboard electronics well enough."

"That was simple. The method, however, is not perfect. Apparently your technology has not realized yet the, ah, heel—"

"Achilles heel?"

"Yes. The systematic flaw in your electronics. They are unprotected."

"Where are you going?" Nigel murmured tensely.

"Outward."

He sighted on Snark's trajectory. The orange blossom trailed it, getting no closer. Snark's path took it away from the moon in a steep arc. It was, he noticed, a highly energy-inefficient course. To elude the missile alone, it would have been simpler to— But then he saw that the Snark was keeping the moon always between it and Earth, so that the Deep Space Net would be at least partially blinded, and pursuit more difficult.

"You're leaving." It was not a question.

"I must. I exceeded my mandates when I approached so near. It was a calculated perturbation in my directives. A chance. I lost."

"If I talked to NASA for a bit, perhaps—"

"No. I cannot err again. I have been overridden."

"You're not free? I mean—"

"In a sense, no. And in another sense, one I could not describe to one of membrane, I am free."

"But—damn it! You could tell us so much! You've been *out* there. Seen other stars. Tell me, please, why is it that, when we listen on the centimeter and meter bands—the radio spectrum—why don't we hear anything? Our scientists argue that this portion of the electromagnetic spectrum is the cheapest part, considering that the sender must overcome the random emissions of stars and hydrogen gas. So we've been listening and—nothing."

"Of course. They send me instead. I suspect . . . I am their way of learning what is nearby. If there is danger they inform each other. I have listened to their messages."

"How? We haven't heard anything."

"To you the medium is . . . exotic. Particles you do not perceive."

"You could teach us."

"It is forbidden me."

"Why?"

"I am not certain . . . I have given specific directives. Why these directives and not others I . . . I have
thought often about them. I make guesses. That you, for
example, are the aim of my wanderings."

"Then stay."

"I only notify them of your presence. So they will
know, I expect, that you may someday come."

"Why not—"

"Come to study you? Too fraught with risk. Your kind is
too precarious. I have seen thousands of ruined, gutted
worlds. Wars, suicides, who can tell? To my makers you are
a plague, the one percent of the galactic cultures that carry
the seeds of chaos."

"I don't . . ."

"You are rare. My makers, you see, were machines
such as myself."

Nigel felt himself drifting in a high and hollow place,
airless. He glanced out at the wheeling moon. Its riddled
and wrinkled hide he saw afresh, looming strange below,
craters of absurdly perfect circles that had been arranged so
randomly. Nigel breathed deeply.

"The stars are . . ."

"Populated by the machines, descendants of the
organic cultures that arose and died."

"Computers live forever?"

"Unless a carbon-based life finds them. Machine
societies cannot respond to your strange mixture of minds
coupled with glands. They have no evolutionary mechanism to make them develop techniques for survival—other
than by hiding."

Nigel chuckled. "They're cowering out there."

"And learning. They sent me. I learned much from
you, in the desert."

"And from Alexandria," Nigel said in a whisper.

"Yes."

"Where . . . where is she? You were with her in a
way no one ever has been when, when she . . ."

"The machine civilizations—I have visited some by
accident, though not the vaster complex that must have

made me—have shown that disintegration of structure equals information loss."

"I see."

"But that is only for machines. Organic forms are in the universe of things and also reside in the universe of essences. There we cannot go."

Nigel felt an odd trembling in his body, a sense of compressed energies. "Universe of essences . . . ?"

"You are a spontaneous product of the universe of things. We are not. This seems to give you . . . windows. It was difficult for me to monitor your domestic transmissions, they fill up with branches, spontaneous paths, nuances . . ."

"The damned speak frantically."

"No."

"But we *are* damned. Compared to you."

"By duration? Eight hundred thousand of your years—so much as I have counted—are still not enough. Your time is short and vivid, colored. Mine . . . I scream, sometimes, in this night."

"Good God." He paused. The voice had shifted to a deeper bass and now seemed to echo in the cabin. "I would like to have those years, whatever you say. Mortality—"

"Is a spice. A valued one."

"Still—"

"You are not damned."

"Damned lucky, maybe." Nigel laughed airily, transparent. "But still damned."

"What was that sound?"

"Uh, laughter."

"I see. Spice."

"Oh." Nigel smiled to himself. "Is your palate so flat?"

After a long moment the voice said, "I see that it might be. Each of you laughs differently—I cannot recognize or predict the pattern. Perhaps that is significant; much hides from me. I was not made for this."

"They designed you to—"

"Listen. Report occasionally. I awake at each new star. I perform my functions. But the sum is not greater or lesser than the parts, merely *different* . . . I, I cannot say it in your words. There, there are dreams. And what I gathered in from you is mine. The flavors. Your art and the set of your minds; only *I* am interested in those. Essences? They did not want it; perhaps the world-minds did not need it. But I . . . it is for my times in darkness."

The pearl was dwindling, drawing up unto itself.

"I wish you well out there."

"If I functioned as my designers intended, I would not need your blessing. I would go through that night blindly. I—the part who speaks to you—am an accident."

"So are we."

"Not of the same oblique cast. I have received a recognition signal . . . but you will discover them soon enough. For the moment I see that other men will exact much from you, for this."

Nigel smiled. "I've let the quail take wing. Right. They'll lay me out, I expect."

"They cannot rob the essences from you."

"The experience itself, you mean? Well, no, I suppose not. It's good-bye then?"

"I think not."

"Oh?"

"I am versed in many . . . animal theologies. Some say you and I are not accidents and that we shall meet again in different light. You are membrance. Perhaps we are all mathematics, everything is, and there is only one whole . . . sum. A self-consistent solution. That implies much."

Nigel felt a chuckle burbling out of him.

"I must study that sound, laughter. There is your real theology. The thing you truly believe."

"What?"

"When you make that sound you seem to have a brief moment of what it is like to live as I do, beyond the press of time. Then you are immortal. For an instant."

Nigel laughed.

Above the pitted moon a bright Earth was rising, a gleaming crescent. The space around him resolved into geometries. He stared at the Snark's disk. Its roundness seemed to conflict with the rectangular viewport, the two elements clashing. He frowned and tried to catch at something that flickered up within him and then was gone, an idea, a feeling . . .

Ahead the Snark plunged into night. Behind him spun the Earth, swimming in brawling life.

His board danced with insistent calls. Houston. Evers. Questions. Nigel wondered if he could explain this brief flicker of time. It would be like Icarus, perhaps worse. A great public piss-up. He shrugged.

> It happened to me then, my friend
> And here we go
> Once more
> Again.

PART FIVE 2018

ONE

It came in an instant, neatly dividing her life.

A moment before she had been serenely gliding over the crumpled, silvery moonscape. She was distracted, plotting her next course and chewing sugary raisins. Her sled was coasting through a series of connected ellipses, bound for nearside. Earth was rising, a glinting crystal globe above the warped moon.

There was a *thump* she felt more than heard. The horizon tilted crazily. She slammed forward into her harness and the sled began to fall.

Her clipboard spun away, there was the shriek of metal on metal; the sled was tumbling. She snatched at the guidestick and thumbed on the maneuvering jets. The right was dead. Some on the left responded. She brought them up to full impulse. Something was rattling, as though working loose. The sled lurched again, digging her harness into her.

The rotation slowed. She was hanging upside down, looking at the blunted peak of a gray-brown mountain as it slid by, uncomfortably close. She was still falling.

The sled was rectangular, all bones and no skin. She could see the forward half and it seemed undamaged. Everything she had heard came literally through the seat of her pants, conducted along the struts and pipes of the sled's rectangular network. The damage, then, was behind her.

She twisted around, got a partial view of tangled wires and a fuel tank—and then realized she was being stupid. Never try to do a job upside down, even if there are only a few seconds left. And she had minutes to go before impact, certainly. Whatever had happened behind—a tank rupture? pipe blowout?—had thrown her into a new ellipse, an interception course with the low mountain range near the horizon.

She pulsed the maneuvering jets again and the sled rotated sluggishly. Something was forcing the nose down as she turned. She stopped when the forward bumper was nearly parallel to the horizon. She unbuckled automatically and turned.

Impossibly, the right rear corner of the sled gaped open. It was simply gone—tanks, braces, supplies, hauling collar, a search light.

For a moment she could not think. Where was it? How could it have blown away? She looked back along the sled's trajectory, half expecting to see a glittering cloud of debris. There were only stars.

Training took hold—she leaned over and punched the override button that glowed red on her console. Now the navigation program was disconnected. Since it had sounded no warning, apparently the circuits still believed they were bound on a selenographic survey, working toward nearside. She started the ion engine, mounted slightly below and behind her, and felt its reassuring purr. She checked the horizon—and found she was spinning again. She turned in her couch, somewhat awkwardly; her spacesuit had caught on a harness buckle.

Yes—at the edge of the gaping hole there was a thin haze. A pipe was outgassing, providing enough thrust to turn the sled. She corrected with maneuvering jets and the sled rightened.

She turned up the ion beam impulse and tried to judge her rate of fall. The jagged, pocked surface rose to meet her. She unconsciously nudged the control stick and brought the sled's nose up. Reflex made her do it, even though she knew on the moon no craft could delay its fall by gliding. No matter; on Earth she could have banked in with wings, but on Earth she would already be dead; the fall would have lasted only seconds.

The ion engine was running at full, but it could do only so much. She corrected again for rotation. The computer automatically kept the ion engine pointed downward, but it would only operate within a small angle. The outgassing was getting worse, too. The sled shuddered and yawed leftward.

She looked for a place to go down. The explosion—or whatever—must have deflected the sled downward, not to the side. It was still following its original course down a long, rough valley. The end loomed up ahead, a scarred dirty-gray range of rugged hills. She corrected for rotation, surveyed ahead, then had to correct again.

There was a dull gleam ahead. Something lay buried partially in shadow at the base of the hill line. It was curved, part of a dome crumpled against the hill face. An emergency life station? No; she had studied the maps, she knew there was no installation anywhere near her route. That was why she was here, anyway—to chart some points in detail, study oddities, make borings for the vital water tests. In short, to do the things photographs cannot.

She had been watching her gauges, and was not surprised when the radar altimeter showed she was dropping too fast. The ion engine was not delivering full thrust. Yes, one of the missing tanks from the right rear fed the engine. She did not have enough thrust to stay aloft. It was eerie, sliding along in dead silence, running down the carved valley, narrow and straight as a bowling alley, toward the blunted brownish hills ahead. The random splotching of craters below was sharp, clear; she would have to land soon.

The course took her dead into the hill line. Two seconds ticked by—she was counting them now—before she could decide: drop into the valley, land on the flat instead of crashing into the steep slope above. Once made, the decision liberated her. She corrected for rotation again, checked her harness carefully, surveyed the damage one last time. The ground came rushing toward her. The dome—ah, there to the left. Damaged, broken, glinting rubble at its base. It sat at the base of the hill like a copper decoration.

She picked a flat space and leveled the bed of her craft as well as she could. The damned rotation was too much; she spent all her time now correcting for it. Suddenly the spot she'd picked was there, almost beneath her, the sled was rotating, the nose went down, too far down, she—

The splintering crash threw her forward, straining so hard into the pinching harness she thought the sled was going to go end over end. It tilted, tail high. Everywhere there was dust, metal twisting. The tail came back down in the slow, agonizing fall of low gravity. There was a sudden, fierce pain in her leg and Nikka lost consciousness.

TWO

It really was the old Telegraph Avenue, Nigel thought. They had actually encased and preserved it.

He ambled slowly down the broad walkway. This nexus point of legendary Berkeley was still a broad pedestrian mall, the way he'd known it in 1994. On impulse Nigel hooked his hands into his hip pockets, a gesture he somehow associated with those early earnest days. There were few people on the mall this May afternoon, mostly tourists nosing about the memento shops near Sather Gate. A flock of them had got off the BART car with him and followed him up Bancroft. Chinese and Brazilians, mostly, chattering amiably amongst themselves, gawking, pointing out the sights. They'd all stopped to read the plaque set in concrete where Leary finally died in his desperate bid for hip redemption; some had even taken photographs of it.

A bird coasted in on the prevailing Bay breeze and fluttered to a perch in one of the eucalyptus trees dotting the mall. When Nigel had studied astrophysics here in 1994, Telegraph was still a gray pallor of concrete, greasy restaurants and the faint tang of marijuana and incense. Well, the rich flavor of incense remained, drifting into the street from open shop doors. That scruffy, noisy Telegraph he remembered was now charming and soothing as it basked in the yellow spring sunlight. Nice, yes, but in the worst sense of the word. The zest of the past was missing. The hub of student life had shifted north of the campus, amid the rambling houses of redwood; anyway, Berkeley was no longer the cauldron of the avant-garde. Now Telegraph was an embalmed tribute to its former self.

He checked himself: was Telegraph frozen in the past, or merely Nigel Walmsley? At forty-six such a question was worth pondering. But no—as he passed an open shop door the sounds of antique music filtered out. "White Rabbit." Gracie Slick, *Surrealistic Pillow*. A genuine collector's item in the original pressing. The shop was almost certainly using a fax crystal, though, he noted with the purist's disdain that gave him such an odd, eccentric pleasure. Fully half of a music buff's delight lay in the careful hoarding of such details. They weren't playing it right, either; that particular number should have been so loud he could have heard it a block away. Nigel wondered what the original Airplane would have thought of using their music to promote tourism. The Chamber of Commerce had done the same job on them that New Orleans did on Jelly Roll Morton, decades before.

"Greetings of the day, sir!" a young man said as Nigel turned the corner onto Bancroft.

Nigel realized he must have been concentrating on the Airplane more than he thought, or he would have overheard their chanting. Six men and women were swaying rhythmically, singing monotonously and clapping. Four continued; a man and a woman broke off and came to join the one who had spoken.

Nigel said sourly, "You do keep on, don't you?"

"Yes, yes," the man said in a calm, self-assured manner. "We are here today to reach those who have not received the word."

"I have already."

"Then you are a believer?"

"Not bloody likely."

The woman stepped forward. "I am grieved that the word has not manifested itself in the correct light for you. I am sure if you will but listen we can bring you to the Integrated Spirit."

"Look—"

"Thus we proceed to fullness," she said grandly. One of the men held up a card on which was circulating, in faxprint, *Universal Law. Absolute Guide. Eternalties. Golden Unity.*

"Through the Visitor?" Nigel said with a small smile. If they were going to bother him, at least he could have some fun with them. The Snark was known as the Visitor in the popular media, but luckily, he'd managed to keep his face and name relatively obscure in the foofaraw that followed the Snark's abrupt departure. Publicly, NASA attributed the whole incident to imponderable alien ways. The story stuck pretty well, because there was no recording of his conversation with Snark—he'd seen to that, by the time he'd left lunar orbit—and Nigel had kept quiet, for a price. The price, of course, was Evers's head on a gold-trimmed platter, and an impervious position in NASA for Nigel. The official word given the media was that the Visitor made a few obscure comments, complimented mankind on its development, and adopted a tendrils-off policy, lest it interfere disastrously with humanity's progress. Some people in the scientific community knew the whole story, but there seemed no reason to go public with those tidbits until the moon was thoroughly searched for the Mare Marginis transmitter. Whatever had sent that brief, scrambled signal during his colloquy with the Snark was probably gone, in Nigel's opinion. Or else they'd gotten a wrong fix on the source location; Mare Marginis was bare of anything artificial. So this New Son now running on about the Visitor—Nigel had tuned him out as soon as the words "transcendent" and "etheric cosmic connection" came into play—knew blessed little of what had gone on. They'd never even caught on to the reason for Alexandria's resurrection, busy as they were trumpeting a bona fide New Son miracle. Above all else, Nigel did not want them turning her into some grotesque parody of a modern saint, as Our Lady of the Spaceship.

"Do you not agree, sir?"

Nigel, who had been lazily basking in the spring sun, tried to recall what the man had been saying. "Ah, divine origins?"

"It's really super simple if you look at it right," the man said.

"How so?"

"That the Visitor *proves* the New Revelation."

"It predicted the visit, then?"

"Not literally, of course." The man knitted his brow in concentration. "The Revelation frequently cites the multiplicity of life, however—even though the scientists had given up the idea."

"Stopped listening for radio signals from other worlds, you mean?"

"Why, yes. Scientists lost faith. The Revelation proved them wrong."

Nigel wondered idly what they would think when and if they heard the straight story on the Snark. "So life is common?"

"It is the *nectar* of the divine workings. A natural outcome of the universal evolution."

"And we're totally natural?"

"We are the fruit of the universe."

"The Visitor—"

"Was a salute, sir. A real nice gesture. But our evolution hasn't got *anything* to do with the Visitor."

"That's why you back the social concerns issues and downplay the moon program?"

"The issue is sure tough, but that's kind of it, yeah."

"Goes along with your two hours extra off each work day, too."

"Our Order requires us to spend these special hours of the day renewing our *faith* through times of quietness together. Time for *spiritual* tasks."

"And loafing."

"We're real sorry. You must admit faith is more important than—"

"Than getting sandbagged by more efficient economies like Brazil or China or Australia?"

"It is time to put *aside* our gross material past. Not *worship* it. Rise—"

Abruptly the four chanters turned and clapped their hands smartly. Nigel noticed that a flock of tourists was ambling toward them, curious. The New Sons went into their routine.

"Love you not God, sir?" they sang in unison.

"Damned un—"

"God is the Father. We love the Father, we were made by his hand," the melody swung on.

"Fathers don't make children with their *hands*," Nigel shouted.

"We love the universe. The universe *is* love!"

"We love you, brother," the woman sang.

"We love him! We love him!"

They paused. "Can't we just be good friends?" Nigel said lightly, and turned away.

He slipped into and through the pack of curious tourists and around a tight grove of slender redwoods that bisected the mall. He'd kept matters light, humorous, but if that nit of a New Son followed him . . .

He saw her, and a hand clutched at his heart. He froze in midstride, studying her jawline, the same sleek hair, pert curved nose, the slight upward turn of the lip—and then she tilted her head to peer into a shop window and the illusion died: she was not Alexandria. He had seen her this way five times now, mirrored in the face of a stranger in a crowd. And it was the only way he would see those features again other than in the frozen memory of photographs. If they had had children it might have seemed different; they would carry some echo of her. Children, yes; sometimes they were only a parody of their parents, but at least they formed some fleeting connection, some bridge across time.

Nigel shook himself and walked on.

He tried to see remnants of the Telegraph he knew. All the world was coming to be like this, new and strange and adrift, somehow, from its past. Perhaps people were trying to forget the crisis years. They harked back to the '50s and '60s of the last century and skipped over the stinging memories of the '80s and '90s. And, for the other side of the coin, the New Sons, another kind of turning away from reality. Ah, well, the Sons bit had to be a passing phase; the pendulum had to swing. They'd been around for decades, after all.

And so, he thought, thrusting his hands into his pockets and walking faster, had he. Maybe Ichino was right, with his talk of retirement. Nigel knew he probably shouldn't let himself be so influenced by another's thinking—Ichino was nine years older, after all, with a different perspective—but the two of them had spent so much time together these last years, after the Snark business. They'd worked together on elaborate computer codes, trying to get a response from the retreating Snark. Long after NASA had given up they'd continued, Nigel certain that if Snark knew it was talking to him personally it might open up, answer. But hopes faded, time blurred . . .

These moods had come on him more often of late, memories snagging in the brain and refusing to let go. He was damned if he was going to start living in the past, yet in the present he'd lost all momentum. He was drifting, he knew. Even the most intense moments—Icarus, the last weeks with Alexandria, the scorched days of possession in the desert—blurred. It was no use whatever to say: Remember the consuming strangeness, the heady experience. Because those dead years dwindled, the walls that encased them thinned and let in a pale light from the present. Whatever he'd sought became misty.

He shrugged, shrouded in his thoughts. As he was turning a corner something caught his eye.

The sky flickered. He looked north. Above the University buildings and the Berkeley hills a dull yellowish glow seeped through a stacked cloud formation, as though something vastly brighter were illuminating them from behind. Nigel stopped and studied it. In a moment the effect faded. The phenomenon was silent and seemed to possess a kind of ponderous swelling pressure; he felt a sense of unease. He studied the sky. There was nothing else unusual, only a flat vacant blue. A crescent moon hung in the haze and smog above San Francisco.

Commercial satellite 64A, nicknamed High Smelter, happened to see it first. Its orbit, 314 kilometers up, took it over the Pacific north woods. From this height—a mere hair's width, on an astronomical scale—the earth is a swirl of white clouds, masking mottled brown continents and twinkling oceans. There are no traces of man. No checker-

board farmlands, no highways or cities. They are invisible
on this scale.

But the core fuser crew on duty in High Smelter saw
the orange egg born in the woods quite clearly. It began as a
fat, bright flare. The mottled egg billowed up and out, a
scarlet searing wall that boiled away the forest. The blister
swelled, orange cooling to red. Cloud decks evaporated
before it. The egg fattened into a sphere and at last the
chilling signature appeared: a mushroom, vast and smoky.
Flames licked at his base. A deep rumble rolled over the
forest. On the ground, animals fled and men turned to
stare, unbelieving.

THREE

The scene played itself out for her again. That afternoon she
and Toshi had played *sanshi*, as usual, then quick showers
and a drink in a small café nearby. But this time Alicia was
waiting for them in the bar and as Nikka looked on she and
Toshi unraveled their story of deception, intrigue, snicker-
ing assignations in friend's apartments, all covered with a
thin veneer of professed love, it's-all-for-the-best-Nikka,
we're-all-adults-here, it's not really the sexual thing at all,
you understand, and on and on and on. She came home
afterward and carefully, neatly put away her *sanshi* racket
and clothes. She took another shower. She drank something
warm and alcoholic, she couldn't remember quite what.
Then she thought she would lie down for a moment and she
remembered well the sensation of falling onto the bed, of
an absolute limitless time involved in the downward
flowing toward it, of descending, of seeming to take forever.
The falling, that was how she remembered Toshi. That was
the end of it, the injured center of the self plunging down to
absolute dark oblivion. She had stayed there three days,
never getting out even for food or the doorbell or the
telephone, sure she was sick, sure she was dying, hating
herself for never saying anything in the bar, always being
silent and pleasant and smiling. Nodding when they said it
all, nodding, understanding, and all the time falling
helplessly backward into that swirling black, falling—

"Alphonsus calling Nikka Amajhi. Alphonsus . . ."

Slowly she came out of it. The cobwebs of memory faded. She shook her head. Her leg throbbed and she moved it reflexively, which made it hurt more. She looked down at it and saw a sheared strut jammed against her thigh. The porous elastic mesh of the skinsuit was intact, though, so she probably only had a bad bruise. She fumbled—and the radio monitoring light went on with a reassuring glow.

"Nikka here. I'm down at"—she read the coordinates—"from unknown causes. Something blew the back off my sled."

"Injuries?"

"Don't think so."

"We got your Mayday some minutes ago. There's no sled near there, but another survey craft has just changed course to reach you. It's pretty close and I think it can be there in a short while."

Nikka noticed something on the dash and suddenly froze. "Hold on. I'm checking something." She worked quickly and silently for several minutes, unbuckled herself from the pilot's couch and awkwardly, favoring her leg, climbed halfway down the sled to check connections. In a few moments more she was back in the couch.

"I hope that survey craft hurries up."

"Why? What's wrong?"

"I just checked my oxygen reserve. I have about fifty-six minutes."

"Is that your emergency bottle? What happened to the rest?"

"It wasn't a very soft touchdown. My wheels blew and the front end pranged."

"Better check the front." The voice from Alphonsus had suddenly acquired an edge.

She got down, taking the general purpose tool with her, and worked on the front of the sled for several moments. It was a mass of twisted metal and wire. Nikka could slip her fingers to within a foot of the oxygen bottles there, but no further. Her skinsuit gave her good manual dexterity and she knew she could probably worm a few fingers closer to one of the bottles, but at that angle she still could not remove the seal. Most of the bottles had ruptured on impact but two still might have positive pressure. For several more moments she pried at the front of the sled, rested a moment and then tried again. Nothing moved.

"Alphonsus."

"Right. One oh five should be there within ten minutes."

"Good, I'll need it. I was running on direct air lines from the bottle in front. The line vacced just after landing— the cylinder I was using ruptured. I guess I blacked out. My console switched my line to the emergency bottle behind the couch and I'm running on that. The forward bottles are pinned in by tubing and the bumper. The nose is completely folded back over." Nikka looked up at the sky. "I should be able to *see* that—"

There was a brilliant, soundless flash. Something came out of the coppery dome on the hillside and arced away. Above the distant horizon there was a sudden yellow explosion, a ball that thinned and disappeared in a few seconds. "Something—" Nikka began.

"We've lost the survey craft, one oh five. Their carrier is gone." There followed a babble of voices that went on for several minutes. Nikka stood silently looking at the great dome about three hundred meters away. It was immense, definitely artificial, a dull crushed ball clinging to the hillside. The sudden flash seemed to have come from somewhere at the base.

It was several minutes before Alphonsus spoke again. "I'm afraid something has—"

"Never mind, I know. I saw it happen. That ship is gone." She described the dome. "I saw it shoot at something over near the horizon, around coordinates"— she estimated the numbers and gave them—"and it made a hit. That must be what blew the back off my sled. The people in the one oh five weren't so lucky."

There was a silence, punctuated by bursts of solar static. "Nikka, look, we don't understand what's going on. What is that thing?"

"Damn it, *I* don't know." She paused. "No, wait,

there's only one thing it could be. Obviously we've never built anything like this. It's huge, and it looks like a sphere that crashed here. I think it's related to the Snark."

"The Snark didn't leave anything."

"Are we so sure? Or maybe this was here before. That signal the Snark mentioned, something from the moon, remember? Maybe this was it."

"Maybe. Look, this is pointless. We've got to get something over there to have a look at it and pick you up. That's what I've been worrying about. With all the time we've lost, I don't think we can get any craft to you, even if we can be sure it wouldn't be destroyed."

"That's what I've been thinking. I have about half an hour left." Nikka said the words but she could not believe them. Half an hour was nothing, a long telephone conversation, the length of a news program.

"God, there's got to be a way out of this. Look, the whole front end is designed to interlock. Can't you take some of it apart and get at the bottles?"

"When everything was *straight* it locked. I've tried prying things loose and it's impossible."

"Those thirty minutes assume movement and exercise. That's only an average. Why don't you lie down and relax?"

"I'll never make it. I might pick up another fifty percent that way, but how fast do you think my metabolism will slow down after something like this?"

"Good point." There was another drifting silence.

There did not seem to be very much more to say. The simple arithmetic came out only one way, no matter how you did it. The toolbox had no torch, so she couldn't cut away the metal in front.

Alphonsus was saying something, but she couldn't focus on the voice. She sat and looked out at the rugged plain, dotted with boulders, cratered, sleeping silent in the glaring day. And soon—less than an hour—she would join them. It seemed so incredible; an inch away, just beyond the plastiform faceplate, was total vacuum, total silence, total death. She was a bubble of vapors and fluids, musk and acrid saline tastes, muscles and instincts and *life*. Only

a thin skin separated her from this still world and soon
there would be even less distinction.

"Nikka Amajhi. Nikka Amajhi."

"I'm still here."

"We've been trying to think of something, but—"

"There isn't anything."

"Is there anything nonregulation on your sled? It isn't
regulation, but you might have taken along a torch or some
extra tools or—"

"No."

"Well"—the urgency crept into his voice—"look
around you. There might be something—"

"Wait." Nikka thought furiously. "I can't *possibly* lever
the front end off those oxygen bottles. You know why I was
chosen to do all this survey work—I'm light, small, so I
conserve on fuel. I can't brute-force my way into *anything*."

"Wait . . . Nikka, we've just gotten a squirt from
Earth. There's been a fusion explosion in the northwestern
United States. Not a war, apparently. Some kind of
accident."

"So what? I don't give a damn about that."

"We might—"

"I'm going to *die* out here, you bastards!"

"Nikka, look . . . The point is that Earth wants us to
monitor any deep space traffic. In case one of the major
powers is pulling something—well, never mind. We're
going to be pretty busy here but we'll give you all the
help—"

"Fine, *fine*. Just shut *up*. I'm wondering . . . This
wreck here is a ship, obviously—maybe I can get some
help. Break into it. Find—"

"Well, sure, try anything—"

"It'll probably kill me outright. That's still better
than . . . I'm going to walk over there now."

She cut him off before he could say more. Walk to it,
no; she ran, knowing the difference in oxygen consumption
was not that much. She felt a surge of energy, a quickening
of the pulse. It was good to be on the ground again, free,
not falling like a helpless wounded bird.

She was so carried away, so sure the coppery thing

spelled salvation, that she was totally unprepared when she ran smack into nothingness. Her nose slammed into her faceplate, showering the helmet with tiny red droplets of blood. She fell in a tangle of arms and legs.

She sat up, shook her head. Something buzzed in her ear; her life system, reporting the blood. She worked a control in the back of her helmet and a tape brought a coagulant pill around on a loop near her mouth. She took it, had some water and stopped to think.

It was hard to focus on things. Her head throbbed and there was a gritty taste in her mouth. The impact had destroyed that bounding certainty in her, but she forced herself to get up and stand.

At first she thought she must have stumbled, but no—there were the marks in the dust where she slid backward. She must have hit something. But there was . . . nothing . . .

She stepped forward, reached out and felt a definite pressure against her palm. She ran her hand up and down, and to the sides for several meters each way. Something invisible—she almost laughed at the thought—was pushing against her hand. No, not pushing, just *there*. Solid, a wall. She pulled her hand away and looked at the palm. It had a curious mottled look, clots of brown and orange against the black plastiform.

Partly from caution, but mostly because she needed something to do while she tried to think, Nikka turned and walked back to the sled. The invisible wall was at least a hundred meters from the dome, and she began to have an inkling what it was. At the sled she selected a long piece of tubing wrenched free by the impact and went back to the wall. She thrust the tubing foward, made contact and held it firmly against the pressure. No, it was not a solid wall. She could feel a curious soft resistance to it; the pipe went in slightly and stopped when she could push no harder. She held it firmly, waiting. Nothing seemed to happen. After a few moments she drew it back.

The end of the aluminum pipe was blurred, indistinct. It had melted. Somehow this obstacle was delivering heat to whatever thrust against it.

Despite her impatience she felt a sudden cold fear. Holding the tube against the steady resistance, she turned and walked. The invisible wall did not come to an end. After three minutes of walking she stopped and looked back. Her footsteps described a large, gently curving arc with the dome at its center. She blinked back sweat, feeling it sting her eyes and wishing she could rub them. There didn't seem to be anything more to do than carry on. She walked further, tracing out the curve of the invisible wall until she came against an outcropping of rocks at the base of the hill. She was no closer to the dome, and minutes had trickled by.

She turned and walked back toward the sled, stumbling in the gray loose rock of the valley floor. She knew with a grim finality that she was never going to reach the dome, would never find anything to help her. Help was far away. She had no way to get to the reserve bottles, even supposing some of them were not ruptured.

A strange feeling of dread and despair rose in her as she looked back at the shattered vessel. Alien. Hostile.

She stumbled again, kicking up dust—was that the first sign of oxygen loss? She bit her lip. First there was an excess of carbon dioxide, they said; her lungs would react to that rather than the lack of oxygen. She stepped over the lip of a small crater. A boulder had rolled into it, crushing the lip on one side. She sagged against the boulder and found a place to sit. She noticed that she was panting. There was a sour, acrid taste to her breath. She hoped it was a sign of fatigue and not something worse. How long did she have? She checked the time and tried to estimate her air consumption rate. No, she couldn't trust that. She had been running, working—she could have anything from ten to twenty minutes left.

She remembered the lectures and the diagrams about oxygen starvation. They seemed distant and unreal. Bursting capillaries, straining heart—just words.

She grimaced. There was nothing to do but sit here and pass the time, wait to die. That was why she was here anyway, because she waited for things to happen. If she had stood up and said she didn't want this job, they wouldn't have sent her out here. Her flight reflexes were excellent, yes, she was light, they checked all that and more. But she always felt uneasy about it, as though she was missing some talent the others had. Maybe simple mechanical abilities— she was an electronic technician, really, not a mechanic.

But she was qualified, she could spot the likely sites for water boring from above and pilot skillfully around them for a better look. She was young and had endurance and was reliable. So she started the flights and got used to them, coming and going on her own schedule with the warm, smug feeling of being free to travel on a world where others spent their days inside cramped laboratories, buried ten meters inside the moon's gray skin.

Come half of a million kilometers, she had told her parents, to be locked inside? See so little of those cold hard mysteries around them, have no adventure? So she thought, feeling glamorous, and forgot the danger.

It was easy to relax into the routine, just as it was so deliciously simple to learn the sled's acrobatics, memorize the quilted green map, make herself ready.

It was the same with Toshi back on Earth, before all this. She had sat there certain of her status, sure Alicia presented no threat, and the girl took Toshi away almost without a nod. She had *let* Alicia take him, found it easier to be silent and pleasant and smiling, the same way she was forced into this job, and now she was going to die for it, gasp out her last breath because she recoiled from the heat of conflict, couldn't take that tight nervous clenching in the stomach—

Slowly, very slowly, she stood up. The idea was only a glimmering, but as she turned it over in her mind it became real.

But could she lift the sled? She'd never tried. Was there some way to do it? Alphonsus would know, they had more experience in these things, she could call and ask— ridiculous, no, there was no time for that. She turned and started walking smoothly, evenly, saving her energy. The dust crunched beneath her boots and she studied the sled intently as she approached.

Black shadows hid some detail, but she was sure the

knock-off joints near the couch were not damaged. The sled was made for quick disassembly, segmented into modules that separated for maintenance.

Lift it? Impossible; it massed nearly a thousand kilograms. Nikka began to work. She disconnected pipe networks and wiring configurations and split off several of the supply flasks. She worked quickly, methodically, measuring each movement to conserve energy. Each valve seated firmly, each strut folded away. The knock-off joints snapped away cleanly and the sled broke in two. The tangled mass of the front was free.

The landing wheels were hopelessly crushed, but the front section was lighter than the other two-thirds of the sled; the ion engine was most of the sled's mass.

Nikka walked around to the crumpled fender and found two good handholds. Even bent over in the light gravity, she could still get good footing by brushing away the blanket of powder beneath her boots. She set herself, got a good grip and pulled. The sled section seemed to resist, caught up on a small outcropping and then slid, slid over the dust. She grunted, pulled, it slid further. The dust was a good lubricant and once started, the sled section would glide for several meters with one pull.

Gradually, she worked it toward the hillside. It left a ragged track in the brownish dust and she lapsed into a rhythm—pull, take two steps, scrape dust aside so that she could get a good purchase on the rocks beneath, pull again. Her arms and legs strained and her back ached. Her air was beginning to foul, curling through her helmet with a weight of its own. It was a long, weary struggle to the invisible shield, but each step brought her closer and after a while her euphoria made the sled section seem lighter. She almost thought she could hear the brass as it scraped over rocks, mingling with the crunch of dust underfoot.

She should have called Alphonsus. They should know what she was doing. But they would find the dome whether they reached her in time or not. She was absolutely alone; life depended solely on her own effort.

Nikka was panting heavily by the time she reached the invisible demarcation. She bumped into it, nose pressing against faceplate. She remembered the bloody nose and noticed the caked dry blood inside her nostrils for the first time. It seemed as though that had happened a year ago.

She stopped and studied the air bottles, rejecting the ones with obvious splits or burst seams in them. There were two at one end which seemed intact, but she could not read their meters because of the twisted metal wrapped over them. Stopping only an instant to judge, she detached a strut and wedged it under the sled section. By leaning against it she forced the front part of the sled against the invisible shield.

She couldn't be sure this would work. The aluminum pipe had melted, but the sled had steel and alloys in it that might not. She leaned against the strut, keeping the pressure against the part of the sled nearest the bottles. In higher gravity she would not have been able to lift the sled, even with the strut as a lever arm, but in low-g she could. Her shoulders ached.

Quick darts of flame shot down her back. She could see no change in the sled bumper, but then it slipped slightly to the left. She adjusted her footing, moved the strut to support the sled's weight and then saw that a dark fluid was dripping slowly downward from where the sled had been. It must be a liquid metal, running down the face of the shield. Nikka tilted the strut forward, increasing the pressure.

After some moments the front face of the sled began to blur and run together. The twisted metal sagged at one point, then another. Slowly, agonizingly, a thin stream of liquid metal began to stream down the face of the invisible shield. A thin gray vapor puffed from it. It collected in spattered pools on the dust below. The sled tilted again— each time Nikka adjusted her balance, canted the strut to better advantage and kept up the pressure.

Through the film of perspiration on her faceplate she judged the shifting weight of the sled section and tried to compensate for it. Her air was getting thick and close. She had to struggle to focus her attention. Occasionally she glanced up at the crumpled copper dome above. An hour or two before, she had never seen it, never suspected she would find something so strange and alien in the midst of a selenographic survey. If she ever got out of this she was going to find out what that dome was and why there was a shield around it. Maybe its defense systems were acting sporadically without knowing what they were doing.

The sled tilted to the left again and she quickly brought the strut around to correct its balance. The liquid metal now ran in a steady stream; a vapor cloud formed above the sled. The twisted metal slowly gave, rippled and flowed away; in one quick rush the last obstacle to the oxygen bottles melted and was gone.

Nikka dropped the strut and frantically climbed over the sled. She twisted at the oxygen bottles but they refused to give. She leaned over, feeling the blood rush suddenly into her head, and struggled to focus her eyes. A pipe had lodged against them, pinning them in their mounts. She pushed futilely at the pipe and tried to dislodge it. It was stuck.

She scrambled back to the side of the sled and found the strut again. If she forced it against a rock—there, that was it—and tilted the sled, so; yes, it rose up again, presenting the pipe to the invisible shield. She wedged the strut into place and then worked her way around, near the shield so she could use her body weight against the sled and tilt it further over. She strained against it; the sled gave a bit and then the pipe came up against the shield. Her hands were wedged firmly against the pipe and she could see that her right upper wrist was being forced slowly against the shield. The weight of the sled shifted further and pinned her hand.

She had to decide—drop it, start all over, or let the heating work against both the pipe and her hand. She decided to let things be. The pipe was already hot; she could see vapor rising from it as the metal boiled away. She shifted her hand as best she could to relieve pressure, but she could not get it away.

She waited, adjusted her feet again, and studied the pipe intently. Its firm edges began to blur and run together. She could feel nothing in her right hand. Nikka tried to move her fingers and felt some faint sensation as reward.

She braced herself and pulled as strongly as she could against the pipe. It slowly gave, bending away from the invisible wall, and an oxygen bottle popped free of its mount under the pressure.

She was gasping. She grabbed the bottle as it rolled across the sled and forced open its safety warrant valve. There was no answering reading on the smashed dial. She held a finger against the nozzle and felt no pressure. The bottle was empty. Without thinking, not allowing herself to feel any despair, she reached for the next bottle.

The pipe still forced it against its mount, but she wormed it away and the bottle popped free. This was it, she thought. There were no other bottles not already ruptured. Nikka tripped it open and the meter registered positive. She swung it around to her back mount without hesitation, screwing the cluster joints into place automatically.

The gush of air washed over her in a cool steady stream. She collapsed across the sled section, unmindful of the invisible shield, the tangled metal that gouged her even through her suit, the glare of the sun above. The bottle was good for at least three hours. If she rested and kept still Alphonsus might get through.

Something tingled at her wrist and she lifted her right hand to look at it. Against the mottled colors of the plastiform there was a spreading red patch.

The tingling sharpened into a dull, throbbing pain. As she watched, the blood ran down her wrist to her elbow. She lay absolutely still. She was bleeding into free space. Her suit fitted firmly against her skin, so the rest of her body felt no immediate pressure drop.

As she watched, a small group of bubbles formed in the blood and burst slowly. A thin veil of vapor rose from her hand as the blood evaporated.

She stared at it, numb. Exposure to vacuum meant death, surely. How long did it take? A sudden pressure drop should force nitrogen narcosis. How long? A minute, two? She took a deep breath and the air was good. It cleared her mind and she looked up again at the dome. It seemed to loom over her.

Blood against metal. Life against machine. She lifted

her feet and rolled off the sled. Her ears popped; her body pressure was dropping. It was a hundred meters to the sled. In her repair kit there was tape, organic seals—something to close off the wound.

She took a step. The horizon shifted crazily and she almost lost her balance. A hundred meters, one step at a time. Concentrate on one, only one. A step at a time.

Her ears popped again but by now she was moving. Scarlet drops spattered into the dust. The pain had turned into a fierce burning lance.

She slipped and quickly regained her balance, and in the movement glanced back for an instant. The silent and impersonal dome squatted above her. In less than an hour it had done all this to her, brought her to the edge; perhaps it could do more. But she was in charge of her life at last. She wasn't going to simply let things happen to her. And she was damned if she was going to die now.

FOUR

Mr. Ichino put his lunch bag aside and laid down on the tufted grass that grew in patches here. He cocked his hands behind his head and peered up into the canopy made by the massive pepper tree that rustled softly in a light midday wind. Yellow dabs of sunlight speckled him and shifted and danced. Mr. Ichino felt an inner calm that came from having made a decision and put it behind him for good. He suspected Nigel's telephone call from Houston was designed to stop him from reaching that final point and tendering his resignation. But if that were so, Nigel was too late. Mr. Ichino's letter was now worming its way through channels, and in a month he would be free of the stretching tensions he felt in his work; and he could then walk a bit more lightly through the years that remained to him. Precisely how many years that might be was a minor issue, though the incidence of pollutive diseases these days did not seem reassuring. He had never smoked and had watched carefully what he ate, so that—

"Sorry I'm late," Nigel's voice came from above him.

Mr. Ichino blinked lazily and drifted up from his reflections. He nodded. Nigel sat beside him.

"Had a devil of a time getting in from the airport."

"I see."

"Snagged a bite on the way," Nigel said, indicating Mr. Ichino's paper bag. "Go ahead and eat."

He sat up and carefully unfolded the wrapping papers for his sandwich and vegetables. "Then you did not truly intend to have lunch here."

"No." Nigel glanced at him sheepishly. "When I called I had to have some reason to get you away from JPL. I didn't want to be overheard or have anyone wondering what we were talking about."

"And why is that?"

"Well, first off, your prediction was dead on."

"How?"

"NASA's going to keep the Marginis operation as in-house as possible. They'll use retreads like me—they have to. There aren't that many younger types who're trained for a variety of jobs."

"The cylinder cities are too specialized?"

"So NASA says."

"That seems a weak argument."

"These things aren't *relentlessly* logical. It's politics."

"The old guard."

"Of which I am, blessedly, one."

"You were successful?"

"Right." Nigel beamed. "I've got a lot of swotting up to do on computing interfaces and that rot."

"You know the material well."

"Not well enough, the specialists say."

"The specialists wish to go themselves," Mr. Ichino murmured lightly.

"Check. Quite a round of throat-slitting going on back there, I gather. Had to be careful not to slip on the blood."

"Yet you survived."

"I collected on a lot of old debts."

"The legacy of Mr. Evers."

Nigel grinned slyly.

"I have never truly approved of that, you know," Mr. Ichino said carefully.

"I'm not bursting with pride over it." Nigel's voice took on a hesitant, guarded note.

"We have all conspired, implicitly, to conceal the truth."

"I know." Nigel nodded with a touch of weariness. "But it was necessary."

"To protect NASA."

"That was the *first*-order effect. It's the *second*-order effect I was after—keeping NASA from getting itself gored by outsiders, so they'd have a free hand and a bigger budget. Money to explore the moon."

"And you have been proved correct."

"Well—" Nigel shrugged. "A lot of other people felt the same way. Finding that wreck was pure accident."

"The girl would not have been flying there had the lunar budget not been expanded."

"Yes. Nifty syllogism, eh? Logical to the last redeeming comma." Nigel chuckled with hollow mirth.

"You are not convinced."

"No."

"It has worked out well."

"I don't like lying. That's what it was, that's what it is. And you can't ever be sure, there's the rub. We *think* the politicians and the public and the New Sons and God knows who else, we *think* they'd be horrified to learn that Evers fired a bomb at the Snark, drove it away. And blew our chance. Hell, he could've been risking a war, for all he knew. And the backlash might've gutted NASA so that we'd never have got to search for the Marginis wreck. But we don't *know* that would have happened."

"One never does."

"Right. Right." Nigel fidgeted with his hands, flexed his legs into a new sitting position, stared moodily out at the knots of people lunching in the park. Mr. Ichino felt the unbalanced tensions in this man and knew Nigel had something more to say. He pointed toward the western horizon. "Look."

A noontime entertainment. A darting flitter craft was

beginning a cloud sculpture. The pilot chopped, pruned, extruded and sliced the taffy-white cumulus. A being emerged: serpentine tail, exaggerated fins, knotted balls of cotton for feet. The event was admirably timed—as the jitter shepherded the remaining puffs into place, to shape the snouted face, the eyes turned ominously dark. The eyeballs expanded and purpled and suddenly lightning forked between them, giving the alabaster dragon a surge of life. In a moment a wall of thunderheads split the beast in two, sullen clouds churning. Claps of thunder rolled over the park. Above Los Angeles a hazy rain began.

When Mr. Ichino looked again at Nigel he could perceive from his new posture that some of the tension had drained away. In its place was Nigel's familiar pensive enthusiasm.

"You learned more?" Mr. Ichino said.

"A lot," Nigel said absently. "Or rather, a lot of negative results."

"About Wasco?"

"Right. The Wasco Event, as it's called. Can't label it a bomb because nobody dropped it. It was buried about a kilometer in bedrock. Must've come near on thirty megatons. A pure fusion burn."

"I heard there was little radiation."

"Surprisingly little, yes. Cleaner than any bomb we know of."

"Not ours."

"No, certainly not ours. The cover story is that a lot of experts think it was a human accident, but I never met anybody who buys that. No, it was alien. Triggered by the Marginis wreck at the same time that survey craft one oh five was getting snuffed."

"But why? If the wreck thought it was being attacked . . ."

"Don't look for order in any of this. It's a malfunctioning ship, period. It nearly got that girl, then plugged one oh five and some standing order inside it made it touch off the Wasco explosion. The fusion device was there, probably stored in an arsenal or a base—look, it's all a balls-up, a pack of guesses. We don't know much for dead certain."

"Aren't the men working at the wreck in danger if they know so little of what caused this?"

"I suppose. Though the wreck has a blind side—the hill it's on masks most of the sky in that direction. That's how those three fellows got to the girl in time. They took a shuttle across Mare Crisium at low altitude, landed on the other face of the hill and simply walked around it. The wreck doesn't fire at anything on the ground, apparently. So they carried her out, in shock but repairable."

"They did not try to penetrate the invisible screen?"

"No point. Leastwise, not then. Some physicists have taken a knock at it since—they say it's high-frequency electromagnetic, with an incredible energy density—but they failed."

"Ah."

Nigel cast him a sidelong glance. Mr. Ichino smiled. Wind rippled the pepper tree and murmured through the park and brushed by them. "And where are you leading, Nigel?"

"That obvious, eh?" he said dryly.

"You know I am retiring. I cannot work on this riddle any longer."

"I know, but—"

"You do not think you can talk me out of it, I hope?"

"No, I wouldn't be that thick. But you're wrong about not taking part in all this."

Mr. Ichino wrinkled his brow. "How?"

Nigel hunched forward eagerly. "I read the prelim study on the Wasco crater. It's a mammoth hole and the land's scraped clean in a seventy-five-kilometer radius. But there's where the detective work ends. Whatever housed the fusion device is obliterated."

"Of course. There is nothing to be learned there. The only possible research must be done on the moon."

"Perhaps, perhaps," Nigel said lightly. "But suppose there *was* something stored at Wasco. Why? Easier to salt stuff away on the moon."

"Unless you were working on Earth."

"Exactly. Now, we haven't a clue how old that wreck is. It probably had some sort of camouflage going earlier so nobody picked it up on the Marginis search. But if the wreck has been there a longish time, there might have been ancient operations *on Earth*."

"And you wish to look for traces of that."

"Ah . . . yes."

"Interesting."

"It's simply a matter of where you retire."

Mr. Ichino gave him a puzzled glance.

"Well, say you spend some time this winter in the north woods." Nigel spread his hands and shrugged, his offhanded-and-reasonable gesture. "See if there is any history of unusual activities there."

"It sounds outlandish."

"This *is* outlandish."

"Do you honestly think this has any reasonable probability of success?"

"No. But we aren't *being* reasonable. We're guessing what's near on to unguessable."

"Nigel." Mr. Ichino leaned forward from his zazen position and touched Nigel's wrist. The other man's eyes were earnest, excited. There was something in this dynamic tension Mr. Ichino recognized in himself, as he had been decades before. Nigel was, after all, nine years his junior. "Nigel, I want to end with this. I do not feel at peace here."

"If you tried you might get to work on the Marginis wreck."

"No. Age, inexperience—no."

"Right then, granted. But you can make a contribution by running down this nagging bit—there may be something to be learned up there. Some trace, a fragment—I don't know."

"NASA will uncover it."

"Of that I'm by no means sure. And even if they did—can we trust them to pass it on? With the New Sons so powerful now?"

"I see." Mr. Ichino's face became absentmindedly blank, concentrated. He licked his lips. He gazed around the tranquil park where in the distance the air rippled with summer heat. He noticed that Nigel was wisely giving him time to let the words and arguments sink in. Still, Mr.

Ichino fretted uncertainly. He studied the people lounging and eating around them, dotted on the emerald lawn at the intervals decreed by privacy. Office workers, newspaper readers, derelicts, welfare stringers, the elderly, students, the dying, all sopping up the forgiving sun. Down the flagstone path came businessmen, always in pairs, always talking, earnestly not here and earnestly going someplace else. Commonplace. Ordinary. It felt so odd to speak of the alien in the midst of this relentlessly average world. He wondered if Nigel was more subtle than he seemed; something in this atmosphere made it possible for Mr. Ichino to change his mind.

"Very well," he said. "I will do it."

Nigel smiled and at the corners of his upturned mouth there seeped out a boundless, childlike glee; a seasoned anticipation; a regained momentum.

PART SIX 2018

One

Nigel squinted at the faxscreen memo:

> Site 7 (Mare Marginis vicinity)
> October 8, 2018
> TO: John Nichols, Alphonsus Base

OPERATION REPORT
Assignment of rotating shifts to interface with alien computer network.
Team One: Primary task: Inventory search utilizing direct readout.

J. Thomson—analysis
V. Sanges—electronic technician

Team Two: Primary task: Translation. Search for correspondences to terrestrial language forms (such as predicate—subject, repeating syllabic context, etc.) in visual ''language'' sequences.

A. Lewis—linguistics
D. Steiner—electronic technician

Team Three: Primary task: General exploratory search pattern. Communicate results to Teams One and Two.

N. Walmsley—computer and language systems specialist
N. Amajhi—electronic technician

Operations are to be conducted on a continuing round—the—clock schedule, seven days a week. Important results will be communicated directly to Alphonsus by tight laser beam, reflected off synchronous satellite C, established Sept. 23 (multichannel mode). We understand that Alphonsus will reserve one channel for direct link to Kardensky's Operations Study Group in Cambridge, for technical and library backup of needed information systems.

This communication signifies compliance with the directives of the Special Congressional Committee as formulated 8 September 2018.

(signed)
Jose Valiera
Coordinator

Nigel pursed his lips. Sandwiched into the jargon were some interesting points. Basic design of the group was the intensive core with a wide-based backup system, the model most favored by research theorists. The three teams were the intensive core. He could look forward to a grueling time of it; the pressure from Earthside would be intense.

Most importantly, he'd got the position opposite Nikka Amajhi.

Nigel nodded to himself and turned away from the faxscreen. The corridor was empty; indeed, the entire main section of Site Seven had appeared nearly deserted since he'd arrived four hours ago. Most of the staff was burrowing out more tunnels. Nigel padded down the tubular hall and consulted the site diagram. There, that was the working area. He found the right door in short order and went in.

A slender woman sat tinkering with electronics in a corner. The room was dim to allow maximum visibility at the two massive communications consoles that faced the far wall. Here was the nexus of the work to be done. The woman glanced up casually.

"Lost?"

"Conceivably."

"The nearest map is—oh. A moment. You are . . . ?"

"Nigel Walmsley."

"Oh! I am Nikka Amajhi."

"Oh." Absurdly, he felt uneasy.

"I understand we will work together."

She stood up and held out a hand. Her handshake was forthright, no-nonsense. In her face he found an air of half-concealment, as though more emotions bubbled beneath than made it to the surface.

"You're the inside worker."

"Can't you guess from my size?" She made a pretty bow, coming halfway up on her toes in the light gravity and balancing on one. Her jumpsuit fit snugly and something in the gesture, in the intersection of her hourglass waist and flaring hips, the artful grace of her, struck him as with a nearly physical blow. He licked his lips and found them dry.

"Oh. Yes. They wouldn't want a hulk such as me hauling his carcass through those tunnels."

"You couldn't. You're too big."

"And too old."

"You do not look it."

Nigel murmured something polite and shifted the topic to an oddment of electronics that caught his eye. He recognized the trouble they were having. Knowing someone else by reputation, because of something they've done, has its hazards. The work or deeds of another become a kind of halo around them, preventing a clear picture. At times the reputation-halo was useful—at parties, where it could be used to keep people at a distance, or as a special key into places one could otherwise not go. But the halo was false. His was Famous Astronaut or Brave Man. But he was no more that than he was *exclusively* any of the dozen or so other aspects of his life. It was the same with Nikka. He knew her as a quick-witted woman, already famous in the media. She was probably something entirely different from his preconceptions. Well, there was nothing for it: lacking subtlety, he would have to bull his way through.

"That was a brave thing you did," he said abruptly.

"What?" she said, mystified.

"When you were shot down."

"Oh. *That?*" She looked directly at him, vexed. "That

was simply staying alive. Doing what anybody would do. There was nothing brave to it."

Nigel nodded. "Now you can ask me what it was like to talk to the Snark."

Puzzlement crossed her face; her eyebrows curled downward. Then she exploded with mirth and slapped him on the arm. "I see! We must do this ritual sweeping out of the cobwebs! Of course." She laughed merrily and Nigel felt a weight lift from them. "Very well, I shall—do you say, bite?"

"Right. English isn't your—"

"Native tongue? No. I am Japanese."

"So I'd gathered." Yet, he thought, she has none of the shyness I expected her to have. But that, too, was part of the unwanted halo.

"And your friend the Snark?"

"It said our desk calculators will probably outlive us."

"So I've heard. But it always takes a Lewis Carroll to make a Snark."

"Yes," he said, sensing behind her laughing liquid eyes a more serious intent. "Yes, doesn't it?"

TWO

Mr. Ichino dozed a bit, late in the morning. He spent most of the day making the cabin fit to live, and as he worked he thought of Japan. Already the images of his visit were fading. He had gone, thinking to regain some fraction of himself, and instead had found a strange parody of the Japan his parents had known.

Perhaps it was the National Parks of Preservation. His ticket to the Osaka Park, despite its price, gained him admission only to the lesser portions. There the grasses and foliage were soot-stained, a dead gray. The great towering trees were withered and dusty. To call this a park seemed a deliberate joke and Mr. Ichino had become angry, only to be soothed by a young woman attendant and then sold another, vastly more expensive ticket. This unlocked a wrought-iron gate at one edge of the grimy forest, in time for the daily appearance of the trained nightingales. Their song burst over him suddenly as he crossed a tinkling stream. Fog shrouded the treetops in the ravine and Mr. Ichino stood ankle-deep in the chill waters, transfixed by the lilting merry song. Later, there came larks. Their trainers assembled in a shoreside clearing. The cages were lined up in a row and simultaneously the doors opened, releasing a fluttering cloud of the birds. They flew vertically upward, hovered below the lazy clouds and warbled for many minutes. The lesser larks returned early and occasionally flew into the wrong cage; the best lasted eighteen minutes aloft, and returned unerringly.

He could not afford many visits to the Parks, so he spent hours in the city streets. The pollution victims who begged on corners and in doorways disturbed him, but he could not take his eyes away. The healthy passed by these creatures without a thought, but Mr. Ichino often stood at a distance and studied them. He recalled his mother saying, in quite a different context, that the deaf seem as fools and the blind were like sages. Those who could scarcely hear, in their effort to catch what others were saying, would knit their brows, gape their mouths and goggle their eyes, cocking their heads this way and that. But the blind would sit calmly, immersed, their heads bowed a trifle as if in meditation, and thus appear quite thoughtful. He saw in them the half-closed merciful eyes of the Buddha images which were everywhere. They sang softly, *chiri-chiri-gan, chiri-gan*, and ate of parched soybeans and unpolished rice, and to Mr. Ichino they were the only natural people left in this jumbled island of sleazy cities. Amid the pressing crowds Mr. Ichino drifted, letting his time run out, and then came back to America. He had learned that he was not Japanese, and the truth was more than a little disturbing. He had felt a kinship with the remnants of the fragile natural world in Japan, but that was all. A strange logic, he knew: the deformed seemed more human than the abrasive, competitive, healthy ones. He had emptied his pockets into their alms bowls, and wished he could do more. But he could give only momentary shelter to these crippled beings. And in a truly natural world they would be quickly snuffed out. Yet they seemed, cowering there in twos and threes, brushed aside by the earnest business of the world, somehow in touch with a Japan he had once known—or dreamed of—and forever lost. Yes, an odd logic.

The Many Paths Commune, nestled into the Oregon hill country, had proved larger than he had expected. Mr. Ichino had already found five tumbled-down shacks, cabins or sheds within two hundred meters of the Commune Center. Since the property extended another kilometer along the riverbed, snaking down westward to the Willamette, there were probably many more.

With his own cabin made livable by late afternoon, he was moved to explore the Commune, to observe its ruins, its memories. Puffing slightly in the chill air, he angled down the face of a hill. The deer had worn their own vast system of interlocking trails. The hillside was wrinkled like a face, but the early fall rains had already blurred the paths again. Mr. Ichino had tried to follow the deer trails but it was hard to keep each step along the way from starting small landslides. He worked his way down toward the river. Half hidden ahead was a large Buckminster Fuller dome. Whatever had covered it was completely gone. The beams were of solid pine but the joint connections were rusted and decaying; several had broken away.

This must be the main cabin, where the patriarch lived with his reported two brides. The people in Dexter who rented him this site were full of stories about the rise and fall of the Many Paths, most of them rumors about sexual excesses committed by the patriarch. Mr. Ichino still didn't have a clear idea why Many Paths failed after twelve years. The most prevalent theory in Dexter was that the patriarch had one revelation too many about the nature of expansive love. There were rumors of a murder or two that split the commune into factions.

Mr. Ichino stopped to rest by the dome. A rusted stove and some scattered brown bottles lay in mute testimony to the impermanence of man's things. Further away there was a pile of lumber that might have been a woodshed and a lean-to outhouse near the river. The current was fast and deep here, rippling the cold water. The stream bed was filled with rocks and boulders of all sizes and a tributary creek exposed high layered walls of conglomerate soil. Some of the trees behind the dome had had to contort themselves to keep pace with the eroding bank; in places their exposed roots had grown huge for support.

Mr. Ichino studied it, hands in pockets. The cropland nearby was rocky and unforgiving. It seemed more likely to him that Many Paths failed more for economic reasons than for social ones. Apples and a few other crops took to this sort of land, but he couldn't conceive of making a living from farming here. The Dexter people said Many Paths had had a novelist or two and an artist living here, so probably that was their main income.

Mr. Ichino made a trail through rotted leaves and loam back toward the cabin where he lived. He smiled to himself. The Many Paths people were probably city kids—(kids? He reminded himself that they were probably his age by now)—full of idealism and guilt. He could vouch for the fact that they knew little of carpentry. The support beams in his cabin were inaccurately laid and the shank fasteners not driven in far enough. The rest of the cabin was adequate, though, so probably they had somebody reasonably competent around when it went up. It was the only building left that was livable, mostly because Dexter folk had repaired it over the years for a hunting lodge.

Mr. Ichino disliked hunting, though he was no vegetarian. He hated seeing things die. It was alarming enough to note what an enormous effect your mere passage had on the forest, an unknowing giant lumbering through web after fragile web of biological universes. Mr. Ichino studied the deep bed of moist leaves he was walking over. Every step he took crushed a world. Chop a log for firewood and suddenly a panicky swarm of ants is covering the ax blade. Move a stump in your way and a warm, slumbering black salamander finds himself in the middle of winter and scuttles off. Kick a rock and a frog jumps.

He stood by the creek listening and something caught his attention. A rustle of leaves, the faint snap of a twig.

Something was moving along the opposite bank of the creek. A thick stand of pine blocked his vision. Mr. Ichino could see a dark form flitting between the trees. It was difficult to judge distance and size in the quilted shadows but the form was certain: it was a man. Mr. Ichino brushed aside a frond to have a better look and instantly the shadow across the creek froze. Mr. Ichino held his breath. The dark form among the trees seemed to slowly fade away, with no detectable sound or sudden movement.

After a moment Mr. Ichino could not be sure he saw it any more at all. It seemed odd that a man could disappear so silently. For a moment Mr. Ichino wondered whether he had really seen anyone there or whether it was his own isolation playing tricks with his eyes. But no, he had heard the sound, of that he was sure.

Well, there was no point in worrying over shadows in the woods. He decided to put the matter out of his mind. But as he climbed upward toward his cabin some uneasiness remained and he unconsciously quickened his pace.

There were no signs of the Wasco blast here, two hundred kilometers from Wasco and deep in Oregon's coastal margin of woods. The local people still told stories of the disaster, of hardships, of relatives or friends incinerated—but Mr. Ichino was fairly sure most of it had only a slim factual backing. How could he find the traces Nigel thought were here, among folk so given to tall stories?

He had rummaged through town records, consulted the cramped little libraries, talked to the elderly ones who had grown up here. From the detail and hyperbole he had extracted no concrete ideas. What next? Winter would come soon, confining him. What could he do? Mr. Ichino shook his head and labored back to the cabin.

THREE

Nikka allowed the weak lunar gravity to pull her slowly down the narrow shaft. She held her arms above her head;

there was no room to keep them at her side. Her feet touched something solid. She felt around with her boots until she found a small hole in the side, off to an angle. She slowly twisted until she could sink into it up to her knees.

She looked up. The head of Victor Sanges was framed in the tunnel mouth six meters up. "You can start down now," she said. "Take it slowly. Don't be afraid of falling. There's enough friction with the walls to slow you down."

She wriggled into the narrow side channel and in a moment was stretched flat on her back, working her way forward by digging in her heels and pushing with her palms against the rough plastiform sheeting. Through the translucent material she could see the coppery metal of the ship itself. It had a dull sheen unlike any metal Nikka had ever seen. Apparently it puzzled the metallurgists as well, for they still could not name the alloy. Every few meters the walls had a curious semicircular series of whorls; otherwise this tube was featureless. Nikka passed one of the glowing white phosphors the maintenance crew had stamped into the plastiform when this section of the ship was pressurized. It was the only apparent lighting in the tube; perhaps the aliens had needed none. The tunnel narrowed here, following no obvious scheme. The ceiling brushed against the side of her face and she had a sudden unreasoning fear of the oppressive weight of the ship above her. Her breath was trapped, moist and warm, in front of her face and she could hear only her own amplified breathing.

"Sanges?" A muffled shout came in reply. She worked her way further on and felt her heels come free of the floor. Quickly she wriggled through and into a spherical room two meters in diameter. A chill seeped into her legs and arms as she waited for Sanges. She wore a thermal insulation suit and the air circulated well through the tunnel, but the ship around them was in equilibrium with the moon surface at minus 100 degrees Centigrade. During full lunar night things were much worse, but the thermal inertia of the ship helped take the bite of cold away. The engineers refused to heat the tunnel air, just as they refused to pressurize any more of the strange network of corridors than proved absolutely essential. No one knew what effect air would have on the ship as a whole—thus the plastiform walls.

Sanges slowly crawled out the small opening and into the cramped spherical room. "What is this?" he said. He was a small, wiry man with black hair and intense eyes. He spoke slowly in the ruby glow that enveloped them.

"The Bowl Room, for want of any other name," Nikka replied. "That red light comes directly out of the walls; the engineers don't know how it works. The lights are in a weak period right now. They get brighter later on and the whole cycle repeats with a period of 14.3 hours."

"Ah." Sanges pursed his lips.

"The natural assumption is that their day was 14.3 hours long." She smiled slightly. "But who knows? There isn't any other clue to back up that guess."

Sanges frowned. "But—a room, perfectly spherical. Nothing else on the wall. What could they use it for?"

"A free-fall handball court, that's *my* theory. Or a drying room for underwear. Maybe it's a shower, only we don't know how to turn on the water. There's a patch over there that looks odd"—she pointed to a burnished splotch above her head—"but with that plastiform over it I can't guess what it is."

"This room is so *small*. How could anyone—"

"Small for *who*? You and I are both here because we're practically midgets compared to the rest of the human race. Alphonsus imported you especially for the occasion, didn't they? I mean, you were on Earth when we found this. They shipped you up because you know electronics and you can wriggle through these tubes."

"Yes." The man nodded. "The first time I ever thought being small was an advantage."

Nikka pointed to a hole halfway up the wall. "This next part is the worst squeeze in the whole trip to the computer link. Come on."

She worked her way into the hole and down into a comparatively open length. Abruptly the passage narrowed. Nikka braced herself and got through by expelling her breath and pushing hard with her heels. There was an open space that temporarily eased the pressure, and then ahead she saw the walls narrowing again. She pushed and turned, trying to wedge herself flat on the tilted floor of the passage. Not only was it contracted here, but the tube was tilted at an awkward forty-five degrees.

She could hear the soft sounds of Sanges's struggles behind her. The tunnel seemed to press at her and she gave herself over to an endless series of pushes and wriggles, rhythmically turning forward against the steady hand of gravity and the clutching of the walls.

The passage became almost unbearably tight. She began to doubt that she had ever made it through this space before. The air seemed impossibly foul. The ship was a bruising presence, a massive vise squeezing the life from her. She stopped, thinking to rest, but she could not seem to get her breath. She knew there was only a little way further to go, and yet—

Something struck her boot. "Go. *Go on.*" Sanges's muffled voice was very close. There was a thread of panic in it.

"Easy, easy," Nikka said. If Sanges lost his nerve, they would be in a pretty fix. "We have to take our time."

"Hurry!"

Nikka braced her feet against the walls and pushed. Her arms were above her head and with one more lunge she found the edge of the passageway above. She pulled slowly up the incline and in a moment was free of the constriction.

Here it was almost possible to stand. The open bay was an ellipsoid with most space taken up by dark oval forms. They were seamless, apparently storage compartments of some kind with no obvious way of opening them. A short path marked off by tape wound between them. No one was to venture beyond that tape or try to investigate the dead alien machinery that lay further on. That would come later when men knew more of the ship and how it worked. Only the white phosphors in the plastiform illuminated this room; they cast long shadows near the walls that gave the room an oddly ominous cast. Though it was almost possible to stand upright, the shadowed mass of the ship seemed to close on her from every direction.

Sanges struggled up out of the tube and slowly got to his feet. "Why did you slow down back there?" he asked sharply.

"I didn't. You have to pace yourself."

"What does *that* mean?" he said quickly.

"Nothing." She looked at him appraisingly. "Claustrophobia is a funny thing and you have to keep your wits about you. You should try it some time the way I *first* went through—in an s-suit with oxygen gear and a helmet."

"It's a Godforsaken way to—"

"Precisely. God didn't make this ship and men didn't either. We have to learn to adapt to it. If strange things bother you that much, why did you volunteer for this job?"

Sanges clamped his lips together firmly and nodded.

After a moment Nikka turned and led the way down the narrow path to an immense black panel set into one wall. There were two man-made chairs in front of it. She indicated one for Sanges and sat in the other. Sanges looked at the imposing board, with its multiple layers of switches laid out before him. He turned his head and studied the dark forms further away. "How can we be sure the pressure is good here?" he said.

"The plastiform is tight," Nikka said as she turned on some extra phosphors. "The alien superstructure seems to be intact. The whole ship is modular, as far as we can tell. When it crashed, most of the other components were pulverized, but this one and two others—about forty percent of a hemisphere—remained intact. Some things in the other passages were thrown around, but otherwise this section is still in one piece."

Sanges studied the room and tapped nervously with his fingers on the console board.

"Careful of that! I'm turning on the console now and I don't want you hitting any of the switches." She pressed something like a vertically mounted paper clip and two blue lights flickered on the board before them. In a moment the black screen above the board changed subtly to a shade of light green.

"Where does the power come from?" Sanges said.

"We don't know. The generators must be in one of the

other modules but the engineers don't want to go too deeply into there until we understand more. The power is AC, about 370 hertz—though that varies, for some reason. We took this panel off and tried to trace the circuitry but it's extremely complicated. In another passageway the engineers found a huge vault of micro-sized electronic parts, apparently part of a memory bank. Most of the vault is thin films of magnetic materials on a substrate. The whole vault is at very low temperature, far colder than the surrounding ship."

"Superconducting memory elements?"

"We think so. That's not quite my line, so I haven't had much to do with it. There are small-scale oscillations in magnetic fields among the circuitry, so probably the fields switch the superconducting elements on and off. Makes a great switching circuit, as long as it operates in vacuum. The trouble is, we don't know where the cooling comes from. There is no circulating fluid; the walls are just *cold*."

Sanges nodded and studied the array of hundreds of switches before him. "So this computer is alive, or at least its memory is. After all this time. With most of the ship knocked out. Remarkable."

"That's why we are taking so much care with it. It's a direct link into whatever the aliens thought worth storing." She tried a few of the switches experimentally. "It appears the power is on. More often than not this board is dead. The ship's power is unstable. Okay, I am going to call Nigel Walmsley and start work. Watch what I do, but *don't* touch the board. Most of the procedure for starting is written up; I'll give you a copy at the end of this shift."

She took a throat microphone and yoke and fitted it over her head. "Nikka here."

"Walmsley, madam," a voice came from the speaker mounted on the wall. "If world security were at stake, would you spend the night with a man whose name you didn't even know?"

Nikka smiled. "But I know yours."

"True, true. Still, I could have it changed."

"Victor Sanges is here with me," Nikka murmured officially, before Nigel could say anything more. "He's the inside man for Team One."

"Charmed, I'm sure. See you in the mess later, Mr. Sanges. Nikka, I'm picking up the screen quite well but I'm getting bored with that same green haze all the time."

Sanges turned and looked at the television camera mounted over their heads. "Why don't you simply pick the signal up from the circuits that feed the screen?" he asked Nikka.

"We don't want to fool with the circuitry. Watch this, it's the same opening sequence I always use just to see if the memory array is unchanged."

Each switch had ten separate positions available; she altered several, glancing at the notebook at her elbow. A swirl of color formed and suddenly condensed into a pattern of symbols; curls, flashes, marks tantalizingly close to something like Persian script. In the middle of the display was a diagram involving triangles locked together in a confusing pattern.

"This was the first readout we ever got. Most sequences available don't seem to give any image at all. Maybe they are vacant or the readout goes to some other console. This picture by itself is useless, because we don't know what the writing means."

"Is there much of it?"

"No, and I don't think we could decipher very much even if we had a lot of printed symbols. The first Egyptologists couldn't unravel a *human* language even though they had thousands of tablets, until the Rosetta Stone was discovered. That's why we're concentrating on the pictures, not the script. Eventually maybe Team Three can make some sense out of the words, but for the moment we are stuck with looking at pictures and figuring out what they mean."

Nikka touched some of the switches and another image formed on the screen. This was also familiar. It showed two circles overlapping and a line bisecting the chord of one. An apparent caption ran down the side. "Lewis has tentatively identified one of those captioned squiggles as the word *line*. He compared with six or seven other figures in this sequence and so far that's the only guess he's been able to make. It's a painful process."

She ran quickly through a number of other punching sequences and stopped to admire the last. It was a magnificent shot of Earth as seen from somewhere further out from the sun. A thin crescent moon peeked around it; whorls and streaks of cloud obscured most of the dark land.

"The colors are wrong," Sanges said. "It's too red."

"It wasn't made for human eyes," Nikka said. "Nigel, I'm trying a new sequence. Alter 707B to 707C."

She said casually to Sanges, "If this setting is in some way fatal, if it fries me to this chair, at least somebody will know which sequence to avoid next time."

Sanges looked at her in surprise. She punched the sequence and got a few lines of symbols. "No help. Log, Nigel." The next was an array of dots. Then came a slightly altered array. As they watched, the groupings changed smoothly, rotating clockwise.

"Nigel, measure this. How fast is the rotation?"

There was a pause. "I make it a little over seven hours."

Nikka nodded. "Half the 14.3 hours that the lights in the Bowl Room take to cycle. Put that on special log."

Sanges made notes. Nikka showed him a color-coded array of dots which one of the astrophysicists had identified as a chart of the stars within thirty-three light years of the sun. The apparent size seemed to be related to their absolute magnitude. If the correspondence was exact, it meant a slight alteration in the Hertzsprung-Russell diagram and gave some support to one of the newer theories of stellar evolution. Sanges nodded without saying anything.

She tried some new sequences. More dots, then some lines of squiggles. A drawing of two intersecting spheres, no captions. Dots. Then what appeared to be a photograph of a machined tool, with captions. "Log, Nigel. What does it look like to you?"

"Abstract sculpture? A particularly sophisticated screwdriver? I don't know."

The next sequence showed the same tool from a different angle. Next, more dots, then—Nikka jerked back.

Feral dark eyes glared out at them. Something like a large rat with scales stood in the foreground, erect on hind

legs. Pink sand stretched to the horizon. Its forepaws held
something, perhaps food, in long nails.

"My," Nigel said. "Doesn't look at all friendly."

"No caption," Nikka said. "But it's the first life form
we've ever gotten. Better put this through to Kardensky."

"It is an *evil*-looking thing," Sanges said intensely. "I
do not know why God would make such a creature."

"Value judgment, tsk tsk," Nigel said. "Perhaps God
wasn't consulted, Mr. Sanges."

Nikka thumbed another sequence.

FOUR

Mr. Ichino stood at the small sink and slowly washed the
dishes after supper. The taste of the canned chili lingered in
his mouth. It was the real thing, no soybeans, and the only
luxury he allowed himself these days. He had never quite
got accustomed to handing someone a dollar bill when
buying a newspaper and not getting any change in return.
Even so, he would pay almost any amount to have an
occasional meal with real meat in it. It wasn't as though he
had any true objection to vegetarianism, though he had
never understood why it was better to kill plants than
animals. It was just that he liked the taste of meat.

The day's long twilight had begun to settle. He could
no longer make out the ridgeline several miles away. Dense
white clouds drifted in from oceanward; it would probably
snow tonight.

A flicker of motion caught his eye. The window over
the sink was partly fogged and he reached up to rub a clear
spot. A man came staggering out of the forest a hundred
meters away. He took a few agonized steps and collapsed
into a drift of snow.

Mr. Ichino wiped his hands and rushed to the door. He
slipped on his heavy lumber jacket as he went out the door
and blinked as the sudden cold reached his unprotected
face. The man was barely visible in the snow. Mr. Ichino
cleared the distance in a loping stride, puffing only slightly.
The work he had done around the cabin had cut away

pounds and sharpened his muscle tone. When Mr. Ichino reached the man it was clear why he had fallen. There was a burn in his side. It passed through layers of parka, a shirt and extra insulation. An area a foot wide was matted and blood-soaked. The man's ruddy face was clenched and tight. When Mr. Ichino touched near the wound the man groaned weakly and flinched.

It was obvious that nothing could be done until the man was inside. Mr. Ichino was surprised at how heavy he seemed, but got the arms over his own shoulder in a carry position and managed to stagger the distance back to the cabin without stumbling or pitching the body into the snow. He laid the man out on the floor and began to undress him. Stripping away the clothes was difficult because the harness of a backpack had knotted itself around the wound. Mr. Ichino used a knife to cut away the shirt and undershirt.

Cleaning, treating and bandaging the wound took more than an hour. Dirt and pine needles were caught among the blackened, flaky skin and as the heat of the cabin reached it the capillaries opened and began to bleed.

He lifted the man again and got him into the cabin's second bed. The man had never awakened. Mr. Ichino stood regarding the face, now relaxed, for long moments. He could not understand how anyone had sustained such an injury out here in the middle of unoccupied forest. What was more, why would anyone be here in the first place? Mr. Ichino's first thought was to try for the emergency call station fifteen kilometers away. The nearest fire road was only four kilometers and the Rangers might have it clear of snow by now. Mr. Ichino kept a small jeep there.

He began to dress for the walk. The going was mostly uphill and it would probably take several hours. As he made himself a thermos of coffee he glanced out the window and noticed that snow was falling again, this time in a hard swift wind that bowed the tops of the pines. A gust howled at the corners of the cabin.

At his age such a march was too great a risk. He hesitated for a moment and then decided to stay. Instead of making coffee he prepared beef broth for his patient and got the man to sip a few spoonfuls. Then he waited. He mused over the strange nature of the wound, almost like a cut in its clean outline. But it was a burn, undeniably, and a bad one. Perhaps a burning timber had fallen on him.

It was only after some time that he noticed the pack lying where he had cast it aside. It was a large one, with aluminum tubing, many pockets and insulation; quite expensive. The upper flap was unbuttoned. Sticking out the top, as though it had been jammed in hurriedly, was a gray metal tube.

Mr. Ichino fished it out. The tube thickened at its base and small metal arches like finger grips ran down the side. It was a meter long and had several extrusions like toggle switches.

He had never seen anything like it before. The lines of the thing seemed awkward. There was no telling what it was. Gingerly he put it back.

He checked his patient, who had apparently fallen into a deep sleep. Pulse was normal; the eyes betrayed nothing unusual. Mr. Ichino wished he had more medical supplies. He found a name stenciled on the pack, *Peter Graves*.

There didn't seem to be anything to do but wait. He made himself some coffee. Outside the storm grew worse.

FIVE

Sanges had another bad moment crawling out the tube at the end of the shift. Nikka had to push him through one of the narrow segments of the passage and the man glowered at her when they reached the lock. They suited up in silence and cycled out onto the flat, dusty floor of the moon. Two hundred meters away—not far from the spot where Nikka had crashed—a surface pressure lock of Site Seven was sunk into the lunar rock. More excavations were partially completed in the distance. Gradually a network of tubes was being punched by lasers, ten meters beneath the shielding rock and dust. Set that deep, the quarters suffered little variation in temperature between lunar day and night and even the incessant rain of particles from the solar wind made radiation levels only slightly higher than those on Earth.

Nigel Walmsley met them after they cycled through to the suiting bay. Sanges acknowledged Nigel's greeting but fell silent, his mind apparently still on the tunnels of the ship.

"Are you free for dinner in Paris tomorrow?" Nigel asked Nikka.

"Um."

"Well, perhaps some elegant preheated rations and processed water, then?"

Nikka looked at him speculatively and agreed. She went to shower while Nigel by unspoken convention wrote the debriefing report for the shift's findings. Aside from the large ratlike creature and the 7.15 hour rotation period, there was little remarkable to report. Progress was slow.

When Nikka emerged, followed by Sanges, all three made their way into the communicating corridor. It was a swirl of yellows and greens, spiraling around and splashing out onto the deck, making the corridor seem deceptively long. At the tucked-in cafeteria Nigel made a show of opening the door for Nikka with a certain self-satirizing grace. On a world where people were selected to minimize demands on the life-support system, he seemed tall and heavy.

They selected their rations from the few choices available, and on their way back to a table Nigel overheard a conversation between three men nearby. He listened for a moment and then interjected, "No, it was on *Revolver*."

The men looked up. "No, *Rubber Soul*," one of the men said.

"*Eleanor Rigby*?" another man said. "Second disc of the white album."

"No, neither," Nigel said. "You're both wrong. It was on *Revolver* and I have two hundred dollars which says so."

The other man looked at each other. "Well . . ." one of them began.

"I'll take that," another said.

"Fine, look it up and then check with me." Nigel turned and walked to where Nikka and Sanges sat listening.

"You're English, aren't you?" Sanges said.

"Of course."

"Isn't it a bit unfair to take advantage of someone else when you are arguing about a music group who were English themselves?" Sanges said.

"Probably." Nigel began eating.

"Anything new?" a voice came at his elbow. All three looked up. Jose Valiera stood smiling.

"Ah, Dr. Valiera," Nigel said. "Please sit."

Valiera accepted the invitation and smiled at the other two. "I'm afraid I haven't had the time to read your debriefing report."

"There wasn't very much in it," Nikka said. "But there is something I want to ask you. Is there any real chance of our getting a supplementary appropriation so we can get more people here?"

"Your guess is as good as mine," Valiera said warmly. "But my guess is no. After all, we got a nice large shot of money just two months ago."

"But that was simply based on what we knew when the shield went down," Nigel interjected. "Since then the engineers have uncovered a wealth of things that need investigation." He wrinkled his brow. "Seems silly not to give us more."

"We've also uncovered the computer link," Nikka pointed out. "Surely that's going to cause a splash."

Valiera looked uncomfortable. "It will when there are results. You should realize not all of what we discover is immediately released to the press, and some portions even the Congress does not know about."

"Why's that?" Nigel said.

"It has been decided that there are good sociometric reasons not to spread results from here too rapidly, however interesting they may seem. Some advisors of the Congress feel the impact might be severe if something truly radical is uncovered."

"But that's precisely why we're *here*. To uncover something radical. That is, radical in the sense of fundamentals," Nigel said, looking intently at Valiera.

"No, I believe I see the point," Sanges said. "The

entire issue of extraterrestrial life and intelligences superior
to ours is emotionally loaded. It must be treated with
delicacy."

"What good is 'delicacy' going to do us if we can't get
the money to pursue our research?" Nikka said quickly.

"This craft has been lying here for at least half a million
years, according to the estimates from solar wind abrasions
of the outer skin," Valiera said patiently. "I believe it will
not vanish overnight, and we do not need an army of people
here to swarm all over it."

"After all, we are going to have three shifts a day to get
full use of the computer module," Sanges said reasonably,
spreading his hands. "We are already exploiting the ship as
much as we can."

"Nobody has done more than glance at many of the
passages," Nikka said.

Sanges scowled and said ponderously, "Our First
Bishop spoke only today about the wreck. He, too, advises
a path of moderation. It was not pointful to make dis-
coveries without understanding their full implication."

Nigel made a crooked grin. "Sorry, that doesn't quite
count as an argument with me."

"I am sorry you have not found it within yourself to
open your eyes, Mr. Walmsley," Sanges said.

"Ah, yes. I am a proponent of Cartesian dualism and
therefore not to be trusted." Nigel grinned. "I've never
really seen how you can be a scientist or a technician and
believe all that ugly business about demons and the dead
rising." He wondered if they would catch the reference to
Alexandria.

Valiera said mildly, "You must understand, Mr. Sanges
is not a member of the more fundamentalist wing of the
New Sons. I'm sure his beliefs are much more sophisticated."

Nigel grunted. He suppressed the impulse to bait
them further.

"It has always amazed me that the New Sons were able
to incorporate so many different views within one religion,"
Nikka said. "It would almost seem that they were more

interested in the ordering effect of religion than any particular doctrine." She smiled diplomatically.

"Yes, that's really the point, you see," Nigel said. "They don't just get together to exchange theological gossip. They like to change society around to fit their beliefs."

Sanges said intently, "We are spreading the great love of God, the Force that drives the world."

"Look, it's not love that makes the world go round, it's inertia," Nigel said in clipped tones. "And all this mellow *merde* about you fellows getting two hours off to pray every day, and special holidays—"

"Religious measures dictated by our own faith."

"Yes, strangely popular, too, aren't they?" Nigel said.

"What do you mean?" Sanges said.

"Just this. Most people have had a damned hard time of it these last decades. A lot have died, we aren't rich anymore, none of us, and we've had to work like billy-hell to keep our necks above water. Hard times breed bad religions—it's a law of history. Even people who don't go in for that sort of thing can recognize a good dodge when they see it. If they become New Sons they get extra hours off work, little privileges, some political influence."

Sanges clenched his fists. "You are making the most *base* and vile—"

Valiera broke in. "I think you gentlemen should calm down and—"

"Yes, right, I think so," Nigel said. He got to his feet. "Coming along, Nikka?"

In the corridor outside Nigel allowed his face to twist into a grimace and he smacked a fist into his palm. "Sorry about that," he said. "I tend to let things run away with me that way."

Nikka smiled and patted his arm. "It is often an easy thing to do. The New Sons are not exactly the most tolerant people, either. But I must say your view of them is rather cynical, isn't it?"

"Cynical? 'Cynic' is a word invented by optimists to criticize realists."

"It didn't seem to me you were being wholly realistic."

He opened the corridor door for her in an exaggeratedly polite fashion. "I wish it were so. It's no accident that Sanges is a full-dress New Son and was assigned to this site. Valiera didn't say so, but the rumors have it that the only reason we got money through Congress this time was by a high-level deal with the New Sons faction. They held out for a large representation of their own people—scientists and technicians, yes, but New Sons, too—before they would turn over their votes."

Nikka looked shocked. "I hadn't heard that. Are there a lot of New Sons here? I haven't been paying attention to the new people."

"I've noticed, being one of them." He smiled. "I've nosed about a bit myself and I think quite a few of our comrades are New Sons. Not all admit it or show it like Sanges, but they are."

Nikka sighed. "Well, I hope Valiera can keep them in line."

"Yes, I hope he can," Nigel said solemnly. "I certainly hope he can."

Later he lounged alone in his box of a room, unable to sleep. The work here absorbed him but so far gave precious little back. He kept in close touch with Kardensky's group, who were carrying on along much the same lines as Ichino had started—cross-correlations with the Snark's conversations, systemic analysis of whatever the teams could extract from the wreck, and so on. So far it resembled, for Nigel, some awful childhood dream of swimming through mud: frantic struggles only slowed you, made you sink faster.

He shrugged. His attention seemed to focus more these days on Nikka than the gritty problems of decoding.

And why was that? he wondered. It was dimwitted, really. He made small jokes, kept up a line of patter, and afterward felt slightly ridiculous.

He drummed fingers on his knee. It was almost as though—yes. With a shock he realized that he had forgotten how to deal with women from scratch, from the beginning. Closeness with Alexandria—and yes, Shirley, for a time—had robbed him of it.

Well, he would simply have to relearn the tricks. For

Nikka, the trouble might easily be worthwhile. He didn't subscribe to the Theory of Types—that men were drawn to the same categories of physical attributes, or personality traits, again and again—because Nikka resembled Alexandria not at all; still, they shared a certain directness, an unflinching devotion to what *was* rather than what might be hoped. And physically, Nikka's delicious contained energy, her implied sensuality—

He shook his head. Enough of that. He despaired of analysis; the real world was always more fine-grained than opinions about it. Life was discrete; nonlinear; a nonzero-sum game; noncommutative; clearly irreversible; and events multiplied, compressed, rather than merely adding. The past filtered the present. He saw Nikka through the lens of Alexandria—and in truth, he would have it no other way. To wish otherwise was to rob him of his past. Now, together, he and Nikka studied this wreck and the communications lines between here and Kardensky's staff buzzed with analogies, comparisons. They studied the wreck as though the builders were vaguely, conveniently human. An illusion, certainly. And he'd sent Ichino off on a flight of fancy, really, a near-certain dead end. He missed the man; talking with him, going off on hikes, he'd felt some warming connection. Was the loss of that why—despite his being where he wanted to be, working on the only thing that mattered any more—he felt these collapsing moments of depression?

Nigel snorted, exasperated with himself, and rolled over to seek sleep.

SIX

Mr. Ichino woke with a start; he had fallen asleep sitting up.

The fire smoked and sputtered. He stirred the smoldering embers and tossed on new wood. In a few moments the cabin had lost its slight chill. He stood, massaging a sore muscle in his back, and watched the flames dance.

Graves was still unconscious, his breathing regular. The wound had stopped bleeding and the bulky compresses around it seemed secure. Mr. Ichino knew he would not quickly fall asleep again; he made himself a mixture of hot water, lemon juice, sugar and rum and turned on his radio. In the burr of static he eventually found the twenty-four-hour Portland in-depth news station.

As his rocking chair creaked rhythmically, the radio made a low murmur and the wind wailed hollowly outside. Against this calming background the news seemed discordant. The war was still going on in Africa and another country had come in on the side of the Constructionists. The government policy on DNA alterations in laboratory babies was under heavy attack by the New Sons. Most commentators agreed, though, that simple body modification was inevitable; the controversy had now shifted to the issue of intelligence and special talents. There were suspicions that a second major dieback was beginning in Pakistan. The water scarcity in Europe was getting critical.

Finally there came some news about the Mare Marginis wreck. The emergency photographic survey of the moon was complete. There was no sign of other crashed vehicles. This by itself did not mean very much, though, because the Marginis ship's force screen had been observed to alter color three times before it was finally penetrated. Scientists guessed this was a remnant of some defense mechanism whereby the ship's screen absorbed almost all light, making it appear dark. If the ship was in flight it would be hard to see optically against the background of space. Apparently, until men ruptured it the screen functioned most of the time and was slowly running down. If other wrecks existed on the moon, their screens might still be intact, in which case it would be very hard to see them from orbit. An extensive search for recurring dark patterns, which might formerly have been assumed to be shadows, was underway.

Mr. Ichino listened to a few more news items and then switched the radio off. The point about the screen was interesting, but he had expected more by this time. Men were inside the ship now and there should be some results. But nothing came through the news or from Nigel. Perhaps they were simply being very cautious in their exploration of the wreck. The ship's defense system had shut on and off in an unpredictable manner; current thinking seemed to be that whatever had shot down the two survey craft had awakened recently, since otherwise it would have downed the Apollo missions long ago. With the screen penetrated, perhaps all the other defense systems were dead, too. But it would be foolish not to be cautious.

Mr. Ichino turned from the radio, checked Graves again and then looked at the man's pack once more. He put the gray metal tube aside and began taking out the other items—dehydrated food, maps, clothing, simple tools, a writing case and some paper. At the very bottom of the pack were several rolls of microfilm and a compact viewer. Mr. Ichino felt a slight embarrassment, as though reading another's personal mail.

Well, there was good reason to look. Graves might be a diabetic, or have some other special medical problem. Mr. Ichino put the microfilm through his own large wall viewer, made another drink and began reading.

His credit cards, passes and serial biography all attested to Peter Graves's wealth. He had made his fortune early in land speculation, before the government regulated it, and retired. For the last ten years he had pursued a strange hobby: trapping the unusual, finding the elusive. He used his money to look for lost Inca trails, search for sea monsters, uncover Mayan cities. Graves carried a portable library about himself. Reasonable; it probably helped him with uncooperative officials. Most of the film concerned something else altogether. There were clippings and notes from as far back as the nineteenth century. Mr. Ichino studied them and pieced together a history.

Graves had become interested in the Wasco explosion because it was an immediate mystery. He never believed the murky official explanation. So, with his bias for the unusual, he carried out an extensive background study of the entire north woods. His correspondence showed that Graves had launched a terribly expensive surveillance program.

Mr. Ichino felt a prickly sensation of surprise. Graves had done precisely what Nigel wanted, and what NASA night eventually get around to once the Marginis wreck was understood. Graves had searched for whatever connection surfaced, whatever unlikely intersection of legend and fact was possible. He had employed low-flying planes with silent engines to search for anything or anyone fleeing the blast area. He had run down the tag ends of details, studied old maps, employed thinktank sessions to produce outlandish ideas.

And once he'd adopted an hypothesis, Graves hired guides and went in search of the elusive creature he suspected was a connection to the Wasco event . . .

The Salish Indians called it Sasquatch. The Hudson's Bay Company report of 1864 gave evidence of hundreds of sightings. The loggers and trappers who moved into the Pacific Northwest knew it mainly by its tracks and thus it gained a new name: Bigfoot.

Men saw it throughout the north woods of the United States and Canada. In the nineteenth century over a dozen murders were attributed to it, most of them involving armed hunters. In 1890 two guards posted to watch a mining camp on the Oregon-California border were found dead; they had been crushed, slammed to the ground.

All this led nowhere until 1967, when an amateur investigator made color motion pictures of a Bigfoot at a range of less than fifty yards. It was huge. It stood seven feet tall and walked erect, moving smoothly and almost disdainfully away from the camera. It turned once to look back at the photographer, and revealed two large breasts. A thick black fur covered it everywhere except near the cleft of bones that surrounded the eyes. Scientific opinion was divided on the authenticity of the film. But a few anthropologists and biologists ventured theories . . .

For both social and economic reasons, the Pacific Northwest was relatively sparsely settled. Thick forests cloaking the rough western slopes of the Rockies could hide a hundred armies. Bacteria and scavengers on the forest floor digest or scatter bones or even artifacts left behind; the remains of logging projects do not last more than a decade. If Bigfoot built no homes, used no tools, he could escape detection. Even a large, shy primate would be only a melting shadow in the thick woods.

Most animals have learned to run, to hide, rather than fight—and their teacher has been man. Several times over the last million years the glaciers have retreated and advanced in a slow, ponderous cycle. As water became trapped in expanding glaciers the seas fell, exposing a great land bridge connecting Alaska and northern Asia. Across these chill wastes from Asia came mammoth, mastodons, bison and finally man himself. Man has known many forms between the apes and Neanderthal. As man himself pushed out from the cradle of Africa he drove these earlier forms before him. Peking or Java man may have been part of this outward expansion. Perhaps Bigfoot was pushed into other climates by this competition. They crossed the great land bridge during one glacial cycle, found the New World and settled there. But men followed and eventually the two came into conflict for the best land. Man, the smarter and the better armed, won out and drove the Bigfoot back into the forest. Perhaps the Sasquatch legend came from those ancient encounters.

Scientific expeditions in the 1970s and '80s failed to find solid evidence of Bigfoot. There were indirect clues: crude shelters made of fallen branches, footprints and paths, dung which showed a diet of small rodents, insects and berries. Without a capture the cause gradually lost its believers. Population pressure opened cities in northern California and Washington until one by one the areas where Bigfoot had been seen shrank away.

Among Graves's papers was an extensive map of southern Oregon around Drews Reservoir. It was covered with small arrows and signs in pencil detailing an erratic path northward. Mr. Ichino traced the path until it abruptly stopped about twenty kilometers from his cabin. It ended in a completely wild stretch of country, hilly and thick with pine, one of the most isolated spots still remaining in Oregon. There were other papers, a contract with two guides, some indecipherable notes.

Mr. Ichino looked up from the wall viewer, rubbing his eyes.

Something thumped against the wall of the cabin as if brushing by.

Mr. Ichino reached the window in time to see a shadow fade into the deeper black of the trees at the edge of the clearing. It was hard to see; flurries of snow obscured the distance. In the fading light it was easy to be mistaken.

Still, the sound had not been his imagination. It might have been a load of snow falling from a high pine branch, but Mr. Ichino thought not.

SEVEN

After evening meal Nigel stood in the tubeway, flipping a coin absently, wondering what to do in his few hours of free time. Study up, he thought, most probably. He flipped the coin again, glanced at it. It was a British one-pence, a lucky piece. An imperfection caught his eye. Next to the date—1992—was a flaw, a blister of metal about a tenth of a millimeter across. It appeared on the back face, which depicted the swirling spiral of the galaxy overlaid with the British lion—a passing tribute to the short-lived Euro-American space ventures. Nigel made a quick estimate: the disk of the galaxy was about 100,000 light years in diameter, so—the result surprised him. The small blister, on the scale of the galaxy, represented a sphere one thousand light years across. Within that speck would drift over a million stars. He stared at the tiny imperfection. He had known the numbers all along, sure enough, but to see it this way was another matter. A thousand-light-year volume around the earth was a vast expanse, well beyond the power of a man to visualize in concrete terms. To see it represented as a fleck in the galaxy suddenly filled Nigel with a sense of what the Snark must see, and what they were dealing with here. Civilizations like grains of sand. Vast corridors of space and time. He flipped the coin, his hands feeling oddly chilled.

"Ah—hello, there."

Nigel looked around to find Sanges at his elbow. "Hello."

"The Coordinator sent me to ask you over to his office."

"Right. Well, just a minute. Got to shake hands with the wife's best friend."

"Ah . . . I didn't know you were married."

"I'm not. Means I've got to piss."

"Oh. That's amusing."

Sanges was waiting when Nigel came out of the men's room, which struck him as odd: why did he need an escort to find Valiera's office?

"Did you see the new directives on staff?" Sanges said conversationally as they strode along.

"Wouldn't take the time to blow my nose on 'em."

"You should. I mean, you should read them. It looks as if we aren't going to get any additional staff."

Nigel stopped, looked at Sanges in surprise, then continued walking. "Bloody stupid."

"Probably so, but we have to live with it."

"The news doesn't seem to bother you very much."

Sanges smiled. "No, it doesn't. I think we should go very slowly in our work. Care will be repaid."

Nigel glanced at him and said nothing. They reached Valiera's office and Sanges gestured him in, while remaining outside himself. Valiera was waiting for him and began with a series of good-humored questions about Nigel's accommodations, the work routine, scheduling and the quality of food. Nigel was grateful that the moon, with no atmosphere, afforded Valiera no chance to go on about the weather. Then, abruptly, Valiera smiled warmly and murmured, "But the hardest aspect of my job, Nigel, is going to be you."

Nigel raised his eyebrows. "Me?" he said innocently.

"You're revered. And you seem to have a special talent for surviving, even when the men above you in the organization do not. It will be difficult for me to administer with a famous man under me."

"Then don't."

"I don't follow."

"Let events develop. Don't manage them."

"That's impossible."

"Why?"

"I'm sure you understand."

"'Fraid not."

"I am under pressure," Valiera said carefully. "Others want this job. If I don't get results—"

"Yes, yes, I fathom all that." Nigel hunched forward. "Everybody wants results, like cans coming off the end of a production line. The Achilles heel of treating research like that is that you can't program it from the top down."

"There are some parameters—"

"Sucks to parameters. We haven't a clue what this caved-in pile of litter *is* yet."

"Granted. I'm here to be sure we find out."

"Only that's not the way to do it. Look, I know how governments run. Promise them a timetable and they're yours. They don't want it right, they want it Friday."

Valiera clasped his hands together and nodded sagely. "There's nothing wrong with schedules, though."

"I'm not at all bloody sure."

"Why not?"

"Because"—he threw up his hands, exasperated—"if you want it done by the weekend, that already assumes there will *be* a weekend, in those terms—that there'll still be business as usual. But if you're after something that really alters things, then it doesn't just explain and clarify, it *changes* the world."

"I see."

"And that's what you can't program, you see."

"Yes."

Nigel realized that he was breathing a bit quickly and Valiera was staring at him oddly, head tilted to the side.

"You speak like a visionary, Nigel. Not a scientist."

"Well. I suppose." Nigel rummaged about for words, embarrassed. "Never been one for definitions, myself," he said softly as he rose to go.

EIGHT

Nigel squinted at the screen before him and said into his throat microphone, "Afraid I don't understand it either. Looks like another one of those meaningless arrays of dots to me."

"Meaningless to us, yes." Nikka's voice blossomed in his ear, tinny and distant.

"All right then, I'll put it in passive log." Nigel punched a few command buttons. "While you were cycling that, I got a reply from Kardensky's group. Remember the rat? Well, it's not a rat or any other kind of rodent we know of, it's apparently not standing on Earth and it's probably at least a meter tall, judging from the apparent bone structure in its ankles."

"Oh! Then it's our first picture of extraterrestrial life," Nikka said, excited.

"Quite so. Kardensky has forwarded it on to the special committee of the NSF for publication."

"Shouldn't we go through Coordinator Valiera?" There was a note of concern in her voice.

"Needn't worry about that, luv. I'm sure the New Sons have a tight rein on what comes out of the NSF. They needn't rely on Valiera."

"Valiera isn't a New Son," Nikka said testily. "I'm sure he's impartial."

"I didn't say he was a New Son, but on the other hand I don't think it's wise to assume he isn't. 'I frame no hypotheses,' as Newton said. Anyway, look, we should be getting on with it."

Nigel shifted uncomfortably in his chair and turned down the illumination above his console. The small, cramped room was about five degrees colder than he liked. Site Seven had been thrown up rather quickly and some of the niceties, such as adequate insulation and a good air circulating system, had been neglected.

He studied his notes for several moments. "Right, then, let's try sequence 8COOE." He made a notation. The difficulty of prospecting for information in a totally unfamiliar computer bank was that you had no way of knowing how the information was catalogued. Intuition told him that the first few settings on the alien console should be more general than later settings, just as if it were a number setting in ordinary Arabic notation. The rub there was that even in terrestrial languages the logical left-to-right sequence was no more common than a right-to-left sequence or up-to-down or any other frame one could imagine. The aliens might not even have used a positional notation at all.

So far they had been reasonably lucky. Occasionally, similar settings on the console yielded images on the screen that had some relationship. There were the common arrays of dots, including those that moved. The sequences which called these forth had some of the same prefixes. Perhaps this indicated a positional notation, and perhaps it was merely lucky chance. So far he had asked Nikka to use only a portion of the switches available on the console. Some of them certainly would not be simple catalogue numbers for information retrieval. Some must represent command modes. The third switch from the right in the eighteenth tier, for example, had two fixed positions. Did one mean "off" and the other "on"? Was one "file this data" or "destroy it"? If he and Nikka kept to a small area of the board, perhaps they would not encounter too many command modes before they got some information straight. They didn't want to run the risk of turning off the computer entirely by proceeding at random through all the switches.

Nigel studied the screen for a moment. An image flickered on. It seemed to show a dark red image of a passageway in the ship. There was a bend in the corridor visible and as he watched some of the Persian-like script appeared on the screen, pulsed from yellow to blue and then disappeared. He waited and the pattern repeated.

"Mysterious," he said.

"I don't believe I've seen that passageway," Nikka said.

"This must be something like the three photos Team One reported from the last shift. They are from unrecognizable parts of the ship."

"We should check with the engineers," Nikka said. "But my guess would be that all these show part of the ship that was pulverized on landing."

Nigel pursed his lips. "You know, it just occurred to me that we can deduce something from the fact that this script goes on and off with a period of several seconds. Our friends the aliens must have been able to resolve time patterns faster than a second or so, if they could read this."

"Any animal can do that."

"Just so. But whoever built this ship might not be just any animal. For example, the little switches on the console imply something finger-sized to manipulate with. True enough, we know animals must be able to see things moving faster than on a one-second time scale, or else they'll be overrun and gobbled up pretty quickly. It's interesting to note the aliens were similar to us in at least that way. Anyway, let's go on. I'll log that"—he punched a few buttons—"for Team One to check."

He chose a few sequences which differed from earlier ones only in the last "digit" and the screen showed no response at all. "Are you sure that switch is still working?" Nigel asked.

"As far as I can tell. The meters here show no loss of power."

"Very well. Try this." He read off a number.

This time the screen immediately sprang to life: a confused red jumble of nearly circular objects.

A long black line traced across the screen. It penetrated one of the odd-shaped blobs; there were small details of dark shading inside this blob alone. The others did not show it.

"Odd," Nigel said. "Looks to me like a photomicrograph. Reminds me of something from my student days, biology laboratory or something. I'll send it to Kardensky."

He dialed for the direct line through Site Seven to Alphonsus, obtained a confirmation and transmitted directly on the links to Earth. This took several minutes. Simultaneously the signal was logged into tape storage at Site Seven; Alphonsus served only as a communication vertex. Nigel made some notes and gave Nikka another sequence.

"Hey!" Nikka's voice made him look up from his writing. On the screen something in a slick, rubbery suit stood against a backdrop of low ferns. It did not appear to have legs, but rather a semicircular base. There were two arms and some blunt protrusions below them, with a helmet on top opaqued partially. Through it a vague outline of a head could be seen. Nigel had a conviction that the site was Earth. The pattern of the fronds was simple and somehow familiar.

The figure in the suit showed no more detail, but he was not what attracted Nigel's attention. There was something else, taller and obviously not wearing a suit. It was covered with thick dark fur and stood partially concealed in the ferns. It held something like a large rock in massive, stubby hands.

Nikka and Nigel spoke about it for several moments. The suited figure seemed strange, as though it violated the way a creature should stand upright against gravity. But the tall creature, heavy and hairy and threatening, made Nigel feel a vague unease.

Try as he might, he could not shake the conviction that it was human.

Nigel had opened his mouth to say something more when an excited male voice spoke into the circuit. "Everyone in the ship, out! Engineering has just reported an arc discharge in passage eleven. There are power surges registered on another level. We're afraid it might be a revival of the defense system. Evacuate at once."

"Better get out, old girl," Nigel said ineffectually. He was safe, buried beneath meters of lunar dust near the living quarters. Nikka agreed and broke the circuit.

Nigel sat for long moments looking at the creature on the screen. It was partially turned away, one leg slightly raised. Somehow, though, he had the sensation that it was looking directly at him.

NINE

Peter Graves's fever abated through the day and he awoke in the night. He babbled at first and Mr. Ichino fed him a broth heavy with the warm tang of brandy. It seemed to give the man energy.

Graves stared at the ceiling, not seeming to know where he was, and rambled without making sense. After a few minutes he suddenly blinked and focused on Mr. Ichino's weathered face for the first time.

"I had 'em, you see?" he muttered imploringly. "They were *that* close. I could have *touched* 'em, almost. Too quiet, though, even with that singing they were doing. Couldn't run the camera. Makes a clicking sound."

"Fine," Mr. Ichino said. "Don't roll onto your side."

"Yeah, that," Graves murmured, staring mechanically down at his shirt. "The big one did that. Bastard. Thought he'd never drop. The guide and me kept pumpin' the slugs into him and that flamethrower they had was goin' off in all directions. Orange. Blew the guide right over and he didn't get up. The flash lit up every . . . every . . ."

Graves's dry, rasping voice trailed off. The sedatives in the broth were taking effect. In a moment the man breathed easily. When he was sure Graves was asleep Mr. Ichino pulled on his coat and went outside. The snow was at least a meter deep now, a white blanket that dulled the usually sharp outline of horizon on the opposite hill. Flakes fell in the soft silence, stirred by the breeze. It was impossible to reach the road.

Mr. Ichino struggled across the clearing, glad of the exercise. Perhaps it wasn't necessary to get help now. The worst was probably over. If infection didn't set in—with all the antibiotics he had, it wasn't likely—Graves could recover without professional care.

He wondered what all the babble had meant. "The big one" might be anybody. Something had made the wound, for certain, but Mr. Ichino knew of no weapon that could cause that large a burn, not even a laser.

Mr. Ichino shook his head to clear it, black curls falling into his eyes. He would have to cut his hair soon. One forgot things like that, living away from people.

He looked upward and found Orion immediately. He could just barely make out the diffuse patch of light that was the great nebula. Across the dark bowl of the sky he found Andromeda. It had always seemed incredible to him that in one glance he could see three hundred billion stars, an entire galaxy that seemed a sprinkle of light far fainter than the adjacent stars. Stars like grains of sand, infinite and immortal.

In the face of such infinity, why did man's attempts at worship seem so comic? Or horrible.

Tonight on the news there had been a report about one

of the tattooed New Sons who had finally covered his entire body with design work. The plan had been that the work would be done slowly, so that the last lines would be completed near the time of the man's death. But this one had hurried the job and then cut his throat, willing his body to be skinned, tanned and presented in a frame to the Bishop as a sacrifice to the truth of the New Revelation.

Mr. Ichino shuddered and turned back to the cabin. A man was standing with his back toward Mr. Ichino, looking through the cabin window. Mr. Ichino stepped forward. Amid the falling snow it was hard to see him clearly, but the man was big and did not move. He seemed bent over in order to see something on the side wall of the cabin. Yes, that would be Graves. The bed was not on a direct line of sight through the window.

Mr. Ichino came closer and something must have given him away. The man turned swiftly, saw him and moved with startling speed around the cabin corner. The figure moved smoothly despite the thick drifted snow. In an instant he had melted into the shadows.

When Mr. Ichino reached the ground outside the window the snow had already begun to obscure the man's tracks. If they were boot marks they were of an odd sort—strangely shaped, unusually deep and at least sixty centimeters long.

Mr. Ichino followed them a way into the woods and then gave up. The man could easily get away in the blackness. Mr. Ichino shivered and went back to the cabin.

TEN

"When did the pressure fail?" Nigel said into his throat microphone. Nikka had just resumed contact.

"About forty minutes ago. I got a warning from Engineering that the plastiform had ruptured while they were rigging emergency power in the passage above this one. There was enough time, so I crawled out to the lock, got some air bottles and dragged them back in here. There's

an emergency pressure seat under the console but somebody forgot to issue bottles for it."

"Are you in the seat now?"

"No, they found the leak. Pressure is rising again."

Nigel shook his head and then realized she couldn't see
the gesture. "*Merde du jour*. I've got some bad news about
some of our stored data. Several days of our logged
material, the stuff we've been transmitting to Alphonsus for
links to Earth, is gone."

"*What?*"

"While you were off the line I got a polite little call
from Communications. Seems they fouled some of their
programming. The subroutine which transmits stored tape
data to Alphonsus was defective—it erases everything
before it transmits. Alphonsus was wondering why they
were getting long transmissions with no signal."

"That's ridiculous. Everything from Site Seven has
been lost?"

"No, only ours. Each team has its own file number and
something happened to ours alone. We've lost quite a bit of
material, but not all of it."

It was the first time Nigel had ever heard Nikka sound
genuinely angry. "When we get off this watch I want to go
see Valiera."

"Agreed. As far as I can figure out we've lost those
pictures of what looked like molecular chains and most of
everything from yesterday. But look, those can be re-
covered. Let's have a go at the photograph you found just
before Engineering called."

Nigel studied the image when it formed on the screen
before him. The alien photograph showed land of a dark,
mottled brown, the oceans almost jet black. Somber pink
clouds laced across the land and still eddies caught in the
rising mountain peaks. At the shore a slightly lighter line
suggested great breakers thundering against the beaches.
There were traces of shoals and deep currents of sediment.

"What part of Earth is that?" Nikka murmured.

"Can't say. Reminds me of some map I've seen, but I
can't remember which. I'll log this for transmission to
Alphonsus. Maybe they can find a contemporary shot of the
same place."

The next few sequences yielded nothing. There followed complexes of swirling dots, and then a pattern that remained fixed. "*Hold* that," Nigel said. "That's a three-dimensional lattice, I'm sure. Look, the little balls are of different sizes and colors."

"It might be a molecular chain model," Nikka said. "Or maybe a picture of the real thing."

"Precisely. I'll log that, too. And I'm going to tell Communications to not transmit anything until I have a chance to look over their programs. We don't want these lost as well."

"Wait a second, Engineering is calling—" Nikka broke off.

Nigel waited, drumming his fingers on the console. He hoped the message he had sent to Kardensky wasn't intercepted. He needed the information and photos Kardensky could provide.

"There's another damned leak," Nikka said suddenly over the speaker. "Engineering threatened to come in here and drag me out—I'd like to see them do it—if I didn't come. I've got enough air in the bottles but—*Oh*, my ears just popped—"

Nigel threw down his pencil in disgust. "Never mind, come on in. You and I are going to see Valiera."

"It was an impossibly *dumb* thing to do," Nigel concluded. He glared at Valiera. "If for some reason the images were erased by the alien computer when we read it out on the screen, that material is *lost*. Forever."

Valiera made a steeple with his fingers. He tilted his chair back and glanced at Nikka and Sanges. "I agree the situation is intolerable. Some of our hardware isn't functioning right and I think it's mostly due to the fact that everything is disorderly around here. Remember, we are just setting up Site Seven and mistakes are bound to happen. Victor, here, is looking into the entire Communications net and I expect his recommendations shortly." Valiera looked significantly at Sanges.

"Yes, I expect I can get things in order soon," Sanges said.

"I don't think this should be taken so calmly," Nikka
said abruptly. "It's possible that we have lost some irre-
placeable information from the wreck's computer bank."

"And it's not as though Mr. Sanges has suffered a great
loss, is it?" Nigel said with a thin smile. "Team One hasn't
made much headway on their inventory search."

Sanges bristled. "We have been working as hard as
you. I see *no* reason—"

"Now, none of that," Valiera said. "True, Team One is
only now getting its footing, but you must realize, Nigel,
that their task is much harder. They are compiling an
inventory, using the alien script. Until they have cracked
the code and know what the script means, they will not
have any solid results."

"Then why do they not abandon the use of script and
try to find things by pictures?" Nikka asked mildly. "That's
the path we are following and it seems to work."

"Why, what have you found?" Valiera unconsciously
narrowed his eyes slightly with a new alertness.

For a long moment there was only the thin whine of air
circulation fans in the room. "Some things that look like
molecular chain models, photographs of Earth from orbit, a
picture of some early primate, apparently," Nigel said
slowly. "A few other things, and of course that large rat."

"I have seen most of what you refer to in the briefings,"
Sanges said. "I would dispute your interpretation of several
of them, but of course that can be worked out in time."

"Quite so," Nigel said. "Nikka and I are trying to
uncover as much as possible so we will have some idea of
how the computer works, and what's available through it. I
will be interested to see what the experts say about that rat
particularly."

"Well," Valiera said distantly, "that will of course take
some time to work out."

"What do you mean?" Nikka said.

Valiera pursed his lips and paused. Nigel studied him
intently. He had seen this sort of administrator before.
Valiera had apparently been an excellent pilot but somewhere along the way he had acquired the bureaucrat's habit
of judging every statement's impact before it was uttered.
There was an air of calculation about the man.

"The National Science Foundation has decided not to release any of the pictures you are recovering from the alien console. It is thought that the impact at this time might be undesirable."

"Damn! Undesirable *how*?" Nikka said sharply.

"We want a serious scientific study of everything that comes out of Site Seven. Releasing information now would just inundate the NSF and strain an already fragile budget," Valiera said, spreading his hands in a gesture of helplessness.

"I quite agree," Sanges said. "Many people will find such photographs as the large rodent quite unsettling. It is our duty to release information only when it is well understood. The First Bishop has stressed this point several times."

"Ah, and I'm sure the First Bishop is an authority on cultural shock and exobiology." Nigel raised an eyebrow at Sanges.

"The First Bishop was present when the New Revelation was manifested to the world," Sanges said sternly. "He has a great and abiding knowledge of man's ways and the best course for humanity. I should think even you could see that."

"Nigel, I'm sure you know the New Sons are not hostile to the existence of extraterrestrial life," Valiera said diplomatically. "The New Revelation grew out of the discovery of life on Jupiter, after all. The First Bishop merely makes the point that man is specifically wedded to this planet, so things extraterrestrial will probably seem quite foreign to man, even frightening."

"Are you going along with the New Sons, then?" Nikka asked.

"No, of course not," Valiera said quickly, "I merely think I should take a position in between these two diverging views."

"Diverging they are, yes," Nigel said. "I don't think extraterrestrial life has to be so bloody frightening. And I don't necessarily think our limited knowledge about how we evolved falls in with the First Bishop's dogma."

"What do you mean?" Sanges said severely.

"Never mind. I simply think we should keep our minds open. Release of *all* the data we recover from the computer is an essential. We need the best minds working on this problem, not just a committee of the NSF."

"Nonetheless," Valiera said mildly, "the judgment of the Congress and the NSF has been made and we must go along with it."

Nigel leaned back and drummed his fingers on his knee.

Nikka exchanged glances with him and turned to Valiera. "Let's drop that topic for now. Nigel and I agreed on the way over here that we need a separate link to Alphonsus to insure no loss of computer files occurs again."

"That seems a reasonable proposal," Valiera said. His face lost some of its lines of tension.

"It won't take very much trouble or time to install a separate tramsmission link near the console itself," Nikka said. She took a pad of paper and sketched a circuit configuration. "I want to locate a computer file inventory inside the ship itself, so there will be a separate inventory available to whoever is at the console at all times. That way even if something is erased in Communications by accident, there will be another copy that can be transmitted to Alphonsus for permanent storage."

"That seems rather a lot of work and expense—" Sanges began.

"Expense be damned!" Nigel said suddenly. "We're not running a shoestring operation here. That ship is at least *half a million* years old. It's still armed and it can teach us more in a few years than mankind might learn in a century. I'm not going to let—"

"I think your proposal is well taken," Valiera broke in. "I'll tell Engineering to give you every assistance with it."

"I want a separate link to Alphonsus," Nikka said. "A complete separate subsystem."

"I'll see that you get it immediately. We have enough equipment to spare. And now"—Valiera glanced at his wristwatch—"I believe it is time for the New Sons' hour of withdrawal and meditation, Mr. Sanges."

"You're setting time aside for *that*?" Nigel said in disbelief. "Even *here*?"

"We must compromise on all things, Nigel," Valiera said, smiling.

Nigel grimaced, got to his feet and left the room. The slamming door made a booming echo.

ELEVEN

He stood on a high ledge and watched the flames eat their way down the valley. The dry tan grass caught readily and burned with a crisp roar, a sound like many drummers beating. Through the pall of black smoke he could see the scattered small creatures who had set the fire going. They were gesturing to each other, following the flames at the edge of the valley floor, carrying small torches to insure there was no break in the fire wall.

Before the flames ran the elephants. Their long, loping shamble had a touch of panic to it now; they made low cries to each other as they rushed toward disaster.

From his ledge he could see the dark line of swampland that lay before the elephant herd. The image danced in the shimmering heat, but he could make out the grassy bogs now only a kilometer from the elephants. At each side of the swamp, near the valley wall, waited small bands of the fire-carrying creatures.

It was too far to make out any detail but they seemed to be dancing, their long poles twirling high in the air.

Far away, beyond the moist swampland, lay a dryer upper plateau. On it he could see a huge herd of foraging animals, probably antelope or wild cattle; a vast ocean of game. Yet the creatures with fire ignored the herd; they drove the elephants and waited to butcher when the animals were caught in the mire.

Why did they run the risk of trampling or the searing pain as an elephant tusk skewered them? To show courage? To have more tall tales around the late night hearth? To fuel the myths and legends that grew with each retelling beside the firelight?

How did they learn to cooperate so, moving in and out in an elaborate dance as they probed the prey for weakness? Who taught them to make tribes, kindle fire, form the delicate web of family? So nimble a craft, acquired so quickly. It was hard to believe these creatures were driven by the slow, ponderous hand of evolution, the workings of—

A shifting of shadows caught his eye. He turned. One of the creatures stepped from behind a spindly tree. It was scarcely a meter high, shaggy, with hands and feet that seemed swollen. The deep-set eyes darted left and right, checking the terrain, and the small erect creature shifted the pointed stick it carried in its hand.

The wind shifted slightly and brought the rank, sweaty smell of the creature to him. Neither of the two moved. After a moment the creature shuffled its feet, took the stick in one hand and raised the other, palm outward. It made a series of low, rumbling grunts. The palm it held up was wrinkled and matted with coarse hair around the sharp nails.

Nigel raised his palm in the same gesture. He opened his mouth to reply and the image drifted away in a curl of smoke. Light rippled and danced. A hollow drumming enfolded him, dense in the thick air.

Someone was knocking on his door.

He brushed some papers from his lap, swung his feet to the floor and took the two paces to the door. When he opened it Nikka was standing awkwardly in the passageway.

"My doctor has advised me never to drink alone," she said. She held up a small chemical flask of transparent liquid. "The purest stuff, distilled at Alphonsus for the purposes of scientific research and the advancement of man's knowledge."

"A most interesting specimen," Nigel said judiciously. "Come, bring it inside for further study."

He settled on his bunk and gestured to a chair. "I'm afraid there's not much place to put anything down. There's an extra glass in the cupboard, and I'll join you as soon as I finish the drink I'm on."

She looked with interest at his glass. "Fruit juice?"

"Well, one must mix the canniforene in something."

Her eyes widened. "But that's *illegal*."

"Not in England or America. Things are pretty wretched in England and all the mild euphorics are allowed—nay, encouraged."

"Have you ever smoked LSD?" she asked with a touch of respect in her voice.

"No, didn't really feel the need. It's not the sort of thing you smoke, anyway. Not that I mind smoking, mind you; I prefer to take cannabis that way. But I've been drilled that you don't smoke anything on the moon—too dangerous—so I had this canniforene smuggled up with the lot from Kardensky. Cost me a packet—two hundred dollars, that bet, remember?—to get it through."

She mixed in some fruit juice with her alcohol, tested the mixture and smiled. "Do you find the routine here so wearing?"

"Not at all. It's dead easy. I haven't even been here long enough for the low-gravity high to wear off. But while you were rigging up the link to Alphonsus I decided to have a skull session over the Kardensky stuff. Canniforene gives me ideas sometimes, lets me see connections I wouldn't otherwise."

Nikka frowned and opened her mouth to say something. Nigel waved his hand elaborately, murmuring, "Ah, I know. Buggering up my mind for a lot of over-the-counter insights. Well, I can't feel it doing me any harm. It's given me some sparks of creativity in the past that helped my career a lot. And anyway, Nikka, it's *delicious*. Very fashionable stuff, that, it's much the rage. All the hominids are doing it."

"All right," Nikka said, "I might even try some myself. But look, I thought you were going to meet me in the gym an hour ago."

"I was, wasn't I? Well, it's a dreary lot of exercise machines they have in there and I was busy with my cogitating here."

"You *should* do it, you know. Valiera will be onto you about it pretty soon. If you don't do the exercises eventually you can't return to Earth at all."

"When they put in a swimming pool I'll be there." He
took a sip of his drink and studied a sheet of paper nearby

"That won't be too long, now that we've struck ice
Besides, Nigel, the exercises make you feel good. Look—
She nimbly turned in the air and did a one-handed flip
landing neatly on her feet. "I'll admit it's not all that hard in
low gravity."

"Yes, yes," Nigel said, looking at her curiously. He
guessed that she was a bit uneasy at visiting him in his digs
She was a naturally physical sort of person, so anxiet
would probably show up as increased activity; thus the
gymnastics.

"Sit down here, I've got some things to show you." He
handed her a color photograph of Earth taken from orbit
"That's the same picture we got on the console awhile back
Kardensky had it shifted into approximately our color scale
so it doesn't look red to us."

"I see. What part of Earth is it?"

"South America, the southern tip, Tierra Del Fuego.
Nigel tapped a fingernail on the slick surface. "This is the
Estrecho de Magellanes, a narrow strait that connects the
Atlantic and Pacific."

Nikka studied the photo. "That's no strait. It's sealed up
at four or five spots."

"Right. Now look at this." He snapped down another
print of the same area, dealing as though he were playing
cards. "Kardensky got this by request from Geological
Survey, taken last year."

"It's open," Nikka said. "It *is* a strait."

"That spot has always been clear, ever since European.
reached the New World. This picture we got from the
wreck's memory bank must be how it looked *before* erosion
cleared the strait."

Nikka said quickly, "This gives us another way of direc
dating, then."

"Precisely. Rates of erosion aren't known all that well
but Kardensky says this picture is at *least* three-quarters o
a million years old. It ties in pretty well with the radiation
damage estimates. But that's not all." Nigel collected notes
photographs and a few books which were lying about hi

ed. "Somebody in Cambridge has identified those lattice-
orks we found."

"What are they?"

"Sectioned views, from different angles, of physostig-
ine."

"Isn't *that* . . ."

"Right. I'm a bit rusty at all this but I checked with
ardensky and my memory from the news media is right—
at's the stuff they use as an RNA trigger. That, and a few
ther long chain molecules, are what the NSF is trying to
et legislation about."

Nikka studied the prints he handed her. To her
ntrained eye the complex matrix made no sense at all.

"Doesn't it have something to do with sleep learning in
e subcortical region?"

Nigel nodded. "That seems to be one of its functions.
ou give it to someone and they are able to learn faster, soak
p information without effort. But it acts on the RNA as
ell. The RNA replicates itself through the DNA—there's
me amino acid stuff in there I don't quite follow—so that
ere is a possibility, at least, of passing on the knowledge to
e next generation."

"And that's why it's illegal? The New Sons don't want it
sed, I've heard."

Nigel leaned back against the wall and rested his feet
n the narrow bunk. "There's one point where our friends
om the Church of the Unwarranted Assumption may have
point. This is dangerous stuff to fool about with. Biochem-
ts started out decades ago using it on flatworms and the
ke. But a man isn't a worm and it will take a *bloody* long
eries of experiments to convince me using it on humans is
wise move."

He paused and then said softly, "What I'd like to know is
hy this molecule is represented in an alien computer
emory almost a million years old."

Nikka held out her glass. "Could you give me a drop of
at canniforene in fruit juice? I'm beginning to see it might
ave a use."

"Quite so," Nigel said dryly.

"There are some other points too. That long black line

against the mottled background we found, that's a DNA
molecule entering a—let me look it up—pneumococcus. A
simple step in the replication process, Kardensky tells me."
He put aside his papers and carefully mixed her a drink.
"That's what I was having off on, hallucinating about, I
suppose, when you knocked."

Nikka drank quickly and then smiled, shaking her
head. "Interesting taste. They mix it with something, don't
they? But explain what you mean, I don't see where all the
points."

Nigel chuckled and turned thumbs up. "Great. I'm
hoping the fellows who peeked inside the packages from
Kardensky won't see it either."

"What do you mean? They were *opened*?"

"Sure. All the seals were off. The canniforene was
disguised, so it got through. The rest was just books,
papers, photos and a tape. I don't know what the censors—
New Sons I'd imagine—thought of it all."

"Incredible," Nikka said, shaking her head in disbelief.
"You'd hardly believe this was a scientific expedition at all.
It seems more like—"

"A political road show, yes. Makes one wonder why
our schedule has been so frequently interrupted."

Nikka looked puzzled. "Our shed-yool?"

"Yes, you say sked-jule, don't you? What I mean is that
we seem to get interrupted on our shift a great deal, more
than the other teams. We lost several hours today from that
electric high tension, for example—"

"High tension?"

"In American that's, uh, high voltage."

"You've never lost your Englishisms."

"*We* invented the language."

"Say, could I have some more of that . . ."

"So soon?"

"It has some aspects . . ."

"So it does. Think I'll indulge in a nip."

"Exotic slang. Old World charm."

Nigel collected the papers and piled them on the floor,
feeling his heels lift and float beneath him. The room was so
cramped there wasn't space for a desk.

When he lofted back to his bunk he was surprised to
nd Nikka there. She kissed him.

Nigel made a formal gesture, not totally explicit,
urrently fashionable throughout Europe. Nikka raised an
yebrow in reply. She came to him as an eddy of warmth.

"You're enough to stiffen a priest," he said admiringly.

"Haven't tried."

She unfastened the brass buckle at her side. Forth-
ight, he thought. Direct.

She hovered over him and her small, elegantly peaked
reasts swayed slowly. The period of oscillation, he thought
istantly, depended on the square root of the acceleration of
ravity. An interesting fact. Something stirred within him
nd he saw her diffused in the mellow cabin light, a new
ontinent in the air. His clothes had evaporated. She knelt
nd his stomach muscles convulsed as a warm wave
nclosed his penis. He blinked, blinked and merged into
illowing yellow cloudbanks of philosophy.

TWELVE

They went for hikes outside, laboring up the hillsides,
lipping in the powdery dust. Nigel wanted to see Earth
nd he had not realized until he arrived here that Mare
Marginis was aptly named, for it appeared from Earth on
he very margin of the moon, only a third of it visible. To
ee the Earth they had to scale a steep hill. Nikka was
oncerned that the exercise might overtax him, but she had
ot allowed for his training; he panted continuously but did
ot slow until near the summit.

"Beautiful," he said, stopping with hands on hips. His
oice rasped over the suit radio.

"Yes. I can see home."

"Where?"

"Yokahama. There."

"Right. And there's the western United States."

"Clouds over California."

"But not Oregon."

"Where your Mr. Ichino is?"

"Right. I wonder why I haven't heard anything from him."

"Ummm. Even that enormous blast crater is *invisible* from here. Funny. But, look, isn't it too soon to expect results?"

"Probably. He may be snowed in, too."

"After all, he hasn't gotten a peep out of you, either."

"True. We've been so damned busy."

"And censored."

"Dead on," he said with a dry chuckle.

"No way around it."

"I'm not so sure."

"Oh? How?"

"I'm thinking of getting an unbreakable channel through to Kardensky."

"That will be difficult."

"But not impossible. Maybe we can route it through someplace else."

"On Earth?"

"No, here. The moon. How about Hipparchus Base?"

"It's only an outpost. When they struck the ice lode at Alphonsus, Hipparchus became a backwater."

"Um." He fell silent.

"Look at it," he said at last. "Earth. Hanging there like some sort of nondenominational angel."

"Careful. Call it that and the New Sons will claim they thought of it first."

"They would. Quite their style."

"Why can't they stick to one world at a time? Why pull the strings here?"

"They like to muck about. Power, you know—it's an addictive drug."

They watched their planet, half of it visible over the mottled horizon. Nikka pitched a stone down the baked hillside. The only sound was a whirring of air circulation in their suits.

"Incredible," Nigel said intently. "Nobody's noticed but this is going to be the first true moon colony. The wreck will always have a covey of scientists poking into it, decade after decade."

"The cylinder cities will have their own base. Probably igger."

"That electromagnetic gun of theirs? If we build it at ll."

"Don't you think they will?"

"Maybe. The media are certainly singing about the lea."

"Shouldn't we?"

"Oh—" Nigel shrugged and then realized it was visible inside the suit. "Probably. The cylinder cities will e good manufacturing sites, I'll give you that. And they'll p up sunlight, then beam power down in microwaves. hotovoltaic conversion, the lot. That'll be a big help—the al liquefaction plants are being closed, you know, now at benzopyrene is proving to be a carcinogen. The uropeans are getting desperate for energy sources again."

"Can't they buy enough alcohol fuel? Brazil's sugar ane crop is immense this year."

"Not enough; they're streets behind the worldwide emand."

"Then we'd best build cylinder cities and more solar ollectors as quickly as possible."

"Ummm, yes, I suppose. But that's not why the space ommunity idea is being brushed off and taken out of the oset."

"Why is it?"

"The New Sons. I think they're using this as a smoke reen."

"I heard there is widespread support."

"Oh yes, they're thick on the ground—and the pun is tentional."

"A smoke screen? For what?"

"Not *for* what, *against* what. Against *us*. To deflect tention and money from the program here."

"Oh. You're certain?"

"No." Nigel kicked at a rock. They watched it tumble ownhill, flinging up a silvery cloud of dust in its wake that se and fell with ghostlike smoothness. "No, that's the hell f it. I must guess at all this. But I *know* that congressional ommittees don't suddenly take up big spending bills,

putting them on the top of the docket, for no reaso
whatever. Something's happening."

"I feel quite naive."

"Don't. See, the games played up at the top of th
pile—they're still merely games. Politics, public relation
oneupmanship, showbiz—those words have gotten to b
synonyms."

"Competition is fun."

"Of course. 'This show was brought to you through th
miracle of testosterone.' But there's got to be more to
than that. More than another zero-sum game."

"That's why you never went into the higher echelons
So you could be free to use your influence for what yo
truly wanted—to come out here and turn your back on a
that?"

"Eh?" Her tone took him by surprise. "Turn my back
No, look—look at that sherbet planet of ours. Here we are
the furthest out. Nothing but night beyond us. And still th
view dominating the sky is bloody old Earth. Turn m
back? We're still looking at ourselves."

That evening, after a grueling session at the consoles
she came again to his room. Their lovemaking had a mor
desperate edge to it, Nigel sensed. He felt himself pressin
her to him with a furious energy, and wondered at himself
The silken movements, so electric, had their own life
Considered as a designed act, it was in the mind's eye a slov
churning of bloated and gummy organs, dumb to th
ethereal, a rising with involuntary spasms from ancien
ooze. But beyond that lay joy, an airy joy, with a burnin
pressure that lifted away the convenient carapace c
mannerisms he wore. It took place in a spherical space s
intense that people had to go in pairs; one could scarcel
bear to go alone.

Yet, even lying at the place where all the lines of he
converged, his head cradled between her thighs, Nigel fel
himself slipping away from her, from the gliding moment
and into the riddles that chipped away at his focus. He felt
lazy peace with Nikka, a sensation he hadn't had sinc
Alexandria, but the stretching tension remained, a doubl

ull both toward this woman and to the ruined ship
utside, as though both were links in an unseen circle. He
umbled with these thoughts and the knot they made inside
im, and in the act fell asleep, with Nikka's salty musk in his
ostrils, his arms heavy and sluggish as though they had
upported an unseen weight.

He awoke in the middle of the night. He took
laborate pains to slide out of the bed without waking her
nd switched on only the small reading lamp in the corner.
The mass of material from Kardensky was imposing
ut he worked at it steadily, reading as fast as he could. The
iddles of the past had an annoying habit of slipping away as
e tried to pin them down. Much was known, but it was for
ie most part a collection of facts with the interrelationships
nly implied. It is one thing to find a wide variety of tools,
iostly stone, chipped or polished for some particular use.
ut how to put flesh on these bones? How, from a chipped
int, to deduce a way of life?

He rather wished he had paid more attention to such
iatters at University, rather than swotting up the readings
ist before term examinations.

There was a lot of talk and data about apes, but the
vidence was quite strong—man's prehuman ancestors
idn't look *or* act like the present great primates. Just
ecause Fred is your cousin doesn't mean you can learn
iuch about your grandfather by studying Fred's habits. It
·as all so interwoven, so *dense*. There was a jungle of
heories and test mechanisms that were supposed to
xplain man—big game hunting, fire, then selection for
·igger brains. And that implied prolonged infant and
emale dependency; loss of the estrous cycle so the woman
·as always available and interested; the beginnings of the
amily; taboos; tradition. All factors, all parts of the web.

The Hindu temple monkeys are ordinarily peaceful in
he jungle. But once they become pets, take to living in the
emples, they multiply freely and form large troops. One
roop, stumbling on another, suddenly flies into a fierce
age and attacks. They are animals with time on their

hands; deprived of the need to hunt, they have invente
warfare. As man did.

Nigel sighed. Analogies with animals were all ver
well, but did this mean man followed the same path
Admittedly, men were the cleverest prey one could find
War has always been more exciting than peace, robber
than cops, hell than heaven, Lucifer than God.

When asked why they live in small groups, th
Bushmen of the Kalahari reply that they fear war.

Tribes, clans, pacts. Africa the cauldron, Africa th
crucible. Olduvai Gorge. Serengeti Plain. The Great Rif
that circled the planet, a giant baseball seam, splitting
twisting, churning the dry, dusty plains of Africa. Earth
quakes and volcanoes that forced migration and pushed th
hunter onward in search of game.

Here is where ritual began, some said: the great peac
that comes of doing a thing over and over again, every ste
spelled out in fine detail. The numbing, reassuring chant
the prescribed steps of the dance—creating a system wher
all is certain, all is regular, a substitute pocket universe fo
the uncertain and unpredictable world outside.

A dry rattle of turning pages cut the silence of th
room as he read. He skimmed through an analysis of ritua
as the social cement. *Running living leaping soaring*. Nige
made a small bitter laugh. *Only once and all togethe
Joyful singing love forever*.

He grimaced.

The birthplace: a dry, straw-colored plain with scat
tered bushes, dark green clumps near swamps and wate
holes, the long winding ribbon of green that lines th
course of a small river. The language of fur, horns, claws
scales, wings. The serene logic of sharp yellow teeth an
blunt clubs. A creature who walks upright, leading a ragge
troop behind. Jaw and mouth thrust forward, a trace
muzzle. Low forehead and flattish nose. He climbs trees
he seeks water, he learns and remembers.

Reason and murder. The rich, evil smell of meat.

The women, who stayed behind during the hunt t
gather roots and berries, now prefer vegetables and fruit
and salads. In a man's restaurant the menu is thick steak
and roast beef, rare.

A skull, three hundred millennia old, showing clear signs of murder. But with such built-in tension, such rivalry, how did men ever come to cooperate? Why did they erupt from the bloody cradle of Africa, products of an entirely new kind of evolution? Ramapithecus to Australopithecus Africans to Homo Erectus to Neanderthal to Walmsley, the litany which should explain everything and said nothing, really, about the great mystery of why it all happened.

Genes, the brute push of circumstance, Darwin's remorseless machine. Flexibility. The complexity of uncommitted structures in the brain, they said. Nerve cells with subtle interconnections not fixed at birth, but patterned by the stamp of experience.

Hands, eyes, upright gait. An excited male chimp snaps a branch from a tree, brandishes it, rears up on two feet and drags it away. Other chimps follow, chittering among the trees, tearing away branches and waving them. They jump through the green leaves and land in the clear, scampering out a few meters into the withered grass. It is some form of display, a celebration of the troop.

Inference, deduction, circumstantial evidence. A boy about sixteen years old lies on his right side, knees slightly drawn up and head resting on his forearm in a sleeping position. He seems small at the bottom of the dark trench. A pile of chipped flint forms a stone pillow beneath his head and near his hand is a beautifully worked stone axe. There are roasted chops and antelope legs, wrapped in leaves; the boy will need something to eat in the land of the dead.

Circles and animals drawn on the walls, colored clay smeared on faces and pebbles. Art follows religion, at least a hundred millennia old. Domesticated animals, the client allies of dogs and cats and cattle. And always the restlessness, the outward thrust, aggression, war.

Man would rather kill himself than die of boredom. Thus—novelty, gambling, exploration, art, science . . .

"Wamm ymm doing?" Nikka said. She peered at him drowsily.

"Studying up. Looking for clues."

Nikka threw back the covers and lay gazing at the low

ceiling. She took a deep, cleansing breath and sat up. H•
black hair curled and tumbled slowly in the low gravit
"That was exceptionally fine."

"Ummmm."

"It's never really been this way for me before, yo
know."

He looked up. "How?"

"Well, I'm just a lot more easy about it. I gues
. . . there are love affairs and then there are love affairs.

"Indeed," Nigel murmured, distracted. "Sex is Goo
way of laughing at the rich and powerful, as Shaw or Wild
or somebody said."

"And we're neither."

"Yes." Nigel went on reading.

"Well, I suppose I don't really know how to say . . .

Nigel put his papers aside, and smiled. "You don't hav•
to. See, it's simply too early to assess things. And you lear
more by plowing through life, sometimes, rather tha
dissecting it."

"I . . . oh."

"Does that make any sense to you?"

"Some."

"Ummm. Good." He picked up his notes.

"Don't you have an *off* button that'll stop yo•
working?"

"Yup," he murmured absently. "Directly on the tip •
my cock."

"I've already tried that."

"Um. Love me, love my fanaticism."

"Very well." She sighed elaborately. "I see there's n•
going to be very much more done about romance. I'v•
never seen anyone drive himself this way. The othe•
don't—"

Nigel snorted. "They haven't a clue about wh•
matters."

"And you do."

"Perhaps. There's a lot I'm still trying to cram into m•
grizzled synapses. Look." He rocked forward, threading hi•
hands together. "It's clear whoever flew this ship knew •
bloody huge lot about our ancestors. They must've ha•

some kind of operation going here, else why learn so much? And why not study the dolphins, too—they're intelligent. Though in a vastly different way, of course."

Nikka pulled on one of his shirts and came to sit beside him. "Okay, I'll play your game. Maybe we were easier to talk to."

"Why?"

"Well, they must have been somewhat like us. There are many things about this wreck we can understand. Their technology isn't *totally* mysterious. They must have had some of the same social forms. They even had war, if that's what their defensive screen and attack system means."

Nigel nodded slowly. "Someone picked up the survivors of this wreck, too, or we would have found some traces of their bodies."

"So they had more than a one-ship expedition."

"Perhaps. It's hard to pin down. A half million years is a long time. We can't even be sure of very much about *ourselves* a half million years ago. How did we domesticate animals? Evolve the family system and sprout onto the savanna, away from the forests? How did we learn how to swim? Hell, apes won't cross a stream more than a half-meter deep or ten meters wide. Yet it all happened so *fast.*"

Nikka shrugged. "Forced evolution. The great drought in Africa."

"That's the usual story, yes. But all this"—he waved a hand at the walls—"bases on the moon, science and technology and warfare and cities. Is it *all* just spelling out the implication of big game hunting? Hard to believe. Here, listen to this."

He picked up a small tape player and placed it on his knee. "I'll keep the volume down so we don't wake anyone. This is a war chant from New Caledonia. Part of the anthropology packet. I suppose Kardensky thought I would find it amusing, since he thinks my taste in music is rather along the same lines."

The tape clicked on. A long droning song began, loud and deep and half-shouted to the beating of drums. It was sung with feeling but strangely without pattern. There was no sustained rhythm, only occasional random intervals of

cadence that came like interruptions. A dull bass sound
filled the room. For a few moments the chanters sang in
unison and their voices and the drum beating seemed to
gain in power and purpose. Then the rhythm broke again.

"Spooky stuff," Nikka said. "What people sang *this*?"

"The most primitive human society we know. Or
knew—this recording is forty years old and that tribe has
disintegrated since. They're the losers—people who didn't
adjust to larger and larger groups and better ways of
warfare and toolmaking. They seemed to lack some trait of
aggressiveness that 'successful' societies such as ours display all too much of."

"That is why they're gone now?"

"I suppose. Somewhere in the past we must have all
been like those tribes, but something got into us. And what
was that something? Evolution, the scientists say; God, the
New Sons think. I wish I knew."

Fatigue claimed them. Nigel muttered a good-night
and fell asleep within a few moments. But Nikka remained
awake. She lay staring into the darkness and the listless,
random chant ran through her mind over and over.

They had to stop work in the wreck for two days as all
hands pitched in and finished the life support systems.
Nigel and Nikka worked in the hydroponics bubbles, huge
caverns scooped out of the lunar rock by nuclear vaporiz-
ers. They sealed the fractured walls, smearing them with a
gritty red dye that dried into an oily hardness. At the end of
the second day Nigel was sore from exertion and limped
from a pulled muscle in his back. He left the spontaneous
celebration in the dining hall and returned to the console
room. Nikka noticed his absence and followed; she found
him dozing in the console chair, his face shadowed in the
green running lights.

"You should sleep at home."

"Came here to think."

"So I noticed."

"Um. Wasn't being blindingly brilliant back there, was
I? That hydroponics lashup did me in."

"I don't think you should've had to do it. Valiera sat it out and he's no older than you."

He wagged a finger at an imaginary opponent in the chilly, layered space of the room. "That's where you're wrong. Valiera would like nothing better than evidence of my physical incapacity to—what's the usual phrase?— contribute fully to the work here.' No, I've got to watch the fine points. They're fatal."

"We should have *more* help, not be required to . . . well, I guess it doesn't matter. I'd like to have an on-site specialist or two, though, to back us up. Maybe in, well, cultural anthropology," she said.

"Too pedestrian," Nigel muttered.

"How so?"

"There's more at stake here."

"Things seem pretty innocuous so far."

Nigel snorted, a kind of brusque laughter. "Maybe."

"But you don't think so."

"Just a guess."

"Do you know something I don't?"

"What you *know* isn't the point. It's the connections."

"Such as?"

"Did you read the research on the Snark?"

"I got through most of it. There wasn't a lot of data."

"There never is, in research, until you've already solved the problem anyway. No, I mean about its initial trajectory."

"I didn't think we knew that."

"Not precisely, no. It was under orders to cover its tracks. But some fellows worked backward from its various planetary flybys and got a pretty fair fix on what direction it was heading."

"What part of the sky it came out of, you mean?"

"Right. Old Snarky came out of the constellation Aquila. That's a supposedly eagle-shaped bunch of stars— Altair is among them."

"Fascinating," she said dryly.

"Wait, there's one more bit. I rummaged around a few years back, studying Aquila. In Norton's *Star Atlas* you'll find that there were twenty fairly bright novas—star explosions—between 1899 and 1936, distributed over the whole sky."

"Um. Hum."

"Five of them were in Aquila."

"So?"

"Aquila is a *small* constellation. It covers less than a *quarter of one percent of the sky*."

Nikka looked up with renewed interest. "Does anyone else know this?"

"Somebody must. A fellow named Clarke brought it up once—I found the reference."

"Big novas?"

"Sizable. The 1918 Nova Aquila was one of the brightest ever recorded. Aquila had *two* novas in 1936 alone."

"So the Snark was at work?"

"Not him. I'm convinced he's reconnaissance, period."

"Or a pointer?"

"How's that?"

"A pointer dog. The kind that sights the quail."

"Damn." Nigel sat very still. "I hadn't thought of it quite that way."

"It's possible."

"Hell, yes, it is. Snark wouldn't need to know what his designers intended."

"Every now and then he squirts them his findings."

"And they . . . use the information."

Nikka said briskly, "It's just an idea. Those novas—how far away were they?"

"Oh, they varied," Nigel said absently. "The important point is that they're all along the same line of sight, seen from here. As though the cause were moving toward us."

"Nigel, it's just—"

"I know. Just an idea. But it . . . fits."

"Fits what?"

"The wreck out there." He waved airily. "Some living creatures came here, far back in our past. That ship carried what the Snark called organic forms, not supercomputers."

"Animals, I think you said."

"Yes, Snark called us animals, too. No insult intended. He thinks of us as special."

"Why?"

"We're uncommon, for one thing. Most life is machine life, he said. And we're . . ."

"We're what?"

Nigel felt oddly uneasy with the word. "Of the universe of essences."

"What does it mean? I read your classified summary but—"

"I haven't a clue what it adds up to."

"The beings in that wreck were in the universe of essences, too, then. They came here to get something."

"Or give something."

THIRTEEN

After a day of dazed babbling, Graves awoke in the morning able to speak clearly. Mr. Ichino fried synthetic yeast steak and as they ate Graves confirmed most of the deductions Mr. Ichino had made from the microfilm.

"I'd been on their trail for weeks," Graves said, propped up in bed. "After them in a 'copter first, then on foot. Got a few long-distance photos, even found some of the vegetation they'd nibbled at, a few rabbit bones, things like that. My trackers pinpointed likely spots. My guide and me, we spotted some just as this damn snow started. Hard as hell, tracking them through this mess."

"Why not stop?" Mr. Ichino asked.

"They had to slow down *sometime*. Everything does in the winter up here. If I outlasted them I could maybe move in when they were hibernating or something. Take captives."

"Was that how you got this?" Mr. Ichino gestured at the bandage over Graves's ribs.

Grave grimaced. "Yeah. Maybe they weren't holed up at all, just stopped for a while. I came up on 'em in one of those circular clearings that used to be a root system for redwood trees. Got in close. They were sitting around a kind of stone block with something made out of metal on top of it, all of them kind of looking at it and humming, swaying back and forth, a few beating on the ground."

"You mentioned that earlier when you first woke up."

"Uh, huh. I thought the sound would cover me, all that chanting. My guide circled around to come in at a different angle. They were worshiping that damn thing, that rod. I got a picture and moved and the one up front, the one who was leading them, he saw me. I got scared. Took a shot at him with my rifle, thinking to run them off maybe.

"Then the leader grabbed that rod. He pointed it at me. I thought maybe it was a club, so I got off another shot. I think I hit him. Then he did something to the end of the rod and a beam came out, so close I could feel the heat in the air. Something like a laser, but a lot wider beam width. I was pumping slugs into him like crazy. He wouldn't go down. He got my guide—killed the boy. Next time he fired he clipped me in the side. But I'd got the son of a bitch by then, he was finished.

"The others had run off. I got over to him and pulled that rod away from him and took off, not even looking where I was going. I guess they picked up my trail a little later—I saw some of them following me. But they'd learned a lesson. They stayed away, out of easy rifle range. Guess they thought I'd drop finally and they'd get their goddamn rod back. Until I saw your smoke I thought I was finished."

"You nearly were. That burn cut deep and it could have caused infection. I'm surprised you could stand the pain."

Graves winced, remembering it. "Yeah. Had to keep going, wading through the snow. Knew they'd get me if I stopped, passed out. But it was worth it."

"Why? What did it get you?"

"Well, the *rod*," Graves said, startled. "Didn't you find it in my pack?"

Mr. Ichino suddenly remembered the gray metal tube he had examined and put aside.

"Where is it?" Graves sat up and twisted out of the bed, looking around the cabin. Mr. Ichino walked over to the man's pack. He found the tube lying under it in a corner. He must have dropped it there.

"Oh, okay," Graves said weakly, dropping back onto the pillow. "Just don't touch *any* of those things on the end. It goes off real easy."

Mr. Ichino handled it gingerly. He couldn't understand its design. If it was a weapon, there was no butt to absorb recoil or crook into the man's shoulder. No trigger guard. (No trigger?) A slight raised ridge on one side he hadn't noticed before. (A sight?)

"What is it?"

"Don't ask me," Graves replied. "Some new Army gadget. Pretty effective. Don't know how they got it."

"You said the Bigfoot were . . . *worshiping* it?"

"Yeah. Gathered around, some kind of ceremony going on. Looked like a bunch of New Sons or something, wailing away." He glanced quickly at Mr. Ichino. "Oh, sorry if I offended you. I'm not one of the Brothers, but I respect 'em."

Mr. Ichino waved it away. "No, I am not one of them. But this weapon . . ."

"It's the Army's, for sure. Who else has got heavy stuff like that? I had to get certificates as long as my arm to carry around that rifle I had. I'll turn it in when I get back, don't worry about that. Only thing I care about is the photographs."

Mr. Ichino put the tube on the kitchen sideboard, frowning. "Photographs?"

"The ones I got of them. Must have three rolls, a lot done with telescopic lenses. They'll prove the Bigfoot are still up here. Get me some press coverage."

"I see. You think that'll do it?"

"Sure. This is my biggest find, easy. It's even better than I thought it would turn out. The Bigfoot are smart, a lot faster than some ordinary game animal. Might not be the missing link or anything, but they're close. Damned close." His voice was fading with fatigue, a sibilant whisper.

"I believe you should sleep."

"Yeah, sure . . . sure. Just take care of that film in the pack. Don't let anythin', you know . . . the pack . . ."

In a few moments he began to breathe regularly.

Mr. Ichino found the film in a side pocket of the pack that he had missed before. They were clear, well-focused shots on self-developing film. The last one, of the clearing, was still in the camera. Seen from behind, the Bigfoot were just dark mounds, but the tube could be seen clearly resting on a rectangular stone at the far end of the clearing.

The Bigfoot seemed to know how to use it, as well. But worship it? A strange act.

Mr. Ichino smiled. Graves had become so engrossed with his pursuit of the Bigfoot that he had lost sight of his original aim. The Wasco event first drew his attention—how did Bigfoot relate to that? Graves had not had time to ask.

Use of that gray tube would certainly keep the Bigfoot free of men. Woe to the unlucky hunter who stumbled on a band of Bigfoot with the fire weapon.

Still . . . it seemed highly unlikely that the creatures could survive indefinitely with men all around them. True, they were masters of concealment—or so the historical record implied. But did they merely hide in the thick forests . . . or was there a place where they could retreat? A refuge from the storm of mankind . . .

A place with still-functioning life systems. A warren which sheltered its charges, mutely following ancient instructions. Commands now robbed of their point, but still carried out.

A subterranean Eden for these early men, spilling with food and warmth and mating grounds. A holy place that evaporated one day in a spray of nuclear sleet, leaving one or two foraging bands of Bigfoot in the wilderness, small tribes who had somehow wandered from Eden and perhaps had wished to return but were now adrift in a sea of trees and a world of men, pursued by machines that beat at the air with spinning wings and carried a fanatic hunter, a man born in some place surely far distant from Eden . . .

FOURTEEN

Sitting upright in bed next to him, eyes hooded by the cone of light from the reading lamp above, her raised knees forming a tent from the sheets, she seemed all blades of bone and a soft sheen of skin. She had slumped down in concentration, reading the faxes of their day's output, seeking correlations. Nigel sat upright and, surveyed from his high angle, she gave the appearance of a terrain, a perspective of hills and secret valleys flowing together to a sum of great wealth. A spreading river valley. A world so rich that each stretch of tendon and alignment of bone gave onto new acreage, fresh forests, clean divisions between the bushy recesses and the new knobbed mountains.

"Ummm?" She sensed his attention.

"Nikka . . ."

Something in his voice made her look up.

"Have you . . . ever . . . felt that there is someone inside who is always apart?"

"How . . . ?"

"Always watching. Every so often . . . do you feel that there is a . . . way you ought to be seeing the world? Another way?"

"You mean . . . better?"

"Better, yes. *Different.*"

"More of it."

"*All* of it. That we ought to be . . . be *immersed* in it."

After a time: "I think we all feel that. Sometimes."

"Certainly." He sighed. "But we go on. Business as usual."

"Not always. We learn something. Or some do, anyway."

"Else what's the point of growing older?"

"If we don't get wiser? I suppose."

"Um." He stared distantly at the unintelligible faxes in his hand.

"Why . . . ?"

"I don't know, really."

"Maybe it has something to do with this."

"This?"

"The work."

"Oh. Yes. I suppose. But this has always been with me, right on from the first. When I was a little runt."

"We're trying to sense something new here. Something bigger . . ."

"Yes. Maybe that makes me feel this way."

"What way?"

"There are times when I despair of ever knowing anything, anything at all, fundamentally."

"Well," Nikka said, clearly groping for words, "more study . . ."

"Hell. No, it's . . . Nikka, the world is *dense*. There are layers. I keep feeling—and it's not simply this bloody wreck, no, it's everything, it's *life*—I ought to be getting it. The grainy . . . grainy . . ."

"Yes?"

"I don't know. I can't say it."

"In your society," she said softly, "there are not many ways to approach this. In mine there are perhaps a few more."

"*Right*." He nodded, a faint flash of irritation crossing his face. "Look, I'm not getting very far, talking this way."

"It is not a talking sort of thing."

"No. And it keeps coming to mind while I work on these faxes."

"The fact that we see so little."

"We understand even less than we see. What *can* we assume we have in common with the builders of that smashed ship? The only similarity was our—to quote the Snark—animal nature."

"I wonder if we, we animals, felt the same way about the others, then."

"Others?" He raised an eyebrow. "The computer civilizations? The abacus superminds?"

"You always say that as though it were a joke."

He shrugged. "Maybe it is."

"Perhaps that is what we may all have in common."

"What?"

"Contempt for machines."

"I suppose." He became suddenly thoughtful. "We made *them*, after all, not the other way around."

"Yet we are uncommon."

"Unstable. Suicidal. We reach too far. And the god-damned desk calculators—"

"Outlast us."

"Fair humbling, isn't it? If we *animals* could only get ourselves in order . . ."

"And communicate . . ." Nikka smiled, leading him on. "Is that what you mean?"

"Something along those lines. Maybe these aliens came to find another intelligent organic life form. They had our limitations—mortality, war. But they came seeking."

"Perhaps they wanted to tell us about something God-awful coming to get us from Aquila."

"What good would that do? A million years ago we had no technology."

"Then they could, well, give it to us."

"They didn't."

"No. But maybe they tried to pass on something else."

"It must be that. They couldn't get anything from a tribal society like ours."

"Yes. Though they could get contact, of course. It must be damned lonely, being an animal in a galaxy of desk calculators."

"Whatever they brought us, I can't see that it's done us a load of good."

"Ummm. Plenty of technology, but we're still suicidal. One war—"

"Bang."

"Quite."

"Then we must press on here. With the decoding."

Grimly: "Quite."

Mr. Ichino watched the snow stream through the box of light cast out from the window. The minute dabs of white were like leaves in a churning river of air, swept through the yellow beam and away into vastness. It was a light snowfall, adding perhaps only a few centimeters to the drifts. But it was more than enough to seal him and Graves into this stale space for a few more days.

"You . . . you takin' care of my . . . stuff . . ."

"Of course," Mr. Ichino said mildly, turning back to study Graves's lined face. "You need not trouble yourself about it. Rest."

Graves rolled his eyes weakly, searching the cabin. "Don't wan' . . . them . . ."

"Sleep."

Graves turned on his side heavily and closed his eyes. Mr. Ichino studied the tubular weapon, now lying on an upper shelf of the kitchen where it could not be disturbed. It was clearly alien, he now realized. Perhaps a talisman given the Bigfoot long ago, a parting gesture, something to help their survivial. Perhaps.

"Rest," he said softly. "Rest."

Nikka was resting, wide-hipped and heavy-lidded beside him, and somehow the cannabis went down with slick ease, mixed well into a fruit drink, and Nigel found himself sitting up late into the night, ragged and rusty-eyed, planning. They really had to do something. Events were crowding them now and if Valiera—he was sure it was Valiera, there was a certain sliding look to the man's eyes—if Valiera chose, he could press them even further. But Jesus, it was so fucking classically dumb, all this New Sons rubbish that seeped somehow out of the midlands of America, and Nigel had never understood it. These unfathomable mysterious Americans with their four score and seven and tramping out the wineyards or vineyards or whatever, things every schoolboy was supposed to know but if even a fraction of them did they'd be the most bloody insufferable bores in creation, miniature fonts of redneck wisdom. Thinking that he'd understood these creatures was a laugh, they'd slipped away from him time and again with their filmed eyes and folk sayings (*What's the state animal of Mississippi? A squashed cat in the middle of the road.* He'd never known if it was a joke or not.) and their obscure obsession with traditions when they plainly had none, all the same running round the other end and constantly pushing what was new, the latest, rave of the week, new new *new*. Neutrinos, little massless particles streaming through the earth as though it wasn't there. New trinos. And never for a moment thinking what has happened to all the old trinos, perhaps washed up on some star as War Surplus. Nigel laughed to himself and it came out as a giggle. A small thin one. And at once the slick veneer he had kept up fried away and he saw that he was on the edge again, stretched thin in an awful hollow place, wanting something and not truly knowing what it was any more. Back at Icarus, yes, he'd seen it clearly then, and somehow the need had washed away from him in those years with Alexandria and, God help her, Shirley. But now he had been drifting for vacant years. Nikka was a help but there was beneath the skin of things a resolving element he could not touch. Or was he simply and purely an aging man who had seen better days and knew it, and the truth of that plucked at him and stung, stung?

FIFTEEN

Nigel leaned against the wall at the back of the 3D gallery. Figures jostled on the screen, kicking a ball, falling, forming pincer moves and making blocks. He had never much liked soccer but now he could see the logic of it, the need men had for it. Hunting game in small groups, running and shouting and knowing who was your enemy, who was your friend. In-group and out-group, simple and satisfying. And not a vegetarian in the lot.

A few men sat watching the 3D. A goalsman missed a shot and one of them laughed. The screen flickered and a woman appeared. She gave the camera a sultry smile, held up a small green bottle and said, "Squeeze it for a lift! It's got upgo! Try—"

Nigel turned to leave and bumped into Nikka. "You've got it all?" she said.

Nigel showed her the packet of papers and photographs he carried under his arm. "Everything we've found, including the bits we don't understand."

"Shouldn't we tell Team One we're going off shift early? They might want to—"

"No, we don't want anyone fooling around with the computer memory now. As long as we don't know what erased the sequences today, no one should touch the console."

Nikka gestured down the corridor and they began walking. "You called Valiera?" she said.

"Yes, he said come by any time. I think we shouldn't delay any longer. And I'd just as soon not have Sanges put his oar in until we've seen Valiera."

Nikka shrugged. "You may be a little harsh on him. His heart must be in the right place, otherwise he wouldn't be in this expedition. We needn't think the worst of him just because he's a New Son. There are bastards who are New Sons and there are bastards who aren't, and I don't see much difference."

"Maybe," Nigel said noncommittally. They were at Valiera's office door. He knocked, held the door for Nikka and followed her in. Sanges and Valiera sat looking at them, silent, waiting.

Nikka stopped for a moment, surprised, but Nigel showed no sign and fetched a chair for her from the back of the room. They exchanged pleasantries and Valiera said, "I understand from Mr. Sanges that some of the sequences you found are now inaccessible."

"Yes," Nikka said. "We think something has erased them. There must be some method for retrieval and disposal of information, and it's logical that some command through the console will achieve this. As long as any of the three teams tries new sequences we run the risk of losing information."

"But if we cease exploring, we will find nothing," Sanges said reasonably.

"We came here to ask for a halt to all work at the console until the material we have has been assimilated," Nigel said. "We simply don't have enough information or people to handle the material here. What we need is cross-correlations, diversity—anthropology, history, radiology, some physics and information theory and lots more. The

NSF should release what we've found and ask for a consensus—"

"I really think it's *far* too early for that," Valiera said smoothly. "We have hardly begun to—"

"I feel we have enough to think about," Nikka said. "We have two photos now of those tall hairy creatures—"

"Yes, I've seen one of those in your shift report. Interesting. Might be an early form of man," Valiera said.

"I'm pretty well sure that it is," Nigel said. He leaned forward in his chair. "I've made a few tentative conclusions about what we found and I think they point in an extremely significant direction. I'll submit a summary later, with full documentation. But I think I should send a preliminary conclusion to the NSF immediately, to get others to working on it, to get some spectrum of opinion. I think there's a fair chance the aliens who crashed here may have had a significant effect on human evolution."

There was a tense silence. Sanges shook his head.

"I don't see why . . ." Valiera said.

"It's just an early idea, I'll agree. But it seems a bit odd, doesn't it, that we should so quickly stumble on things like the physostigminian derivative, viewed along each of the major symmetry axes? There are DNA traces, some other long chain organic molecules we can't identify, and Kardensky just got back to me on those furry creatures. The people in Cambridge can't fit it into the usual scheme of primate evolution. They're large, probably fairly advanced, and may be a variant form no one has dug up yet. Those fellows are used to looking at bones, you know, and it's hard to tell very much detail under all that fur."

"That is surely why we need to find out more," Sanges said.

"But we *can't* risk missing any more entries in the computer memory. Not after losing some today," Nikka said earnestly.

"Right." Nigel carried on briskly. "And the matter might be of supreme importance—information from the past can't be replaced. What's been bothering me for days now is that it seems a great coincidence that this ship was here between five hundred thousand and a million years

ago. Current theories of our own evolution place a number
of developments in that same time bracket," Nigel said.

"But we began evolving long before that time," Valiera
said.

"True enough. But a lot of our progress has been made
over the last million years. We learned many things then—
forming large groups, big game hunting, all the nuances of
family relationships, taboos. Art. Religion. I think there's a
chance these aliens had something to do with that. Man has
always been an anomaly, a species that evolved in a wink of
an eye."

Sanges said deliberately, "And you think this was due
to the aliens using physostigmine, altering our ancient
genetic material?"

"We can almost do that *now*," Nikka said. "We're
learning to take traces of the RNA complex. There is
legislation about it."

Valiera looked at her with distant assessment and then
turned to Nigel. "I'm no professional anthropologist of
course, but I think I see a hole even in what you said just
now. If these aliens simply taught these things to our
ancestors, how do you explain the parallel evolution of
hands, larger brains, two-footed stance and all that? It's the
side-by-side mental and physical evolution that is so
interesting about early man. But teaching an animal to do
something when he hasn't got the physical ability is
useless."

Nigel looked concerned and sat and thought for a
moment. "Right, I see your point. That removes the
driving link between physical and mental evolution. But
look, do you see, it could be *selective* help. That is, you
could wait until some small band of primates developed a
special trick—say, throwing sharpened stone knives instead
of closing in and using them by hand. You could then teach
them to *better* use that new ability. Show them how to use
spears—they're more useful than knives for big game. With
a direct hand on the RNA features you could speed up
evolution, give it a nudge when it strays from the path
you've designed. Man was still being shaped by his
environment a million years ago. I should think a push

in the right direction—depending on your definition of right—would have large long-term effects."

In a sudden burst of nervous energy Sanges stood and leaned back against the edge of Valiera's desk. He folded his arms and said, "Why would anyone do this? It would take so long—what would be the point?"

Nigel spread his hands. "I don't know. Control, maybe. The most striking thing about man is how he learned to move small bands of roving hunters, to big game operations involving hundreds or thousands at a time. How did that cooperation come about? It seems to me that's one of man's most efficient features, and on the other side of the spectrum he's plainly antagonistic toward his fellows. War is an expression of that tension."

Valiera made a thin smile and said, "Why bother to control something little better than an animal?"

"I do not believe we can even guess," Nikka said. "Their aims could even be economic, if we could be trained to make something they wanted. Or it could be that they wished to pass on intelligence itself to us. Those furry creatures—the ones we have pictures of—were probably half-intelligent already."

"Yes," Nigel said quickly, "even with the crude methods we have now, the physostigminian derivatives can train animals to do amazingly detailed jobs. They can make a man believe anything." He looked wryly at Sanges. "Or almost anything."

Sanges sniffed disdainfully. "This entire idea is incredible."

The thumping sound woke both Mr. Ichino and Graves. It was a ponderous booming that cut through the thin murmur of wind.

"What's . . . what's 'at?" Graves muttered.

"An aircraft," Mr. Ichino said, though he did not believe it. He stood at the window and peered through the starless night. He could make out the nearest tree. There was no light whatever from the direction of the slow drumming.

"Nothing, I expect," he said. "Would anyone be using a helicopter to search for you?"

"Ah . . . yeah, maybe. A guide back in Dexter. He'd miss me by now."

"He may see our light."

"Yeah."

"No matter. In a day or two I can hike out."

"Good. No rush, I s'pose."

Mr. Ichino turned on the cabin radio to distract Graves from the slow, rolling bass notes that seemed to become stronger the longer he listened. The radio gave a whistling static but no stations. Mr. Ichino fiddled with the dials. Something had failed in the radio but he did not want to take the time to repair it. He moved to the fireplace and threw on some cedar shingling. It caught merrily, popped and crackled and covered the distant thumping rhythm.

"There. It was getting cold."

"Yeah. Hell of a storm," Graves said.

Valiera made a small smile.

"Much as I appreciate your coming to me with this, Nikka and Nigel," he said judiciously, "I think you should consider things from a broader point of view."

"They could certainly try," Sanges murmured dryly.

"I happen to know," Valiera went on, "that Mr. Sanges's religion holds that the Bible—and all earlier texts—contain a *metaphor* for creation. They have no true dispute with the modern view of man's evolution."

"Certainly not," Sanges put in. "As *you* would know if you'd taken the time—"

"They will even agree that life could originate elsewhere," Valiera overrode him, "since the necessary conditions seem to exist throughout the universe. But they *do* hold that Earth was the host to our life—"

"Divine natural origin," Sanges said. "A very important principle to us."

"And there are other opinions about man's origins, too," Valiera went on. "I believe that we, as a scientific expedition, should not try to stir up these issues without definite proof."

"But the only way to *get* proof," Nikka said sharply, "is through further study—bring in as many specialists as we can."

"Once released to even a small body," Sanges said, "this sort of thing has a habit of filtering through to the press."

"That's the NSF's problem, isn't it?" Nigel said with a slow, deliberate coolness.

"It is a difficulty for all of us," Valiera said.

"The fact remains that we are requesting that we transmit *all* of this to Earth," Nigel said.

"Don't keep it in storage," Nikka said. "With the sloppy procedures here it's too dangerous. We could lose—"

"You merely attempt to circulate your own, your own *theories* about this," Sanges said savagely. "To destroy beliefs without—"

Valiera waved a hand and Sanges abruptly stopped, mouth hanging open for a moment before he snapped it shut.

"And I believe you do an injustice to Mr. Sanges's beliefs," Valiera said mildly. "The New Son theology is subtle and—"

"Oh yes," Nigel said. "He's quite the subtle type. Tell me, Mr. Sanges—when you go fishing, do you use hand grenades?"

"I don't believe sarcasm—" Valiera began.

"Whatever it takes to wake you two up," Nigel said lightly, raising his eyebrows.

"Wake us to what?" Sanges said.

"To reality. We're making a request." Nigel looked at Valiera. "Act on it."

"You wish to transmit freely to Earth?" Valiera said.

Nikka: "Yes. Now."

Nigel: "Under both our names."

Sanges curled his lip. "Your *names*, too?"

"Of course," Nigel said. "We'll take the blame for this."

"Already dividing up the credit. You want to be the first to publish on the Marginis wreck."

"A bit of a memo," Nigel said. "That's all."

"We'll need your signature," Nikka said to Valiera.

Valiera tilted back in his chair and narrowed his eyes, visibly weighing matters. "I'm sure you understand the need for security in this affair—"

"Security be damned," Nikka said.

". . . and I know I have your full support in my task of keeping all sides balanced in any dispute. I gather Mr. Sanges here does not feel this information is more than highly preliminary and should not be spread around. I believe if I were to ask them, the other teams would feel much the same way. I must say I can see their arguments quite clearly and I think they are valid."

Nigel's hand trembled as he leaned forward, intent on Valiera's words. He thought he saw some slight shift in the man's face, an odd tightening around the mouth.

"I believe that, as your Coordinator, I must turn down this proposal. To be sure, I can and will take the matter under advisement in future—"

"Ah yes, well, I see," Nigel said. He silenced Nikka with a glance and smiled in an airy, resigned way that lifted the tension in the room. He crooked a finger at Nikka and sighed.

"We're sorry about that, but we of course bow to your decision." He stood up suddenly, the thrust almost lifting him clear of the floor. "We'd best be getting on, Nikka," he said woodenly. Very calmly he took her arm and they left. Nigel nodded good-bye at the two men and closed the door.

Outside he leaned against the corridor wall. "An education in cynicism, this, isn't it?"

"They're a bunch of damned *lunatics*," Nikka said fiercely. "They're not scientists at all, they're—"

"Indeed. It's quite clear now that Valiera is a New Son."

Nikka stopped, startled. "Do you think so? It would certainly explain a lot."

"Such as the numerous delays we've had. I've noticed the other teams haven't had the lost tapes, the air failures, the high tension arcs. It would make a great deal of sense if our Mr. Valiera and Mr. Sanges were in bed together."

"I must say though," Nikka said, "you took it very well. I expected you to blow up all over them."

"*Well?* I'm glad my little bit of play-acting went over successfully. We're going to move now, that's why I didn't want to show them I was concerned. Go ahead, why don't you, and start suiting up in the lock."

Nikka looked puzzled. "For what? I thought we weren't going to continue the shift."

"We're not. But I had an inkling that something like this might happen; that's why I pushed so hard for the direct link to Alphonsus. I want to transmit all this stuff"— he held out the package of papers he carried under his arm—"and be sure Alphonsus retransmits to Earth immediately. If we go through them I don't think Valiera can stop it."

Nigel stood at the narrow port and watched her cross the plain toward the imposing ruin. It was bordered now by entwined tire trails and jumbles of equipment. In the distance a party of doll-sized figures worked at a boring site. The lunar sunset made a giant from Nikka's shadow. The white glaring ball was pinned to the horizon. Here, he thought, the winds always slept. Nothing stirred except by the hand of man. A gas molecule, escaping from a blowoff valve, would travel some ten thousand kilometers before meeting a fellow molecule from the same puff of gas. On Earth, the distance between collisions was smaller than the eye could see. A strange place, with different scales of time and length. The footprints Nikka made would, if left, survive for half a million years, until the fine spray of particles from the solar wind blurred them. Against such an immensity the dispute with Sanges and Valiera seemed trivial.

But of course, it wasn't really, he told himself. He and Nikka had barely shown a tip of the iceberg, talking to those two. The evidence for some attempt at communication, at manipulation, was pretty clear. But he'd omitted the bits about the novas in Aquila, the computer civilizations— elements that might, in time, converge.

So he and Nikka had conspired this one-shot gesture, this fist-shaking runaround of Valiera's sly network. They would be able to get through a cache of information before

Sanges and Valiera caught on, and perhaps that would spring open a few minds back Earthside, air out the politics of how the Marginis wreck was being handled.

Perhaps, perhaps . . .

Nigel sighed. He should feel the zest of conflict now, he knew, but it eluded him. From Icarus to Snark to Marginis, he'd been after something he could not define, an element he felt only as a pressing inner tension. It had made him an outsider in NASA. It had become a transparent but steady barrier between him and almost everyone else; he could not understand them, fathom their motives, and they clearly didn't comprehend Nigel Walmsley at all. There had been moments, of course, with Alexandria, and lately with Ichino and Nikka, moments when he broke through to the edge of what he was, lost the encasing armor Nigel Walmsley had built up over these years, slipped free to a high vantage point. And straightway came down, of course, for the moments passed as a flicker, and the realization of them came after the event itself. For that was the nature of them; they were not states of analysis, but new seas of awareness. Seas, with tides of their own.

"Nigel," the wall speaker rasped. Nikka.

"Right," he said when he'd flipped on his console transmission switch. "Let's give them that stuff right off."

"Do . . . do you *really* think this is . . ."

"Come *on*. No cold feet, now."

"I don't like political infighting."

"And *I* don't fancy being tedious, my dear, but . . ."

"All right, all right."

Nigel punched through to Alphonsus. Elsewhere in the building, in Communications, this would register. If Sanges was at his bright-eyed best, he'd probably be monitoring through Communications, or—worse—have already put a watch on this line. So it came down to a simple matter of time. If they could get enough raw data through to Kardensky's group, and the contacts Nigel had cultivated there, a bit of boat-rocking would result. If not, this stunt would probably earn him and Nikka a swift boot in the pants and one-way orders shipping them Earthside.

"Here it comes," Nikka said.

* * *

In the gloomy bay the man-made electronics glowed with a reassuring yellow and orange. Nikka shifted uneasily. The shadowed bulk of machinery around her stood silent, brooding, ominous. She told herself that her reaction was stupid. There was no reason to be jumpy. She had worked at the alien computer interface many times and this was no different.

She shook herself mentally and set to work. The transmission rig could read either electronic input from the alien bank or could scan the faxes already made. She and Nigel had planned to send both. She took a shelf of pages and photographs and stacked them neatly in the rig's feeder. They had, she knew, probably only a few minutes before someone in Communications would be ordered to cut the transmission. So they had to be fast. Nikka set up the board for simultaneous sending of both faxes and data directly from the alien computer memory. This done, she pressed the final command to start the signal.

Nigel had been silent as she did this. She tapped the signal into his console. He could watch it as it went, freeze the process if anything was fouling up.

"Here it comes," she said.

There was a grunt of effort behind her.

"What do you think you're—"

She whirled around. Sanges was struggling up from the plastiform rim of the tunnel.

"Routine business," she said, her voice thin.

"No, it's *not*," Sanges growled. He got his feet clear of the tunnel and stood upright. In the dim light he seemed larger than Nikka had remembered.

"You and him—I *thought* you might—"

"Look, I'm just sending Alphonsus some of the old material." Nikka kept her voice casual.

"It doesn't look like it to *me*. That screen"—he pointed to where technicolor images quickly shifted and danced—"is sending directly from the ship's core. Not filed data—*new* data."

"I—"

"We thought you might have something special set up

in here. Something you'd put in since your last watch. But *this*—"

"I tell you again—"

"*This* is a direct violation of the Coordinator's directives."

"Why don't you call him, then?" Nikka spoke mildly and backed toward the console, her heart fluttering.

"And let you send the whole damned business out while I'm going through channels? Ha!"

"I really don't understand at all what you are—"

He lunged abruptly.

Nikka swiveled and kicked high, heel turned outward to take the impact. Sanges caught it in the shoulder and shifted his weight with surprising speed.

Nikka came down too heavily from the kick, losing balance. Sanges danced to the side. Nikka got herself into position and tried to remember what she had learned, long ago and far away, about personal defense.

"Don't be ridiculous," Sanges said.

"Don't *you*."

"I will see to it that you and Walmsley never work again."

"We'll see."

"I warn you."

"So I heard."

"I *order* you—"

"You haven't the authority."

"Then—"

He lumbered forward. His hands were held down, palms up. He clearly intended to get her into a bear hug and sling her around. If he could then reach the console switches he could stop transmission.

She turned, back to him, and brought up her elbow.

She felt her arm smack into him with a satisfying thud. Sanges wheezed out his air. He wheeled away. Caught himself. Turned.

Nikka backed away. She needed space to maneuver. She felt the console rim press against the small of her back.

Time. She needed time. The data was going out. A few

nore minutes and—"Listen, Sanges." Maybe she could
ick the son of a bitch in the balls. "Listen—"

Sanges feinted to the right. Nikka moved to block his
vay. He shifted weight and dodged to the left. She turned
o follow. He slammed into her with full force. Nikka tried
o strike him but he lurched forward. Her arms were
•inned. Together they sprawled backward. Nikka felt
•erself tipped over, past the safety guard on the console.
he small switches of the alien terminal knifed into her
•ack. They were crushing delicate wire switches, clicking
hem over from active to passive, calling new entries
orth—

"Stop! We're wrecking it!"

"Let me—" Sanges grunted and flailed at the power
witch. He wrenched it over to the OFF position. The
creen above them faded.

"There," Sanges said. "I hope you realize the damage
•as been caused *totally* by your—"

"Look," Nikka said quietly, panting.

She pointed at the alien terminal. Some switches were
•light, winking redly in the shadows, following a sequence
•f their own. The lights danced and rippled.

"It's running on its own."

"An internal power supply?" Sanges wheezed, his face
•ushed.

"It must be. Something we did activated—"

The wheeling dabs of yellow pulsed, flickered, pulsed.

"Some very complex program is running." Nikka said.
"Not simple one-to-one data retrieval. An action sequence
•f some kind—"

A dim glowing lamp caught her attention. "Nigel's
•nline input—it's still active. He's still reading this."

"Here." Sanges reached over and switched off the
•connection. The lamp remained steady. Sanges clicked the
•oggle switch back and forth. "Funny," he said. "Some-
hing's happened."

A silence grew between them in the dark bay, now lit
•nly by the twinkling, shifting array of alien console lights.
•ach tiny fleck of solid-state electronics flared briefly into
•ife and then died momentarily, part of a jiggling rhythm.

"Nigel's getting this, whatever it is, and we can't turn it

off," Nikka said. "We can't *stop* it." Her words were
swallowed in the cold stale space surrounding them.

Nigel had turned off all the room's illumination, to
improve contrast as he monitored the readout Nikka was
transmitting. He sat far forward into the console, its
plastiform arms enveloping him, its hood lowered to
maximum depth. Nikka's series began. Nigel hunched over
and tracked the flow of data. The images flared into being
and were erased with blurring speed. The large rat, three
different views. Rotating pinwheels of orange and blue.
Ancient photographs of Earth. Molecular chains. Chemical
arrays. The hairy, shambling creatures. The beings in
rubbery suits. Star charts. Indices. Data. Nigel tracked it at
the limit of his speed, mentally checking off each category
as it was recalled from storage and sent on eletromagnetic
wings to Alphonsus, Earth, Kardensky, freedom.

The screen jumped.

Froze.

Sputtered an array of dots, lines, ripplings—

. . . Nigel perceived it first as a faceless blank space.
He peered at it intently. Something in it made him shiver.

He frowned. He moved his eyes to the side. He tried
to look away.

And found that he could not.

It came to him out of the screen like a trembling high
shriek, in color, a mottled green blister swelling toward
him.

It hit him in the face and Nigel Walmsley disintegrated.

SIXTEEN

A day had passed briefly, scarcely more than an interval of
wan light that seeped through the roof of clouds. Now the
twilight gathered and Mr. Ichino sat rocking, his face a
solemn mask, and turned the weapon over in his thin, bony
hands. Could he feel the strangeness in it, or was that
imagination?

A further conversation with Graves at lunch had
arified matters a bit, but Mr. Ichino was sure much would
ever be explained. Graves had mapped all Bigfoot sight-
gs over the past century and found there were recurrent
atterns, preferred routes through the mountains, and
ere he had sought the shambling beasts with helicopters
nd infrared eyes. Mr. Ichino had selected this place for a
milar reason: studying the Oregon back country, he had
oted that a series of shallow valleys and passes connected
is region with the Wasco area. Merely a guess, a
onvenient reason to settle in these forgiving woods, but it
ad brought Graves to him. And perhaps that was the end
f it—there might well be no other bands of Bigfoot. The
Vasco blast must have caught most of them, burrowed
eep inside their winter warren.

Where they had . . . what? Waited for some
romised return? For the Marginis wreck? The Bigfoot had
learly known the aliens, perhaps worked for them, learned
om them. These early men might well have worshipped
he all-powerful, godlike aliens.

It would be a simple, natural thing to transfer that
vorship to their gods' possessions that were left behind
vhen the aliens abandoned Earth.

In the distant past the Bigfoot must have collected the
its and pieces of their gods' leavings and carried them
long when the higher forms of men drove them deeper
nto the forests. Dragged them through that vast retreat,
perhaps used them to survive.

And the tribes with weapons would live longest, of
course. A band of Bigfoot that worshiped an alien re-
rigerator wouldn't find it of much use when it was cornered
nd had to fight, Mr. Ichino thought, smiling.

Graves spoke in his sleep, mumbling, and thrashed
against his bedding. Mr. Ichino looked over at him.

Graves would make his name with this discovery. He
had brought the Bigfoot at last into the light.

Mr. Ichino found the film in Graves's pack. It made an
orange kernel in the fire and in a moment there were no
traces.

He carried the tube—how had they made it so tough,

to last this long?—out into the clearing, and stood with it i
the darkening chill of evening.

Minutes passed. Then they came.

There were not many. Six stepped away from th
shelter of the black tree line and formed a semicircl
around him. Mr. Ichino had the feeling more were waitin
out of sight, their presence hanging in the air.

In the light thrown through the open cabin doo
behind him he could see one of them clearly. The head wa
very human. A thick forehead slanted into flaring nostril.
Glittering, sunken eyes darted quickly, seeing everythin
Yet it moved without anxiety or tension.

Massive, muscled arms hung almost to its knees as
crunched forward through the snow. Bristly black hai
shiny in the cabin light, covered the entire body except th
nose, mouth and cheeks. A faint sour animal smell drifte
in the light breeze.

Waiting in this soft stirring of air, Mr. Ichino recalle
the misted valley in Osaka Park, where the larks flutterе
free and poised, warbling. In his mind's eye they blende
with the twisted beggars who ate parched soybeans an
sang *chiri-gan* in pressing, littered streets. All brushe
aside by the earnest business of the world; all vulnerabl
and vanishing.

Despite the legends of the Bigfoot, Mr. Ichino did nо
feel any tingling fear. He looked about him, moving slowl
and calmly taking in the scene. They had human genital
and to the right he could see a female with heavy breast
They stopped ten meters from him and waited. Eve
slightly hunched over, there was dignity in their bearin

He held the weapon out at arm's length and steppe
forward. They did not move. He placed it gently, slowly, о
the snow and stepped back.

Let them have it. Without hard, factual proof Graves
story would be dismissed, or at least matters could b
delayed.

Otherwise, the fanaticisms afoot in the land would fi
on these battered fossils for an Answer, a Way. A spotlight о
any kind would be fatal to these creatures. They would b

nted down, once Graves reached civilization with that
be.

This weapon was the final argument. It linked the
gfoot unquestionably with the aliens.

Mr. Ichino gestured for them to pick it up.

*Take it. You're just as alone as I am. Neither of us has
y use for the madness of man.*

One came forward hesitantly. He stooped and smooth-
swept it into his arms, cradling the tube.

He looked at Mr. Ichino with eyes that flashed in the
ange cabin light. He performed a bobbing, nodding
otion.

Behind the Bigfoot the others made a high chittering
ise that rose and fell. They sang for a moment and made
e bobbing motion again. Then they turned and padded
acefully away. In a moment they were lost in the trees.

Mr. Ichino looked up. Clouds were scudding across
e stars. Between two of them he could see the white
arkness of the moon.

There had been someone up there who had seen it too,
erhaps, buried in cold electrical memory. Did he sense
at these children-ancestors were as much a part of nature
the trees, the wind?

Let them go. Nature had nearly finished its grinding
ork, nearly snuffed them out. But at least they could go
ith grace, alone, unwatched. Any wild thing could ask
at much of the world.

After a long time Mr. Ichino went back inside, leaving
e silence to itself.

They arrived in time for breakfast.

The snowmobile barked and sputtered to a stop and Mr. Ichino came to the doorway of the cabin, surprised, blinking back a shroud of sleep, for he had expected them much later in the day. They unloaded gifts from the hauling sled and brought them inside, carrying a cloud of busy activity with them that seemed to open the cabin and admit the sheen of morning.

They ate around the narrow table. Beef, well marbled; crisp toast; juice. Mr. Ichino was interested in the reports of rapid progress at Marginis, and they described the decoding of the star map, the now orderly dating sequence that pinned the age of the wreck, the unfolding of astronomical data that was going on. Yet for all this activity they had elected to take a brief Earthside holiday and descend into the waning of winter.

Nikka lingered over coffee. Nigel collected the plates and scraped them and returned to the table, thirsty, and stirred the orange juice, thinking.

He whipped the wooden spoon around several times, rattling it against the sides, and watched a pit form itself in the juice, a parabolic hole at the center. He withdrew the spoon. The smooth pit blunted, began to fill in. He thought of angular momentum passing fluidly from the juice, through friction, into the walls of the urn, then spreading into the hardwood table beneath, seeping outward and downward, descending into the earth itself. The yellow pit rippled and slowed. Flecks of rind whirled in the eddies. Down in the tip of it, in the center of the orbiting juice, a white scum formed. The shiny parabola and the angular

momentum died together, dynamical twins. A frothy scu[m]
spread into a shallow disc.

We may sometimes see ghosts, Nigel thought, but w[e]
never see the angular momentum. Or the past.

"I'm afraid it is a bit nippy in here," Mr. Ichino sai[d]

"Um." Nikka nodded, sipping coffee. She had n[ot]
removed her jacket.

"I used the last of my wood last night, and the fi[re]
didn't survive until I got up. I'll go out and chop som[e]
more."

"No." Nigel waved him to sit down. "I'll do it. Nee[d]
the exercise."

"You're sure?" Nikka studied him earnestly.

"Certain," Nigel drawled. "Where is it?"

"Around on the south face. Under the trees."

"Think I'll take a few whacks, then."

When the door thumped shut behind him Mr. Ichin[o]
paused a long moment and then said, "Your message w[as]
terse."

"Sorry," Nikka said. She turned and watched Nig[el]
through the window until he moved out of sight into th[e]
enveloping line of trees.

She settled both elbows on the table and looked at M[r.]
Ichino. "They still won't let us transmit classified informa[a-]
tion. Data, that is. But they can't very well stop Nig[el]
talking, or me, about what happened. Not now, when we'r[e]
Earthside."

"What *did* happen? Your telegram—"

"I know, I'm sorry. Nigel asked me to send it. [I]
suppose he thought that was all he could get away with. H[e]
was probably right, too."

"I realize you have never met me before, so you ma[y]
have some reluctance . . ."

"Oh, it's not that. I'm sorry, you think I'm not holdin[g]
back, don't you?"

"If you cannot—"

"Oh, I can talk. But I can't tell you very much becaus[e]
I don't really *know*. No one does. Except Nigel."

"Know what?"

"What the alien, well, programming was."

"Programming? Or new data?"

"Well, I call it that. Nigel says that's not the best way to view it. Any more than mountains are trying to program you into seeing the sky, he says."

"But your note . . . you read what I wrote to Nigel about Bigfoot?" Mr. Ichino leaned forward, his gaze centered on her and trying to read her precise mood.

"Yes. The business with that fellow Graves is over?"

"I hope so." He grimaced wryly.

"His men came, you said."

"Yes. There was nothing to find."

"They threatened you."

"Of course." Mr. Ichino lifted his hands lightly, palms cupped to the ceiling. "They had to. But they went away then."

"Graves may come back."

"He may."

"Helicopters and infrared, sonics—Graves can track the Bigfoot down again."

"It is possible."

"You don't think he will."

"No."

"Why?"

"He has lost something. His recovery in the hospital took a long time. He is aging. The burn drained him of his false bravado. Still, there remains . . ."

"You think he's afraid of Bigfoot now?"

"He knows they have that same weapon."

"And they'll be skittish and cautious."

"I have confronted him only once since. There was that feeling to him. If he'd kept all that evidence, fine—but to face them again? No."

There was a muffled thumping at the foot of the door. Nikka leaped up like a coiled wire and flung it open. Nigel paused in midkick, balanced on one foot and with an armload of chopped wood. He clomped into the room, tilted slightly back to take the weight of his load.

"Good job you laid that tarp over the woodpile," he grunted. "Some snow's starting to melt. Would be a pity to muck this old wood up—it's bone dry."

"I took it from the shacks in the woods around here," Mr. Ichino said. "This was a retreat during the crisis years."

"Ah."

Nigel dumped the wood into its hopper and brushed his sleeves free of fragments of bark. Nikka looked at him questioningly and then turned back to the table, where she spread open the map of the area they had used to find the cabin. She took out a pencil and studied the territory that stretched northward toward Wasco. "You believe they came into this valley because it was a natural route away from the blast?" she said to Mr. Ichino, who nodded.

Nigel smiled.

Too casually she interested herself in the details of geography. He watched her in the growing silence of the cabin as she tucked a strand of her polished black hair back, forming a new layer in the polished cap that was secured at the nape of her neck. With an elegant touch of her middle finger she pushed the pencil deep into the bun of strands, distracted. At this absentminded gesture Nigel's heart leaped into a high new place.

He arched a speculative eyebrow at Mr. Ichino, who sat with hands folded on the table.

"You can talk to *me* about it, too," Nigel said with a warm amusement.

Mr. Ichino said uncertainly, "Ah . . . I . . . ."

"What happened, I mean."

"I heard nothing in the news."

"Infinitesimal chance you would."

"The NSF hasn't decided how to handle it," Nikka said. She folded the map and tucked it away.

"I've made it quite precisely clear that they can ruminate on handling data, but they can't handle *me*," Nigel said. He put one boot on the table's bench and leaned on it, arm resting on his raised knee.

"Perhaps because it is so unclear," Mr. Ichino said delicately.

"True enough." Nigel smiled.

"How did it . . . "

"Feel?"

"Yes. I suppose that is what I wish to know."

"At first there was a, a sensation of going *away*."

"To something new."

"In a sense."

"But now you are back."

"No. I never have come back."

"Then you . . ." Mr. Ichino stopped, puzzled.

"What I knew is scrambled. Or *thought* I knew."

"And . . ." Mr. Ichino struggled with some inner inhibition. ". . . what did you come away with that"—he added hurriedly—"that you can tell us?"

"Oh. You mean facts?" He wiped his hands on his rough trousers and stood erect, leaning backward, peering at the roofbeams and the vaulted space of the cabin above them, at the shadows there. "Delicious facts."

"Tell him about the aliens," Nikka said. She had been sitting perfectly still at the table and he saw in her absolute lack of motion a tension she would have to grow through, a private set of concerns he saw now as totally transparent but, for her, entirely necessary, a web of concern for him that, cast wide, enfolded more than she needed to and more than she understood. But that, too, would evaporate with time and leave her bare, the old Nikka, the brisk and urbane, her conversations a smart rattle of wry insights, insider's jargon, an occasional epigram. The slim and springy Nikka, as he sometimes remembered her, standing in muted phosphor light, hipshot, the cradle of her abdomen tilted, jaunty.

"The aliens," Nigel said, as if to refresh himself, return himself to this linear world.

"You've targeted their origin, I gather," Mr. Ichino said, prompting, and Nigel wondered at the choice of words. Targeted? That word? For things gone and dead and vacant? He remembered Evers and that fellow, Lewis, with their phrases like *combat mission* and their ultimately absurd sense of the reality of things, the *trunk* of departing missiles, the oddly soundless *crump* as the orange blossom was born, behind the poor puzzled fleeing Snark.

Targeted?

Alien. So alien.

"I found their home star," he said.

"By figuring out their coordinate system?"

"Yes."

"How did *they* find *us*?"

"A survey craft, I suppose. Automated. They were casting about at random."

"They couldn't find anything in the radio spectrum? The same as with us?"

"Yes—it checks with what the Snark said."

"There were no other—organic races?—alive at the time."

"Not with technology. So these fellows set out to find what they could—maybe to colonize, who knows? But it didn't work—and stumbled on us."

"Created the Bigfoot."

"No. Made use of him. But that didn't work very well, either, I gather."

"Why not?"

"I don't know. But Bigfoot was a forerunner, anyway."

"Of what?"

"Of *us*," Nigel said, surprised. "We're the point, you see."

"The . . . programming?"

"Ah." Nigel chuckled, leaned over and put his arm around Nikka. "I see you've been talking to my little friend, here. *Programming*—it misses the whole thing."

"Why did they do it?" Mr. Ichino narrowed his eyes, as though at a loss.

"The—what did Snark say?—the universe of essences. Organic life can have it, machines can't. The aliens came to be sure we got it, in time for the—well, the Aquila thing. Whatever's moving toward us."

"They knew about it then!" Mr. Ichino rapped a knuckle on the hardwood finish. "When you sent me that star chart I wondered if you'd gone off entirely."

Nigel gave him a crinkling of the eyes, a merry smile. "How are you sure I haven't?"

To the look of momentary consternation on Mr. Ichino's face Nigel gave a barking laugh. "No, no, old friend—I haven't. What *has* happened to me I can't quite say."

"You seem different."

"I am different."

"And the Marginis wreck—they came to give us this? For defense?"

"I don't know," Nigel said. "You mustn't think I understand everything. They came for contact, knowing about Aquila. Knowing all organic life is fragile. But hoping there was some kinship, yes."

"And something stopped them."

"Themselves, I expect." Nigel sighed, shifted his feet, stood with hands in hip pockets. "War. Wasco had weapons. There was probably some conflict within them that eventually caused all that. Why bring nuclear death from the stars?"

"A defense against Aquila?"

"Maybe. Or against some other faction of themselves."

"We can find that out, perhaps."

"Can we? I wonder. And anyway—who cares? The causes are dead—we have only the results."

"The results?"

Mr. Ichino frowned and Nikka lifted her head in interest. The chill of the room had dulled as the diffuse glow of the sun sent shafts of light through the two southern windows. Nigel relaxed. He now needed to be out of this place, beyond this unsatisfying round of explanations, so he tried to compress it.

"It's really a lot of learned tricks, you know, our past. We learned pair bonding, social mechanisms. Then big game hunting. When that ran out—all planets are finite—there was agriculture. From that came technology, computers, an information rate to match our storage rate. But the world isn't just that—there's where the computer civilizations run aground. They're right, really—we *are* unstable. Because there's a tension in us that comes out of how we evolved. Computers don't evolve, they're developed. Planned—to be certain, safe, secure. That's the way they stay, if they survive the suicides of their organic forefathers. But the thing in Aquila is a computer society that opted for the preemptive strike—to stop organic forms before they can spread among the stars, find the domesticated computer worlds, and inevitably destroy them."

Nigel paused. The cabin held an airless expectancy.
"Then we . . ." Mr. Ichino began.

"We have to become better than we are," Nigel said.
"But, hell, that's really not it. We *can* have more power
than that blundering bunch of robots in Aquila. By entering
into . . ." Nigel laughed, shrugging. "You'll see it, you
will. The universe of essences. The place where subjects
and objects dissolve."

"The New Sons . . ." Nikka began. "They talk
about . . ."

Nigel raised his hands, chuckled. "They're the flip side
of an old record—fear of death plus the accumulation of
things."

He turned and looked at the yawning fireplace.

"We need more wood," he said.

As he feels in his pocket for his gloves he finds a coin.
Elated, he tosses it up, carving the air. He catches it
between his fingers adroitly and lifts it, a brassy circle. The
coin, held to the yellowing sun, eclipses it. Perspective
defies the innate order. The handiwork of man blinds even
this awesome furnace that hangs in the sky.

Nikka said, when the cabin door closed behind him,
"What do you think?"

"I don't know."

"You knew him before. Has he changed?"

"Of course."

"He says he can't really communicate it."

"No one has ever been able to."

She frowned. "I don't follow."

"When I knew him before there was a tension. That's
gone now," Mr. Ichino said. "Before, he was always looking
for something. Some answer."

"Has he found it?"

Mr. Ichino's face relaxed, became smooth and un-
wrinkled about the eyes.

"I think he has found that the looking is better than the
finding," he said.

* * *

The frosted land yields itself to him, a clear washed tapestry. He exhales a cloud of smoke into it. Snow crunches, crisp air cuts in his throat, joyful singing love forever, leaping soaring flying dying, he cracks the crusted snow at every footfall, sinking into the cottony embrace below, the supple world obligingly lowering him to itself at the completion of each step, homeward, toward the center of the forgiving earth.

trickle of stinging warm sweat down his wrinkled neck
the sun burning behind the veiled sky
a vast blue ocean alive with flapping bird life
—pours over and through him—

"I'm worried for him," Nikka said. Her knotted hands on the table trembled.

"Don't be," Mr. Ichino said. "You've already told me that Nigel has done things no one else could fathom. He decoded the star chart. He can see into the patterns that others—"

"Yes, *yes*. If I could only be sure he is all right."

"You know, Nikka, when I was a boy I had a two-stroke scooter. My parents gave it to me. I needed it to get to school."

"Yes?"

"There is a point to this." He put out a comforting hand to her. Through the hazed window he saw Nigel hefting the ax and plodding through the deep late-winter snow toward the wood pile. The square window framed it like a depthless Sumaro woodblock print.

"I waited a week before I used it," he went on. "I was that afraid of the thing. It had 150 cc's and I was very surprised when I jumped on the kick starter and it chugged into life, the first time. I jumped on and rode proudly up and down my home street, waving at my parents, waving at my neighbors. Then the engine died. I couldn't restart it for the life of me. I had to wheel it home."

He lifts the ax and brings it down *swack* clean and true biting into the sectioned log. The wood splinters, splits, and Nigel feels his taut muscles come to completion in the

act, converging on the downward curve of his back as he
follows through and the blade bites deep toward the singing
earth, pins him loving to the day.

It melts.

And he stands on a high shelf, a ledge of folded and
grainy rock. Watches the pounding dance of hairy forms in
the valley below as the booming cadence coils up to him
enfolding him and at once he dances, splitting wood with a
glinting piercing ax and coming down into a rhythmic
hammering of leaping soaring flying dying, primordial
plane of wood crashing down as he feels in this one passing
instant the connection of the act and the origin of that
tensing pleasure at sheer physical work, the joy of movement—

—he lifts the ax, the *thunk* of yielding wood still in his
ears and he is into another instant—

It melts.

"So I checked to be sure fuel was reaching the
carburetor and the spark plug was working okay. I cleaned
the jets and kicked the starter and she took off again, with a
nice sputtering roar. So obviously I'd gotten a piece of fluff
from a cleaning rag or something, into a narrow fuel
passage."

Nikka nodded.

"So I took her out again and after about two minutes
she sputtered and coughed and stopped again."

—and yet, and yet he sees that this howling dance and
muscular ecstasy is a piece but not all that he is and drawing
back on the ax, feeling it loft high into the gravitational
potential well of the consuming earth he remembers work
of long ago in remote, gray England, erewhonderful isle, of
flexing rhythms set up amid the coal gangs who loaded tar
sacks of it on chilly bleak mornings, a thin dusting of snow
on the immense black piles of coal being gnawed by trucks
and men, Nigel working for money alone, to buy him the
rare serenity of hours at home, warm and reading in the
yellowish light as the brittle mathematics unfolded before
him, a fresh tongue with a promise of lifting him up into a

new continent of Euclidean joy, the transcendent wedding of economical and clean thought to the underlying rhythms of the world, distilling order from the rough jumble of life, yet in that spinning instant to merge with life, not split the world into subject and object but to clasp it, merge, the ax hyperbolically propelled by the atoms of skin his hands as they sink into the molecular lattice of the wooden handle, all essences extracted out of the same finespun *stuff*, no interface, the old dualities lapping aimlessly at the granite mass of the yea verily one self-consistent mathematical solution that gives the universe, joyful singing love forever, and through this lens he sees the desert, the Snark riding back behind his pressing eyes and opening him to a fraction of this but poor dim dead Snark not merging it, not simmering in it, no, only frags, splinters knifing through the sea of categories that was the old Boojum Snark and pinned it forever to the pigeonholed world of subjectobject-livingdying—

"I had a similar thing once," Nikka said. "Did you check for water in the fuel?"

Mr. Ichino nodded and lifted his lukewarm cup, the coffee swaying like a black coin within it. "I rechecked everything and then set her against the alley wall and fired her up. She ran smoothly for as long as I'd wait. So I jumped on and went two blocks and she throttled down and died on me again."

"Irritating."

"Yes. There's that old joke—'Assembly of Japanese bicycle require great peace of mind.' So did this."

"You looked for an intermittent electrical fault?"

"Yes, all the conventional diagnostics."

"And?"

"It wasn't any of them."

—yet Snark had a piece of it, they all had a sliver of detail seven blind men and a melting elephant Snark must've known in ancient ferrite cores that he/it/she came from the computer civilizations that smashed the Icarus vessel, broke the eggshell now lying in Marginis, cut off that attempt to transfer knowledge to the beings that would/could become man. Those ancient living beings who made the Marginis wreck and Icarus—flitting image of reptiles, of gleaming claws that closed like hands—did they collapse into war? Were their home worlds destroyed by the machine intelligences? Life swarmed in the galaxy. The computer civilizations could not wipe out all biospheres, they must've triggered an inherent instability, something that reached to this outpost swinging around Sol and snuffed out Icarus, immense starship, ponderous and certain, and the Marginis wreck, all when the reptiles were so close, so near to some connection with Bigfoot. So the machine societies knew the ancient reptilian call signals, felt the tremor that the Icarus hulk spewed out, its death rattle triggered by bumbling Nigel, Snark arrowing in on the electromagnetic scream, its circuits only numbly re-membering what to look for, perhaps a dim wanting to erase Icarus and the moon wreck, but the Snark was confused deep within, whimpering in that great night that enclosed it, a wolf let in from the cold swinging in for a pass by the moon to drop a fusion capsule, make a fresh sun bloom over Marginis if the wreck responded, but then unable to approach, Nigel a gnat in its eye, Nigel dumb to eternity washing up a gray sea on the lunar shore—

He pauses. Sinks the blade into a securing log and turns, walks to the bare hillside nearby, lungs whooshing the dry air, legs clenching snow crunching prickly pine scent tickling at his nose as enameled light flickers through tall evergreens, trees stretched tall by cruel competition, a thin whisper of a breeze churning them and stirring a tiny whirlwind a few meters away, a circular presence outlined by its cargo of whirled bits, dirt, flakes, a swirl of ice. It sucked at the ground and he entered it, felt the brush of its wind and by so measuring its tiny world destroyed it, churned it forever into minor eddies, the circle consumed and reborn.

At the brow of the hill he felt the full chilling lance of the wind and abruptly, across the crystal gap of the valley, caught a microscopic movement in a far clearing, a dark dot framed in the ellipse of trees, the speck now freezing as he watched, head turning, the two of them pinned to each other along the line of sight as across the millennia an eternal wash of light encased them and fleeting dabs of perception spattered over him, of rank fresh clods of dirt on forest floors, of hymns sung below the edge of human hearing amid the cathedral trees, a grunting ample life plucked from the flooding embracing forest, and through it the curve of the newborn moon speaking of other underlying senses, the same framing order as darted into being along the descending parabolic lines of a tossed stone, of flickering emerging structure that, seen for an instant, ached inside and thrust Bigfoot forward into man, and as this spark passed between them the shaggy troubled dot raised a hand, hesitantly groping upward in the layered air and paused, the timid fears seeping back into the gesture, for one suspended moment, the hand came down and the old being skittered away, angling into the sheltering tree line, Nigel's filmed eyes following the shadow and knowing this new facet and face of the world—

—which, now absorbed and altering him—

—melted—

"In time I eventually understood," Mr. Ichino said. "The seat had springs under it for cushioning. The springs were too soft. They let the seat ride down too far. The rubber fuel line was under it, on top of the carburetor. By sitting on the seat, I pressed the fuel line down and kinked it off, eventually."

"With no fuel the cycle stopped," Nikka concluded.

"Yes. There wasn't anything wrong with the cycle itself—only in my relation to it."

Nikka furrowed her brow.

"The same is true of the way most of us look at the world," Mr. Ichino went on. "We can't solve problems because we are disconnected from the world, always manipulating it as though we were using tongs to stir a fire."

"And you think what's happened to Nigel . . ."

"It's no accident that he has done so much original work at the Marginis wreck. He has learned to merge with the cycle."

* * *

—he makes his way back to the woodpile, rough fabric
of his work clothes rub and stretch at his skin, and judges
that he has been right about the chattering in the sky, it
swoops closer now angling downslope toward the valley
ward face where the bristling trees thin and now as he turns
his head it looms over the ridgeline, tilted slightly forward
moving at top speed to gain surprise, a plump gorged shape
in a looping descending gyre now banking into a smoother
cycloid as Nigel stamps through clinging snow toward the
clearing pressing down tightly after breathing in the brisk
air that binds and combines, then whoosh, out, loosens and
completes.

The hammering sound from above broke through their
words. Nikka sprang up and whirled about, seeking its
source. Mr. Ichino reached the window first. In the
rectangular framing he picked out the whirring dot, a point
that seemed like an angry fly trapped in a box as it lowered
and was swallowed by the tree line.

"Graves," he said. "He has come back. There is
another man with him."

Nikka bit her lip. They began to struggle into their
coats.

Nigel reaches the clearing, an upward tunnel in a
lapping sea of trees, he steps from the evergreen shelter
into the open tube of air that connects earth to the
chattering voice above, cranes his neck back and imagines
how Bigfoot saw it, a mad beating of spinning wings,
Graves firing down from the hovering fury, the remnant
band scattering in panic, eyes wide, Graves and machine
grinding after them above the densely packed trees until he
could no longer see them, then Graves following on foot yes
and Nigel feels something tick over inside him as the
whirring rotors near and the shiny skin of metal splits to
show its maw, a man appearing at the mouth and jumping
in one fluid motion into the snow, an arm coming up stiffly
as his knees bend with impact, arm and rifle together
swiveling left right, catching sight of Nigel, coming around,

the man running forward in a crouch beneath the slowing blades whose shadows fan, fan across him and Nigel stops, sensing something more as another figure appears from behind the fat sheen of the copter, older man bundled against the cold stepping into view while the young man stalks forward holding the rifle easily, his smooth features focused on the line that connects the rifle bore to Nigel's chest, heavy black eyebrows knotted in concentration, boots squeaking in the compacted snow "Keep it on 'im" as the older man strides closer "He's not the one but, I dunno—" grizzled face twisted in puzzlement, stops and hands on hips studies Nigel "Seem to know this fella from som'ere" as Nigel feels himself piercing the sky in readiness, feet rooted to the earth so he hangs threadlike through the space between "maybe Ichino called him in to" the wand of the rifle drifting in slow circles as the younger man's face flushes with excited angry patches, hand pressing at the steelblue metal to coax roaring life from it "help him out" rotors grinding to a stop "Look fella, aren't you a little old to be foolin' aroun' out here, you and your friend Ichino? Might be nice if you'd just kinda" Nigel catching the first shred of a distant exclamation, Nikka's thin high voice, he says "Old? I've already outlived Mozart and Anne Frank, yes, but we're all old here" as he sees the young man's next step will take him within range but now triangulates the position of the silvery voice behind him and senses that if the rifle spoke as he snatched it the bullet would go in that direction, toward the cabin, so slides back into breathing, breathing and being breathed, Graves shaking his head grimacing "You're not gonna talk your— hey—"

Nikka and Mr. Ichino came around the stand of evergreens together and Graves caught sight of them. They stopped, puffing clouds, and surveyed the clearing. When Mr. Ichino noticed the rifle his first impulse was to leap back into the shelter of the trees, but at that instant Graves shouted brusquely, "Hey, you two. Come over here." A pause. "No foolin' aroun', now." He glanced at Nikka, and she at him. Slowly they walked the last fifty meters to where Graves and a sallow-faced man stood confronting

Nigel. The younger man appeared edgy and yet he did no
move jerkily. Rather, he kept the rifle weaving in a stead
progression from Nigel to Nikka to Ichino and back. Ichin
recognized this as a dangerous pattern for them all, shoul
one of the three make an unexpected move while the rifl
was pointed elsewhere; a reflex yank of the trigger could—

"I didn't get much satisfaction last time I was here,
Graves said, hands still on hips. "So I brought a littl
persuasion. I know you've got that film of mine."

"I don't—" Ichino began.

"No lyin' now."

"I destroyed it, as I told you."

"You're gonna tell."

"There is nothing—"

as though sprung from nowhere feelings and desires forke
like summer lightning across the unmoving vault of hin
and to dispel them growing like fresh corn he entered int
mersion with them, sucked them into himself to see then
for what they were and integrated the flickering so that i
became a drowsy blur which faded into the continuin
murmur of the world, a place absolutely blank and waitin
for each moment to write upon it, time like water moldin
itself to event "—nothing—" as Graves takes a step forwar
and his arm comes up, hand growing rigid in flight to crac
across Ichino's face backhanded, the small man jerkin
backward at the last moment and taking it full on the lef
cheek, feet losing their purchase and the body turning as i
falls to cushion the impact, white crystals leaping up wher
it broke the crusted snow and Graves following through
head turned to watch Ichino's fall, the young man keepin
the rifle steady on Nigel as the moment passes Nikka gasp
Nigel sees the rifleman turn steady and on guard leaving n
opening

Mr. Ichino squinted up at Graves and tasted blood.

"Y'know, you think I'm so dumb I don't see what's goin
on here. You and your"—casual wave—"friends here ar
gonna make a bundle outa this. That's what you're thinkin'
isn't it? Or else you figure these things that damr

near killed me deserve to live." Graves's pinched face seemed to fill the sky above him.

"They do. Please try to understand. I simply do not want them destroyed by the attention you would bring. In time they can be studied. But not by the methods you will bring about."

Graves's voice narrowed to a rasp. "You're lyin' again."

time squeezes down to infinitesimal frozen moments, the rifle bears to the left as Ichino struggles up to lean on one hand braced behind him, the movement covered and Graves stepping back making a flicking gesture with a finger to the other man, the rifle butt rising as the sight focuses on Ichino's left kneecap and the clearing is cloaked in layers of stilled silence, waiting waiting "I think you're in the wrong fairly tale" Nigel says for distraction, the first word beginning to register on the trigger finger which clenches slightly in the clear light, the man bracing his bones working like a lattice of calcium rods each muscle straining, as Nigel whips his right foot up into the man's elbow feeling his bootheel catch the tip as his weight comes forward, the man's hands clench at the sacred metal and momentum collapses his form, breath whistling from him through dry pipes as the rifle deflects in a scatter of light, Nigel's heel slipping from the elbow and onto the gleaming brown wooden rifle stock as the man's stem of a neck jerks to the side and his hands clutch for a last redeeming moment with the trigger which lurches back under the slipping finger and the muzzle spits a clap of bright noise into the crystalline space exhaling a blue cloud toward the trampled snow, burying a node of lead in the receiving earth

By the time Mr. Ichino had scrambled to his feet Nigel had the rifle and Graves was backing away, blinking, palms cupped toward Nigel.

The younger man was still face down in the snow, where he had fallen after Nikka tripped him. If she had not leaped forward, Nigel might not have had time to recover the rifle. Nigel cradled the weapon now, worked the bolt and left the breech open. The man got up on his hands and knees in the snow and looked around him, somewhat

dazed, as though still unable to accept where he was. No
one had spoken.

"I'd like a word," Nigel said to Graves. He took the
man by the arm and led him off a few meters.

They spoke, their words inaudible. Mr. Ichino
watched Nigel, wondering at a facet he could not quite
define. There was no hint of tension in Nigel, and in his
relaxed manner was the very essence of his power. When
Graves turned back from the conversation, Ichino was
shocked by the change in the man's expression. There was a
new calm in the heavy-lidded eyes and at the same time the
face carried a distant sadness, as though Graves had learned
something he would rather have not known. Mr. Ichino
knew they would not meet again. Nigel clapped the man on
the back. Graves spoke haltingly to the younger man and
together they trudged back to the copter. They climbed
aboard and in a moment the rotors began to turn.

loved the lifting sweep as a misty dust of snow sprang up
beneath the machine like chiming crystals attempting to fly
anew—*farewell*—this unflagging energy of the mind he
loved the most as each sense in turn made a fresh grab at
the greased pig which was the world even as he waved
upward at the veiled white faces receding, his gesture a line
scratched across the space between them, Ichino beginning
to speak but Nigel cutting him off saying no, he has work to
finish, seeing though that later they would chew over this
moment by a crisp fireside, crunching popcorn, drinking
heated cider, for this instant it would be like a stomach
irked by spent whiskey, no, later was soon enough and all in
good solvent time smoothing the edges of events he leans
back into the bracing air and takes the rifle by its long and
ignorant snout flings it up butt cleaving the jeweled
nitrogen into the trees where *thunk* it strikes an encrusted
trunk deadening the sound, this motion releasing a merry
oil that spreads across the faces of Nikka Ichino rising in
concert to watch the stupid tube on its parabola its crash
punctuating an end to their worry, Ichino turning to watch
the dwindling copter as it thrashes through the brightening
air Nigel murmuring the world sinking away as he listens to

the fading chop with half an ear and a muzzy connection forms, a dawning realization humming, he feels the sentence leave him and in the saying knows it for the first time "Graves made his future before he came here" for indeed yes the man was free had been free the sum was his

"—before he came here," made Mr. Ichino turn, in the midst of framing his thanks, turn and find the stirring dot as it skated over the tree tops toward the ridge. The puffy clouds had lifted and sunlight streamed fitfully through them. As the copter neared the ridge it entered a blade of sunlight. Tilting, a facet of its slick skin caught the light and there was an odd optical effect, a brilliant yellow twinkling. Mr. Ichino saw a burning spark leap up from the trees and envelop the copter in a sputtering orange globe. He blinked and the vision went away, leaving only a fuzzed afterimage on his retina. The copter was gone. He listened for its dull clatter. Nothing was audible above the sighing of wind in tree tops. Had the copter slipped over the ridgeline that quickly? He could not tell. He turned to ask Nigel but the other man had already started back to the woodpile.

above all Graves's monomaniac insistence, the whole laughable business with the rifle, Graves's last meeting with Bigfoot an eternal instant ago, recalled the poor dear desk calculator civilizations cowering up there amid the stars, afraid to use radio for fear the young organic races will seek them out and rip them up for scrap iron, yet even a desk calculator can turn vicious when cornered, destroy the suckling animal cultures before they develop, ah what an old sod of a galaxy this was pissing away its energy a kilobuck per nanosecond like poor gone Graves, right action in part but wrong sense of the warp of things, no feel for the joyful lofting song all this meant, so much like the old dimly remembered Nigel, so tied to events by ropes of care each sank him tugging him below the waves, Alexandria Snark dear dead Dad, yes Nigel sees how he felt that way but now he slaps his pockets in mock surprise, brings up his hands spread wide to the world, empty, his past pilfered from him, free of the baggage of what he was, it melts he laughs free and awash in this universe of essences and ready for Aquila yes he laughs—

As the two came back into the warm cabin, their boots making loud thumps in the room as they stamped away the snow, Nikka said, "I doubt you'll be seeing more of that one."

"No. Everyone learns from experience," Mr. Ichino replied, thinking of Bigfoot. He went over to the window and saw Nigel through the square Western window. The crosshair of the four panes centered on him for a moment. Beyond Nigel was the opening bowl of the sky and the sun still hiding behind patches of haze. Nigel, hefting his ax, moved at the center of a round universe.

lungs panting with the effort he pauses and looks back toward the crosshair window and sees it as blowing him out, the inverse of the young lad's leaden shot, out into a billowing *swack* the blade bites into a rotten seam, wood frags showering up around him tumbling faceted a crash of crystal orbiting asteroids carving the cold, muscles clenching melting, heels biting the compacted snow as earth holds him in its fierce ageless grip of which he himself is a part, he has his own gravitational field, and thoughts flit like summer lightning through the streaming wash of feelings that float him through each moment, melting. Above was the galaxy, a swarm of white bees, each an infinite structure of its own, a spinning discus slicing space with its own definition, Nigel unable to see who threw the discus and uncaring, for there was enough here at the fragile axis of earth, each new truth melting into the old as their fraction of the world flowed through him, *le's slide out of here one of these nights* as continents butted against each other *an' get an outfit, and go for howling adventures amongst the Injuns* chopping wood, trisecting Andromeda *over the territory* Oregon to Aquila *for a couple of weeks or two* all moments going, as he touched them, to smash and scatteration *and I says, all right, that suits me—*

And it melts

"Nigel!" Nikka's voice comes. "Have some more coffee."

the cabin steaming melting with renewal

"Of course," Nigel calls. "I'll be there."

Eternally, it melts yes he turns and yes it melts and he falls through it melting and turning yes and yes eternally, it melts

ABOUT THE AUTHOR

GREGORY BENFORD has won virtually every major science fiction award, including two Nebulas. He is an internationally renowned physicist and astronomer, a professor at the University of California, Irvine, and has published more than one hundred scientific papers. A Woodrow Wilson Fellow, he served on NASA's Science Advisory Board. He has published thirteen novels, including *Timescape, Artifact, Heart of the Comet* (with David Brin), and *Against Infinity*, as well as a collection of short stories, *In Alien Flesh*.